RIGHTEOUS FURY

Sequel to The Mistress of Auschwitz (Book 2 of 3)

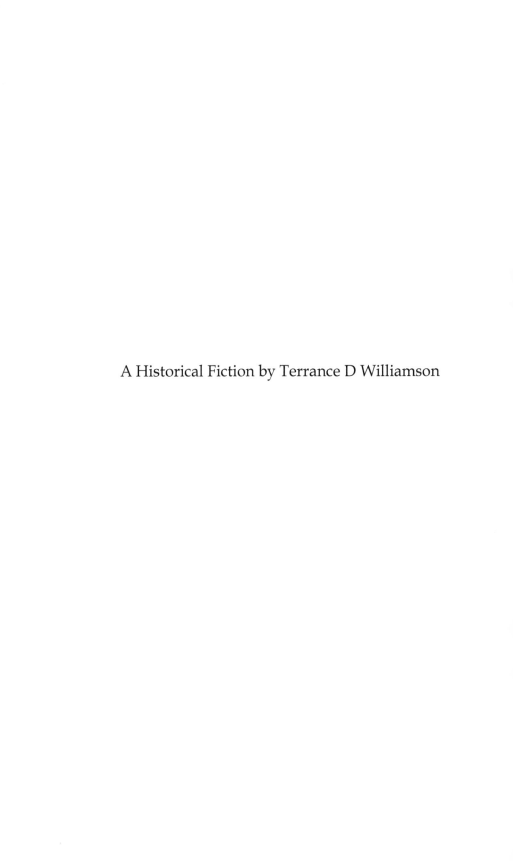

A Historical Fiction by Terrance D Williamson

Dedicated to:
My eternal son,
My loving daughter,
And my patient wife.

Introduction

This book begins just before the point where the previous book, The Mistress of Auschwitz, ended. While I strove to be as accurate as possible, liberties were taken to tell the story.

With regards to Eleonore's story after the camps, I exercised this liberty to its full extent as there is almost nothing to rely on for information. There is no accounting of what happened to her after the Allies unshackled the camp inmates. Apart from how her true story ends, large parts of her records have been left blank, and I have taken it upon myself to create the drama which could've happened.

In contrast, the new character introduced into this book, Hanns Volker, has a thorough and compelling historical accounting. I have, however, hidden his true identity out of respect for his living relatives. I hope that I've done this wonderful man a great service for the sacrifices he made to bring justice into the world. All of the events that occurred in this book are based off of his real experiences.

Actual excerpts, statements, quotes, and arguments have been extracted by the prosecution and defence with respect to the Belsen Trials. I must stress that if you endeavor to read the immensely interesting trials, that you read them in their entirety.

DISCLAIMER: While certain events are taken from Hanns Volker and Eleonore Hodys' life, this is the fictional telling of the historical events and are, in no way, the actual representation of either Eleonore or Hanns. I would encourage anyone interested to research and read about the extraordinary events that have been fictionalized in my book.

Chapter One:
Liberation

Deep in earth my love is lying
And I must weep alone.

Edgar Allan Poe

"Sit," the Allied officer ordered Eleonore gruffly after he opened a door to a small interview room with large, clear windows.

Eleonore froze in the doorway at the sight of the cement floor stained with blood. Her fear intensified when she spotted the shackles fastened to the gray, iron table and she shuddered to think of the malicious purpose of this room.

With a slight nudge, the officer guided Eleonore inside and brushed past her as he pulled out a chair for himself. Despite his impoliteness, Eleonore found herself trusting this man and didn't detect that he wished her any harm. Besides, manners were forgotten in the hell of a concentration camp, even from the liberators.

Sitting across from him, Eleonore winced at the strain on her stomach and held her belly as she positioned herself on the chair. The Nazi doctor had been careless with the stitches on her stomach and they caught on the fabric of her borrowed dress, causing great discomfort with even slight movements.

Abruptly, the man threw his satchel onto the table and retrieved a black pen, a frayed leather notepad, and a pack of cigarettes. Lighting his cigarette, the man didn't offer one to Eleonore, who half-expected the gesture to be customary.

"May I have one?" Eleonore asked with longing. In normal circumstances, she wouldn't dare be so bold, but her time at Auschwitz had altered her sense of propriety.

"No," the man shook his head quickly as he wrote.

"What are you writing?" Eleonore grew annoyed at his rudeness.

Irritated by the interruption, the man closed his eyes as he muttered to himself softly, struggling to remember something pertinent which Eleonore had inadvertently driven away.

"Right," he nodded and continued writing, ignoring Eleonore's question as she sighed at the disregard.

"How do you know German so well?" Eleonore continued to pester him. "Your accent is familiar."

"My name is Hanns Volker," he finally replied and sat up straight while looking at her with disinterest. "I grew up in Berlin."

"You're Jewish?" Eleonore asked, but felt herself feeling faint from exhaustion and trauma.

"I am. As were those American soldiers who wanted to kill that Nazi officer."

"Then why did you stop them?" Eleonore squinted.

"A dead Nazi can't talk," Hanns looked out the window at the Allies busying themselves with raiding the other offices across the hallway and collecting the documents and evidence that weren't destroyed, "and the world needs to know what has happened here."

"I'm still confused as to why you need me," Eleonore shook her head. "Why did you single me out?"

"Vengeance," Hanns spoke coldly.

"I'm not much use when it comes to violence," Eleonore huffed. Being rather petite, Eleonore was of little threat to anyone, even in her best physical condition.

"Rudolph Hoess," Hanns blurted the name and Eleonore froze in terror at the mention of him. "He was the father, wasn't he?" he nodded to her belly.

Eleonore's eyes welled as she thought of her child. The Nazis had stolen that future from her, and she felt the absence of her baby with every breath. She tried to speak, but the words wouldn't form. Instead, she replied with a simple nod.

"The Commandant of Auschwitz has escaped, and I have been tasked with tracking him down," Hanns leaned in and folded his hands as he spoke quietly.

"Escaped?" Eleonore frowned.

"Yes," Hanns nodded quickly.

"How does his escape involve me?" Eleonore shook her head.

"Will you help me hunt him down and bring him to justice?"

Eleonore stared at Hanns in complete shock. She didn't believe that she had heard him correctly. Then, swiftly, Eleonore reached across the table, grabbed Hanns' cigarettes, took one out of the package, and held it to her mouth as she waited for him to light it.

With his hands folded, Hanns studied her for a moment. Then, reluctantly, he reached into his satchel and retrieved some matches. Lighting one, he held it against her cigarette as she stared into his eyes, testing his character.

Inhaling deeply, Eleonore leaned back in her chair before exhaling a cloud of smoke that swirled about in the stagnant air. The room began to spin as she closed her eyes. She was hungry, desperately, and it had been an age since her last cigarette, which she now savored.

A shout from outside the room startled Eleonore, and she looked through the window to see a young soldier, no older than eighteen, shaking and scrambling to pick up the documents that he had accidentally scattered in the hallway. A senior officer shouted impatiently at the blunder, which only increased the unsteadiness of the boy.

Clearing his throat, Hanns regained Eleonore's attention. While she wasn't the best judge of character, Eleonore read well enough into Hanns' expression that he wasn't relishing the request for assistance from her. He seemed, to her, to be emotionally distant and calculated, but Eleonore surmised that this was due to him being overwhelmed with what he was experiencing. Regardless, it made her question the purpose of him asking her for help.

Not to mention that the disparity between them made her feel rather self-conscious. Nearly twice his age, Eleonore sat across from him as a shadow of herself in a tattered, bullet-filled dress, while he was clean-shaven with a smart, pressed uniform in perfect order. She would've preferred to have been afforded the dignity of being interviewed as his equal but understood that he viewed her as pitiful. It wasn't his fault, she realized, as her sad appearance evoked an emotional response that only a few would be immune to.

Although young, there was a maturity in his gaze. Eleonore could sense a mischievous spirit about him which, she supposed, made him adept at his job. If he was going to hunt down Nazis such as Rudolph Hoess, then he had to be cunning and carry a sharper wit than his 'prey'.

"Well," Hanns became impatient, "will you help me find Rudolph Hoess?"

"That depends," Eleonore tapped her cigarette gently, shaking off the ash as Hanns continued to stare at her with a grave expression. She assumed that this was his first experience with the barbarity of the Nazis, and he was trying to compensate by covering up his emotions.

"On what?" Hanns shrugged.

"What do you believe I can contribute?" Eleonore squinted as she took another puff.

"You were his lover, no?" Hanns crossed his arms.

"No!" Eleonore frowned and shook her head quickly, disgusted at the very thought.

"But you carried his child," Hanns looked at her suspiciously.

"That doesn't require love," Eleonore spoke softly as she looked away.

"He took you by force then?" Hanns' intrigue grew, and Eleonore spotted a plot forming in his mind. The severity of his frown lessened, and Eleonore noticed his opinion of her shifting faintly.

"Not necessarily," Eleonore swallowed, wishing he would use a little more tact in his questioning. It was an uncomfortable discussion even in the best of circumstances.

"I'm not following," Hanns watched her intently.

"I offered myself for the sake of another," Eleonore returned to staring into his eyes, "but to say I had a choice in the matter would be false. He didn't force me through physical means, but he didn't offer me the opportunity to deny him, either."

"Well, Miss Hodys," Hanns returned to folding his hands as he leaned in, unmoved by Eleonore's trials, "I'm offering you the opportunity to exact revenge on this man. Will you not assist me?"

"What can I do?" Eleonore shook her head in bewilderment.

"You knew him best," Hanns tilted his head. "Did he mention anything about where he would go, places he could hide?"

"I didn't know him best!" Eleonore grew indignant. "I barely knew the man at all!"

"You knew him a hell of a lot better than me," Hanns pointed to her still swollen belly.

"How dare you!" Eleonore stood but regretted the rash movement as the room began to spin around her. "You have no idea what I did to survive! Or what I did to alleviate another's sorrows!"

Hanns remained silent as he watched her for a moment before slowly taking out another cigarette and lighting it as he stared into her eyes. One would hardly need to be perceptive to decipher his thoughts as he looked at her with a slight scowl. He believed that she had behaved dishonorably and taken the path of convenience rather than principle. She might have assumed the same, Eleonore supposed, if she was in his position.

Then, while still holding his cigarette, Hanns reached into his satchel and produced a small, brown envelope which he handed to Eleonore. Watching him warily, Eleonore sat and opened it as she pulled out the documents enclosed. Written in English, Eleonore struggled with the complexity of the wording. She could understand a moderate level of English, but legal jargon was challenging to comprehend. She could, however, decipher the words 'War Crimes Investigation Team'.

"What's this?" Eleonore looked up at him.

"I have been tasked with gathering information for the upcoming war crime trials in Belsen," Hanns spoke softly. "I believe that you have valuable information which, if we catch him, will help us bring Rudolph Hoess to justice."

"If you catch him, then don't hesitate to hang him," Eleonore spoke with unwavering hatred. "And if he runs, don't miss when you squeeze the trigger. I can't provide you with more valuable information than that," Eleonore passed the envelope back to Hanns.

"You won't help me?!" Hanns shot his head back in surprise. "Why? Do you still love him?"

"I didn't love him then and I don't love him now!" Eleonore's eyes bulged at the outrageous accusation.

"Then why won't you help me?"

"My life has been uprooted enough," Eleonore's lips trembled as she spoke. "I need to go home. I need to return to my flat, to my shop. I need to eat. I need to rest. I need my life back."

"Berlin is in ashes," Hanns spoke bluntly. "Whatever life you once had is now gone."

It shouldn't have come as a surprise, but to hear Hanns utter these words shattered whatever fabrication she clung to that life could return to 'normal'. The beautiful city where she had grown up, where her lovely little shop had been, where Ruth and Alex had given her many wonderful memories, was now destroyed. What was she if not the seamstress of *La Venezia*?

"There is nothing for you there," Hanns continued to speak without much emotion but waited patiently for Eleonore while she absorbed the devastating news. "If you don't believe me, then ask anyone, including some of your previous captors. They continued with these camps even when it was clear that they had lost the war. They persisted in murdering my people, and those like yourself who resisted, even when the orders had ceased."

"How did you know that I'm from Berlin?" Eleonore watched him with increasing mistrust.

"I know a few things about you, Miss Hodys," Hanns lifted the envelope and waved it briefly before slapping it back down on the table. "But I also know that Berlin is not your native home. Your accent isn't natural to you. It's close, but there are a few words here and there that give you away."

"Vienna," Eleonore explained, impressed with Hanns' investigative abilities, giving her confidence that if anyone could catch Rudolph, it would be the man in front of her. "Alright, what do you need from me?"

"To start, a statement. Then, once the trials commence, it would be beneficial to have you take the stand as a witness."

"Absolutely not," Eleonore shook her head. The thought of her being near to anyone involved with Auschwitz gave her immense anxiety.

"We can discuss that later," Hanns held up his hand to calm her. "Can we begin, at least, with your statement?"

"You said Rudolph Hoess escaped?" Eleonore took another puff from her cigarette.

"That's right," Hanns nodded.

"He wanted me dead while I was at Auschwitz," Eleonore glanced down at her still swollen belly, indicating the reason. "If I give you this statement, it's likely that he will try to have me killed."

"We'll protect you," Hanns opened the tattered notepad and prepared to write. "He can't hurt you anymore."

At this, Eleonore burst into tears and turned away to hide her shame. Her hand trembled as the ash from her cigarette fell to the floor. Rudolph, she felt, was ever-present. He was the shadow in the corner of the room, the unsettling feeling that someone was behind her. How could Hanns be so arrogant to assume that he could protect her? The damage that Rudolph did was irreversible.

"Eleonore," Hanns continued with a little more sympathy, "this is the right thing to do," he relaxed his shoulders and showed, for the first time, a genuine emotion. "You can help bring justice to an untold number of lives who have been affected by this Nazi plague."

"I'm so tired," Eleonore leaned back in her chair and took another puff of her cigarette.

"We're all tired, Miss Hodys," Hanns spoke casually but, by the look he received from Eleonore, knew that he should've kept silent.

"You've still got meat on your bones," Eleonore muttered bitterly under her breath and closed her eyes.

"I didn't intend to insult you," Hanns shook his head and paused before continuing as Eleonore sensed a rage rising within him. "Truth is, I heard about the camps, but nothing could've prepared me for this. I want to find this bastard, and I want to find him now before he gets too far away."

"I understand," Eleonore wiped the tears from her eyes. "I'll tell you my story, but on one condition."

"What's that?"

"Hide my identity, to some degree at least."

"I need your name," Hanns looked at her with regret.

"Just use my initials," Eleonore leaned forward. "Please."

"E.H.," Hanns spoke faintly as he wrote on the top of the page.

"Thank you," Eleonore sighed and grabbed another cigarette. "Could I possibly have something to eat?"

"Uh…sure," Hanns thought for a moment and then reached into his satchel and placed a red, tin can on the table.

Without reservation, Eleonore shoveled the spam-like product into her mouth. She must've looked mad to Hanns, but she didn't care. She simply closed her eyes and chewed as quickly as possible to quiet her aching stomach.

"Thank you," Eleonore nodded to Hanns as she wiped her face with the sleeve of her borrowed dress.

"Proceed when you're able," Hanns held his pen at the ready. "Just tell me your story as best as you can remember it."

"Well," Eleonore puffed her cigarette, "I owned a seamstress shop in Berlin, *La Venezia*, that was used as a secret meeting place for Socialist Democrats, of which I was a patron. I also employed two Jews at the store, Ruth and Alex, who were the sweetest people I've ever had the privilege of knowing. Despite the race laws that came into effect, I refused to terminate their employment."

"So, you were arrested, then?" Hanns spoke as he wrote.

"Not directly. I was warned by a Nazi official that I was on their 'list' and that he would be returning within twenty-four hours to arrest me. We were childhood acquaintances, so he gave me the courtesy of a warning. As expected, we panicked and attempted to flee the country. Ruth, Alex, and I were duped into believing that we had an avenue to freedom with a certain gentleman who convinced me to forge Nazi party papers," Eleonore shook her head as she remembered the crippled man who had deceived her. She wondered where he was now, and if he had been caught by the Allies, or if he even knew the conditions that he was cheating people into. If he had willingly sent people to the camps knowing how wicked they were, then Eleonore hoped that he was dead, as cruel as that sounded.

"They arrested me under the charge of falsifying documents and took me to Auschwitz under this pretense, and packed me into a stock car on a train brimming with prisoners."

"Stock car?" Hanns looked up from the paper.

"It was hell," Eleonore began to shake as she recalled the horrific experience. "There was no room to lie down or even to sit. They packed us in like cattle, and we had to stand amongst our own waste. The man beside me died standing upright."

Eleonore paused as she waited for Hanns to finish writing. The trembling in his hand made it difficult for him to maintain the same speed he was able to employ previously. She could perceive how difficult it was for him to accept her story. Not from the sense of fabrication, but from disbelief that such a tragedy could occur. It was one thing to comprehend that death happened on a mass scale, but to uncover the details of how it was carried out, and the conditions that he himself had barely escaped, was disturbing.

"What happened when you arrived at the camp? Were you aware of the gas chambers?" Hanns dabbed the sweat from his forehead.

"Not at first," Eleonore squeezed her eyes shut as she tried to remember. Such dreadful images were not something she was anxious to recall. "I saw the crematoriums, but I didn't understand their purpose until it was revealed to me some time later."

"Did you ever witness anyone taken to the gas chambers?"

"I saw those who were selected," Eleonore recalled the poor souls doomed to death in such a terrible manner, "but initially I wasn't aware as to why they were selected."

"And who was selected?" Hanns sat back and took a quick breath as he tried to steady his anger.

"The weak, the young, the elderly, anyone who was 'useless' in their eyes."

Hanns paused after he had written down her last sentence, and Eleonore watched as he tried to comprehend what she was telling him. She assumed that if he was asking her about the gas chambers, then he was aware of their purpose, but to hear her describe who was taken was difficult for him to process.

"What were the conditions like at Auschwitz?" Hanns asked after he had gathered himself, but his eyes remained fixed on the paper. Eleonore understood that he needed to document her statement and these horrible facts with as little emotion as possible, as difficult as that was for him.

"Shocking," Eleonore stared at the ceiling as she recalled. "Similar to what you've seen at this camp. They shaved our heads, humiliated us, and herded us into bunkers without insulation or heat. Many died of sickness or exhaustion or starvation. If you didn't work, then you died, but some of the inmates were worked to death. Death was everywhere. Death was more common than breathing."

"What were your responsibilities in the camp?" Hanns asked as he looked at her with rising sympathy.

Eleonore paused as she looked back at Hanns. There was a denial lingering over him. She could see it in his eyes. The enormity, the unrepentant malice, and the brutality of these camps were not easily understood. Eleonore wondered if she herself fully understood what had happened.

"I worked in the hospital, under a cruel Kapo. My responsibility was to change the bedpans."

"Why…" Hanns scratched his head as he took a moment to think, "why didn't anyone fight back?"

"We tried," Eleonore shook her head slightly as she recalled the bravery of her sweet Ella, "but we had to be careful. I tried to help the resistance movement, but I was caught in a place where I shouldn't have been and the Kapo who ran the hospital sent me to die in the standing cells."

"A standing cell?" Hanns looked at Eleonore as though he wished her not to answer.

"It's a cell about the size of this chair," Eleonore shifted in her seat and began to shake. She closed her eyes and clenched her hands into fists as she recalled the clanking of metal against metal and the groans of starvation from the other inmates that were with her. She could still hear their screams for even just a drop of water.

"How did you get out?"

"Chance?" Eleonore shrugged as she opened her eyes and took a deep breath. "Perhaps it was fate? Rudolph's wife, Hedwig, was searching for a seamstress to work at the Villa. A certain lieutenant thought he could raise his standing with the Commandant by providing what Hedwig was looking for."

"That was kind of him," Hanns narrowed his gaze, sensing there was more to the story.

"The lieutenant," Eleonore cleared her throat as she recalled Jung, "he discovered my talents when I restored his uniform. I bartered my release from the standing cell in exchange for the repairs."

"So, you worked at the Villa?"

"For a brief spell," Eleonore scratched the back of her neck to ease some of the awkwardness.

"Why brief?"

"Rudolph Hoess took notice of me and began to pursue what he hoped would be a mutual relationship. Hedwig put a quick end to this and terminated my employment," Eleonore cleared her throat.

"So, you engaged in relations with the Commandant at the Villa?" Hanns frowned.

"No," Eleonore shook her head and swallowed, "but Rudolph wasn't deterred by my removal from the Villa. He provided me with a private cell back in the camp where he could visit me at night."

"I was under the impression that relations between an officer and an inmate were prohibited. How did he visit you?"

"Not without risk," Eleonore tilted her head. "He was almost caught on one occasion. He would come late at night after sending the guards away."

"Then your relationship was sexual?"

"I'd like to discuss as little of this as possible," Eleonore glanced away, displeased with the casualness of his tone.

"I don't mean to be indelicate," Hanns put the pen down, "but you must understand that anything and everything we can use against this man will help bring him to justice. If his relationship with you was sexual, then we can build a case around that mistreatment."

"There is no justice," Eleonore spoke bitterly as she stamped her cigarette out.

"Not fully," Hanns stared into the table. "Yet, I'm certain that we can both agree that this man needs to be placed into custody."

"Yes, the relationship was sexual," Eleonore became agitated as she grabbed another cigarette, "but not by choice. He threatened to kill another inmate, one of the leaders of the resistance and a dear friend of mine, if I didn't sleep with him. Once it was discovered that I was pregnant, he must've panicked as I never saw him again. He sent me to the standing cell and ordered that I be starved to death."

"You were sent to the standing cells twice?" Hanns began but was interrupted by an engine roaring to life outside the building.

Eleonore clasped her hand to her chest in fright as the windows began to rattle. The Allied guards outside the room abandoned the documents and exited the building with weapons at the ready. Even Hanns stood quickly and placed his hand to his pistol, further terrifying Eleonore's nerves that something sinister was transpiring.

Hanns tried to speak to Eleonore but he was drowned out by the noise. Seeing that communication was useless, he gathered his belongings into his satchel and motioned for Eleonore to follow him.

Trembling as she left the interview room, Eleonore walked closely behind Hanns as they sped towards the exit. The earth beneath their feet began to rumble and Eleonore imagined that the Nazis were launching a counter assault. She was so close to being freed from this hell, but Eleonore feared that she had hoped too soon.

They left the building quickly but were met immediately by a wall of soldiers with their backs to them, watching something that was just beyond Eleonore's view. They held their weapons down by their sides which was a relief to Eleonore that there was no threat, but the source of the noise was still curious. Passing through the group, Hanns moved to get a glimpse of what was happening, and Eleonore followed closely behind him.

Pushing their way to the front, Hanns and Eleonore stopped abruptly when they realized the cause of the commotion. Holding her hand over her eyes to block out the sun, Eleonore witnessed a sight that, although she had lived in the camps, she still could not believe.

A bulldozer had been brought into the camp and it was digging into the earth, creating a large pit. Beside this pit were bodies that had been piled into a heap. Malnourished, pitiful corpses awaited their final resting place in this mass grave. Men and women were nearly indistinguishable from each other with nothing but skin clinging to their skeletons.

The sight was gut-wrenching, and Eleonore held a hand over her mouth as tears began to form. Even after all the time she had spent in Auschwitz, she could never be desensitized to such horrors. Soldiers wept as they carried out the terrible business of hauling the bodies to the pile, prisoners watched vacantly with some being days away from death themselves, and commanders shouted orders while concealing their emotions to complete the awful task at hand.

Eleonore and Hanns and the soldiers with them stood in silence as they watched. There were no words to dispel the terror, no comforts to be spoken which could eradicate the shock. The earth shook underneath their feet, the divine seemed absent, and the weight impressed on everyone's heart was irreversible.

In the face of such overwhelming malevolence, Eleonore was unable to articulate what she was experiencing. Even her ability to think clearly had been stripped away and all she was left with was the capacity to react.

Glancing at Hanns, Eleonore spotted tears in his eyes. But these were not the tears of sorrow. These were the tears of unbridled hatred and the unrestricted desire for revenge. She recalled the same yearning in Ella and remembered how desperately she sought retribution for what the Nazis did to her husband. Eleonore had cautioned Ella against resentment, but now, when she looked at the faces of those gathered, she understood that their honorable vengeance would not be impeded.

"I'll take you to the American camp," Hanns spoke softly after the roar of the engine had been cut.

"Now?" Eleonore looked at him curiously.

"I don't want to be here any longer than necessary," Hanns spoke with seething resentment as he remained fixated on the bodies. "We need to continue your statement so that I can catch the devil who is responsible for all this."

Eleonore nodded as a desperation arose within her to escape. She wished that she carried the tenacity and courage to remain and help those who were less fortunate than herself. She had spent months in the camp witnessing the horrors of Auschwitz, but still, some had lost more than their dignity.

She remembered Em who had lost her son, and Ella who had lost her husband. Perspective, she understood, was fatal to self-pity. Her trials were greater than she could've imagined facing in her lifetime, but they failed in comparison to the loss of loved ones, especially the most precious amongst them.

Signaling for her to follow him, Hanns led Eleonore back to the camp gates. They walked past American soldiers who were shouting orders to one another, but Eleonore could only make out a word or two of English. Yet what she could comprehend disturbed her greatly: disease, pestilence, quarantine. An emptiness grew in Eleonore's stomach with the sense that the release from her trials may not be as close at hand as she perceived.

"Stay here," Hanns paused just before they reached the gates. "I'll speak with the guards and explain the importance of having you released immediately."

In agreement, Eleonore stood at a respectful distance, feeling the pains of her exhaustion. She tried to listen to their conversation, but her fatigue was dominating her mental capacities and she eventually gave up trying to translate. They seemed, however, to be deliberating brashly and Hanns' voice was growing louder and louder as he pointed wildly at Eleonore.

Then, out of the corner of her eye, Eleonore spotted a horror that she wished to forget. A woman and her child, who was no older than ten, were sitting upright against the wall near the gate. Both were naked and dead, and both were skin and bones. The child had tragically died some days ago, but the mother had kept him near her breast which, Eleonore spotted, had a recent wound from a bullet. She had been shot maybe only hours ago and Eleonore fumed at the cruelty of the Nazis who had killed her within moments of liberation.

Moved with pity, Eleonore went over to the lady and knelt in front of her. *I wonder what your name was,* Eleonore reached up and brushed the dirt away from the woman's cheek. *What a shame that they killed you hours before your release, but at least you're with your child.*

Yet, Eleonore found it odd that the woman didn't look sorrowful, but rather, resilient. Despite the loss of her child, this woman carried a strength that, even in death, Eleonore could only dream of.

Then Eleonore noticed a faint line on her ring finger which, she assumed, once carried her wedding band. Running her hand along the line on her finger, Eleonore thought that she heard a groan. Studying the woman for a moment, Eleonore held her breath as she waited for another noise, but then the woman twitched her finger and Eleonore nearly fell backwards in surprise.

"H-Help!" Eleonore shouted towards Hanns who was still arguing with the guards. "She's alive!"

"Hey!" Eleonore shouted again, forgetting his name in her panic. "Hey!"

Finally, Hanns took notice of her alarm and rushed over to help. Picking up the woman with little effort, Hanns scanned the camp, desperate for anyone that could assist.

"Her child!" Eleonore looked at the boy.

"Leave him! He's riddled with disease!" Hanns shouted over his shoulder as he darted for the makeshift medical tent which was being hastily erected in the corner of the camp.

Ignoring Hanns, Eleonore picked up the boy, despite the strain on her stomach, and followed as briskly as she was able. Her famished state and recent 'surgery' were taxing under his weight, but Eleonore would not part a mother from her son.

"Help!" Hanns shouted in English when he arrived at the tent where he was swiftly met by the medical staff who pointed to a cot where he could place the woman.

A doctor ran over to Eleonore where he took the boy in his arms. But by the weight of the child, and the limpness of his limbs, the doctor understood that the boy was deceased, and he froze in place. The doctor looked down at the boy as if he was gazing upon his own son, and a tear rolled down his cheek.

Clumsily, the doctor turned and entered the tent. He shook as he placed the boy beside his mother. He was terrified but wanted to fulfill his duty, yet the shock had rendered him incapable of decisiveness. An anxious nurse shouted at him to provide direction, breaking him from his trance, and he replied with orders that might save the mother.

"We need to have you assessed," Hanns pulled Eleonore into the tent and showed her to a cot.

"You mentioned the American camp," Eleonore looked up at Hanns. "Can we not go there instead?"

"Well," Hanns sighed, "we might have a problem with that."

"What do you mean?" Eleonore began to panic.

"Your release has not been permitted," Hanns looked at her sternly, but with a hint of compassion.

"I don't understand," Eleonore watched him intently and started to believe that she would never leave.

"The camp is overwhelmed with typhoid," Hanns glanced back out at the pile of bodies, "and we need you to be quarantined until it's safe for you to leave."

"Sounds familiar," Eleonore spoke bitterly and rubbed her eyes in exhaustion. "I'm a still a prisoner."

"No, I-"

"Then can I leave?" Eleonore interrupted.

"No," Hanns shook his head and glanced down at his feet. "But we need to rebuild Germany. Releasing a pandemic of typhoid would be detrimental."

"I can't stay here," Eleonore shook her head as the tears formed. She sat on the edge of the cot and began to rock back and forth as the dread overwhelmed her.

"They are bringing food and water and supplies. You'll be taken care of."

"No," Eleonore clenched her jaw and began to raise her voice. "I need out!"

"It's not possible," Hanns raised his hands to shed off the responsibility.

"You can get me out," Eleonore looked at Hanns intently.

"How?" Hanns shrugged.

"You'll think of something," Eleonore nodded.

"I'm going to help with the bodies," Hanns removed his satchel and set it down by Eleonore. "We'll talk later. You're safe now. I promise."

Chapter Two:
Lest We Forget

Monsters exist, but they are too few in number to be truly dangerous. More dangerous are the common men, the functionaries ready to believe and to act without asking questions.

Primo Levi

Privacy was absent in the medical tent as it swelled with a growing number of patients that were malnourished or diseased. Makeshift cots had been arranged when the ones supplied had run out, and some patients even slept on blankets on the ground.

The chaos within the tent reminded Eleonore of her time in the hospital at Auschwitz, yet here, in contrast, the medical staff cared for the well-being of their patients. Nurses urged calmness to some of those who were in shock and didn't trust anyone wearing a doctor's lab coat. To these poor souls who were delirious, the physicians reminded them of the cruelty that they had experienced and believed that they were about to be the subjects of another wicked experiment.

"Sir, sir, you can't eat that quickly," a nurse beside Eleonore begged a patient. "You need to take your time."

The patient ignored the warning and turned his back to her as he ate the food like a ravenous beast protecting its kill. He spilled the contents of the rations everywhere as he shoveled the food into his mouth, desperate for relief.

"Where am I?" a woman asked groggily, and Eleonore noticed that it was the same woman they had saved from near the gates.

"You are under our care," a nurse spoke sympathetically to her.

"And my boy?" the woman looked at the nurse with deadened eyes, scarcely able to open them.

"Uh," the nurse sat at the foot of her cot as she tried to soften the blow, "your child has perished, ma'am."

"I know," the woman replied without emotion. "Where's his body?"

"He's being laid to rest as we speak," the nurse replied softly.

At this, the woman burst into sobs like a dam breaking under the insurmountable weight.

"I need to see him," the woman tried to sit up, but she was too weak.

"Ma'am, you need to rest," the nurse stood and put a stern, yet caring, hand to stop the woman from moving.

"I need to see my boy. Why did you help me?" she looked at the nurse full of rage.

"Some kind people spotted you in your condition and brought you here. They saved your life."

"They didn't save me," the woman sobbed bitterly. "They condemned me to a life without my son. They should've left me."

Sitting at the edge of her cot, Eleonore turned away from the woman to allow her some dignity. She wondered if the woman was right, and if she should've let her go in peace.

But Eleonore distracted herself from such thoughts by staring out the front of the tent as she watched Hanns clearing the camp. He was relentless in his effort to restore some dignity to his people. Anyone could see the emotions building within him, but they remained barricaded behind the fortified wall of duty.

Eleonore watched as Hanns grabbed the arms of a deceased prisoner while another soldier assisted him by grabbing the legs. With a heave, the two lifted and carried the body to the hole which had been dug by the bulldozer. Swinging the body, they tossed it into the mass grave while other soldiers followed suit and threw other bodies in as well.

It was disturbing to watch, and Eleonore didn't know how to process what she was witnessing. The Nazis had been so calculated and hateful in their murder, revoking all emotion or elements of humanity. The Allies, too, were required to suppress their emotions, otherwise they would be reduced to weeping from morning till night. Yet, in opposition to the Nazis, the Allies concealment of rage and hurt was noble. They would press on in the hopes of protecting others and saving whoever had been left.

Still, Eleonore sensed that there was an urgency to complete the task. No one wanted to be in this environment for longer than necessary, and understandably so. While the war was horrific enough, who could these men tell about what they had seen? This was not a great war story to share with their children who were eager for grand tales of adventure. They would bear these burdens and live with them in quiet resentment.

Then, Hanns and his fellow soldier went over to the body of a teenage girl, likely no older than fifteen, who was a mere few feet from the medical tent. Eleonore's heart broke for her and she recalled the two teenage girls who had been murdered by lethal poison in her cell by Dr. Mengele. She remembered how beautiful they were and how unrepentant their murderer had been. Eleonore wished with all her heart that Dr. Mengele had been captured and that he would get his just punishment for what he had done.

This time, however, the soldier with Hanns collapsed and fell to his knees beside the teenage girl.

"Get up!" Hanns shouted.

"I...I can't" The soldier clutched his chest breathlessly.

"Yes, you can!" Hanns looked at him with incredible rage.

"I've got nothing left to give," the soldier looked up at Hanns to be lenient. He was a young man, not much older than the girl he was kneeling beside, and Eleonore wondered if she reminded him of someone special back home.

"She has nothing left to give," Hanns pointed to the body of the girl lying in front of him. "You're still breathing."

"I just need a minute," the soldier wiped the sweat from his forehead.

"No! Up!" Hanns remained adamant.

"These are our people," the soldier held the dead girl's cold hand. "I don't mean just that they were Jews, but they were German as well. My family escaped, and your family escaped, but this could've easily been us. It could've been my brother's body that they were throwing into a mass grave or my mother who had been found nearly dead at the gate. The American Jews are mad at what was done to our people, and rightfully so, but this is on a whole different level for me and you."

Kneeling beside the soldier, Hanns spoke softly, "Then let's lay her to rest. Now is the time for action, we can reflect later."

Agreeing, the soldier stood to his feet and summoned the strength as he placed his hands under the girl's arms. With a heave, the two took the girl and set her down gently in the pit that had now been filled with bodies.

Suddenly, a great commotion arose just out of Eleonore's view but coming from near the tent. Some of the guards outside the tent took notice as well and left their posts immediately and ran towards the scene. Eleonore watched as even Hanns ran in the direction of the chaos. Curious, Eleonore left her cot and peeked her head out the entrance to catch a glimpse.

About fifty yards from where Eleonore was, a group of Allied soldiers were escorting a Nazi doctor towards the pit. Her heart leapt with terror when Eleonore recognized him as the same doctor who had performed the abortion on her. About ten men guarded him against their fellow soldiers who were determined to cause the doctor harm. A soldier or two were fortunate enough to land a punch against the doctor's jaw or face and some even grabbed chunks of his hair.

The Allied soldiers began arguing amongst themselves about how to deal with the doctor. Many were enraged that this devil was permitted to continue drawing breath, others were eager to commit him over to a slower, more painful end. Still, others were resolved to defend him, knowing what their superiors intended as his punishment.

Eleonore watched as Hanns stood at a slight distance, observing the doctor with hateful malice. He held his hands in his pockets as he smoked, and to most, Hanns would appear oddly calm, but Eleonore knew different. She had only recently been acquainted with this officer, but he held the same terrible gaze on the doctor as he did when talking about Rudolph.

Eventually, the escort stopped in front of the pit which was filled to the brim with bodies and the doctor, shaking from fear, was forced to confront the horrors of his labors. Two guards, one on each side of the doctor, held onto his arms and if he so dared to lower his head or close his eyes, he was delivered a swift strike from their batons. The soldiers who were of a more vindictive disposition quieted their thirst for retribution when they realized the chastisement at hand. They backed away as they allowed this just torment to unfold.

A stillness fell upon everyone at the camp as they watched the Nazi doctor, who had taken the oath to do no harm, standing before his mountain of sins. The only sound was his pathetic sobbing, and Eleonore believed that his whimpering was not from regret, but from trepidation of what awaited him.

"You killed my husband!" a shout arose, cutting against the silence, and Eleonore saw a woman, on the other side of the pit, pointing wildly at the doctor. "A curse be on you!"

"You took my daughter!" another woman beside the first cried out. "You took my daughter! You took my daughter!"

Soon, the camp erupted into bitter cursing as one by one the other inmates joined in the condemnation of this doctor until no one was silent. They called out the names of those he had killed, filling heaven with their lamentations. Eleonore wanted to shout the names of Ella, Em, Ruth, and Alex, but her voice was caught in her throat and she remained silent.

Then, amidst this uproar, Eleonore noticed with marvel as a Rabbi and a Priest entered the camp. They strode together in unison as both religions tread upon the unholy earth beneath their feet. The Catholic Priest was adorned with a purple stole around his neck and the Rabbi wore a double star on his tunic. Both holy men were white as ghosts and their legs became as heavy as lead as they walked into the camp. They covered their noses with their hands to drown out the stench, but both were too shocked for words and were lost on how to convey their emotions.

Slowly, the camp returned to silence as they took notice of these pious men and awaited their reaction. Many looked to them to answer an impossible question. These men bore the unbearable burden of being the bridge between heaven and earth. Yet now their pious professions seemed so inadequately prepared to answer on God's behalf for this level of devastation.

Then, suddenly, a famished inmate who was near Eleonore left the tent and approached the Rabbi. He was more than half-starved and bruised from beatings, and the Rabbi's breath was stolen from the horror of seeing a human in such a dreadful condition.

"The dead walk," a tear fell from the Rabbi as he looked on the inmate with immense pity.

Gently grabbing the Rabbi's tunic, the inmate felt the double star and broke out into sobs as he stroked the badge of faith and cried, "Rabbiner, Rabbiner."

Taking the inmate's hand into his, the Rabbi whispered something to him that Eleonore couldn't hear. Then, gently, the Rabbi placed his hand on the inmate's shoulder before leaving the crumpled man with a seed of resolve that he didn't possess before.

Walking towards the mass grave, the Rabbi and Priest didn't so much as offer the whimpering Nazi doctor a glance. He didn't exist in their eyes, and Eleonore assumed what they were likely thinking: his soul was lost. Then, the two men stood, alone, before the mass grave and gave the signal for it to be filled with earth.

Eleonore watched as soldiers and former prisoners stood and observed the burial silently, no one daring to say a word. Eleonore spotted the Rabbi weeping as the grave was filled. Regardless of their religion, the soldiers removed their helmets while the officers removed their caps and held them by their sides. All but the nurses and doctors who were busy saving their patients had ceased their work.

Eleonore was moved at the emotion of the Rabbi and, to pay her respects, held her hands gently in front of her and bowed her head as he recited the Kaddish. Some other inmates from the tent joined her outside as well and she could hear them quietly reciting along with the Rabbi.

Eleonore was amazed that anyone could believe in God at a time like this. Where was He when she was placed in the stock cars packed with people? Where was He when Em's son was taken to the gas chambers? Where was He when Rudolph took advantage of her? Where was He when so many of His own people were killed?

A sharp cynicism raged within her and she couldn't understand why the divine had been so absent. The Priest and Rabbi seemed to be sharing in her disbelief as they paused at certain parts of their prayers, seeing that the words were inappropriate for the circumstance.

"Blessed be His name," the Priest cleared his throat and swayed awkwardly as he fumbled with the prayer book in his hands, unsure of how to continue.

But, after the Catholic and Jewish prayers were recited, the bulldozer roared to life again as it started on the next mass grave. There was still much work to be done, and many bodies required proper burial.

"Take this," a nurse handed a bowl to a patient near Eleonore.

"Here," another nurse handed Eleonore a lukewarm bowl of broth and some dry bread.

"Thank you," Eleonore looked at the nurse with genuine gratitude. Though, she wondered if she could eat. The broth rolled around slowly which reminded her of how kind Mrs. Felix had been to give her the simple gift of a bowl. Without such a basic necessity, she would've faced a torturous death by starvation.

Snap!

Eleonore looked up from her bowl, startled by the sound, to see a photographer kneeling and taking a photograph of her and the others around the medical tent. Irate that the man showed no sensitivity during such an event, Eleonore stormed back into the tent.

"If we could just gather the few of you together for another picture," an interpreter spoke to those who had remained outside.

Returning to her cot, Eleonore fumed at the tactless photographer. *How could he be so rude?* She thought as she clenched her jaw and wished that she had the strength to confront him.

There are bigger things to focus on, Eleonore reminded herself and calmed a little, feeling a bit selfish for her reaction. Dipping the bread into her soup, Eleonore took a bite and felt the broth burn her dry throat.

"Ah, Rabbi," a nurse called, and Eleonore looked up to see that the Rabbi had entered the tent.

She studied the man with interest mixed with admiration. Many in the camp were looking to him for answers which, she assumed, he was searching for as well. Yet she also found it odd that he, as a chaplain, was armed with a pistol holstered at his side. Should she have found herself in a healthier state, both spiritually and physically, she would've loved to engage this intriguing man in conversation.

But the discussions she wished to participate in now seemed inconsequential. Philosophy, theology, and other such existential subjects felt so impractical and trivial that she was almost embarrassed that she ever concerned herself with them at all. The pursuit of happiness and the concerns of daily life had fallen silent at the feet of a singular purpose: survival.

"Someone was asking for me?" the Rabbi looked kindly at the nurse, but Eleonore could tell that he was in shock and, mentally, he was still standing before the mass grave.

"That's right," the nurse led him to the back of the tent. "There was a baby boy born about a week ago and the mother would like him to be circumcised."

A baby born here? Eleonore shook her head. *Thank God the Allies arrived in time.* But just as the thought entered her mind, another thought arose in contention. *Thank God? Why thank Him? What about the other thousands of babies or pregnant women killed by the Nazis? What about your own child that the Nazis aborted when you arrived here?! Or how about the reason for your pregnancy in the first place?! Where was God then?!*

"Good," a familiar voice spoke, and Eleonore looked up to see Hanns standing over her. "You need to regain your strength," he nodded to her bowl of broth.

"Howard, there you are," a nurse came over and spoke to Hanns in German, though she talked slowly and a bit haltingly as it wasn't her native tongue.

Why did she call him Howard? Eleonore wondered, but was distracted by a young girl, no older than five, clinging to the nurse. Her hair had been shaved, she had scars and bruises on her face, and there were dark circles under her eyes from malnutrition. Still, there was something familiar about her that Eleonore couldn't quite identify. She gave a slight smile to the girl, but she only clung tighter and looked away from Eleonore.

"This little one claims that her mother was shipped to another camp just last week," the nurse put her hand behind the girl's back and edged her forward.

"Last week?" Hanns looked down at the girl who replied with a nod, but still without much emotion.

"What's your name?" Hanns asked quickly but the girl was too shy to answer.

"I'll need a name if I'm to find your mother," Hanns continued, but the girl looked vacantly back at him.

"There are millions of people now displaced throughout Europe," Hanns spoke in a hushed tone to the nurse. "Finding this girl's mother will be nearly impossible."

"Howard, we must try," the nurse persisted.

Why does she keep calling him Howard? Eleonore squinted as she looked at Hanns suspiciously, curious as to what he was hiding from her.

Studying the girl, Hanns retrieved a notepad from his satchel and knelt in front of her, "Can you write?"

The girl nodded.

"Can you spell your mother's name?"

Again, the girl nodded.

"Good," Hanns put the notepad down on the foot of Eleonore's cot. "Write it for me and I'll try to find your mom, okay?"

"Go on," the nurse encouraged her and pointed to the notepad.

Cautiously, the girl walked to the foot of the cot and, taking up the pencil, wrote her mother's name. Her writing was large and clumsy, but legible enough for Hanns to read it properly.

"I'll find out what I can," Hanns spoke to the nurse as he studied the girl's writing.

"God bless you!" The nurse grabbed Hanns' arm.

"Don't invoke the Almighty in a place like this," Hanns' face grew red with rage.

"Sorry," the nurse covered her mouth with her hand, distraught that she had overstepped.

"Miss Hodys," Hanns turned towards Eleonore, "I place this girl in your care until I've had the opportunity to investigate. In the meantime, I'll continue helping with the bodies. Nurse, please see that they are cared for."

"Of course," the nurse tried to hold the girl's hand and lead her towards Eleonore, but the girl dug in her heels and refused to be coerced.

Stunned at the turn of events, Eleonore watched Hanns swiftly exit the tent.

"I have other patients to attend to," the nurse gave a polite, but substantial push for the girl to leave her care and enter that of Eleonore's.

For a moment, Eleonore and the girl faced each other at a complete loss for how to interact. While children were naturally attracted to Eleonore, she found herself increasingly unsure of how to entertain them. In a setting like this, where the girl was as alone and as frightened as Eleonore, she wished that she had had a say in the change of her occupation.

"What's your name, sweetie?" Eleonore asked eventually.

The girl didn't answer but stared at Eleonore with an emptiness that no child should ever understand.

Suddenly, the bulldozer roared to life and the girl jolted towards Eleonore, terrified at the sound.

"I've got you," Eleonore put an arm around the girl whose attention was locked on the machine digging another grave.

"Don't watch," Eleonore gave a warm smile as she turned the girl's face towards hers. "It's not something little girls should see."

"I want momma," the girl spoke, but her voice was harsh and raspy.

"I can imagine that you do," Eleonore spoke as an immense pity swelled within her.

"Do you know where she is?" the girl looked intently into Eleonore's eyes.

"No," Eleonore shook her head, wishing that she did, "but the officer will help you find her."

"What?" the girl asked, her mind searching for comprehension.

"The officer that was here with us," Eleonore pointed at the spot where Hanns had been standing, "he will help you find her."

"Do you know where she is?" the girl asked again.

"I wish that I did," Eleonore patted her shoulder, and, in that instant, she understood the familiarity. Something about this girl, something not entirely concrete, reminded her of Ella. There was a powerful wrath hidden underneath exotic beauty. This girl was a fighter, she just didn't know it yet.

"What's your name?" Eleonore moved off the cot and knelt before the girl.

"Hannah," the girl replied shyly.

"And your last name?"

"Kerestesh," the girl replied.

"Hungarian?" Eleonore threw her lips upside down. "You speak German quite well."

Hannah returned to a blank expression and Eleonore assumed that she was thinking again of her mother.

"Come up here," Eleonore returned to the cot and patted the spot beside her as she sat on the edge, but Hannah refused to even acknowledge her presence.

I'm not sure how to talk to her, Eleonore thought. *I feel like there's some trick or phrase I should be saying.*

"You miss your mom?" Eleonore persisted.

At this, Hannah welled up and began to sob.

Now I've done it, Eleonore grew crimson with embarrassment. *What a stupid thing to say. Of course she misses her.*

"Come here," Eleonore held her hands out, but Hannah pulled away violently.

Sighing, Eleonore slapped her hands against her thighs in defeat. *They should've asked me first before leaving her alone with me,* she shook her head. *Think, Eleonore, what did you like as a girl?*

"Do you know that I make dresses?" Eleonore leaned in.

Still, Hannah continued to sob, but she gave a glance of interest and that was enough for Eleonore to continue.

"I owned my own shop in Berlin. Do you know what it was called?"

Hannah shook her head as she calmed a little and looked expectantly at Eleonore.

"*La Venezia.* Do you know what that means?"

"Venice," Hannah spoke through sniffles.

"That's right! How did you know that?"

"Father showed me pictures," Hannah began but broke into sobs again. "Have you seen the pictures?"

You poor thing, Eleonore's heart broke for the child, and for all the children who had been robbed of their lives and their families.

"We'll find your mother," Eleonore whispered and held out her hand to Hannah who looked at her outstretched hand, judging if she could trust her. Eventually, the girl took hold and Eleonore hoisted Hannah onto the cot to sit beside her.

"Big dresses?" Hannah mumbled.

"What's that?" Eleonore leaned in.

"The dresses, were they big?"

"The biggest," Eleonore exaggerated with her voice.

Hannah smiled a little and Eleonore noticed her leg start to sway a bit. She marveled at how adaptive children were. The bulldozer roared outside the tent, stirring dust into the air. Yet Eleonore was able to distract Hannah and shelter her, to a degree, from the horror just outside the tent.

Chapter Three:
Purpose

"The purpose of life is not to be happy. It is to be useful, to be honorable, to be compassionate, to have it make some difference that you have lived and lived well."

Ralph Waldo Emerson

"Eleonore," Hanns whispered.

"What's wrong?" Eleonore awoke and opened her eyes slowly as she looked at him.

"We need to go," Hanns offered her his hand to help her up.

"Go where?" Eleonore became confused.

Although half asleep, she noticed that the medical tent was empty, and she was the only one left. In fact, the tent had been stripped bare and her cot was all that remained. She wondered how everyone had vacated without disturbing her. She felt a chill on her arms, and she shivered as a wind rushed through the empty tent.

"Come," Hanns grabbed her hand forcefully and led her out.

"You're hurting me!" Eleonore tried to break free, but his grip was too strong.

"Where are we going?" Eleonore looked up at Hanns as they walked through the camp, which was also deserted, but he didn't reply as he stared blankly at something in the distance.

Curious as to what had stolen his attention, Eleonore looked in the direction of his gaze when she noticed that they had suddenly left the camp and were walking in a dry, vacant wasteland. The sky above was darkened with black, wrathful storm clouds and the earth at their feet was coarse, gray sand stretching for miles in all directions. They were isolated from the world, and a loneliness began to crush Eleonore's soul.

Then, in the distance, Eleonore noticed a single building situated on a hill. In her heart, Eleonore knew what it was, but she prayed that she was mistaken. It was Cell Block 11 and she understood that she would spend eternity suffering in that standing cell.

"Hanns!" Eleonore panicked. "Stop! Please!"

She looked up at him for mercy, but her heart gave out when Hanns looked back at her and his face transformed into that of Commandant Hoess. A wicked smile grew on Rudolph's face knowing the torment that he would bring her.

Eleonore tried to run away, but her legs were locked on some sort of track and she had no control over her movement. Then, in an instant, they were before Cell Block 11 and Rudolph grabbed her by the arm as the metal doors opened by themselves to reveal a dark, bottomless pit. Screams and wailing arose from within and the terrible clanking of metal against metal echoed from the inmates trapped inside.

Rudolph grabbed her shoulders, and pulled her towards him as he looked at her with a lustful gaze. Repulsed, Eleonore turned away, but he grabbed her by the jaw with a coarse, blood-stained hand and forced her to look at him. Then, with one hand gripping the back of her head, Rudolph took his free hand and clasped it over her mouth and nose. Eleonore looked up at him with fearful eyes, but there would be no clemency as he began to suffocate her.

Eleonore shot awake.

Sitting upright, Eleonore looked around to see that she was still in the medical tent and the dream was nothing more than a fabrication, however real it felt. Apart from the pale orange light hanging from the entrance, the tent was completely dark, and Eleonore noticed only a couple of nurses quietly checking on the patients.

Pondering as to the meaning of the dream, and wondering what time of night it was, Eleonore laid back down but was surprised by a lump beside her which groaned slightly at being disturbed. *Hannah!* Eleonore recalled and gently inspected the girl to see that she was still sleeping soundly.

A smile crept onto Eleonore's face as she watched the sweet girl. Eleonore ran her hand over the girl's bald head as she slept peacefully, glad that she found her as a source of comfort. A part of Hannah reminded Eleonore of Rudolph's daughter and she marveled at how different their existence was. Because of the coincidence of birth, one lived in paradise while the other was forced to endure hell.

"Can I help you?" a nurse called, and Eleonore looked up to see that Hanns had slipped into the medical tent.

"No," Hanns spoke in a hushed tone and pointed towards Eleonore, "I'm here for her."

"For what purpose?" the nurse crossed her arms and examined Hanns guardedly. She spoke so loudly that Eleonore was surprised that she hadn't disturbed the other patients.

"That's classified," Hanns replied briefly as he brushed past the nurse.

"Classified?!" the nurse huffed and then walked briskly to the exit. "I'll go call the doctor."

"No, wait!" Hanns turned towards the nurse but she had already left.

"What are you doing here?" Eleonore asked.

"We have to go, now!" Hanns whispered harshly and looked around to make sure no one else would question his purpose.

"Where?" Eleonore asked, not entirely awake yet, and the image of Rudolph was still lingering. Her body was tense, both from the disturbing sleep and from the stress of her recent and forced abortion.

"Where do you think?" Hanns grew impatient and pulled Eleonore to sit upright as she winced at the sudden movement. "Can you carry her?"

Eleonore shook her head apologetically and Hanns grunted as he picked up Hannah who stirred and whined but fell back asleep with her head on his shoulder.

"The truck is waiting," Hanns held open the flap to the medical tent and Eleonore noticed that the sun had not yet risen.

Truck? What truck? Eleonore frowned, but then she spotted a military transport waiting near the gates. A man was sitting in the driver's seat with his hands gripping the steering wheel and his eyes were wide and panicked.

"Hey!" the nurse shouted after them. She had made good on her promise and was now returning with the doctor who looked less than pleased.

"Quickly," Hanns gripped Eleonore's arm firmly and sped her on.

Swiftly, they reached the truck and Hanns let down the tailgate as he checked over his shoulder to gauge the distance between themselves and this persistent nurse. Hanns placed Hannah down gently, and Eleonore marveled at her ability to remain sleeping, and then climbed into the back herself. Sitting on the bench, Eleonore pulled Hannah onto her lap and rested her head on her shoulder.

"You didn't say anything about her," the man in the driver's seat whispered sternly to Hanns with somewhat awkward German. He carried an accent, but the pronunciation, at least, was accurate.

Glancing at the man, Eleonore caught his sharp, dread-filled eyes in the rear-view mirror.

"Just drive," Hanns whispered back.

"I don't like this, Howard," the driver shook his head. "I need to know what's going on."

"She has agreed to help us," Hanns explained briskly, "so I'm helping her."

"And who is she?"

"Someone who has invaluable information on Rudolph Hoess."

"Is that right?" the driver turned around and faced Eleonore as he studied her with growing interest.

"Now, can we go?" Hanns pointed impatiently.

"Alright, alright," the driver threw his hands in the air and put the truck into drive. "I just want to be informed is all."

"Just keep quiet," Hanns spoke over his shoulder to Eleonore. "Strictly speaking, it's not permitted for me to take you out of the camp."

Eleonore's heart began to race, and her stomach churned as the truck jumped to a start and made its short trek to the gates. She had been sent to Auschwitz by the deceitfulness of a man she thought she could trust, and she wondered if being captured trying to escape would land her in another prison. Though, she assumed, the Allies would be much more lenient. *I just need to get out,* Eleonore rubbed her eyes.

Stopped by the guards at the gate, Hanns handed them some papers which they checked over thoroughly. Straightening her back, Eleonore peeked out the front of the truck and caught the sight of the guard sifting through the documents. Yet, to Eleonore, these guards still seemed shell-shocked by the day's events and she wondered if they were even conscious of what they were reading. The guard gave a rather unconvinced look up at Hanns and then called to his fellow guard.

I wish I knew English better, Eleonore huffed as she bounced her leg anxiously. *Though I suppose I didn't believe I would ever have use for it.*

"Stop them!" a distant shout echoed throughout the camp and Eleonore spotted the nurse closing in.

At this, the guard asked Hanns and the driver a few heated questions which Eleonore gathered by their reactions that the fabrication was quickly falling apart.

Hanns began shouting at the guards and an intense exchange took place which only increased her anxiety. Then, one of the guards raised his rifle and aimed it directly at Hanns. A small cry escaped from Eleonore and she clasped her hand over her mouth to stifle any further outburst.

"Go, go, go!" Hanns shouted to the driver who floored the gas pedal and they sped out of the camp.

"Get down!" Hanns shouted to Eleonore who obeyed without hesitation and lay flat on her back on the bench, waking up Hannah who began to cry at the disturbance and the shock of not knowing where she was.

"It's alright," Eleonore tried to calm Hannah down while she waited for the bullets to pepper the back of the truck.

After what felt like an age, Eleonore realized that no shots had been fired. She glanced up at Hanns who had turned around in his seat and was looking nervously out the back.

"I think we're in the clear," Hanns breathed a heavy sigh of relief and then began to chuckle and laugh.

"You could've handled that better," the driver berated Hanns.

"What was that about?!" Eleonore shouted over Hannah's crying.

"I forged some papers for you," Hanns rubbed his cheeks which were growing sore from laughter.

"What kind of papers?" Eleonore frowned.

"Travel papers," Hanns settled a little but still had a large grin. "They are required to travel anywhere in Europe. I guess they were poor imitations. I really thought they were going to shoot at us," Hanns turned to the driver and burst into laughter again.

Still, the driver was unamused, as was Eleonore.

"So, what does that mean for me?" Eleonore sat up again on the bench and tried to rock Hannah who was still crying. "How am I to travel anywhere without papers?"

"We'll sort something out," Hanns shrugged and then pointed to the driver. "This solemn creature is Lieutenant Colonel Genn, by the way."

"Nice to meet you," Eleonore said quickly, and Genn gave a quick nod in reply.

"Where are we heading?" Eleonore asked Hanns.

"First, to find the girl's mother," Hanns answered.

"You know where she is?" Eleonore asked with surprise. She had assumed that such a feat was impossible and, likely, that Hannah would be in her care for some time.

"I know where she was sent, so we'll start there. The mother, along with some others, were shipped out to a camp outside of Hanover called Wolfsburg. Hopefully, that's where she still is," Hanns glanced knowingly at Eleonore.

"Did you hear that?" Eleonore put Hannah upright on her knee, but the girl was in a sorrowful state and simply put her head into Eleonore's shoulder. "We're going to look for your mother!"

"Ya?" Hannah looked up at her through red, swollen eyes.

"Ya!" Eleonore looked at her excitedly, hoping that she wasn't providing false assurances.

"I'm hungry," Hannah began to cry again.

"Do you have anything for her to eat?" Eleonore asked Hanns.

"Do you think she'll enjoy crackers that taste of sawdust and mold?" Hanns joked and Genn slapped the wheel as he laughed, abruptly changing his mood.

"That's not amusing!" Eleonore frowned. *He was so callous yesterday, how can he be so dismissive now?*

"Here," Hanns reached back with a small package of crackers. "They're actually not too terrible."

Hannah nearly jumped out of Eleonore's lap as she snatched the crackers from Hanns who chuckled at her eagerness. Eleonore smiled as she watched Hannah shovel the food into her mouth, but again, wondered why Hanns was acting so nonchalant. He had behaved solemnly in the camp, but now it seemed as if he was a different person entirely.

"There's a uniform for you to change into," Hanns pointed to the opposite bench and Eleonore spotted a neatly folded brown uniform. "It will likely be too large, but I didn't have time to pick out a size."

"I appreciate it," Eleonore smiled slightly as she set Hannah down on the bench beside her, who bounced her leg happily as she ate.

Sliding to the opposite bench, Eleonore held the uniform in front of her as it unfolded naturally to reveal that it was a one-piece jumpsuit. Glancing at the front of the vehicle, Eleonore made sure that neither man was looking. Satisfied with the little privacy afforded her, and the cover of the dark, early morning sky, Eleonore began to undress.

But, as she slid her arm out of the sleeve, something happened that Eleonore didn't quite understand. For whatever reason, she couldn't rid herself of this dress with the bullet hole. Maybe it reminded her of how close she herself had come to being the one with a bullet through her chest. Maybe she wanted to do some service to the previous owner. Whatever it was, Eleonore kept it on as she slid the jumper over top and rejoined Hannah on her bench.

Silence fell upon the company as they traveled through the countryside while the sun gradually rose. The truck jostled and swayed on the roads, which brought on a sort of calm. With a big yawn, Hannah leaned her head on Eleonore's shoulder and fell back asleep within minutes. While the bench was uncomfortable, Eleonore didn't dare shift her position. She wanted Hannah to have a decent sleep. She couldn't provide this sweet girl with much, but if she could alleviate some degree of sorrow from Hannah, then Eleonore would gladly do so.

She only wished that she could afford her with better clothes than the rags she wore now. Spying a small, navy-blue blanket on the floor of the truck, Eleonore judged whether it was too far away for her to grab it without waking Hannah. She tried to lean over, but the strain on her stomach was unbearable. Stretching out her foot, Eleonore nabbed it with the toe of her worn shoe and inched it closer to her. Sighing out of victory mixed with exhaustion, Eleonore covered Hannah and grinned at her success.

But the blanket must've been too coarse for Hannah, or too itchy, and she stirred, grumpily, and tossed it aside before falling back to sleep. Eleonore chuckled and shook her head, considering the effort she went to ease Hannah's troubles only to discover that she had created another.

This must be what other parents feel like, Eleonore thought but her smile faded, and she put her hand to her empty womb. *I wonder if I would've made a good mother. I just wish I knew whether you were a boy or a girl. Not that it would've mattered, but I would've liked to have known. Whatever the case, I'm sure you were perfect.*

Staring out the back of the truck, Eleonore watched as a landscape destroyed by war passed by their view. The leaves had been burnt off of the trees, which now stood as sad, lonely reminders of what once was. The earth, which had once been green and vibrant, was now a mixture of browns and grays.

It was then that Eleonore contemplated the peculiarity of how much she trusted Hanns. She had known him for less than a day, yet, she grinned as she considered that she likely knew him better than most. She had known Hanns under the worst of all possible circumstances and his character was nothing short of admirable.

Glancing at the officer, Eleonore watched as the two gentlemen conversed in English. She wished to know more about them, but their conversation was rather animated, and she didn't want to interrupt. She assumed that there would be plenty of time to get acquainted. Besides, she was deathly tired and not of the frame of mind to discuss anything significant. She wondered what plots they were forming, or if they were discussing something altogether trivial such as the girls that awaited them back home.

Closing her eyes, Eleonore leaned her head back and stared at the roof of the truck which was just a fastened tarp that flapped in the wind. It reminded her of when the Nazis took her to the trains to be sent to Auschwitz. How different life would've been if she had simply submitted to that wicked regime.

You can't permit such a reflection, Eleonore shook her head. *You did the right thing. It cost you hell, but you obeyed your conscience. Rudolph will get his just punishment, and Hanns will make sure of that. As will Jung, despite his kindness to me. He can't be forgiven for his other sins.*

"We're here," Hanns called back to Eleonore who stirred awake and looked groggily down at Hannah who was still sleeping peacefully. Closing her eyes again, Eleonore felt sleep returning, reaching out to her like a dear friend attempting to rekindle a lost relationship.

"I don't think I'll ever get used to this," Genn muttered, catching Eleonore's attention, and she looked out the front of the vehicle to witness what had, unfortunately, become so familiar to her.

The camp at Wolfsburg had been transformed into a vibrant refuge. Medical tents, transportation offices, and even a dance hall had been built. Yet, despite the conversion, the stains of the Nazi plague remained. Dirt was piled over recent graves, starved ex-inmates riddled with disease were treated by a caring nurse or doctor, and the stench of death was thick.

As they approached the camp, Eleonore frowned when she heard lighthearted music blaring from the loudspeakers. It was a German singer that she was unfamiliar with, but the tune struck her as almost offensive. To play cheerful songs which preached about joy and carefree romance were a foreign language to those who had witnessed the unending death and torture of their loved ones and friends. It reminded her of the shock she received in Auschwitz when the orchestra played gleeful foxtrots after roll call; almost as if the Nazis were mocking their victims.

Eleonore understood the intent of the Allies and this joyful music was aimed as a benefit for the prisoners as much as the liberators. The Allied soldiers who had delivered the camp from the Nazis required the reminder of what the goals in life were supposed to be. Routine, Eleonore understood, was to return to normal as soon as possible for both the redeemer and the redeemed. No one wanted to remain in the camps for longer than necessary.

Stopping at the gates, Genn provided a brief explanation to the guards and showed them his papers. Eleonore watched with suspense as they seemed a little confused as to his purpose.

Suddenly, the flap to the back of the truck swung open, and a guard peeked inside to see Eleonore on the bench with Hannah sleeping on her lap. Eleonore watched in amazement as the guard's countenance morphed from apprehension into compassion as he studied them. She realized what an odd sight they must've appeared. Her condition warranted sympathy on its own merits, but the half-starved and shaved five-year-old girl sleeping on her lap would've moved the harshest of men to pity.

Nodding with a slight apology to Eleonore, the guard put the flap back and called to his fellow guard who was talking to Genn, confirming whatever the Lieutenant Colonel had been advising him. Shrugging, the guard handed Genn a megaphone, who then quickly passed this to Hanns, and they drove into the camp.

"This camp feels a bit different," Eleonore frowned. "Smaller, even."

"This was a labor camp," Genn answered over his shoulder as he drove carefully. "Although, 'slave camp' would be more accurate. They made parts for the car factory about thirty miles from here, but this camp was absent of the gas chambers."

"Really?!" Eleonore grew curious.

"They worked the poor souls to death instead," Genn replied and Eleonore caught the rageful flinch of his eye.

"Strange to think that they would've sent her mother here," Eleonore thought aloud.

"Speaking of which," Genn glanced at Hanns as he looked out the window, "go on, you've got the megaphone. You might as well use it."

Nodding, Hanns rolled down the window and employed the megaphone liberally as Genn drove slowly.

"Violet Kerestesh?!" Hanns called, waking Hannah.

"Momma?!" Hannah called while she was still dazed.

"He'll find her," Eleonore spoke quietly as if any interruption on her part would spell disaster.

There was no reply. Only the recognizable, vacant looks from the ex-inmates and a mixture of concerned and annoyed glances from the Allied staff.

"Stop," Hanns ordered Genn, who seemed annoyed at the command, especially since he was Hanns' superior.

"What is it?" Genn leaned over, trying to see what Hanns had spotted.

"I'm going to check the medical tent," Hanns replied as he quickly left the vehicle.

Eleonore peeked her head through the flap as she watched Hanns inspecting the female patients, asking each of them if they were Hannah's mother. Most were too ill to even understand him, but Hanns persisted and disappeared deeper into the tent.

"Where is she?" Hannah asked as she started to cry.

"I don't know," Eleonore peeked again through the flap as she grew anxious for his return.

"What's taking so long?" Genn muttered as he fidgeted with his thumb on the steering wheel.

Eleonore felt her shoulders tensing and quit looking out the flap. Catching Hannah's worried stare, Eleonore relaxed a little and gave a quick smile. The chances of them finding her mother were next to none, and Eleonore began to prepare what she would say to Hannah.

Finally, Hanns returned to the truck and gave a slight shake of his head to Genn who sighed with disappointment.

"She's not there?" Hannah looked at Eleonore full of worry.

"Don't give up," Eleonore patted her back, but in her heart she knew there was little hope.

They continued throughout the camp as Hanns remained resolute with his megaphone. But as they drove by the dance hall, Eleonore was surprised to find that it was brimming to capacity, mostly with Allied soldiers and a handful of previous inmates who had regained some of their strength. Peeking out the back flap, Eleonore watched with amusement as the people danced ecstatically, even though it was early in the morning. It was then that Eleonore realized the obvious: this was not the beginning of their merriment, but rather, the ending of a good night. They had been repressed for their nature, but now they celebrated with reckless abandon. Soldiers in a drunken stupor pressed their luck with former inmates and, as one would expect, most were rejected. Others, Eleonore discovered, had found their fortune and she held back a sheepish giggle when she spotted a couple kissing passionately outside the hall.

"Violet Kerestesh?!" Hanns shouted again.

Still, nothing.

"She's not here," Hannah slouched as she sat beside Eleonore.

"You don't know that," Eleonore placed her hands on the girl's face. "We must not give up hope."

After they had circled around the entire camp shouting for the girl's mother, there was still no response. Eleonore's heart broke for Hannah as the truck came to a stop and she watched Genn rubbing his eyes in defeat as he turned off the vehicle.

The failure of their mission was palpable, and it rested heavily on their shoulders. There wasn't much hope to begin with, but to witness this beautiful girl deprived of her mother was a crushing blow. Eleonore reached out to take the girl's hand, but she pulled away. There were no more tears for her to shed as her sadness was drowned out by unrestrained rage. She clenched her hands into fists and began to breathe slowly, experiencing a pain that no child should ever know.

"I'm sorry," Hanns slumped back into his seat and spoke softly to Hannah. "I don't think she's here. I'll check to see if they have any records of —"

Suddenly, a cry arose from within the camp and Eleonore turned to see a woman bolting towards the truck.

"Is that her?" Genn peered at the woman.

"Is that your mom?" Hanns called over his shoulder to Hannah, but she was so lost to her anger that she ignored him.

"Let's hope so," Genn spoke under his breath as the woman, about the right age for Hannah's mother, came crashing against Hanns' door.

"I'm Violet Kerestesh," the woman panted as she gripped Hanns' door.

"I believe you are this girl's mother," Hanns pointed into the truck. "I'll have to—"

"My baby?!" the woman screamed and stood on her tiptoes as she tried to see into the back. But, being a petite woman, she was unable to get a good view and ran to the end of the truck where she saw Hannah standing beside Eleonore.

"Momma?!" Hannah called as her rage evaporated and she sprinted into her mother's outstretched arms.

"My baby!" Violet wept as she squeezed Hannah tight.

"Momma!" Hannah bawled as the two were reunited.

A tear fell down Eleonore's cheek as she watched Violet kiss Hannah all over. Yet, there was a slight splitting of Eleonore's joy as, for the briefest of moments, she thought that Hannah might be in her care for some time. While the thought was initially overwhelming, Eleonore now wished for nothing more than to take care of someone or to feel needed. While she was tending to Hannah, she could forget her own sorrows. She could table her own fears and worries and help Hannah fight through hers. Still, Eleonore was overjoyed that Hannah had been returned.

But then Eleonore caught the gazes from the onlookers. Mothers and fathers watched with almost hateful jealousy. They would never experience this rare reunion. Why should one mother be so delighted while the rest must endure in their mourning? One drop of justice, it seemed to Eleonore, rippled and disturbed the vast ocean of injustice.

Glancing at Hanns, Eleonore noticed a sort of distance in his gaze as he watched the mother and daughter. He was a good man, Eleonore understood, although she found his character a little puzzling and a bit gruff. Still, this experience was unlike any other in human history and no one quite understood how to properly and effectively behave or react.

"Howard, we need to leave," Genn cautioned Hanns.

"I know," Hanns removed his cap as he scratched his head.

The truck roared to life and the three exited the camp as Eleonore felt her heart throbbing in her chest. She wasn't able to say a suitable goodbye to Hannah, and it left Eleonore feeling rather unimportant to the girl, as silly as she knew that sounded. She had known her for less than a day, but still, Eleonore's heart clung to her.

"Where are we going now?" Eleonore leaned back on the bench as she tried to distract herself.

"As it happens," Hanns looked over his shoulder at her, "I may have found you some employment."

"Really?" Eleonore threw her head back in shock.

"Have you ever heard of the town of Salzkotten?"

"No," Eleonore frowned. "I don't believe I'm familiar with it."

"I'd be surprised if you were," Hanns replied as he gave a quick salute to the guards as they exited the camp. "Calling it a town is a little generous. The population is next to none."

"What's there for me, then?" Eleonore shook her head.

"Well," Hanns sighed and looked at Eleonore reluctantly, "it's not noble work. There is an elderly woman who needs a lady's maid."

Eleonore smiled at the thought of being needed in such a capacity. It wasn't noble, Hanns was right, but Eleonore remembered her duties with the bedpans at Auschwitz; she was used to the ignoble. Besides, having someone to care for was exactly the sort of employment she needed.

"So?" Hanns watched her eagerly as Eleonore pondered. "She's not an invalid, if you're wondering. She simply needs help with daily tasks. She lost all her family in the war, you see, and is now alone. She has requested help and-"

"Thank you," Eleonore interrupted as she nodded. "I accept."

"Good," Hanns breathed a sigh of relief. "I was worried. I have a feeling you will be a good fit."

"Why are you helping me?" Eleonore watched Hanns curiously and noticed Genn glance at him as well.

"I'll be honest," Hanns looked away nervously, "I may have my own motives for you being the successful candidate,"

"Such as?" Eleonore leaned forward.

"There are rumors that SS guards and some other officers have fled to the northwest of Germany. I would like you to be my eyes and ears in that region. If you notice anything peculiar, I ask that you advise me as soon as possible. My only request is that the information is concrete and certain. I can't be chasing guesses."

"Seems reasonable," Eleonore gave a brief smile.

Such espionage, she believed, would make her feel rather important. Besides, the thought of Ella ran through her mind and she could imagine her approval of this charge.

"Is there any danger?" Eleonore asked.

"No credible threats," Hanns replied, though a little too quickly. "Nothing more than rumors at this time."

"Well, I can't show up like this," Eleonore glanced down at her uniform which was still covering the dress with the bullet hole.

"Quite right," Hanns nodded. "We'll stop in a town along the way and get you some clothes."

New clothes, Eleonore smiled as a happy tear welled up in her eyes. Yet, the moment such bliss arrived it was robbed by an overwhelming sense of guilt. How could she appreciate the trivial after what she had endured in the camps? How could she allow any pleasure to be gained in life when others, like Ella, had paid the ultimate price? Regardless, such thoughts were too heavy for her to contemplate, and Eleonore closed her eyes as she took a deep breath in and out. They had done well with returning Hannah to her mother, and that was all that really mattered.

Chapter Four:
The Dress

Success consists of going from failure to failure without loss of enthusiasm.

Winston Churchill

Rolling down the window, Hanns lit his Dunhill pipe and began smoking as he studied a map of Germany. Eleonore closed her eyes as the wind rushed through her hair which was beginning to reach its former lengths. She remembered the cruelty of her head being shaved while they tattooed her arm, and then being sprayed with freezing cold water while naked and huddling together with the other women. If she focused, even slightly, she found herself standing in that cruel room again, feeling the bite of the cold water against her back.

But even in her recollection there was a warmth that the Nazis could not extinguish. Despite that horrific experience, Eleonore's strongest impression was that of Ella's hand holding hers. She remembered the warmth from standing close to her as they sheltered each other from the unforgiving environment. How she missed Ella's strength now.

For all the misery that Eleonore had experienced, she found one encouragement: Ella had influenced Eleonore to such a degree that she took her wherever she went. Ella's bravery, even against the greatest of odds, had stirred Eleonore to emulate her character. Ella had lost everything, but still, she refused to idly accept the fate handed to her. When others would break under the pressure, Ella stood firm and unyielding. Such a spirit was contagious, and Eleonore admired someone who held onto their beliefs with such unwavering conviction.

"Want one?" Hanns leaned back and tapped Eleonore's arm, and she looked up to see him handing her a cigarette.

"Oh, thank you," Eleonore smiled as she removed one from the package.

"You have a light?" She asked.

"Yep," Hanns replied quickly and retrieved the matches.

"I mean, it's nice to have a cigarette, but it has no purpose until it's lit."

"A new form of torture," Hanns chuckled, but as soon as he spoke, he regretted uttering the phrase and he became solemn. A simple string of words that once held little consequence now reminded him of the gravity of what many endured.

"I think we're the only vehicle on the road," Eleonore said, changing the subject.

"Ya," Hanns squinted at the peculiarity and handed her a small pack of matches. "Though, I suppose we're the only ones who can afford petrol, as the British call it."

"How long did you live in England?" Eleonore asked as she took a puff from her cigarette.

"Not long," Hanns glanced at her. "Just enough to learn the language and attempt, dreadfully, to become accustomed to their diet."

"How different is it, really?" Eleonore smiled as she became intrigued. She loved moments like this where consciousness seems to evaporate as one becomes enraptured in a stimulating conversation.

"They have roast beef and Yorkshire pudding," Hanns furrowed his brow dramatically.

"What the hell is Yorkshire pudding?!" Eleonore shot her head back in surprise. "What about ox tongue or chopped liver?"

"They would be appalled to hear you say such things."

"No!" Eleonore giggled. "You're having me on! Aren't you?! It's not very kind of you to take advantage of my ignorance."

"No, it's true," Genn came to Hanns' rescue.

"I think I would have difficulty adapting," Eleonore took another puff. "I tried to go to England, actually."

"Really?"

"At least, that's where the man who tricked me promised that I would be sent. He even gave me a fake name, but I can't remember it now. Thatcher, was the last name, I believe."

"I'm sorry to hear that," Hanns glanced back at her, and Eleonore sensed that he was sincere.

"You seem to have a good grasp of the English language. How did you learn it so quickly?" Eleonore shifted the conversation back to Hanns.

"He just knows the curse words well," Genn smiled cheekily.

"I had a strict teacher. Mrs. Frank, or Frankie as I liked to call her. She had a little flat looking over St. James' park in London where she would instruct me in all the unusual traits of English. Frankie was kind, but stern. Still, I'll never get the stench of pickled onions out of my nostrils."

Eleonore laughed.

"That's not an English custom," Genn interjected. "Don't confuse the poor thing, Howard."

"I've been meaning to ask," Eleonore tilted her head timidly, "but why did you introduce yourself to me as Hanns when everyone else calls you Howard?"

"Hanns is too Germanic sounding," Hanns shrugged. "Living in England, I thought it would be best to go with something more familiar to their sensitive ears, especially given the political climate."

Eleonore chuckled as she contemplated if she would've been required to change her name as well. Eleonore was a common enough name, though the spelling was a little different than usual.

It was nice to ponder the juvenile again, and she welcomed Hanns' sharp wit and dry humor as very adept distractions. She was beginning to feel drawn to Hanns, but not in a romantic sense. In fact, she didn't believe that she would ever find love, at least not truly. Many suitors had been drawn to Eleonore, but no one could capture her affections, and she didn't believe that a man existed who she could love wholeheartedly.

"How did you enjoy England?" Eleonore shuffled down the bench and sat closer to the front seat.

"I liked it, for the most part," Hanns tilted his head as he recalled. "I miss England, to a degree. The people were kind…mostly. I don't miss the rain though," Hanns glanced at Genn, who grinned.

"I could take poor weather over Nazis any day," Eleonore returned to staring out the window. "I still can't believe what happened. Feels like a dream, or a different life."

Hanns and Genn remained silent.

"Don't you agree?" Eleonore watched Hanns.

"Yep," Hanns spoke quickly and seemed to be on edge as he began to riffle through his satchel.

"What's wrong?" Eleonore studied him.

"Nothing!" Hanns barked and pretended to be looking for something important.

Genn looked at Hanns sharply, then he glanced back at Eleonore with a slight shake of his head letting her know it would be best to leave Hanns be for the moment.

Embarrassed by his outburst, Eleonore wished that she hadn't said anything at all. She needed someone to talk to and empty herself of the terrible atrocities she witnessed. Staying silent would destroy her. Not that she wanted to go into great personal detail, but she needed to expel the toxic memories and not let them take up harbor in her spirit.

He's not the only one who's been through difficult times, Eleonore crossed her arms as she prepared her defence. *In fact, I've been through a hell of a lot more than he has. I was at the camps, not him! Who is he to bark at me like that? I have the right to talk. If he doesn't want to discuss this, that's fine, but he doesn't need to be rude about it. He interrogated me, if he would dare recall, asking the most personal questions, and now he can't be civil by politely declining to talk about these subjects? I wish Ruth was here,* Eleonore teared up again. *She'd give him a word or two. And, not to mention, why am I the one sitting in the back and not in the comfortable front seat? Not very polite.*

The rest of the journey was spent in awkward silence with Eleonore fuming inwardly. Genn, too, remained quiet as he fidgeted with the steering wheel or cleared his throat when he became too uncomfortable with the tension. On occasion, Genn would try to hum a tune but would seem to lose the melody and rhythm after a couple bars and give up the pursuit for a few miles before attempting another song.

Eventually, they came to a little town which had a few small shops, about a dozen houses, and a church. The town was one of the smallest Eleonore had ever seen, yet despite its size, there was a great sadness about the place. The houses appeared deserted, the church's roof had caved in from bombings, and the streets were in major need of repair.

"Let's stop here," Hanns grumbled as they drove along the main street.

"Is there even anywhere to stop?" Eleonore peeked out the front, but she was met by silence from Hanns.

"I'm sure we'll find something," Genn piped in after he realized that Hanns was continuing with his shunning.

"Ah, see," Genn spoke cheerily, trying to 'rouse the troops', when he spotted a shop on the main street.

Pulling up to the store, Genn turned off the truck and, in dismay, let his head hit the back of the headrest.

"What's wrong?" Eleonore asked Genn.

"Just tired," Genn lied as he sighed. He was painfully aware that his effort at changing their disposition was doomed.

"Looks like they could use some restoration," Eleonore leaned over and looked out the window to see that the shop's sign had been split in two and the paint had been stripped.

"What are we waiting for?" Eleonore spoke after a minute of inaction.

"I'm thinking," Hanns replied with spite.

"How can I help?" Eleonore asked as she pressed through his sour attitude.

"Just stay here," Hanns threw open the door and jumped out of the truck.

"Stay?!" Eleonore looked to Genn, disgusted with Hanns' tone of voice. "Whatever for?"

"It's best you don't enter the shop looking like you do!" Hanns shouted as he walked towards the store. "It's upsetting!"

"I have the uniform over top!" Eleonore grew indignant.

"Still," Genn looked at her apologetically.

Huffing, Eleonore glanced away and bounced her leg anxiously. *I've been sitting on this awkward bench for hours,* Eleonore grumbled as she grew eager to escape the vehicle. But, just as the thought entered, another arose in contention, and she felt immense guilt for her objection.

How quickly one forgets, Eleonore pondered after Genn and Hanns left to enter the shop. *I stood in a stock car packed with people for hours on end, and now I'm complaining about having to sit on this bench. What I would've given for a bench to sit on then, even an uncomfortable one.*

Looking out the back of the truck, Eleonore wondered if anyone still lived in the town. Despite the stores having 'open' signs, she was convinced that they were the only customers to be seen. Then, Eleonore caught the gaze from a shopkeeper a few stores down. He was standing in the shop window, staring intently at her without reservation. He wasn't gazing with ill-purpose, but rather, with pleading, begging her to purchase some goods from him.

But then Eleonore was distracted by the clip-clop of a horse on the cobbled street and she noticed a man walking in her direction, leading a horse by the reins. For a moment, Eleonore thought it was none other than Alex himself, the elderly man she had employed at her seamstress shop in Berlin. The man walking towards her was wearing a gray suit with gray pants and his suspenders were so loose that they had lost all purpose.

But as quickly as it arrived, the feeling of familiarity vanished, and the man walked past the truck without so much as a glance at her. The trotting of the horse echoed against the surrounding stores as he walked on by with a blank and lifeless expression and Eleonore felt pity for him.

Unable to contain herself, Eleonore stepped out the back of the truck and stretched as she inspected the town. Startled by some muffled shouting, Eleonore looked through the glass on the door to the shop that Hanns was in. With a raised finger, Hanns was shouting at an elderly couple behind a counter who were growing ever more irritated by his behavior.

What's his problem now? Eleonore rolled her eyes. Entering the shop, Eleonore noticed that the store was nearly empty of supplies. There were only a handful of products on the shelves, and only items that no one cared to purchase. Everything of necessity had already been taken. The couple appeared rather solemn, and not appreciative of Hanns' interrogation, and were even more shocked to see Eleonore in her state in the oversized uniform.

"What's wrong?" Eleonore put her hand on Hanns' arm to calm him, but he frowned at her for the familiarity.

"This doesn't concern you," Hanns spoke to her but continued to glare at the elderly couple.

"I demand to know on whose authority you're asking me such questions," the man replied with a thick, northern German accent.

"Does it matter?" Hanns shrugged.

"It might," the man defended.

"You're not just here for me, are you?" Eleonore shook her head. "You're after information. Why didn't you tell me?"

"As I said," Hanns turned towards her. "This doesn't concern you."

"I may be able to help," Eleonore tilted her head.

"Go pick out a dress," Hanns spun her shoulders and gave her a light push to the back of the store where a single rack of clothes was displayed.

"I'll help," Genn put his hand gently on Eleonore's back as he led her away. "It's just theatrics," Genn whispered as they walked. "An interrogation technique, if you will. He's trying to intimidate them into providing the information that we are convinced they have."

"And what's that?" Eleonore looked up at him.

"Classified," Genn shrugged his apology. "There's not much for selection," Genn held up one of the two dresses. It was a plain, navy blue dress made of cotton and not at all that appealing.

"Better than what I'm wearing at least," Eleonore grabbed it from Genn and held it against her body for measurement.

It was then that Eleonore realized the peculiarity of her behavior. The old Eleonore would've never dared to be so bold as to simply grab the dress out of someone's hands. She was much too timid and polite to be so rash. The past year had changed her, drastically, and the nervous, bashful creature she once was now felt so foreign.

"I'm sorry," Eleonore suddenly became embarrassed.

"Whatever for?" Genn frowned.

"My rude behavior," Eleonore's face flushed red. "Also, I just remembered that I'm penniless and, on principle, I don't borrow money. Though I may have to make an exception today."

"The dress is covered," Genn winked. "Besides, it's not me that you're borrowing from. You can thank the British Government."

"I appreciate it," Eleonore smiled bashfully. Genn was a rather sweet soul and, although the two were close in age, she felt as if her father was being channeled through the man before her.

"It's not much," Genn looked at the plain dress regretfully.

"It should fit nicely," Eleonore held it up again. "Let's go pay before they kick your lieutenant out."

"Maybe let's give them a minute," Genn raised his hand. "Do you want to try it on first?" he asked as he looked around the store for an area where she could change.

"I really think we should pay now," Eleonore hinted heavily.

Studying her for a moment, Genn reluctantly agreed and walked with her to the front of the store.

"Have you tried it on?" the elderly lady asked Eleonore, eager to escape Hanns' questioning.

"I didn't see a place for me to change," Eleonore replied sheepishly.

"Follow me," the woman grabbed a key and led Eleonore to a small room near the back corner of the store while Hanns continued his cross-examination of her husband.

"Will you also be needing some undergarments?" the woman asked quietly.

"If there are some available, that would be greatly appreciated," Eleonore replied as she tried to recall the last time that she had the luxury of undergarments.

"Stupid thing," the woman grunted as she struggled with the door. "I can't remember how many times I've asked him to fix this. There we go," she huffed as she heaved it open.

"Thank you," Eleonore nodded as she entered a small, poorly lit room with a tall, but heavily chipped mirror that was leaned against a wall.

Turning to close the door, Eleonore noticed that the woman remained in the doorway. She simply stared at Eleonore and seemed to be trembling slightly.

"Is everything alright?" Eleonore looked at the woman with wide eyes.

"I need to know if it's true," the woman whispered.

"Pardon?" Eleonore turned her ear, wondering if she had heard her correctly.

"I need to know if the camps were real," the woman continued as her trembling increased.

Studying her for a moment, Eleonore nodded and removed the uniform to reveal the dress underneath with the bullet hole. At this, the woman frowned, but Eleonore could see that she was unconvinced. Rolling up her sleeve, Eleonore pointed at her tattoo; 75, 693. Still, the woman remained skeptical and Eleonore felt as though she would brush off most of her subjective evidence.

Rashly, Eleonore removed her dress and stood naked before the woman who examined her in horror. For the briefest of moments, Eleonore was transported back to Auschwitz where she was seated, naked, in front of the other women as her head was shaved, her arm tattooed, and she was sprayed with ice-cold water.

"They were real," Eleonore spoke softly, and pointed to the bullet-filled dress which lay on the floor. "I found this dress in a pile of clothes, otherwise I would have nothing to wear. I was rescued by the officer talking to your husband."

But the woman paid no attention to the dress. Instead, her eyes were locked on the poor state of Eleonore's stomach.

"And that?" the woman's fingers trembled as she pointed to the scar.

"A lesser man impregnated me," Eleonore swallowed and closed her eyes. She wasn't relishing the experience of telling her story, but this woman clearly carried a guilty conscience and knew some information. "He tried to have me killed by starvation. When that failed, a rudimentary abortion was performed to rid any evidence of the man's involvement."

While shaking, the woman handed Eleonore some undergarments and then withdrew to allow Eleonore some privacy. The light in the room was pale, but enough for Eleonore to get a decent idea of what she looked like. While revolting to Eleonore, the wound on her stomach seemed to be healing properly and she was relieved to see that infection would likely not be an issue. Still, she was furious at the permanent marks the Nazis had left on her body. She was thankful to have survived, but such trivial thoughts were natural, she assumed.

Slipping on the undergarments and the dress, Eleonore tied up the back with the little ribbon attached. A tear fell down her cheek as she inspected herself in the mirror. She remembered the first time that she had seen herself in her sorry state at the Villa. She recalled how kind Roza had been when she gave her a wig and did her makeup, crowning her with her former glory.

While now she appeared a bit healthier, the dress still hung off her scrawny shoulders. She felt as though she looked ridiculous with a dress that, for the time being, was a few sizes too large. And not only did she detest her appearance, but she was beginning to realize just how much she had lost.

She was without money, a residence of any sort, her business had been destroyed, the people she was closest to had been tortured and murdered, and this dress was about to become her single possession.

She ran her hands down the fabric and pressed them over her stomach, careful to avoid the wound as she took a deep breath in and out, feeling the rise and fall of her belly. She remembered her last day in Berlin, laying on the bed in her flat, and pressing her hand to her stomach in much the same manner.

While it would be dishonest to describe the dress as unflattering, Eleonore's seamstress eyes begged to make the necessary corrections to better compliment her form. Still, it was wonderful to feel feminine again and to rid herself of the oversized uniform. Picking up the old clothes, including the bullet-ridden dress, Eleonore exited the change room.

"Well I'll be damned," Genn removed his hat as he looked Eleonore up and down.

Even Hanns' gaze lingered, and he stammered while he tried to regain control of his interrogation. Usually, Eleonore was unaware of the glances and stares from others around her as she kept her gaze at her feet, but now it was impossible to ignore the attention and she blushed.

Still, Eleonore behaved rather dignified in pretending not to notice their reaction. Beautiful women must feign ignorance of their own attraction and wait for men to describe their splendor. Or at least, that's what she had been told as a girl.

"I think it would be best for me to talk to the store owners alone," Eleonore handed the old clothes to Genn who was more than happy to oblige her every request.

"Howard," Genn cleared his throat.

"Sir?" Hanns turned around.

"Why don't you go wait in the truck."

"What? I'm not-" Hanns stopped himself short. Glancing at the couple, then back at Eleonore, Hanns excused himself and gave the door an extra heave as the bell jingled at his departure.

"I must apologize for my colleague," Eleonore smiled repentantly at the couple who remained unforgiving.

"Will this be all?" the woman asked quietly but avoided eye contact with both Eleonore and Genn.

"Do you have anything to change the lieutenant's attitude?" Eleonore smirked, but her attempt at lightening the mood fell flat.

"I've seen men like him before," the man spoke crossly. "They demand this and they demand that. We want nothing to do with the war. We're a simple fami-" the man couldn't finish the word and he began to chew his cheek to contain his emotions. "We're a simple couple who just want to run a store. Nothing more."

"The officer is only doing what is right," Eleonore defended. "Though, he may not have the best approach."

"They all believe that what they are doing is right," the man leaned in and pointed towards the truck. "Nothing good comes out of this sort of resentment. He's after revenge, that's all."

"I believe he's after justice," Eleonore pointed to the bullet hole in her dress that Genn was holding. "He wants to help right the wrongs that happened to his people."

"So, he is a Jew," the man spit on the ground. "They started all of this anyways. I've said all I need to. Purchase the dress, but this conversation is over."

Biting her lip awkwardly, Eleonore knew that there was nothing further she could say to convince them. Tapping the counter, Eleonore glanced at Genn who offered the correct payment.

Handing the receipt to Eleonore, the elderly woman held on with a tight grip and wouldn't let go. Studying her curiously, Eleonore understood that something was burning on her mind.

"The camps were real," the woman let go and turned to her husband.

"It's just propaganda," the man grumbled. "They were retirement communities that the Allies have blown out of proportion."

"There was a young man who came through here," the woman looked sorrowfully into Eleonore's eyes.

"Quiet," the husband turned towards her with gritted teeth.

"I will not be silent!" The woman mirrored her husband by turning towards him as tears fell down her face. "How much more can we lose?"

"There still is a chance," the man warned his wife.

"The resistance is dead," the woman waved him off. "You cling to that because you believe, you have to believe, that our boy didn't die for nothing. But he did, damn you!"

"For nothing?" The man looked at his wife with all the rage he could muster. "He fought for his country, and that is something. That is honorable."

"Look where honor got him," the woman began to weep.

At this, the man charged into the back room.

"The Gauleiter of Luxemburg," the woman continued as she removed a handkerchief to wipe her eyes, "his son came through our store."

"When was this?" Eleonore asked and glanced at Genn who was stunned by the turn of events.

"About a week ago," the woman searched her memory.

"Where did he go? Do you know where he is?"

"I don't know anything more than that," the woman shook her head. "I understand that doesn't necessarily help you."

"It does," Eleonore reached out and took the woman's hand in hers. "What name did he go by?"

"He didn't say a name."

"You're certain that it was this young man?"

"The boy's mother comes from a city near here, and they used to spend time in a town close by. He came to our store because he knew that my husband would help him."

"Did he mention where—"

"Get out of my store!" the husband returned from the back room, holding a rifle.

"We're going, we're going!" Genn held up his hands, signaling for Eleonore to mimic him as they walked backwards out of the store.

Chapter Five:
The Manor

Dictatorship naturally arises out of democracy, and the most aggravated form of tyranny and slavery out of the most extreme liberty.

Plato

"You can sit in the front," Hanns opened the door for her with a smile.

"Thank you," Eleonore spoke slowly as she accepted the gesture, though grudgingly. She was repulsed that his behavior towards her had shifted so drastically now that he viewed her with a more affectionate lens.

"Allow me," Hanns offered his hand to help her step up into the truck.

"I'm alright," Eleonore replied, though she struggled to hoist herself up. She realized how silly she looked as a little woman climbing into such a big vehicle, but if Hanns hadn't offered to lend his assistance previously, then he didn't deserve the triumph now.

"You ready?" Genn studied her with concern.

"For what?" Eleonore returned his concerned gaze.

"For your interview. If you fail and she doesn't employ you, then your care under the British Government ends and we can no longer help you. The justification for us spending our resources and time is that you will be planted as an informant."

"I don't even know who I'm interviewing with," Eleonore frowned. "How can I prepare for what I don't know?"

"Her name is Mrs. Meyers," Hanns answered as he climbed into the back of the truck.

"Now you know as much as we do," Genn nodded as he started the vehicle.

"Can you explain to me, again, the British interest in her?" Eleonore rubbed her hand over her forehead.

"We're not necessarily interested in her," Hanns put his elbows against the back of her seat, a little too close for Eleonore's comfort. "We believe that there are some escaped guards from the camps hiding in and around that area. If you notice anything suspicious, report it to us. They'll likely be lower level SS guards. Nothing serious enough to worry about, but still, worth rounding up. Again, wait until you are certain before contacting us."

"Alright," Eleonore nodded. "I should do well in the interview. Not to brag, but I tend to have a strong rapport with the elderly."

"I'm not sure that's something one generally brags about," Hanns bit his lip as he chuckled and Genn's nose whistled with a quick snort.

"I meant that I shouldn't have an issue securing employment with her," Eleonore grew irritated with Hanns. "Or should I behave as you do and begin the interview by shouting at her?" Eleonore shot a glare at Hanns as she alluded to the elderly couple in the store.

"I think I struck a nerve," Hanns chuckled.

"More than one," Eleonore muttered.

"Listen," Hanns shrugged off his silliness, "I was just doing my job. Sometimes you have to be intimidating."

"And how did that work out for you?" Eleonore spun in her seat and turned to face Hanns.

"Please don't fight again," Genn sighed.

"It was working well until you entered the store," Hanns ignored Genn's concerns.

"Humans are complex," Eleonore rolled her eyes. "Not everyone you yell at will buckle."

"Oh really?" Hanns replied sarcastically.

"Yes, really," Eleonore clenched her jaw, but then relaxed a little as she explained. "One combination doesn't open every safe. You must understand the character of the person you're interrogating. It won't always be as easy as shouting to get your answers."

"Are you writing this down?" Genn spoke over his shoulder to Hanns.

"Continue," Hanns pinched his lips as he tried to maintain his fading position.

"When you yelled at that elderly couple, they shut down and you would've been better off shouting at the wall. When the woman saw me, and saw that the wounds were real, then she understood. Connection, Hanns, that's what you need. Even if it's on a false pretense, they will believe that they can trust you."

"They're animals," Hanns gritted his teeth. "How can someone connect with immorality?"

"You've never carried out orders that you disagree with?" Eleonore raised her eyebrows.

"That's not fair," Hanns gave Eleonore a warning look. "I would never obey orders to kill someone."

"Would you obey orders to burn books?" Eleonore pressed.

"Of course not!" Hanns shook his head. "How little do you think of me?"

"For your circumstances it's simple: you'd be thrown in prison or you could die heroically for your principles. But what if disobeying these orders put your wife and children at risk? What if you had a family that would find themselves homeless, or imprisoned and sent to the gas chambers if you refused to burn books?"

"Hiding behind family is a coward's way of justifying their hatred," Hanns clenched his hands into fists.

"But that's how they rationalize their actions," Eleonore spoke softly. "You have to understand that they believe themselves to be innocent. They see themselves as equal victims to the people unjustly imprisoned."

"That's ridiculous," Hanns looked away, not willing to continue the conversation.

"Of course it is," Eleonore continued, "but you need to understand what these men and women are like if you are going to do a proper job."

"All I need to understand is who exactly is responsible for the murder of thousands of my people," Hanns crossed his arms.

Thousands? Eleonore squinted at Hanns as her heart broke for him. *I wouldn't be surprised if that number is much higher than we realize.*

"If you can understand their rationality, then you can better prepare for your interrogations," Eleonore took a deep breath. "I'm just trying to help is all."

"Might as well tear the whole thing down," Genn piped in.

"Pardon?" Eleonore looked at him with confusion.

"The windmill," Genn pointed out the window as he tried to steer the conversation to a lighter topic.

Eleonore looked out the window to see that a group of men had built some scaffolding around a partially destroyed windmill. It had likely been struck during a bombing raid and, Eleonore agreed, was likely better off to be demolished. But what caught Eleonore's attention was the age of the men working. Boys as young as ten and men well beyond their prime were laboring to complete the repairs. Not one among them was of the suitable age for such work.

"Listen," Hanns sighed, "I'm sorry. This isn't easy for me."

"And you think it's easy for me? Out of the two of us, I'm the one who was at the camps, remember?"

"Oh, I remember," Hanns scoffed and Genn sighed as the momentarily dormant argument resurfaced. "You told me about your time at the Villa and your personal cell. You ate as well as the Commandant did. You stayed in comfort while my people froze in the barracks."

"You half-wit!" Eleonore lost her composure as she succumbed to her temper. "I can't believe that I have to defend myself. Those 'decent' experiences were short-lived. The majority of my stay was in the barracks alongside your people, many of whom I considered as close as my own flesh and blood. I spent months inside that standing cell which was intended to be my coffin. I was naked, I was cold, and I was utterly alone. Do you have any idea what that feels like? I'm not the enemy here. I'd rather you treat me with a measure of respect."

"Respect?" Hanns mocked.

"Is there something you'd like to add?" Eleonore frowned at him.

"You were the mistress of Rudolph Hoess," Hanns crossed his arms. "One of the very men responsible for this."

"You're implying that the relationship was mutual," Eleonore grew enraged by the accusation.

"I'm assuming he treated you well," Hanns defended his position.

"I won't deny that I had it easier than most who endured Auschwitz," Eleonore mirrored Hanns by crossing her own arms, "but I also watched my friends die. Do you remember why I was in Auschwitz?" Eleonore squinted at him. "I had a choice, and I chose with my conscience. I could've easily avoided all of this."

"You believe you're a martyr?" Hanns' expression soured further with disgust.

"I'm…" Eleonore was about to counter but then paused as she studied Hanns. "You're not really mad at me, are you?"

"What?!" Hanns frowned.

"You're channeling your frustration towards me," Eleonore peered at Hanns, "but you're not angry with me."

"I don't know what it is," Hanns' knuckles turned white as he grabbed the back of Eleonore's seat, "but something about you infuriates me."

"Well, that's kind," Eleonore grumbled.

"I'm sorry," Hanns relaxed a little, but the tone of his voice indicated that he may not be all that apologetic.

"No," Eleonore sighed. "I shouldn't push so hard."

"It's just," Hanns paused, but continued angrily, "there's a lot to process here and I'm a rather private person."

"I understand," Eleonore nodded. "I suppose anger is easier to show than fear."

"See," Hanns erupted, "there you go again. I'm not sure if it's just the way you're saying things or if it's that judgmental tone, but I can't say anything without you pushing some button of mine."

"Why are you so upset?" Eleonore ignored his anger and pushed through. "Talk to me."

"Forget it," Hanns threw his lips upside down.

"What are you afraid of?" Eleonore persisted.

"I'm not afraid," Hanns shot her a warning glance.

"Then out with it," Eleonore threw her hands in the air.

"I don't know how to deal with this!" Hanns half-shouted. "I can't bear seeing these camps day after day and witnessing what these wicked men and women did to my own people. There's nothing I can do about it, either. I want to find Rudolph, and I want to find him now and make him pay for what he did. This is my home," Hanns pounded his fist against his chest, "and men like Rudolph destroyed this great country. They destroyed the pride I felt as a German."

After a short silence, Eleonore asked quietly, "Where did you live?"

"Berlin," Hanns looked at her with a soft expression. "Same as you."

"When did you leave?" Genn asked, and Eleonore almost forgot that he was present as she was so focused on Hanns.

"Not soon enough," Hanns gave a worried chuckle. "No one believed that the Nazis were so malicious. There were even some Jews that supported Hitler, at first, that is."

"Ya, I remember that," Eleonore frowned slightly.

"Growing up, I never felt that being a Jew made me all that different, really," Hanns shook his head. "There was the odd comment here or there from some who were unaccepting. This increased, of course, as the Nazi party gained popularity. Otherwise, we went to the synagogue once a year, observed some dietary restrictions, and my family had a Torah, but that was the extent of it. Ironically, we were driven into Jewish society only when the law prohibited us from attending public school or associating with non-Jews. But my brother and I were too mischievous for our own good," Hanns grinned. "We would still sneak in to watch the hockey games. Rather dangerous now that I look back at it. We were surrounded by brown-shirts and Nazi youth who were not exactly a rational sort, but that didn't stop us from enjoying ourselves."

"So, what eventually made you leave?" Genn chimed in again, happy at least that the argument had dissipated.

"We ran into some trouble," Hanns shrugged.

"What sort of trouble?" Eleonore pressed.

"We're Jews in Nazi Germany, what kind of problems do you think we had?" Hanns snickered.

"We don't have to discuss this if it's too difficult for you," Eleonore gave a cheeky grin, playing on Hanns' pride.

"My father was a doctor," Hanns glared at Eleonore but returned a slight grin of his own, "and he carried out his practice at our apartment. One day, a bunch of these brown-shirts decided to target our apartment and gathered outside, blocking anyone from coming or going. They shouted slogans which blamed us for all their problems."

"Was anyone hurt?" Eleonore asked.

"No," Hanns studied the canvas on the truck as he recalled the event, "we were saved by a dear friend. The crowd was becoming quite volatile, but a veteran from the first war came to our rescue. Dressed in his uniform, he lectured the crowd, stating that my father had received the Iron Cross from the first war and that they should disperse at once. Fortunately for us, these thugs respected him and moved away."

"What a courageous thing to do," Genn grew impressed.

"He stayed there all day, thwarting off any others who might want to gather in front of our house."

"So, how did you end up working for the British Army?" Eleonore smiled.

"It was impossible to do nothing while my country was going to hell," Hanns shrugged. "So, I enlisted."

"I'm surprised the British army would take Germans," Eleonore pondered.

"Well," Hanns glanced at her, "there were so many that volunteered that they didn't quite know what to do with us."

"Us?"

"Jewish-German refugees," Hanns explained. "The British created the Auxiliary Military Pioneer Corps for us volunteers. My brother and I, along with fifty other Austrians, became the 93 Company. Our motto: Work Conquers All," Hanns threw his fist into the air in a dramatic recreation.

"Huh," Eleonore frowned. "Rather similar to another slogan."

"What's that?"

"Nothing," Eleonore waved away the thought.

"They didn't trust us with guns, I can tell you that much," Hanns raised an eyebrow.

"No?"

"No, we were the laborers," Hanns scratched the back of his neck as he thought.

"So, you had no weapons?" Eleonore frowned.

"Our company's arsenal comprised of five pistols which were each given to one of the five British-born officers."

"You didn't see much action then?" Eleonore studied Hanns, becoming more and more intrigued.

"Luckily, no. We were part of the war effort in France but, again, it was just manual labor. They didn't carry much respect for us, and we mostly did what the mules and horses couldn't. In fact, our company was also one of the last to be rescued from Dunkirk."

"I heard about that," Eleonore frowned as she recalled. "The Allies called it the 'Miracle of Dunkirk' if I remember correctly. Must've been rather nerve-wracking?"

"Ya I was terrified," Hanns huffed. "My full name and place of birth were on my identity card. If we weren't rescued, I would've been shot as a traitor immediately."

"Hmm," Eleonore thought as she looked at Hanns in a new light.

"Here," Genn handed her some crackers from his rations.

"Thank you," Eleonore took a grateful bite. "And what about you, Lieutenant Colonel? What's your story?"

"Oh," Genn chuckled, "I'm afraid there's not much to tell."

"Don't be modest," Hanns slapped Genn's shoulder. "This man here is an actor."

"Really?!" Eleonore's eyes flew wide with excitement. "On the stage or in film? Please say film. Which films have you been in?!"

"Just a few pictures here and there," Genn cleared his throat as he smiled coyly.

"Oh which ones?!" Eleonore grabbed his arm as her interest soared.

"We're here!" Genn ignored the question as he pointed out the front of the vehicle.

"It's beautiful!" Eleonore was shocked at the aesthetics as they approached their destination.

The largest grin grew on Eleonore's face as she stuck her head out the window and the splendor of the house came into view. Not that one would label the manor as prestigious or grandiose, but it was magnificent by its own merits. Especially when Eleonore compared it to her little flat in Berlin. The main dwelling was four stories tall with attached extensions on its western and eastern flanks. The eastern flank was two stories while the western flank was three and the house seemed to flow in a natural decline and incline as if to mimic the surrounding hills.

Passing through the open iron-barred gate, Eleonore's heart fluttered as they crossed over a century-old stone bridge that guarded a tranquil stream. Most people would find this experience to be of little significance, but to Eleonore this humble, simple path to the manor house filled her spirit with an emotion she didn't believe that she could feel again: hope. Closing her eyes, Eleonore inhaled the sweet, natural scent from the stream and leaned back into the truck.

"I'm home," Eleonore glanced at Genn who smiled back at her, unable to withstand her contagious bliss.

"Let's hope you succeed, then," Genn stopped the truck at the door and threw it into park.

Closing her eyes again, Eleonore attempted to focus her mind when, suddenly, her door opened. Slightly startled, Eleonore pulled back and locked eyes with a butler. He had approached the vehicle so silently that she hadn't noticed him. While younger than most butlers that Eleonore had seen, this gentleman was around her age. His black hair was combed neatly backwards and, while not the handsomest man to come across her path, he carried a certain charm in his dark, green eyes.

"Miss," the butler gave a slight bow and offered his hand to help her out of the truck and Eleonore thought that she detected an Italian accent.

Yet, for all his politeness, Eleonore caught what she thought was a scowl and the tensing of his shoulders. Eleonore was poorly dressed in comparison to the butler and she assumed that he was used to serving a higher class of person.

"Thank you," Eleonore spoke cautiously and slowly exited the vehicle with his help.

"Mrs. Meyers is waiting for you in the drawing room," the butler closed the door loudly, almost with a slam, and Eleonore nearly had to jump out of the way.

"Follow me, miss," the butler walked ahead with long, swift strides that made Eleonore feel his intention was to lose her.

While half running, Eleonore followed the butler up the few stone steps until they came to the main door of the house. Standing in the shadow of the manor, Eleonore felt its intimidation set in her bones. Again, most people wouldn't have given the simple country house much thought, but to Eleonore, this home felt as though it were a living creature.

With a firm grip on the door handle, the butler turned around and was about to speak to her when he spotted Hanns and Genn walking up the steps.

"No!" the butler held out his hand, and it was undoubtable that he was, in fact, Italian. "Only Miss Hodys is permitted."

"She's in our charge," Hanns continued to climb the steps.

"Sir," the butler gave a smug look at Hanns, "either she enters alone, or no one enters at all."

"I don't understand why we aren't permitted?" Hanns challenged as he puffed out his chest slightly.

"It's not my place to understand the demands of my lady," the butler returned Hanns' challenge, "but it is my duty to enforce them."

Taking his hat off, Hanns slapped it lightly against his thigh in defeat, though it made Eleonore happy that he should be so concerned with her well-being. While their brief relationship was one of constant contention, she had grown to admire the young man. Besides, their quarreling had exposed some wounds that needed airing. Not that Hanns' inflictions were all that mysterious, but he needed to express them, and if Eleonore hadn't pushed, he would've left them buried.

"After you," the butler opened the door and, again, offered the slightest, customary bow.

"Thank you," Eleonore returned a slight nod.

But as she entered, Eleonore's breath was stolen from her.

She was met by a wide-open entrance as two staircases, one on the east and one on the west, led to the second floor. Straight ahead of her at the end of long hallway was a small, round table beside a window overlooking a garden. On the table was an orchid which was illuminated by the sun striking it through the window. Everything within her screamed to sit at the table while she enjoyed a warm cup of tea and lost herself in a good book.

"Miss," the butler held out his hand for her to take the eastern staircase.

The stairs creaked as the butler escorted Eleonore while she ran her hand along the dark, mahogany railings. The house was quiet, eerily so, and the creaking echoed throughout. A kettle screeched from deep within the house, and Eleonore watched as a maid rushed out of the west wing below towards what she assumed was the kitchen.

"Before you meet the mistress," the butler stopped when they had reached the top, "there are some ground rules we must establish."

"Alright?" Eleonore looked at him with concern, curious as to what was about to follow.

"Mrs. Meyers is a proud woman, and rightfully so. Her family comes from privilege. They have fought and bled to obtain these advantages and she will not take kindly to you."

"Understood," Eleonore straightened her back as she locked these warnings into memory. Though she was surprised that the butler would be so brazenly rude to her without knowing any of her background or history.

"Now," the butler began to walk again, but briskly, and spoke over his shoulder as they walked down a hallway with a dark green carpet, "when you enter the drawing room, don't speak to her unless she explicitly asks you to do so, don't sit unless she offers you a seat, and, by all means, refuse tea or dainties even if she insists."

That all sounds very pretentious, Eleonore thought as a sense of dread stirred within her.

"Here we are," the butler stopped and squared himself with a closed door. With a deep breath, the butler opened the door and entered. Standing parallel to the door, the butler raised his chin high into the air as he pronounced, "Miss Eleonore Hodys."

Sheepishly, Eleonore entered the dark room as the butler closed the door behind her. Thick drapes hung over the windows, blocking out all light except for one corner where an elderly lady sat at a dainty, round table. While her features remained hidden, the woman's silhouette showcased a large hat with a feather jutting out the side.

A grandfather clock ticked patiently as Eleonore looked out her peripheral to take in the room. Her eyes had not yet adjusted to the darkness, and she couldn't make out much beyond some sofas, a piano, and a fireplace which looked overused with black ash spread about its base.

"Closer," Mrs. Meyers demanded in a harsh voice.

Obeying, Eleonore walked over to the lady, holding her hands in front of her and feeling rather judged, though she hoped it was fairly.

"I cannot see you!" the lady half-shouted, and Eleonore sprung closer.

Now that she was a mere few feet from Mrs. Meyers, Eleonore could appreciate her features. The light from the window leapt off her deep blue eyes and, while elderly, Mrs. Meyers seemed to be absent of wrinkles. Her sharp jaw with a pointed, yet soft nose displayed a rather perceptive intellect.

A jealousy grew in Eleonore's heart as she absorbed this magnificent woman sitting in front of her. How she wished to embody the qualities that Mrs. Meyers so naturally displayed. Not even a minute of their meeting had transpired, yet Eleonore was transfixed. Here was a woman who seemed like royalty yet had been displaced from her throne and forced to become content with the scraps.

"You are pretty," Mrs. Meyers spoke with disappointment.

Caught off guard by the unexpected compliment, Eleonore bounced her eyes down to her feet, but reminded herself of the instruction to remain silent.

"I gave you a compliment," Mrs. Meyers frowned.

"I'm terribly sorry," Eleonore's eyes flew wide. "I was instructed not to speak unless asked."

"And I fear that you have failed," Mrs. Meyers folded her hands in the sort of way prominent women do when they are dissatisfied, accompanied by the jarring of their head from one side to the other. "I have not asked you to speak and now you have blamed your misstep on another. Can you be trusted? Why should I employ someone who would disregard instruction and then blame their faults on a co-worker?"

I'll have to use all my wits with this one, Eleonore drew a deep breath, preparing herself for whatever snare lay waiting next.

"Sit," Mrs. Meyers held her hand out to the chair opposite her.

"Thank you," Eleonore grabbed the chair, fumbling with it slightly in the dark, and sat up straight, holding her chin high.

"Hmm," Mrs. Meyers' shoulders dropped, unimpressed by Eleonore's demeanor. "You may speak freely now."

"Thank you," Eleonore smiled brightly and waited patiently for Mrs. Meyers to continue the interview.

"What are you smiling for?" Mrs. Meyers frowned in disgust. "I asked you to speak, yet you sit before me with a foolish grin on your face. You are here on account of the job application, are you not?"

"That's correct," Eleonore nodded sharply, mirroring Mrs. Meyers' severity.

"That *is* correct. Not that's correct," Mrs. Meyers glared at Eleonore's mouth as if she had cursed. "What do you take me for?"

"My apologies," Eleonore felt her breathing begin to labor and wished she had never agreed to this interview.

"Do you understand what your employment entails?" Mrs. Meyers' voice grew deeper as she leaned her head forward.

"Not entirely," Eleonore spoke honestly.

"Then why are you here?" Mrs. Meyers huffed. "I have plenty of girls to interview, do you believe wasting my time is acceptable?"

"I apologize, Mrs. Meyers," Eleonore raised her hand repentantly. "I wasn't privy to as much information as I would've liked."

"What was your previous occupation?"

"I was detained at Auschwitz, but prior to that I—"

"I'm aware of the camps," Mrs. Meyers interrupted and grew indignant that they should even be mentioned. "Barbaric," Mrs. Meyers turned away slightly and shook her head.

"Prior to this," Eleonore cleared her throat, "I owned my own seamstress shop in Berlin."

"And what did your husband think of this?" Mrs. Meyers turned her nose up slightly.

"I'm not married," Eleonore smiled awkwardly, awaiting the inevitable follow up.

"Not married?" Mrs. Meyers leaned in, believing that she had misheard Eleonore.

"That's correct."

"Rather modern," Mrs. Meyers sat up straight again, offering Eleonore a rather peculiar gaze.

"There were no suitable courtiers," Eleonore shrugged. "I wasn't able to run my shop and have a family."

"What a selfish thought. What is more important than family?" Mrs. Meyers muttered under her breath as she sipped on her tea.

"Pardon?" Eleonore asked. The way Mrs. Meyers had asked the question it almost seemed rhetorical, but she wasn't entirely certain.

"I do not repeat myself," Mrs. Meyers blurted. "If you are going to be employed by me, then you must learn to listen and to listen well."

"Then my answer is nothing," Eleonore shook her head as a tear formed. "Nothing is more important than family."

"Then why did you not have one?" Mrs. Meyers squinted. "I lost my sons in the war, you know. Dreadful thing, but there was nothing so important as having them."

Glancing out the window, Eleonore looked at the beautiful garden and at the flowers in bloom. Then, looking back at Mrs. Meyers, Eleonore gave a slight shake of her head, acknowledging that she had no satisfactory response.

"You may leave," Mrs. Meyers waved to the door.

I failed, Eleonore stood slowly and walked away in defeat. Opening the door, Eleonore strained her eyes as the light blinded her.

"One moment," the butler spoke quickly as he brushed past her into the drawing room.

Standing awkwardly in the hallway, Eleonore looked at the paintings on the walls, remembering the priceless pieces that she saw in the Villa at Auschwitz. Life, it seemed, hadn't really moved on since she had been taken to the camp. Everything before felt a cloudy mess, and now, everything reminded Eleonore of her time at Auschwitz. It was inescapable, or so she perceived. The manor house reminded her of the Villa, the paintings reminded her of Hedwig and her contrasting simplicity against the grandiose, and the uncertainty of the future was ever-present.

"Miss Hodys," the butler returned, "this way," he offered his hand in the direction of the foyer and he walked briskly in front of her.

They walked back down the stairs as Eleonore's heart tore inside. How she wished to claim this manor as her new home. Yet her indecisiveness, her lack of clarity, and her self-consciousness had lost her the opportunity. Though, she supposed, it would be better off if she didn't work for someone as austere as Mrs. Meyers.

Then, the butler surprised Eleonore when, instead of leading her out the main doors, he turned to the west wing of the house.

"Through here," the butler opened the door for her.

"Pardon?" Eleonore frowned and glanced out the window of the front door to see Hanns and Genn pacing anxiously.

"Your quarters," the butler frowned back at Eleonore.

"My," Eleonore was stunned, "my quarters?"

"Correct," the butler nodded and again motioned towards the door for her to enter.

"I'm sorry," Eleonore held up her hand pensively. "I seem to have missed something."

"Oh?" the butler watched her curiously.

"The interview did not go well."

"No?" the butler responded as if he was pretending to be unaware.

"No," Eleonore sighed.

"It went better than you thought," the butler nodded again to the wing.

"Really?" Eleonore shot her head back in surprise.

"Really," the butler tried to smile back but his disappointment in her employment was evident.

"Well," Eleonore let out a slight chuckle, "I should tell them."

"No," the butler shook his head and pointed at his chest, "I will instruct them. You must prepare."

"Prepare for what?" Eleonore watched him warily.

"The instructions are on the bed," the butler replied quickly, his patience wearing thin. "Second floor, third door on the left."

"Alright," Eleonore took a deep breath and entered the west wing where she was met immediately by a winding staircase.

Climbing the steps, Eleonore noticed the lack of lavishness on this end of the dwelling. There were no grand paintings and no trimmings or dressings of any sort. Instead, the walls were an off-white and the stairs were guarded with iron railings. Approaching the second floor, Eleonore stepped off and stared down a dark hallway. Not dark in an unnerving sense, but rather, it felt rather secure, protected. The hallways were of a mahogany that reminded Eleonore of depictions she had seen of Tudor palaces. Along the hallway were three doors and Eleonore made her approach as the floor creaked underneath her.

Arriving at the third door, an excitement grew in Eleonore's chest. This was to be her home, and how very happy she was to even think such a thing. Opening the door, Eleonore entered the bedroom and gasped.

Chapter Six:
New Beginnings

Those who cannot remember the past are condemned to repeat it.

George Santayana

Gasping as she entered her room, Eleonore stood in the doorway and was lost to disbelief. The bright, white walls reflected the light of the sun which brought a natural warmth to the room and a calmness to her spirit. The rustic, iron bed and large bath transported Eleonore back to her flat in Berlin. There was even a small, rickety writing desk beside a bookshelf brimming with novels and other encyclopedic books. There was no running water, but still, Eleonore was glad to take whatever steps necessary to bathe privately again.

Perfecting the room was a large, double door window beside the bed that could be opened to the garden. Without hesitation, Eleonore ran to the window and threw it open as she giggled and inhaled the fresh air while leaning on the sill. Here, at the 'castle' of Mrs. Meyers, Eleonore was determined to revive her old routine of enjoying tea while taking in the morning air. Yet instead of the busy streets below her flat in Berlin, Eleonore would be allowed to relish in the peacefulness of nature.

Right! The instructions! Eleonore turned to the bed with its bright, white sheets. She picked up a neatly hand-printed placard which was resting on top of a uniform that read:

> 5:00 AM. Breakfast. Staff are expected to be ready to commence the duties of the day immediately following consumption.
> 5:30 AM. Bring Mrs. Meyers her breakfast. Tardiness will not be tolerated.
> 6:00 AM. Help Mrs. Meyers prepare for the day.

Eleonore's eyes glazed over as each half hour mark was filled with a scheduled event, leaving Eleonore to wonder when, or if, she would have any time to herself.

I'm still surprised that she hired me, Eleonore frowned and threw the placard back onto the bed without reading further. Picking up the uniform, which was a long, black dress with a white trim around the sleeves and hem, Eleonore wondered if it would fit well enough. Being that she was rather petite, Eleonore thought that maybe the dress might drag along the floor, but her main concern was simply how boring it was. There was no care at all in the design and Eleonore thought that it would be better suited as a robe or a fitting dress.

A faint knock rattled against the door which was so soft that Eleonore questioned if she had imagined it altogether. Slinging her dress over her arm, Eleonore moved to the door and opened it slowly, but no one was there. Peeking out into the hallway, Eleonore almost screamed when she locked eyes with the butler who was standing at a respectful distance from her bedroom door.

"Yes?" Eleonore asked timidly.

"It's 4:30," the butler retrieved his pocket watch and tapped it.

Eleonore frowned as she looked at him in confusion as to why the time was of significance.

"You're late for helping Mrs. Meyers prepare for her supper," he explained.

"Oh," Eleonore's eyes flew wide and she rushed back into her room to look at the placard. Near the bottom of the list read:

4:30 PM. Help Mrs. Meyers prepare for supper in the dressing room.

"Do you not believe me?" the butler called after her.

"I, uh," Eleonore shook her head as she studied the placard again, wishing she had read the full list earlier, and then shouted out into the hallway. "Sorry, this is all happening so fast!"

"Get dressed!" the butler replied, and Eleonore watched as his hand came into view as he stretched over to grab the door handle while keeping his gaze low. She wasn't sure if he was merely being polite by not wanting to see into her room or if he was some sort of puritan.

Either way, he looked rather silly as his hair flopped over and Eleonore took more pleasure than she should've at seeing him in this state.

"Quickly!" the butler shouted before shutting the door.

I need to use the facilities, Eleonore panicked as she slipped off her navy-blue dress and into the new, black uniform. Even with her recent weight loss it was a little tight at the shoulders and around the waist.

"Ready," Eleonore flung the door open to see the butler's raised hand, ready to knock again.

"Let's go!" he snapped his fingers.

"Good sir," Eleonore grew annoyed with his rushed demeanor, "I have been advised of almost nothing since my arrival which, I might add, was less than half an hour ago."

"Follow me!" he sprang towards the stairs, ignoring her concerns, as Eleonore hurried to keep up.

"I wish to be informed!" Eleonore shook her head with annoyance as she chased after him.

The butler gave no reply as he walked briskly and, again, Eleonore got the sense that he was trying to lose her in his speed.

"Can you at least tell me your name?" Eleonore panted as they half-ran down the stairs.

"Mr. Mattaliano," he replied as the name rolled off his tongue with pride.

"It's a pleasure, sir," Eleonore wheezed. "Do you have a first name?"

"Miss Hodys," Mr. Mattaliano spun on his heels and glared at her while she remained a step above him, "we are not on those terms. Nor, do I think, we shall ever be. I objected to your employment, but Mrs. Meyers overruled. I'm not sure why, but I trust that she had good reason. I shall remain professional towards you, and you shall return the favor, but we are not friends."

With wide eyes, Eleonore returned a frightened stare, confused and perplexed by the sudden animosity.

"Andiamo!" Mr. Mattaliano clapped his hands above his head and then opened the door as they left the western wing and returned to the main foyer.

He doesn't know that I understand Italian, Eleonore flinched her eye as she followed behind him. *At least all that he said was 'let's go'. I don't understand why he would oppose my employment, or why Mrs. Meyers hired me. This is all happening too quickly.*

But Eleonore's bitter attitude shifted suddenly when a pleasant smell wafted down the hallway from the kitchen. The fantastic scent of roast chicken reminded her of just how hungry she was and how dearly she missed a home cooked meal. She understood what it was to starve, but still, hunger turns one into a different creature and becomes a personality of its own.

Returning to the hallway with the orchid on the table, the butler veered through a door to the left and they entered the dining room. Lit only by candles, despite the unused light fixture overhead, the dining room was cut off from the world by thick, dark drapes.

In the center of the dining room was a large table with six chairs set about it and six candles spaced out evenly on large candle sticks. The table was made of a beautiful dark wood, but in the dim light Eleonore couldn't perceive whether it was oak or mahogany. Regardless, Eleonore's attention was stolen by the maid that she saw earlier who was setting the table for six people.

"What are you doing?!" Mr. Mattaliano barked at Eleonore.

Curious as to the outburst, the cook and the maid ceased their work to watch how the 'new blood' would handle the butler.

"Following you!" Eleonore barked back, tiring of his attitude towards her, and embarrassed that he would yell at her in full view of people she had yet to be introduced to.

"You are to be helping Mrs. Meyers prepare for supper," Mr. Mattaliano pointed back towards the foyer, indicating the direction, "and you are already late!"

"How am I supposed to know where the dressing room is?" Eleonore threw her hands into the air.

"It was on the placard on your bed!" Mr. Mattaliano shouted even louder as he grew animated. "Did you even read it?!"

"Who would've had time with you pounding on the door, rushing me out before I even had a chance to make myself decent?!"

"Excuses are the—"

"Second floor," the maid interrupted while still holding a plate in her hand. "Mrs. Meyers will be in the dressing room. Second door on your right."

"Thank you," Eleonore nodded firmly to the girl who returned to her work.

"That's how civilized people provide instruction!" Eleonore glared at the butler.

"Then I'll have the maid collect you next time you're late," Mr. Mattaliano narrowed his gaze, but then pointed towards the foyer. "Get on with it."

"I'm beginning to regret this," Eleonore grumbled as she left the dining room and half stomped as she returned to the hallway. Glancing out the front doors, she realized that Hanns and Genn had already left, and couldn't help but feeling abandoned without so much as a farewell from them.

Second floor, dressing room, second door on the right, Eleonore repeated the words of the maid as she bounded up the stairs. *I wish Mr. Mattaliano would speak to me with a measure of respect,* Eleonore frowned as she walked through the hallway on the second floor. *That must be it,*

Eleonore sped along when she spotted a door that was propped half-open and the light of a lamp struck her eye.

Eleonore paused to inspect and, peeking through the opening, saw Mrs. Meyers sitting in front of a large vanity. She had removed her hat and her long, silver hair was draped over her shoulder. Even in this informal state, Eleonore was spurred to envy Mrs. Meyers' natural elegance. She embodied refinement and sophistication, and Eleonore believed that it was impossible for Mrs. Meyers to be without these gifts.

"You are late," Mrs. Meyers spoke sharply and looked at Eleonore through the mirror.

Quickly, Eleonore slipped into the room and began walking towards her mistress. Yet Eleonore found it odd how small and bare the dressing room was and she wondered why Mrs. Meyers would be using this space instead of her own master bedroom.

"Close the door!" Mrs. Meyers snapped as if she had warned Eleonore many times beforehand.

"Certainly," Eleonore pressed the door shut softly.

"Hurry!" Mrs. Meyers waved. "Supper is getting cold."

"Of course," Eleonore ran over and stood behind Mrs. Meyers, still not entirely sure of her duties.

Then, Eleonore spotted a purple dress laid out on the bed and she rushed over to pick it up.

"Put that back at once!" Mrs. Meyers spun around in her chair.

Petrified to violate another unspoken law, Eleonore put the dress back immediately and turned to look at Mrs. Meyers with a loss for how to navigate this treacherous environment. Anything she touched was likely to bring about reproach.

Without another word, Mrs. Meyers pointed to a black dress slung over a chair near the vanity before returning to scrutinize herself in the mirror. She sat with a perfectly straight back and her hands folded neatly across her lap. Turning her head slightly, Mrs. Meyers scowled at a small birthmark near the back of her jaw. It was upsetting for Eleonore to watch this near perfect woman obsess over the slightest of blemishes.

Really? This dress? Eleonore frowned as she held it high and inspected it. Lacking style or refinement, Eleonore thought it resembled her uniform better than an evening dress.

"Stop delaying," Mrs. Meyers stood and held her arms out by her sides.

Again, Eleonore sensed that there was some specific direction or 'ritual' required but knew that Mrs. Meyers was too proud to describe the duties she was expected to perform. Fortunately, Eleonore guessed correctly as she began to undress Mrs. Meyers and she learned quickly that her only reassurance would the absence of rebuke.

"Who are we expecting for guests tonight?" Eleonore tried to make conversation as she helped Mrs. Meyers into the new, plain black dress who, even in the simplicity, appeared the definition of grace.

"Guests?" Mrs. Meyers glanced at Eleonore. "What guests?"

"I saw six plates on the table," Eleonore zipped up the back of Mrs. Meyers' dress. "I was just curious as to the occasion."

Mrs. Meyers didn't answer, but Eleonore noticed that her jaw had clenched, and her lips had pursed. Whatever Eleonore had said disturbed Mrs. Meyers deeply. In silence, Eleonore completed her mistress' ensemble with a black pearl necklace, a black silk scarf that draped across her right shoulder, and a black hat which covered her hair.

Still, even while dressed in the most unattractive color, Mrs. Meyers was a picture of perfection to Eleonore. Her blue eyes radiated against the darkness and the severity of her jaw line cut against any notion of feminine fragility. Standing back, Eleonore threw her hands onto her hips as she studied her handiwork. How she wished to have a sewing machine and some fabric to design a dress or two for this glorious woman.

Without a word, Mrs. Meyers turned and walked towards the door, but not without a glimpse over her shoulder which indicated that Eleonore was to follow.

Keeping pace, but at a distance, Eleonore followed quietly as they returned down the steps and into the dining hall. Mr. Mattaliano was waiting patiently with his hands held firmly, yet politely behind his back. With a slight bow, he pulled out a chair, just beside the head of the table, and seated her.

On cue, the maid, who had helped Eleonore earlier, arrived with a silver tray of food. Setting the tray on the table, the maid removed the cover as the steam billowed. Then, the maid lavished each plate with vegetables and meat, and Eleonore was left to wonder as to the mystery why only one was eating at a table prepared for six.

Eleonore half expected that the servants would be asked to sit at the table as well, but she knew that it was a vain wish. She remembered her brief time at the Villa in Auschwitz where she ate in the kitchen by the wonderful talents of Sophie and wondered what had become of her. She liked to think that Sophie was now in some culinary school preparing to become a master chef.

After the meal was served and Mrs. Meyers was comfortably seated, Mr. Mattaliano poured her a glass of red wine and then retreated as he awaited any need that should arise.

Feeling rather out of place, Eleonore stood patiently and awkwardly behind Mrs. Meyers who seemed to be growing increasingly annoyed at her presence. Mrs. Meyers stared straight ahead without any indication that she was about to eat, and Eleonore wondered if she was waiting for another unspoken obligation.

Eventually, the maid cleared her throat to grab Eleonore's attention and nodded her head to the side, indicating for Eleonore to stand next to her by the window. Immediately, Eleonore walked briskly over to the girl and stood beside her, mirroring her stance with her arms held lightly behind her back.

Finally pleased that all was in order, Mrs. Meyers began eating, slowly, and with a disgusted expression as if it was torture to ingest the fine meal.

"Thank you," Eleonore whispered to the maid.

"Don't mention it," she whispered back.

Out of the corner of her eye, Eleonore inspected the maid briefly. While still likely in her late teens, she was rather plain and just a hair taller than Eleonore, but she carried a natural confidence which Eleonore found infectious. Yet, in contrast to her simple looks, the maid was bestowed with two stunning, bright brown eyes that Eleonore assumed would set any man's soul aflame.

"I hope those plates are for us," Eleonore whispered again to the maid who responded with a look of horror.

Eleonore went pale wondering how she had erred. In her brief few hours at the manor, Eleonore felt that all she had accomplished was transgressing these assumed laws.

"How could you be so heartless?" the girl whispered harshly, attracting an unforgiving glance from Mrs. Meyers for interrupting the silence.

Both Eleonore and the maid immediately held their gazes at their feet, unwilling to provoke any more unwanted attention. Then, Mrs. Meyers held up her hand and Mr. Mattaliano was at once by her side to refill her wine. The mistress began muttering something to the butler that was inaudible to Eleonore but seemed of little importance anyways.

Seizing the opportunity, Eleonore leaned over slightly and whispered, "Please explain."

"You don't know?" the maid looked at Eleonore curiously out the side of her eye but kept her focus on Mrs. Meyers.

"Know what?"

"The plates are for her family," the maid gave a glance of pity and at once Eleonore understood.

How could I have been so stupid? Eleonore slouched as she realized the gravity of her offence.

The room was a den of uncomfortable silence as the only sound was Mrs. Meyers' slow chewing or her gulping of the wine. Cutting into the chicken as though she had no energy, Mrs. Meyers would then gradually lift the fork to her mouth as though it were a great burden. Yet Eleonore noticed that her strength quickly returned when she required another glass of wine.

"What were their names?" Eleonore whispered to the maid when the butler was again re-filling Mrs. Meyers' cup.

"I don't know all of them," the maid glanced at Eleonore apologetically. "I arrived only a few weeks before you did. But I do know the most important name: Paul. He was her youngest and sat just to the left of her."

"Killed in combat?" Eleonore asked as she looked sympathetically at Mrs. Meyers.

"No," the maid shook her head, "he was killed in training. It's a rather tragic story actually, and not one to be told over whispers."

Dabbing her mouth with the silk napkin, Mrs. Meyers raised a limp hand to Mr. Mattaliano, signaling that she was finished. At once, the butler was by his mistress' side and snapped his fingers for the maid to remove the dishes.

"I think I should like to lie down," Mrs. Meyers spoke softly to her butler and Eleonore noticed her eyes glazing over.

For once, Eleonore knew exactly what was required of her and jumped into action. Returning to Mrs. Meyers' side, Eleonore held out her hand to offer her assistance.

"What are you doing?" Mr. Mattaliano hissed at Eleonore.

"The madam would like to lie down," Eleonore explained calmly.

"That is my responsibility," Mr. Mattaliano gritted his teeth.

"Not anymore," Eleonore offered him a stern look of warning.

"Thank you," Mrs. Meyers waved drunkenly and grabbed Eleonore's hand, oblivious to the hushed dispute which occurred only a foot behind her.

"To the drawing room, ma'am?" Eleonore asked as they walked slowly back to the foyer.

"To bed," Mrs. Meyers rubbed her eyes with her free hand.

Eleonore helped Mrs. Meyers back up the stairs who struggled with a step or two and was glad to have Eleonore's assistance. Eleonore felt an odd sense of pride as she helped her new mistress. Mrs. Meyers was strict and unyielding, but not from pretension. Rather, Eleonore suspected that Mrs. Meyers was the class of woman who had endeavored to restrain her own passions and perfect her own shortcomings. She expected nothing less from others.

Because of this, Eleonore was determined to earn Mrs. Meyers' respect. This woman had lost everything, everything important that is, and Eleonore wished to assist her in whatever capacity she could. Besides, seeing her in this slightly inebriated state humanized her to an extent.

Arriving at her bedroom, Mrs. Meyers fumbled in her handbag until she eventually retrieved a key and unlocked the door. But before she opened it, she turned to Eleonore with a severe gaze.

"Since my husband's passing, no one in this house has seen the inside of the master bedroom," she leaned towards Eleonore as the stench of wine spilled off her breath. "Pledge to me that it will stay that way. No one is to know of what you are about to see. I charge you as the keeper of this secret. Is that understood?"

Eleonore gave a quick and nervous nod as she stared wide-eyed at Mrs. Meyers, wondering what could possibly await her on the other side.

With a groan, the heavy wooden door opened as if it was a creature awakening from sleep.

"Quickly," Mrs. Meyers ordered as she rushed inside and waved for Eleonore to follow.

Save for the pale moonlight entering from a large window, the room was entirely dark. A chill ran down Eleonore's spine when Mrs. Meyers closed the door behind her and the two were alone in the darkness. Yet this chill was not isolated to the uneasiness as there was also a draft coming from the open window which was letting in the cool evening air.

Striking a match, Mrs. Meyers lit a candle, but Eleonore's apprehension only grew as the room was illuminated and she saw what the mistress had been hiding. An officer's uniform was laid out on one side of the bed, in the place where Eleonore assumed Mrs. Meyers' husband once slept. Beside the bed, on a small table, was an urn which Eleonore believed to be her husband. In front of the bed, on a long footstool, were four other urns, and Eleonore understood this to be her sons.

It was then that Eleonore grew acutely aware of Mrs. Meyers' gaze, inspecting her reaction. Mrs. Meyers held the candle near her face as she slouched and looked at Eleonore vacantly. Yet, it wasn't an eerie vacancy, but rather, from near exhaustion. Still, Eleonore stared back at Mrs. Meyers, wary of her intentions.

"Help me prepare for bed," Mrs. Meyers spoke as she left to light another candle.

With the added light, Eleonore looked around and noticed that the room seemed to be frozen in time. Nothing had been changed or tampered with except that which was essential. The writing desk beside Eleonore was adorned with unfinished letters, and a pen set neatly beside them. A pair of men's boots lay scattered near the fireplace beside the bed, and Eleonore pictured a Mr. Meyers kicking them off as he sat in front of the fire.

Remembering her duty, Eleonore walked briskly towards Mrs. Meyers who was now waiting at her side of the bed. Undressing Mrs. Meyers, Eleonore folded the black dress in her arm and assumed that she should return it to the dressing room.

"I suppose this is unsettling for you," Mrs. Meyers swallowed as she lowered her guard for a moment, though the wine was aiding a little in this regard.

"Not at all," Eleonore lied.

"I would not blame you if it was," Mrs. Meyers turned and faced Eleonore and raised a finger in warning. "Remember, not a word."

"I wouldn't dare," Eleonore shook her head. "But can I ask, why are you trusting me? Our interview didn't go well, and I was certain that I didn't get the position. Yet now you've let me into a room which no one else has seen? I don't entirely understand."

"You may leave," Mrs. Meyers handed the key to Eleonore. "Lock the door on your way out. I take breakfast at 5:30 sharp. Do not be late."

With the dress draped over her arm, Eleonore blew out the candles and left the room. But, as she was leaving,

Eleonore gave one last peek into the room and saw a heart-shattering sight. Mrs. Meyers had climbed under the covers and was weeping silently as she held the arm of the uniform. Locking the door, Eleonore pondered at the gravity of what she had witnessed and why Mrs. Meyers had entrusted her. Eleonore presumed that if she were in her position, then she would not be able to handle herself with nearly the same amount of grace and didn't guilt her for the overconsumption of wine.

"Where's Mrs. Meyers?" a voice called from behind Eleonore.

Startled, Eleonore turned sharply to see the maid standing at the top of the stairs.

"Oh," Eleonore clutched her chest, "it's just you."

"If Mrs. Meyers finds out that you were in that room, she will kill you," the girl rushed over to Eleonore, full of concern.

"No, it's alright," Eleonore held up the key. "She asked me to put her to bed."

The girl's jaw dropped, and she looked at Eleonore with a mixture of awe and jealousy.

"Why you?" she frowned at Eleonore.

"I asked her the same thing," Eleonore leaned in.

"And?" the girl shrugged.

"She wouldn't tell me," Eleonore shrugged back.

"We have much to discuss," the girl grabbed Eleonore's hand and led her away.

Chapter Seven:
1WCIT

A friend is, as it were, a second self.

Cicero

"Mrs. Meyers has accepted Miss Hodys into her employment," Mr. Mattaliano explained to Genn and Hanns who were waiting eagerly outside the manor.

"That's great!" Hanns sighed his relief.

"I'll collect her belongings and take them to her room," the butler continued.

"She's wearing all that she owns," Genn replied with a reluctant glance at Hanns.

"I see," Mr. Mattaliano stared at Genn but Hanns thought he heard the butler offer a slight, impatient groan.

"Our business is concluded," the butler spun on his heels and walked back towards the manor.

"Wait!" Hanns called out and Mr. Mattaliano stopped to look at him.

"I would like…we would like to offer our farewell," Hanns looked at the butler earnestly.

"Miss Hodys is now in the employment of her ladyship," the butler replied condescendingly, "and she is preparing for her evening duties."

"It'll just be quick," Hanns pressed.

"I do find it curious," the butler took a step towards Hanns, "why the British government, with two German-speaking officers, would be so interested in someone of such little significance."

"As you said," Hanns flinched his eye, "it's not our duty to understand our government's interests, but it is our duty to enforce them."

"I must return and prepare for supper," Mr. Mattaliano again spun on his heels and walked briskly back towards the doors.

"You'll tell her goodbye for me, at least?" Hanns called after the butler, who gave no reply as he entered the manor.

"She'll be fine," Genn spoke confidently and waved for Hanns to return to the truck. "She can take care of herself. She's proven that."

"I don't like it," Hanns shook his head. "I don't like it one bit. And I especially don't like that butler."

"What's there to worry about?" Genn gestured as he started the vehicle. "Besides, if Eleonore happens to discover anything suspicious in the area, then she'll notify us. If not, then we provided a good woman with some employment."

"I suppose you're right," Hanns chewed his lip thoughtfully as they drove back over the stone bridge guarding the stream.

The two remained silent as they drove while Hanns smoked his pipe nervously. There was something about Eleonore that he found rather captivating. Not in a charismatic sense, but rather, there was a pull towards her, and he found it difficult to think about anything other than her safety. He wished now that he had not jumped to conclusions when he first read her file. There was more to Eleonore than being the mistress to Rudolph Hoess.

That reminds me, Hanns dug into his breast pocket and retrieved a letter.

"From a lady friend?" Genn asked.

"Ya," Hanns nodded. "How'd you know?"

"There's only one reason a man would have a smile like that," Genn grinned.

"It's from Ann," Hanns mumbled and his expression turned a mixture of joy and dread.

"Who's Ann?" Genn asked playfully.

"My girl back home," Hanns explained dryly, "and I believe that I can predict the contents of this letter."

"Oh?"

"She's very good at arguing, you see," Hanns retrieved a photo which he showed to Genn.

"You dirty bastard!" Genn became rife with envy. "She's gorgeous!"

"Yes, and very committed," Hanns sighed. "She wants to get married."

"And?" Genn scoffed. "This is what you find worthy of complaint? Thousands of men wish that they could be in your shoes right now with a beautiful girl desperate for their attention."

"I suppose," Hanns examined her photograph.

"You suppose?!" Genn looked at him with incredulity.

"I don't know her, really," Hanns defended. "In the last two years we've only spent two weeks together. I met her at Frankie's house, the one who taught me English. Ann is a Jewish-German refugee as well, you see, and Frankie was tutoring the both of us. We stayed in touch and we've written lots. I do like her quite a bit, but I think I should focus more on getting back home before I set up a home."

"You told her no then?"

"I told her that we would discuss things when I returned."

"Oh no," Genn made a sour face.

"Ya, I know," Hanns hung his head.

"What did she say to that?"

"I'm unsure," Hanns tapped the letter, indicating the answer lay within. "But there are bigger things to worry about right now," Hanns became solemn. "Like what we should eat for supper."

"You're always good for a laugh," Genn gave a generous smack on Hanns' arm.

"We all have our talents, I suppose," Hanns replied as he became lost in thought.

"Well?" Genn looked at Hanns expectantly.

"Well what?" Hanns looked back at Genn.

"Go on," Genn nodded to the letter. "Open it."

"Now?" Hanns studied the letter reluctantly.

"You have something better to do?" Genn shrugged.

"I don't know," Hanns examined the envelope.

"Oh, give it," Genn reached over to grab the letter as the truck swerved.

"I'll do it! I'll do it!" Hanns kept the letter away from Genn. "You just focus on the road."

Genn chuckled as he returned his hands to the steering wheel, waiting anxiously for Hanns to entertain him with Ann's reply.

Opening the letter, Hanns mouthed the words as he read quietly to himself.

"Read it aloud!"

"She's good," Hanns dropped the letter to his side.

"Details, Howard!" Genn gestured. "Details!"

"Maybe she should marry you then," Hanns grumbled.

"We've driven through half of Germany," Genn shot Hanns an unappreciative glance. "The countryside is beautiful, yes, but my sanity is dying for diversion. As your superior officer, I demand that you read the details of that letter."

"That's an abuse of power," Hanns muttered, but obliged Genn regardless. "She's suggesting that we get engaged without the pressure of setting up a date for the wedding."

Genn chuckled, "I think she's a little worried about some other broad snatching you up. She must've forgotten what you look like."

"Maybe," Hanns slunk down in his seat as he ignored Genn's teasing. "I'm not sure if this is a red flag. She wants to get married on my next leave, whenever that will be."

"Why don't you request leave, then?"

"This takes precedence," Hanns rubbed his chin. "Once these cowards have been brought to justice, then I can look to my own needs."

Hanns glanced out the window as he grew thoughtful. A hatred was fermenting in his heart. A hatred for what had happened to his people and his country. He knew that nothing good would come from resentment, but he also didn't believe that he could help what he was feeling. Witnessing the horror of the camps was not something he could quickly forget. He was anxious to begin the work and to bring some justice to the world.

"Here," Genn broke the silence and pulled out sandwiches from his personal satchel.

"Where were you hiding these?" Hanns grew animated.

"Ah, damn!" Genn suddenly grew disappointed.

"What's wrong?" Hanns asked.

"There's no mustard," Genn looked sheepishly at Hanns.

"I think we'll survive!" Hanns burst into laughter. "But, seriously, where were you hiding these?"

"I bought them in the town where we got Eleonore's dress."

"That makes me feel a bit better," Hanns grinned. "Here I thought you were carrying sandwiches around for weeks."

"If that were true, I would've given you both of them," Genn chuckled.

"We're here," Genn tapped Hanns to awake him as they arrived at Belsen, another concentration camp that had been transformed to serve a better purpose.

Groaning, Hanns sat up, not feeling at all refreshed by the long drive. Rubbing his eyes, he knew that there would be no rest granted, and that their duty took utmost priority.

"It was discovered by chance, you know," Genn glanced at Hanns.

"What was?" Hanns asked dryly. He wasn't much in the mood for conversation, but instead craved a hot shower, a warm meal, and to resupply his cigarettes and pipe tobacco.

"The camp," Genn pointed and then saluted to the guards as they drove inside.

"Really?" Hanns grew interested.

"A British officer was running reconnaissance when he discovered it by accident," Genn elaborated.

"I wasn't aware," Hanns rubbed the stubble on his chin which was growing too long for comfort.

"Makes you think, doesn't it?" Genn spoke rhetorically as he parked the truck near the administration offices.

"How so?" Hanns asked but wished that he had remained silent as he really wasn't of the frame of mind to engage in any thought-provoking discussions.

"It's a shame the officer didn't find the camp earlier, or what if he had missed it altogether?"

"The real shame is that the camps existed at all," Hanns shook his head.

"True enough," Genn thought for a moment and then turned the truck off and stretched. "I'll run ahead and make certain that the preparations are as I specified. Bring the satchels."

"Sir," Hanns nodded his compliance and jumped into the back of the truck. But, taking advantage of the solitude, Hanns put his head in his hands as he leaned over and experienced a rare moment of emptiness. He wasn't angry or vengeful as he had been previously. Nor was he sorrowful or broken by what he had seen and witnessed. Instead, he felt hollow. There was a numbness to his soul which Hanns found more unsettling than anything else he had experienced. He knew how to handle his rage and where to point his anger, but he was oblivious as to how to deal with this vacuum.

"Can I help you with anything?" a nasally voice startled Hanns and he turned to see a scrawny officer with thin glasses halfway down his nose standing at the foot of the truck.

"I'll be fine," Hanns replied and returned his attention to his task.

Still feeling the presence of watchful eyes, Hanns turned his head to see that the officer hadn't left.

"I can manage," Hanns reiterated.

Still, the officer stared without expression, his attention fixated on the satchels.

"I'm assuming that you know what's in these?" Hanns looked at him suspiciously.

"My father was at Dachau," the officer continued to stare at the bags. "I want to know what happened, from the people that you interrogated."

"I'm sorry," Hanns threw his hands onto his hips as he looked at the man with sympathy. "These are classified."

"By whom?"

"No. 1 War Crimes Investigation Team."

"Oh good," the officer held out his hand, requesting a satchel.

"What are you doing?"

"I'm part of 1WCIT," the officer looked up at Hanns, "and we always use the acronym."

"In what capacity?"

"I'm an interrogator," the officer replied briskly.

There's no hope for us, Hanns thought but bit his tongue. *He's the least intimidating man I've ever met.*

"Still," Hanns took a deep breath, "these need to be typed up properly. They are under my charge until I hear otherwise."

"Understood," the officer pushed his glasses up his nose.

"If you want to be helpful," Hanns jumped off the truck with the bags slung around each shoulder, "you can show me to the briefing room."

"That I can do," the officer threw his hands behind his back and Hanns smiled slightly at the sight of this little man with such an air of importance.

The two walked towards the main office as Hanns followed just behind the officer, struggling under the weight of the satchels and now wishing that he had taken the officer's assistance.

"I didn't catch your name," Hanns panted as they walked.

"That's because I didn't give it," the officer replied.

"Well," Hanns chuckled, wondering if he was the subject of some prank, "what is your name?"

"Smallwood," the officer replied, "Geoffrey Smallwood."

"Of course it is," Hanns muttered under his breath. *Perfect name for him.*

"Here we are," Smallwood opened the door and entered the building, not considering that Hanns may need assistance with the door as it closed behind him.

"This has to be a joke," Hanns stared at the door, wondering how he was going to open it while so encumbered. Bending over awkwardly, Hanns grabbed the handle and pulled, but he wasn't expecting how heavy the door was and watched in annoyance as it slowly shut again as if it were mocking him. With the second attempt, Hanns gave a generous heave and stuck his foot out to stop the door as he abandoned gracefulness and squeezed his way into the building. Inside he found Smallwood waiting patiently with his hands held behind his back.

"I could've used some help," Hanns panted as he looked at Smallwood.

"I thought you could manage," Smallwood replied with a hint of smugness.

"Would you like to carry one?" Hanns spoke patronizingly to Smallwood.

"No," Smallwood shook his head, but still, reached out and took a single satchel off of Hanns' shoulder.

"Thank you," Hanns gave an annoyed looked at Smallwood who seemed oblivious to the irritation that he was causing.

"To your left is the typists' office," Smallwood pointed as he led Hanns deeper into the building.

Glancing into the room which had large windows all around, Hanns noticed three women each sitting at a desk but only one of them was busy with the typewriter. The other two sat at their desks smoking and slouching from boredom.

"I need the typewriter as well!" one of the ladies inside shouted after nearing the end of her patience.

"No, I'm next!" the other stood and elbowed her way beside the typist.

"My work is just as important!" The first shouted back.

"To the right is our briefing station," Smallwood stopped and turned suddenly.

"It's an empty room," Hanns glanced inside.

"Yes," Smallwood replied.

"Where are the desks or chairs?" Hanns shook his head.

"Coming...hopefully," Smallwood ushered Hanns inside.

"And a new light bulb?" Hanns pointed to the flickering ceiling light.

"Should be fixed shortly," Smallwood cleared his throat.

"Well," Hanns sighed when he entered the room, wondering where to place himself, "we've got to make the best of it I suppose."

Suddenly, a shout came from down the hallway and Hanns recognized Genn's voice. *What's that all about?* Hanns wondered as he set the satchels down in a corner.

Bursting into the room, Genn continued to shout in English, quicker than Hanns could translate, but the few words he did identify were ones not worthy of repeating. Following Genn into the room were nine other officers who appeared, to Hanns, to be just as displeased as their superior officer.

The room became a buzz of activity as the officers chatted vigorously amongst themselves while forming a disorderly semi-circle around Genn. While they all spoke German, some better than others, Hanns noticed that no one had a true German accent and it was likely that he was the only real German in the room.

"May I stand beside you?" Smallwood asked Hanns formally.

"Yep," Hanns nodded quickly, still amused by this character, "but you don't need to ask my permission."

At this, Smallwood grew the largest grin and held his chin high as he stood proudly by Hanns who, while feeling a little guilty for the assumption, guessed that this officer had only a few friends.

Suddenly, a cheer erupted in the room as tables and chairs were ushered in by some younger guards. Hanns clapped his amusement as well as he enjoyed how easily the British were excited by seemingly insignificant events. He remembered his first experience in England and how the English Jews that welcomed them found almost any reason to celebrate.

But Hanns' excitement vanished when a frail, young woman entered the room. The merriness around Hanns fell silent as he watched her with great interest. Famished and exhausted, Hanns mistook her for Eleonore, and was surprised to see her amongst them. Yet there was a fire in her eyes, a resentment which burned within her that would see revenge upon her oppressors, no matter the cost. It was a bitterness that Hanns recognized well and, in that fleeting moment, recognized the dangerous path that revenge would lead him.

"Gentlemen!" Genn shouted as he stepped into their midst and looked at each of them sternly. "This is not a moment for cheer. Our charge is grave and our task is solemn. The earth on which you stand was part of a system that saw an untold number of Jews and other prisoners slaughtered."

His words cut into all of them, and the shame about the room was tangible. Each man either glanced at their feet or at each other, ensuring that they weren't alone in the disgrace.

"To order," Genn commanded.

Immediately, the officers took a seat as the tables had been set about in a square facing each other. Grabbing a spot beside Smallwood, Hanns took out his notepad and pen and was about to write when he noticed that the frail woman had not taken a seat.

"Ma'am," Hanns stood quickly and all looked at him as though he were mad, "please, have my seat."

The woman glanced at Hanns curiously, but her countenance changed to sudden horror when she noticed the attention that had been shed on her and she shook her head quickly.

"Sit, Lieutenant," Genn waved at Hanns.

"Sir, I-"

"Now," Genn gave a warning look, and Hanns slowly obeyed.

Whatever friend Genn had been in the vehicle had retreated behind the hierarchy of command. Then, clearing his throat, Genn struck eye contact with the woman and nodded to an empty chair that was hidden in the corner. Quickly, the woman took her seat in the shadows, feeling rather out of place in this world of men.

"Gentlemen," Genn began as he remained standing, "and lady," he added quickly. "We here have formed No. 1 War Crimes Investigation Team, from here onward to be called 1WCIT."

"Acronyms," Smallwood tapped Hanns' arm.

"Shouldn't we wait for the others?" an officer interjected. He was a rather round gentlemen with a red face and large nose with a jovial expression.

"That's Anthony Somerhough," Smallwood whispered. "Don't worry, his bark is worse than his bite."

"I don't know," Hanns glanced at Smallwood. "His bark looks awfully terrible."

"Others?" Genn scoffed. "You are viewing the team in its entirety. Ten officers, two former prisoners."

A murmur rushed about the room and Hanns assumed they were all as surprised as he was.

"Yes," Genn raised his hands to calm them, "this is the team in its entirety. Our task is—"

"Our task is impossible," Another officer interrupted. "Twelve souls to carry out the job of a hundred? Those devils will slip through our fingers faster than we can count them!"

"Who's that?" Hanns asked Smallwood.

"Not sure, actually," Smallwood frowned.

"Impossible is correct," Genn threw his hands behind his back as he studied the team earnestly. "We are the entire infield war crimes staff for Britain. We have this office to perform our operations. Beyond this, we are on our own. We have but one typewriter, no recording devices, one or two vehicles, and no form of communication with one another."

"Then how are we supposed to accomplish anything?" the same officer became irate.

"The same way we are standing here today amidst victory!" Genn boomed. "Ingenuity! Bravery! Righteousness! Britain entered this war without a standing army. Now, we are planting our feet on enemy territory."

"But as far as I'm aware," another officer crossed his arms as he complained, "there are only two amongst us who have experience in the field of detective work."

"Correct," Genn shrugged. "I, myself, am an actor."

"Banker," Hanns threw his hand into the air.

"Photographer," Another huffed.

"So, Britain and the Allies have no serious intent to catch these criminals?" the officer shook his head.

"Because they aren't fully aware of what happened here," Genn tapped a determined finger against the table. "And that, gentlemen…and lady…is our utmost mission. We must show them, and the world, what happened at these camps. If not, these terrible men will escape the judgement due their crimes."

A hush went around the room as the gravity of the situation became apparent. Everything rested upon these twelve souls, and none of them felt confident that they could complete the task adequately.

"For the items that we are lacking, we will make requisitions from the towns, who so far have shown cooperation, to provide the supplies required. You have the documents?" Genn looked at Hanns who nodded to the corner where the satchels were kept.

"These," Genn grabbed the satchels and set them down on the table in front of the team, "are the statements collected by our very own Colonel Stephens."

All turned to a man sitting opposite Genn and noticed the monocle fixed to his right eye. He carried a rather severe, unforgiving expression that terrified Hanns.

I suppose that's what makes him great at interrogations, Hanns shuddered.

"His nickname is Tin Eye," Smallwood whispered.

"I wonder why," Hanns replied sarcastically.

"It's because of his monocle," Smallwood replied.

"Yes, I know," Hanns became impatient. "I was being sarcastic. The nickname doesn't require much investigation."

"However," Genn continued with a deep sigh, "while these are invaluable to our mission, they will not hold up in court. These will need to be re-taken, typed, and properly witnessed."

"How can this be accomplished with only one typewriter?" another officer complained.

"You were all chosen for this task because of your resourcefulness. I have assigned you to three teams," Genn pointed to the board behind his table where a small sheet of paper listed the names of the teams. "A court is to be held in Belsen at summer's end which will follow British judiciary procedures. Counsel will represent both the accused and prosecutor. Those found guilty can expect life imprisonment or death by hanging or firing squad."

An excitement spread about the room that justice, real and tangible justice was within their grasp. The road ahead would be hard, but it would be worthwhile to bring those hated creatures to heel.

"That's too simple for them," Tin Eye Stephens leaned forward and spoke softly, without emotion. "We should do to them what they've done to us. No trial, no counsel to represent them. We should herd them into a camp, let them starve to death while enduring beatings and torture."

A murmur went around the room. Some found the suggestion disgusting while others seemed to echo the enthusiasm for such revenge.

"We can't become like them," Genn stood straight and threw one arm behind his back. "If we can bring these men to trial, justly, then this will set a precedent that cannot be impeded. It is imperative that we are triumphant in this cause. Failure, lady and gentlemen, is not an option we can afford."

"This will take more time than I believe we are prepared to give," an irate officer interjected. "We have to translate as well, may I remind you, which means that every statement will take twice as long."

"I understand that this is an insurmountable task," Genn leaned on the table, "but I cannot stress enough how vital it is that we do not fail in this regard."

"If we beat the confessions out of them it would speed up the process considerably," Tin Eye glared at Genn with a desire for vengeance.

"The use of violence is unacceptable," Genn paused, "but intimidation and the threat of force should be employed liberally. Form up into your teams and begin work immediately."

At once, the room returned to a frenzy as the officers pushed and jostled their way to the front of the room to see which team they had been assigned to. Thankful that he was rather tall, Hanns stood above the others and, squinting, read his name at the bottom of the list.

"Howard Volker?" a call came out from the front of the room, but Hanns couldn't see who was calling.

"Howard Volker?" the call came again.

"Here," Hanns raised his hand.

"I'm Captain Felix," the officer pushed his way through the crowd and stuck his hand out in greeting, "but most call me Captain Fox."

"Howard," Hanns shook his hand.

"We've been assigned together," Captain Fox rocked on his heels.

He was a smaller man, but in no way did this impede his intimidating qualities. He reminded Hanns of a bulldog that Frankie owned in England. It was small, disturbingly lazy, but built like a machine with rippling muscles. There was a feisty temperament to the bulldog, much like in Captain Fox, that if you dared upset it, then there was nothing which could stop it from unleashing all its fury.

"I'm guessing I'm your interpreter?" Hanns raised his eyebrow.

"Correct," Captain Fox nodded, but then grabbed Hanns' arm as he led him to the back of the room, away from the commotion.

"Listen," Captain Fox began, "I'm about as anxious as any to get started. I suggest we commence with the prisoners at Celle. You think you can be ready within the hour?"

"Hour?" Hanns huffed. "I'm ready now."

"Good," Fox slapped Hanns' arm. "Let's get to it then, shall we?"

Chapter Eight:
Kindling

Grief is the price we pay for love.
Queen Elizabeth II

"Here they are," the maid nearly shouted as she searched through a cupboard in Eleonore's room.

"Here what are?" Eleonore eyed her suspiciously as she sat on the edge of her bed, growing territorial over a room that she had spent less than ten minutes inside.

"Glasses," she turned towards Eleonore and held up two small glass cups.

"Oh?" Eleonore remained confused as the girl set the cups down on the table beside the window.

"And the wine," the girl grunted as she knelt in front of Eleonore.

"What are you doing?" Eleonore looked at her nervously.

"I need to get under the bed," she pointed.

"Oh!" Eleonore stood and made way for her.

"Ah, good," the girl retrieved a bottle and held it high. "It's still here."

"What's that doing under there?" Eleonore shot her head back in surprise.

"I put it there," the girl explained.

"Why?"

"Mrs. Meyers doesn't like the servants to drink, so I hid a bottle," she reached again under the bed to retrieve a corkscrew. "And what better occasion than now to enjoy it?"

"I understand her not wanting the servants to get drunk," Eleonore frowned as she and the girl sat at the table, "but it seems rather draconian to not let us partake in a glass or two here and there. Especially when she is so liberal with her own intake."

"We're like Americans during the prohibition," the girl strained as she uncorked the bottle.

"Before you get too excited," Eleonore put her hand over her glass to stop the girl from pouring, "I know that you want to discuss what I saw in Mrs. Meyers' room, but I should warn you that I've been sworn to secrecy."

"No!" the girl's eyes bulged.

"Sorry," Eleonore shrugged. "I should've mentioned earlier, but I don't believe you gave me much of an opportunity to explain myself."

"I was being sarcastic," the girl smiled. "I'm aware that you can't tell me anything."

"Oh? Really?" Eleonore frowned. "Then why are you here, and why the wine? Not that I mind the company, but I do have to wake up in about six hours. I would appreciate the rest."

"Just one quick drink, then I'll leave," the girl held up a finger as a pledge.

"I don't know," Eleonore glanced at the bed behind her, offering up its promise of comfort and rest.

"When's the last time you had a drink?" the girl persisted.

"It's been awhile," Eleonore glanced at the bottle, feeling a sudden itch in her throat and an impulsiveness in her spirit. *It would be nice to have a friend here,* Eleonore thought as she looked hopefully at the girl.

"It's settled then," the girl began to pour, not waiting for Eleonore to remove her hand which was splashed by the wine.

"Hey!" Eleonore held up her hand and looked around for something to dry it with.

"Sorry," the girl giggled.

"Can you grab me a cloth?" Eleonore remained unimpressed.

"Here," the girl grabbed Eleonore's hand and, with the sleeve of her black dress, wiped away the wine.

"Your dress!" Eleonore couldn't believe what she had witnessed.

"We're going to be living together for some time," the maid shrugged. "We should probably get familiar."

"That's not the point," Eleonore muttered as she watched the girl return to pouring. As a seamstress, she was mortified that someone would abuse their clothing in this manner.

"I'm afraid it's a bit late for me to be asking this, but I don't know your name," Eleonore asked awkwardly as she watched her glass fill with growing eagerness.

"It's Eva," the girl replied as she began to fill her own cup, though Eleonore noticed that she only gave herself about half what she had given to Eleonore.

"Such a sweet name," Eleonore smiled.

"Meh," Eva shrugged. "There were about ten girls named Eva in my class. We usually went by our middle names."

"Just because something is common doesn't mean that it's uninteresting. What does Eva mean?"

"What does it mean?" Eva shot Eleonore a confused glance.

"Ya," Eleonore leaned forward. "What does your name mean?"

"No clue," Eva shook her head indifferently.

"You've never bothered to find out or your parents didn't tell you?" Eleonore frowned.

"My parents didn't name me," Eva bit her lip and became a little uncomfortable with the conversation. "Never knew them, either, so it's a bit late to ask now."

"We don't have to discuss this," Eleonore waved her hand to brush away the discomfort.

"What does your name mean?" Eva asked.

"It means 'the other Leanor'," Eleonore smiled briefly. "Not a very strong name."

Bored with Eleonore's explanation, Eva sighed and slumped down on the bed beside Eleonore. Slightly offended, Eleonore watched Eva and understood that their difference in age and interests hindered the stimulation that Eva was craving. She was a young, wild creature who was longing for adventure while Eleonore was anxious for peace and quiet.

Glancing at Eleonore, Eva took a small sip of her wine, but then gave a foul expression and scrunched up her nose as she studied the glass.

"Eva, how old are you?" Eleonore squinted curiously at her reaction.

"I'm nineteen, why?"

"Is this the first time that you've tried wine?"

"What? No! It's gone bad…I think. Try yours. Tell me if I'm mad."

"Alright," Eleonore held the glass up to her nose and took a sniff. *Smells fine,* she thought as she took a quick sip but then immediately puckered up and spit the wine back into the cup.

"Oh, it's awful!" Eleonore's face went sour and Eva chortled as she took another sip with, again, the same foul reaction.

"Why did you take another sip?!" Eleonore giggled.

"I don't know!" Eva laughed. "Maybe I thought I could push through the disgusting taste."

"Let me see that bottle," Eleonore grabbed it and held it high as she read the label.

"Anyways," Eva put down her glass and looked rather disappointed. "I suppose I should leave you be."

"You were just here for the wine, weren't you?" Eleonore's joy faded as Eva stood. "Well, don't I feel cheap…"

"No, no," Eva shook her head vibrantly. "Don't mistake me. I just feel a little foolish for ruining the evening is all."

"You haven't ruined anything," Eleonore reached out and grabbed Eva's hand. "Why don't you tell me a little about yourself."

"What do you want to know?" Eva shrugged as she returned to sitting.

"You said you only arrived a couple weeks ago, where did you come from? How did you end up here?" Eleonore rested her head on her hand as she awaited Eva's reply.

"It's not a very interesting story I'm afraid," Eva glanced away.

"I doubt that," Eleonore studied Eva.

"I did hear a rumor about you, though," Eva looked at Eleonore with a spirited grin.

"What's that?" Eleonore turned her head as she cautiously waited for what was undoubtedly on Eva's mind.

"I shouldn't say," Eva shook her head.

"You have to now," Eleonore persisted.

"It can't be true, so it's not worth repeating."

"You must tell me," Eleonore grew nervous with anticipation.

"They said that you were rescued by the Americans," Eva looked down at her hands, embarrassed to discuss it, "but that can't be true as the camps are all propaganda anyways."

"Who told you this?" Eleonore grew stern and rolled up the sleeve to reveal her tattoo.

Eva studied Eleonore's arm in horror, "Wait?! The camps were real? I thought they were just retirement camps!"

"Who told you about me?" Eleonore repeated with her countenance growing harsh.

"Eleonore," Eva swallowed, "I had no idea. I thought it was just Allied propaganda! I swear!"

"Who told you?!" Eleonore slapped her palm on the table, startling Eva. Eleonore wasn't entirely sure why she was so upset, but even the mention of the camps made her defensive.

"The butler, Mr. Mattaliano," Eva began to breathe heavily. "He warned me about your troubled past."

"Did he now?" Eleonore crossed her arms as she leaned back in her chair. "What else did he mention?"

"I'm sorry," Eva swallowed as she fought away the tears. "That's all he said."

"It's not your fault," Eleonore offered a limp smile. "He didn't mention anything more than that I was at the camps?"

"No," Eva shook her head and wiped away a tear before it could fall. "But I have to say, it was refreshing to see the way you spoke to him earlier this evening. He has the ear of Mrs. Meyers which makes everyone afraid to say or do anything which might upset him. He feels that you're threatening his position."

"Why does she trust me?" Eleonore squinted.

"Mrs. Meyers?" Eva glanced at Eleonore but then shrugged. "That's what I came here to find out."

"I have a feeling that you're not acting alone," Eleonore raised her eyebrows.

"He asked me to check in on you is all," Eva closed her eyes as she huffed, knowing it would be useless to lie.

"Tell him I'm doing fine," Eleonore smiled cynically.

"He'll hate that," Eva returned the smile. "You can't take it personally, but he despises you. You arrived out of nowhere and Mrs. Meyers is already trusting you with more than she has ever trusted him. Since her husband passed, Mr. Mattaliano has never seen the inside of the master bedroom. He's convinced that there's some sort of secret she's hiding," Eva glanced at Eleonore hoping that her reaction would reveal some clue.

"You've been here longer than I have," Eleonore ignored Eva's bating, "what sort of things does Mrs. Meyers like to do? What brings her joy?"

"I haven't seen her smile once since I've arrived," Eva shrugged, "but Mr. Mattaliano mentioned that he misses music."

"He misses music?"

"I'm told that Mr. Meyers employed the gramophone liberally and Mrs. Meyers used to dance with him every night."

"Really?" Eleonore stared at the ceiling as a plot formed in her mind.

"I hope you're not planning anything rash," Eva studied Eleonore.

"I just want to help is all."

"Mr. Mattaliano also complained about getting a little tubby," Eva searched her memory.

"Tubby?" Eleonore snickered.

"Apparently, he used to accompany Mrs. Meyers on their daily walks into town, and now he's noticing the impact of the lack of exercise."

"I see," Eleonore grinned.

This was it, she felt, this was her purpose. She would try to help Mrs. Meyers and bring her back from grief, if that was possible. Besides, if she could convince Mrs. Meyers to take a walk into town, then maybe she could help Hanns by discovering anything suspicious in the area. Not that she wanted to find anything, but she felt rather useless otherwise.

"I should leave you be," Eva gave a slight, informal curtsy to Eleonore. "I'm glad to have met you, regardless of my false pretense."

"Before you go," Eleonore held up her hand to stop her, "I understand the sentiment of putting out the plates, but does she really need to waste all that food? Seems rather excessive, especially with so many going hungry."

"I suppose it is excessive," Eva agreed, "but who are we to tell a grieving mother to stop feeding her children?"

"Hmm," Eleonore pondered. "What about the story of her youngest? I believe that you said his name was Paul?"

"That's a long story," Eva shrugged, "and it's getting a little late."

"I understand. Tell Mr. Mattaliano to talk to me directly next time," Eleonore nodded to Eva.

With that, Eva left Eleonore in the blessed silence that she so craved. She was happy to be working at the manor, and proud of her charge, but since she had left the camp, she had barely a minute to think. She needed to digest what happened and how her life had changed in so many varying directions since she had been arrested and sent to Auschwitz.

Slipping into the nightgown that was set beside the bed, Eleonore locked her door, turned off the lights, and took a deep breath. But when she was about to get under the covers, she thought that she had heard a voice from the garden below her window.

Probably nothing, Eleonore shook her head and closed her eyes. But then the voice came again and, while Eleonore couldn't decipher what was being said, it was clearly not a pleasant conversation.

I should probably check. I'm supposed to be on the watch for anything suspicious anyways, Eleonore griped as she stood and tried to look through the curtains. But they were too thick, and it was too dark outside to see anything of significance. Grumbling, Eleonore opened the curtain slightly as she pivoted around the opening to try and catch a glimpse of anything unfitting.

Her heart stopped. She put her hand to her mouth to stifle an outburst. At the far end of the garden, Eleonore spotted a man holding a pistol by his side and talking wildly at the gardener who was remaining calm, despite the threat. While the gun and the aggravated behavior was enough to startle anyone, Eleonore's fear was made greater by her knowledge of the man.

It was Jung.

His back was turned, so Eleonore couldn't see his face, but it was undoubtedly Lieutenant Jung. Quickly, Eleonore shut the curtains and hid beside the window, hoping that she had imagined the whole event. Her heart pounded in her chest and she broke out into a cold sweat.

Should I tell Hanns? Eleonore wondered. *No, I didn't get a close enough look. It might just appear like Jung from this distance. Besides, Jung is the reason I survived Auschwitz. Though, that doesn't mean he should be forgiven his other sins. Should I turn him in? He would've beaten Ella to death if I hadn't stopped him. What do I tell Hanns? That I might've seen someone from Auschwitz? What if they come all this way only to discover that the information was incorrect? Oh, what's the right thing to do here?* Eleonore put her head in her hands as she slunk down the wall and sat on the floor.

Eleonore began to shake, feeling the fear that was so familiar to her at Auschwitz. The walls began to close around her, and she felt as if she had returned to the standing cell. A panic arose within her and Eleonore knew that she couldn't stay at the manor.

Standing in a rush, Eleonore nearly tore her nightgown as she stripped. Returning to her navy-blue dress, Eleonore bolted for the door. But, before she could leave, a pressing thought nagged at her to look out the window again. With her hand on the doorknob, Eleonore closed her eyes as she leaned her head against the door frame. She knew that she had to look. She desperately wanted to flee, but she had to know for certain that the man was, in fact, Jung.

Slowly, Eleonore let go of the door and returned to the window as the floor creaked under her. Every noise was exaggerated by the deafening silence. Putting a finger to the slit of the curtain, Eleonore pulled it open as slightly as she was able. There was no one. The gardener and Jung – if that's who he was – had left. Opening the curtain wider, Eleonore looked around the garden but couldn't see anyone.

Well I'm not going to sleep anyways, Eleonore fumed at the prospect of losing more hours to insomnia. *I just want to lie down,* she glanced at the bed which seemed to be begging her to commit herself into its care.

I should find a weapon, Eleonore nodded to herself and looked about the room. It was too difficult to find anything in the darkness, but she didn't dare draw attention by turning on the light. Still, Eleonore assumed that even if she could see better, that the odds of her finding anything useful were slim at best.

Looking again at the door, Eleonore knew that she needed to leave. *If Jung finds me, there is no telling what he might do. He was brutal enough at Auschwitz, but now that he's on the run, he might act rashly. I'll look around to see if I can take some money, then I'll head towards town. But if that man wasn't Jung, then I'll be out of a job and I have nowhere to go. Besides, I don't even know which direction the town is in. I know, at least, that I'll need money and a weapon. Let's start with the basics so that I'm ready, should the time come.*

Leaving her room, Eleonore walked as swiftly and as silently as she was able and passed through the hallway and down the winding staircase of the west wing. Cautiously, Eleonore opened the door and peeked her head out into the foyer. The dark manor offered nothing but an eerie silence as it, too, mourned the loss of its once jovial halls. Satisfied that no one was around, Eleonore closed the door behind her and prepared to sneak back to Mrs. Meyers' room to find some money.

The strike of a match from beyond the front door caught Eleonore's eye and she crouched down, hiding behind the main doors. *That must be Jung,* Eleonore thought as her heart pounded in her chest. Slowly, Eleonore peered through the glass panel beside the door to get a better view of who was out front.

A puff of smoke billowed, and Eleonore knew that someone was having a cigarette, but she couldn't determine who it was. Then, Eleonore froze as someone began talking. She couldn't decipher what they were saying as it was muffled through the door, but she could, at least, distinguish that they were talking to themselves.

Oh, Eleonore sighed her relief when she caught the hint of an Italian accent. *It's just Mr. Mattaliano. Maybe that was him with the gardener? No, the man I saw looked much different.*

Summoning her courage, Eleonore was about to begin looking around, but something pulled at her spirit. It was a familiar feeling, like the impression she would receive around Ella when she had rare moments of the sense of purpose. The notion that maybe her life had led up to moments such as this. Moments that seemed entirely inconsequential but, in the end, proved to be of the greatest significance.

Opening the door, Eleonore stepped outside as a startled Mr. Mattaliano quickly stamped out his cigarette. Like a rebellious schoolboy caught in the act, the butler blushed his shame as he brushed his hair back into place and straightened his vest.

A smile crept onto the corner of Eleonore's mouth at discovering him in this vulnerable state. It was refreshing to see him so powerless and frightened and, to a degree, she found this unusually attractive. A part of her despised him for his curt and unwelcoming treatment towards her, but Eva's explanation of his fears of losing his position provided some justification. Still, while his conduct was abhorrent and inexcusable there was a lure that Eleonore wished she could ignore.

"What are you doing?" Mr. Mattaliano whispered harshly as he looked back into the manor, making sure no one else had spotted him.

"You're not permitted to smoke, are you?" Eleonore smirked with a playful spitefulness.

"And she must never find out!" Mr. Mattaliano held his finger up in warning, not at all partaking in Eleonore's amusement.

"I'm not so sure that I'm in the mood to keep secrets," Eleonore hinted.

"Please," Mr. Mattaliano dropped his shoulders, "this is all I have. I can't go back."

Go back? Eleonore wondered and was about to ask for clarity when she heard the rustling of a bush behind her. Frightened, she turned towards the bush, but saw nothing, only the swirling of the hedges in the wind.

"Are you expecting someone?" Mr. Mattaliano spoke quietly, growing suspicious of the bushes as well.

"No," Eleonore turned back to the butler and tried her best to look unconcerned but knew that she had failed to conceal her trepidation.

"You know who that man was, don't you?" Mr. Mattaliano squinted as he studied Eleonore.

"What man?" Eleonore played dumb.

"I don't know his name," Mr. Mattaliano inched closer to Eleonore, relishing the chance to recover the upper hand. "I tend not to ask questions, but I was curious. Now I think I may understand."

"I don't believe that you do," Eleonore began to breathe heavily and retreated in response to Mr. Mattaliano's advance. She didn't know what his intentions were, but she hoped his approach was limited to intimidation.

"I have a proposition," Mr. Mattaliano stopped and stood tall as he looked down his nose at her.

"Go on," Eleonore nodded, her eyes wide with worry. *This better not be what I'm assuming.*

"You were in the master bedroom, yes?"

"I was," Eleonore nodded.

"I'll protect you from this man in exchange for information," he leaned forward, enjoying the intrigue.

Pausing to reflect, Eleonore stared at her feet as she pondered the correct course of action.

"What if the information I provide isn't what you're after?" she glanced up at him.

"I'm prepared for this eventuality," Mr. Mattaliano stood back.

"Mrs. Meyers swore me to secrecy," Eleonore looked at him with regret. "I can't betray her trust."

"Then I suppose you're on your own," Mr. Mattaliano shrugged.

"At least tell me what you're after, specifically," Eleonore bartered. "Maybe I can discover this information without breaking my word."

"I want to know who will inherit the manor," Mr. Mattaliano spoke bluntly.

"That's it?" Eleonore frowned. "That's all you're after?"

"What do you mean, 'that's all'?" Mr. Mattaliano frowned back at her. "It's a prominent piece of property."

"Oh, I see," Eleonore shook her head in disbelief that she hadn't recognized it sooner, "you believe that she may name you as the successor?"

"I've served her family faithfully for many long years," Mr. Mattaliano put his hands into his pockets as he looked at Eleonore with a rather serious expression. "She has no other family."

"Why don't you just ask her yourself?" Eleonore shrugged.

"I have," Mr. Mattaliano gritted his teeth.

"And?"

"She mentioned that," Mr. Mattaliano clipped his feet together as he mimicked Mrs. Meyers' propriety with sarcasm, "it was improper for me to make such an inquiry and, even so, that the time has not yet come for her to consider succession."

Eleonore tried to hide her smile at his enthusiastic impersonation.

"I need to know if I'm wasting my time by sticking around here or if I should move on to other things."

"Fair enough," Eleonore nodded and stretched forth her hand in offering to Mr. Mattaliano. "I'll make you that deal. I'll do what I can to unravel the truth."

Eagerly, Mr. Mattaliano took her hand, but Eleonore squeezed tight, "on the condition that I won't tell you a word until I'm certain that I'm safe from this man."

"Understood," Mr. Mattaliano returned the squeeze. He nearly crushed her hand, but Eleonore didn't dare reveal the pain he was causing.

"Now, can I have a smoke?" Eleonore broke off the handshake.

"Just wash your hands diligently afterwards," Mr. Mattaliano reached into his vest pocket and handed her one as he took one for himself as well. "Mrs. Meyers can smell tobacco like a bloodhound."

"Why does she forbid smoking, anyways?" Eleonore put the cigarette to her mouth as Mr. Mattaliano lit it for her.

"The Fuhrer was against smoking," Mr. Mattaliano inhaled deeply as if to display his defiance of the Nazi leader.

"And she supports him still?" Eleonore shook her head in wonder.

"Not necessarily," Mr. Mattaliano tilted his head in sympathy for his mistress.

"Hitler is responsible for the death of her entire family," Eleonore threw her hand into the air. "He brought disgrace upon the entire nation."

"It's best that you keep such opinions to yourself," Mr. Mattaliano spoke quietly as he clenched his jaw. "There's much that you don't know about this family."

"Are you a supporter too?" Eleonore watched him warily.

"No," he smirked. "Personally, I don't care for any leader. I think they're all after their own interests, and nothing more."

Eleonore remained silent as she puffed on her cigarette.

"Look, all I'm saying is that I understand a little of what she's feeling and if you were to say such things to her, then it would be detrimental."

"How so?"

"These were my masters. I loved them. To think that they died in vain is not possible for me to comprehend. I can't imagine how she's feeling. She has to believe that they fought for a noble cause."

"I was at the camps, sir," Eleonore grew indignant. "I can assure you that there was nothing noble about the Nazi regime."

"I've heard the stories," Mr. Mattaliano rolled his eyes. "Nothing is to be gained by embellishment."

"Embellishment?!" Eleonore was stunned. "How dare you?!"

"Listen," he stepped forward and pointed his finger in her face, "this is my house. These are my people. I don't care what happens to you. As far as I'm concerned, I will protect you so long as our deal stands. After that, I couldn't care less about your fate."

"The feeling is mutual," Eleonore flinched her eye as she puffed smoke into his face.

"Get back inside," he nodded to the door. "It's not safe out here."

"Are there any guns in the house?"

"That's for me to know," Mr. Mattaliano tapped his chest.

"If I die, these secrets die with me, and you'll continue to wonder if you're wasting your time here," Eleonore persisted. "I need to know how to protect myself in the eventuality that you are not available."

Mr. Mattaliano bounced his leg and Eleonore assumed that he was trying to conjure a reason, any reason, not to tell her but he knew that she spoke the truth.

"In the cellar," he sighed. "In the cellar there are some hunting rifles. They won't do much damage unless at close range."

"Thank you, butler," Eleonore stomped her cigarette on the ground before adding a veiled threat, "my father taught me to hunt. I'm more than capable of handling a gun."

Chapter Nine:
Interrogation

Know thyself, know thy enemy. A thousand battles, a thousand victories.

Sun Tzu

"This place looks nicer than half the buildings in town," Hanns shook his head when they had arrived at Celle Prison.

With white walls and an orange roof, the prison didn't give the intimidating impression that Hanns had hoped it would. He had pictured something far worse for where these Nazi animals were being kept.

"Are you nervous?" Fox glanced at Hanns as the two exited the vehicle and began walking towards the prison.

"Me?" Hanns scoffed.

"It's natural to be apprehensive," Fox peered at Hanns.

"I'm not nervous," Hanns shook his head adamantly.

"You're just quiet is all," Fox commented but then abandoned his pursuit as the two returned to silence.

"I'm a little nervous," Fox spoke after a minute and bit his lip as Hanns studied him curiously.

"You're nervous?!" Hanns asked, full of surprise. "But you're the expert here!"

"Doesn't matter," Fox gave a quick smile to brush away the unease. "I get anxious every time. I could be interrogating a loiterer and I would still be unsettled."

"Then why do you do it?"

"You'll see," Fox smiled as his eyes glimmered in anticipation. "It's addicting. Now, which door do we use?"

Two options presented themselves to Hanns and Fox: there was a large, double arched door immediately in front of them and a smaller man door just to the right. While painted gray, the arch door was still pungent with a wonderful oak smell that flooded Hanns' memory of his old family apartment in Berlin.

"Only one way to find out," Hanns stepped forward and gave a generous knock on the large door.

The two waited patiently, but there was no reply.

"Try again," Fox gestured for Hanns to knock.

"Alright," Hanns gave an annoyed, yet subtle glance at his captain, wondering why the officer couldn't simply knock himself. But, just as Hanns was about to bang against the door, the smaller, side entrance opened swiftly and an elderly, sprightly-looking woman burst out with her hand shielding her eyes from the sun.

"You're the crime investigators?" she asked in English with a thick, Scottish accent, and Hanns was thankful that Fox was with him otherwise all hopes of translation would be lost.

"That's us," Fox confirmed.

"Alright," the woman waved for the two to follow as she held the door open. "Would ye hurry along now? I told you to use the wee door."

"I don't think we received any instruction," Fox defended.

"Well you're receiving it now," the woman beckoned, "so best ye hurry or you'll be at the coo's tail."

"Coo's tail?" Hanns leaned over to Fox for an interpretation as they walked briskly to the door.

"Cow's tail," Fox explained. "It's an expression."

"I think I'm in love," Hanns whispered to Fox who gave him a slap on his chest.

Following behind this elderly Scotswoman, Hanns smiled as she reminded him of some of his teachers: strict and quirky yet too humorless to make light of their own eccentricity.

"So," Hanns called as he sped up and walked beside her, "Where are you from?"

"Heh," she scowled at him, "I'm not here to make chit chat. I'd be surprised if ye could pronounce it anyways. Half of his lot can't pronounce it," she pointed back at Fox.

"Focus," Fox grabbed Hanns. "You'll need your wits."

Agreeing, Hanns put aside his boyish jesting and remembered his mission. He was, at least, pleased to find that the interior of the prison ill-matched its outward appearance. Built in the eighteenth century, the prison was constructed for the purpose of housing the scum of society. Its stone walls were unpainted and some cells were nothing more than a block of concrete. Some were windowless while others had the luxury of viewing a small portion of the sky. Hanns wasn't sure what was worse: to catch a glimpse of freedom or to have it stripped altogether.

"You can use this one," the Scotswoman spoke grumpily when they arrived at an open cell.

"Would you be so kind as to let them know that we've arrived?" Hanns spoke to her in the best English he could afford, but she studied his mouth as though he was speaking in tongues.

"Please let them know that we're here," Fox nodded to her.

"What did ye think I was gonna do?" the Scotswoman rolled her eyes and left the cell.

"I said the exact same thing you did," Hanns threw his hand in the air. "I thought my English was good."

"You are nervous," Fox glanced at Hanns knowingly.

"What makes you say that?" Hanns brushed him off.

"I've only known you for a short time, but I've noticed that you make light of things, especially in circumstances like this."

"Like this, hey?" Hanns smiled uncomfortably.

"Howard, you're about to interview the very people who helped kill an untold number of Jews," Fox spoke firmly. "I like you, Howard, and I think that you show great potential, but you need to confront your own demons before you interview these ones."

Hanns' smile faded as he took Fox's instruction to heart. He knew that he was right, but cracking a joke or two to ease the tension was his field of expertise. As a young boy, growing up Jewish in Germany, he coped with the differences by being wittier than the other boys.

Entering the room, Hanns and Fox found that the cell was furnished with three chairs; two of which were behind a flimsy, brown desk and one sat facing the desk about a yard away. The only light in the cell came from a bulb hanging from the middle of the room. Its pale, orange glow barely gave off enough light for them to see one another let alone read their questions on the page.

Sitting at the desk, the nervousness that Hanns had tried to thwart arose within him unchecked. He had only recently learned English and, while he had excelled in his studies, the responsibility was on his shoulders to translate the statements correctly. He wondered if he had the ability to contain his emotions while he faced these criminals.

Lighting his Dunhill pipe, Hanns let the smoke waft around him as he took deep breaths to calm his spirit. He went over the questions again in his mind, planning his interrogation strategy. *No matter what they say,* Hanns thought as he closed his eyes, *don't react. Don't give them any footholds to use.*

"Remember," Captain Fox took a deep breath and Hanns noticed his leg bouncing nervously, "we need two statements: one in German and one in English. Don't stress that it might take longer to write them out. Better to take the time and have it done correctly now than to rush and botch the whole investigation. Here are the questions that I prepared."

Fox took out a sheet of paper from his satchel and put it on the table in front of Hanns. Each question had plenty of space underneath for ample writing room for the responses.

"When did you have time to write this?" Hanns glanced at Fox curiously.

"I wrote these questions before I even left England," Fox nodded.

Chains rattled as a prisoner was marched down the hall towards them. Hanns took a puff of his pipe to calm himself as a worry arose that he might jump the prisoner right then and there and enact some justice of his own.

But any thoughts of violence were quelled when Hanns was stunned by the man who was ushered into the cell. He seemed rather simple in both appearance and intellect. Not at all what Hanns expected to find in a death camp officer. He had a thick head of hair which was brushed backwards while the sides had been shaven some time ago but were now growing back. He carried a blank expression with plain, brown eyes and a thick nose with lips that turned down slightly at the corners.

"State your name," Hanns began, and glanced at Fox to prepare to write.

"Franz Hössler," the prisoner replied quickly, though he trembled slightly.

Hanns and Fox wrote the name down on their papers, and both tried as best as they could to conceal their unease.

"I would like to be helpful in any way that I can," Franz continued.

"You worked at Auschwitz?" Hanns asked without acknowledgement of Franz's cooperation.

"Yes," Franz nodded and repositioned himself in the chair. "Twice."

"In Belsen we discovered documents about a gas chamber in Auschwitz," Hanns retrieved some notes from his satchel as he referenced the documents. "Do you know anything about them?"

"Everyone knew about the gas chambers," Franz hummed nervously. "But I never partook in the selections of who went to the chambers."

"Who made the selections?" Captain Fox interjected. While he stumbled in German, he was competent, at least, with simple sentences.

"Dr. Mengele," Franz replied quickly.

"You witnessed Dr. Mengele making the selections?" Hanns asked.

"Yes," Franz nodded, "but, again, I had nothing to do with the selections. I was merely there to keep order."

"Why would you have to keep order?" Captain Fox pressed.

"Well," Franz cleared his throat, "some of those selected for the gas chambers knew what to expect. Most were ignorant of the true purpose, but those that were aware could, at times, create quite a disturbance. Especially when, uh, the mothers were separated from their children. That was difficult to watch."

"Why were they separated?" Hanns glared at Franz.

"Men, women, and children were all housed separately," the prisoner replied but avoided eye contact with his interrogators.

"That doesn't answer the question," Hanns pressed.

"If, say, you were to commit a crime, then you, sir, would be separated from your spouse and children. If, say, you broke into a jewelry store and took the merchandise, then you would be separated from your family when you were taken to prison. The same scenario applies to the criminals taken to Auschwitz," Franz defended.

"What crimes did they commit?" Hanns clenched his jaw, astonished that Franz could dare defend the camps.

"My position wasn't to judge," Franz swallowed. "My job was to keep order."

"Who was selected?" Hanns took another puff from his pipe, trying everything within him to contain his rage. He wanted to strangle Franz with his bare hands, irate that he should even consider himself blameless. He wanted to point out the errors in his justification, but Hanns understood that his duty was to collect the information.

"Mostly the sick and those who could not work."

"When would the selections take place?" Fox asked.

"When the prisoners arrived from the trains. Anywhere between two to three thousand would arrive at a time."

"How many did you say?" Hanns nearly fell off his chair when he heard the number.

"Two to three thousand," Franz repeated as he fumbled with his hands. "And about eight hundred would be sent to the chambers."

"And how often did these trains arrive?" Hanns braced himself for the answer, praying that his assumptions were incorrect.

"Sometimes daily," Franz looked down at his feet.

Hanns shook as he wrote the response from Franz. He knew that thousands had died at Auschwitz, but if his calculations were correct, that number was much higher than anything he could've conceived.

"Who was in charge of Auschwitz while you were stationed there?" Hanns asked, and retrieved a picture of Rudolph Hoess, ready to present it to Franz.

"Rudolph Hoess," Franz confirmed and Hanns showed him the photograph which he verified. "I made many complaints to him about the gas chambers, but I was advised that it was not my position to do so."

"So, you're innocent then?" Hanns glared at Franz with such a hate that the prisoner began to sweat profusely.

"Innocent?" Franz fumbled with his fingers. "No. But who is innocent, really? It's not my place, in the army, to protest. Though I never took pleasure in such work. Not like the others, such as Irma Grese. There were even some Jews who worked as supervisors, Kapos we called them, who took pleasure in causing others suffering."

"What's your point?" Hanns gritted his teeth.

"Pardon?" Franz swallowed.

"Why would you tell us about Irma?" Hanns flinched his eye. "Or mention the Kapos?"

"I was just passing along information," Franz shook his head as he appeared rather helpless.

"I don't think so," Hanns crossed his arms and put his pen down. "I think you are trying to shift the blame. I think you wanted to point out that some Jews were cruel as well to convince me that this isn't an issue about race."

"Can I speak to you for a minute?" Fox grabbed Hanns' arm.

"No," Hanns nearly shouted and gave a stern look at Fox.

"We collect the information," Fox continued sternly. "That's it. The prosecutors will know what to do with the evidence if we gather it properly. If we interject with our own personal sentiments, then the whole interrogation could be botched and thrown out of court. Don't give the defence lawyers any ammunition."

"This is ridiculous," Hanns smacked his pipe against the table and stomped out the ashes that fell on the ground.

"That is all," Captain Fox nodded to Franz and signaled for the guards to remove the prisoner.

"I want to help," Franz called as he was led away. "Please."

Left alone in the room, the two men didn't dare speak a word. The thought that their people had been systematically murdered on such an unprecedented level was impossible to fathom. Also, the thought that a fellow Jew, a Kapo, could have an active role in the camp, however minuscule, was beyond belief.

"You alright?" Fox spoke to Hanns after a moment.

Nodding, Hanns tried to brush off the uncomfortableness, but the pressure rose within him and he was unable to contain the emotions any longer.

"Damn them!" Hanns slammed his fist on the table. Standing up, Hanns paced aimlessly around the room until he came to a corner. Crouching down, Hanns put his head into his hands and let out a blood-curdling scream which echoed throughout the prison. This was the cry of thousands who could no longer call out. This was the breaking of a million hearts, and Hanns felt them all at once. He had refused to believe the reports that the numbers were in the hundreds of thousands, perhaps millions. He didn't believe that it was possible. Now, however, he had to face this gruesome fact.

"Do you need a break?" Fox asked calmly after a minute.

"No," Hanns returned to his seat. "No, we must continue."

"Understood. This time let the prisoner speak," Fox spoke quietly to Hanns. "You'd be surprised what happens during an awkward silence. I once kept quiet during an entire interview. Not a word. The suspect ended up confessing everything without so much as a single question from me. I didn't even tell him my name. Guilt needs a channel to out itself."

"Right," Hanns nodded, only partially listening.

Next, the guards ushered in a female prisoner. She was rather plump with severe eyes and a growl that suggested she was ready to employ her fists if the opportunity presented itself.

"Name?" Hanns asked.

"Hildegard," the prisoner replied, loudly and proudly and with the voice of one who had spent her life savings on cartons of cigarettes.

"At the hospital in Auschwitz, you demanded to be called Ma'am, correct?"

The fall of her station had not humbled her in the slightest. Rather, Ma'am, or Hildegard, sat with her arms crossed and a sharp furrowed brow. The intimidation she carried at Auschwitz, however, had no effect on the two men interrogating her now.

"Tell me about yourself," Hanns continued.

"I'm not saying a word," Hildegard shook her head and spoke with such vile that Hanns found himself holding his breath. "The validity of this interrogation is questionable at best. How do I know that you won't tarnish my statement with inaccuracies?"

"You will have a chance to review the affidavits once we have typed them up," Fox waved for her to continue.

Refusing to say another word, Hildegard leaned back in her chair, arms folded across her chest, and her lips turning white with pressed rage.

Glancing at Hanns, Fox gave a slight shake of the head, reminding him to allow for the silence to see what it would produce. Re-lighting his pipe, Hanns also leaned back and the room became a den of silence.

"Are we just going to sit and stare at each other?!" Hildegard bellowed, growing impatient.

"Tell me about yourself," Hanns shrugged.

"I know your type," Hildegard leaned forward and squinted at Hanns. "You're going to twist every little thing I say and blow it out of proportion."

"No," Hanns shook his head. "As my colleague here advised, we will record everything you say, exactly as you say it, then you can review the document afterwards."

"Why don't you have a recording device?" Hildegard snickered. "This isn't even official, is it?!"

Again, Captain Fox and Hanns remained silent, allowing the stillness to pressure Hildegard into talking.

"You call yourselves officers," Hildegard spit on the floor. "You're nothing more than boys."

"Your accent," Hanns squinted as he puffed his pipe.

"What about it?" Hildegard frowned.

"German isn't your native tongue, is it?"

"Polish," Hildegard twitched as she was caught off guard.

"What town are you from?" Hanns leaned in, appearing to be genuinely interested, remembering Eleonore's advice to connect to gain their trust, even if it was on a false pretense.

"Does it matter?" Hildegard resumed her stubbornness.

"How did you learn German so quickly?" Captain Fox pressed.

"My parents," she gave a swift nod. "Good, Polish Jews. Hard working. Never complained. Besides, if you didn't speak German well, then the Nazis lumped you in with the others."

"You worked at Auschwitz as a Kapo?" Hanns asked.

"Worked?!" Hildegard shook her head violently as the fat on her cheeks swayed back and forth. "I'm a Jew from Poland. I suppose you've heard of what the Nazis have done to our people?"

"You're lying!" Captain Fox sprang to his feet and came within inches of Hildegard's face. "We have an eyewitness which places you as a Kapo in Auschwitz. You betrayed your people to save your own back. You are the lowest of the low. Fortunately enough for you," Fox returned to his seat and continued calmly as if he had never erupted, "you are inconsequential to us, in every sense of the word, but there are others who we believe to be of great importance. If you provide information on them, and provide your cooperation, then I can see about alleviating your sorrows."

In shock at the outburst, Hildegard was speechless. She sat staring at Fox in terror that the little man could possess such sudden and violent ferocity.

"You were aware of the gas chambers?" Hanns continued the interrogation, impressed with how well Fox had been able to intimidate her. Also, his German was impeccable when he was angry.

"Of course," Hildegard frowned slightly, but eyed Fox cautiously. "Everyone was."

"Were you involved in the selections?"

"No, why would I be?"

"But you didn't do anything to stop it?" Hanns narrowed his gaze. "You didn't do anything to stop the calculated murder of your own people?"

"What could I have done?" Hildegard shook with rage. "If I had said anything, done anything out of line, I would've joined them in the chambers. The only way I escaped the selections was by speaking German well and volunteering to help. I'm not a soldier. I was hairdresser in Poland. I lived a quiet, humble life. I did what I had to survive, just as you would've done," Hildegard pointed a shaking finger at Hanns. "I'm not responsible for their deaths. Don't you dare accuse me otherwise."

"Then who is responsible?" Hanns asked.

"Rudolph Hoess," Hildegard replied without hesitation.

"Do you have anything to prove this?" Fox asked.

"They were careful, extremely careful," Hildegard huffed. "None of the orders, or any talk of the camps, were ever written down. Himmler was in the camps, on occasion, but I never saw him. Just heard rumors of his visits."

"Thank you," Hanns nodded and signaled to the guards to take the prisoner.

"I want to read it," Hildegard glared at Hanns as she was led away. "Every word of my statement."

"You shall," Hanns leaned back and puffed his pipe.

"Filth," Hanns spit after she had been taken away.

"Yes," Fox sighed, "but I wonder what I would've done in such circumstances. I wouldn't have been cruel to my fellow countrymen, but who knows what compromises I would've made."

"I would've fought," Hanns nodded.

"It's easy enough to say from this side of the barbed-wire fence," Fox glanced understandingly at Hanns, "but until you're in that situation, and your survival instincts kick in, who's the wiser?"

"She was a hairdresser?" Hanns stared into the table as he pondered. "I find that impossible to believe. Seems like she's always been evil."

Watching Hanns for a moment, Fox leaned back and folded his hands across his chest before beginning, "I don't believe there is such a thing, really, as a good person. I believe that we all have the capability to do good and evil."

"That's a rather bleak outlook," Hanns frowned. "Of course there are good people."

"Hildegard was a 'good person' before she was taken to Auschwitz. In her previous life, her flaws would've manifested in small, minute details that no one else would've noticed. Under pressure, these minor, seemingly trivial characteristics became exaggerated and we found out how ugly she really was. She's a flawed person and Auschwitz provided the ideal environment for those defects to manifest as a monster."

"That's no excuse to turn on your own people," Hanns grumbled.

"Hildegard believes that she is justified," Fox shrugged. "She believes that she did right by doing what was necessary to survive. Almost all the people I interrogated in my time as a policeman believed that what they had done was warranted, or that they were pushed into it by their circumstances. Some blamed financial concerns, others poor parentage, but the fact of the matter is that they believed the excuses absolved them of the wrong they knew that they were committing. Some, however, knew that they were wicked and became repentant. Most of our subjects will be similar to the last two that we interrogated. They shifted the blame, believing that their hands were clean. Or, in some cases, they dehumanized their victims by believing the propaganda that they were killing off degenerates."

"Still, I would've fought," Hanns looked defiantly at Fox.

"Because you're a strapping young man," Fox looked understandingly at Hanns. "Hildegard is a simple hairdresser who likely had a family to think about. If she fought and was killed, do you think the Nazis would've cared for her children?"

"Stop justifying hatred!" Hanns threw his hands in the air as he glared at Fox.

"I'm not justifying it!" Fox turned in his chair as he faced Hanns in his frustration.

"You keep passing off their offences as excusable!" Hanns stood.

"You arrogant fool!" Fox stood as well as his chair flew backwards and the two faced each other, though Hanns stood about a foot taller than Fox.

"Why do you keep defending them?!" Hanns pointed to the empty chair where the prisoners had been questioned.

"I'm not defending!" Fox shoved Hanns.

"Then what the hell do you think you're doing?!" Hanns grabbed Fox's uniform.

"I'm trying to understand them!" Fox broke off Hanns' grip.

"Why?!" Hanns stood back and threw his hands into the air.

"I need to understand how this could have happened!" Fox looked angrily at Hanns, but then lost his composure and bent over as he wept.

Silently, Hanns watched Fox weep and realized that his Captain's motives were sincere. Hanns had incorrectly assumed that Fox was emotionally distant or that he somehow felt that Hildegard and Franz were justified. Now, however, he understood that Fox was too invested, and he required that separation between intellect and reaction in order to complete his job properly.

"During my time as a constable," Fox gathered himself and wiped his nose with his sleeve, "I thought that I had already witnessed the worst that humanity had to offer."

Hanns remained silent as he waited for Fox to continue.

"Then I came here," Fox shook his head in bewilderment, "and I realized that I didn't know anything about how ugly humans could be. I need to understand this, Howard, I need to understand how a simple German man could end up working as an officer at a death camp and not do anything about it. Or how a hairdresser with no aspirations beyond her current station could allow her own people to suffer and even play some part in their misery. The only way for me to reconcile these inconsistencies is to believe that man has both the light and the dark and at anytime we could be forced to decide between the two."

"Sorry," Hanns spoke quietly. "I suppose that I don't want to understand. I only want to know who did what and have them pay the penalty for their crimes. Then I can go home and forget any of this ever happened. It's not possible for me to comprehend that both Franz and Hildegard believed that they aren't wicked and that they were just acting on orders. That's a terrifying thought."

"Do you hear that?" Fox turned his ear upwards.

The two of them paused to listen as a woman could be heard singing as she approached the cell.

"That's a Nazi song," Hanns felt his blood boiling.

"That must be our next prisoner," Fox rubbed his eyes in despair.

"You're familiar with her?" Hanns frowned curiously at Fox.

"Irma Grese," Fox slapped her file on the table. "The newspapers are calling her 'The Beautiful Beast'."

"What?!" Hanns shook his head. "Why would they romanticize a woman like her?"

"Especially when the inmates called her 'The Hyena of Auschwitz'," Fox raised an eyebrow. "Some of her Nazi compatriots refused to work with her because she was so brutal. Something tells me we won't get far with this one."

With her legs limp from protest, Irma was dragged into the cell by her arms and then seated, forcefully, on the chair facing Hanns and Fox. Wearing a long, plaid dress and high, black boots, Irma had a harsh and intolerant appearance. About the same age as Hanns, who thought of her as more of a beast than a beauty, Irma continued to sing loudly and defiantly.

"What song is she singing?" Fox leaned over and whispered.

"It's the battle song of the National Socialists," Hanns replied.

"State your name," Fox began, but Irma continued to sing.

"You worked at Auschwitz?" Hanns asked as well, but Irma only sang louder and grew bolder.

"Your mother killed herself when you were thirteen," Fox blurted, and Irma immediately grew silent as she looked at the captain, startled that he would know this personal information.

"Says here that she committed suicide when she found out your dad was having an affair with the local pub owner's daughter. Is that correct?"

"What does that have to do with anything?" Irma spoke quietly.

"Nothing," Fox shook his head. "I just wanted you to shut up."

Irritated, Irma crossed her arms and began to stare at the wall, childishly pretending that Hanns and Fox were not present.

"I also note that you had multiple affairs with Nazi officials, including Dr. Mengele," Fox continued, and Hanns discerned that he intended to embarrass her, "and you would often select beautiful female prisoners to be sent to the gas chambers due to your jealousy."

Irma remained silent, which Fox had anticipated.

"Of course, your crimes don't end there," Fox cleared his throat. "Eyewitness statements have accused you of raping other female prisoners, watching with pleasure as your dogs mauled others, and whipping women with a specially made whip. You even had lampshades made from the skin of dead prisoners."

Still, Irma remained defiant and began to chew her nails, but Hanns thought that he had spotted a slight, proud smile, which she had banished quickly.

"Listen," Hanns leaned forward and folded his hands, "you can cooperate willingly, or we can beat the truth out of you."

"Oh," Irma began to laugh, "we both know that beatings are not permitted."

"Are you certain?!" Hanns stood quickly, but Irma was not threatened in the slightest and began to snicker.

At this, Hanns lost all patience and began to walk towards Irma when Fox grabbed him.

"She's not worth it," Fox pulled Hanns in close.

"Like hell she's not," Hanns pushed Fox away, but Fox was undeterred and continued to keep Hanns at bay.

"We're done," Fox called to the guards who collected Irma as, again, she refused to walk by her own volition and began to sing loudly.

"Maybe Tin Eye Stephens is right," Hanns sat back down and began to shake with rage. "Maybe we should beat the truth out of them."

"C'mon," Fox began to gather his belongings and threw his satchel around his shoulder. "We're done for today. We will travel to Schwarmstedt tomorrow at first light."

"Whatever for?" Hanns studied Fox.

"A Nazi doctor is being held at the hospital there. We need to question him."

After advising the hospital staff of their intentions, Hanns and Fox were led to a secure ward that was heavily guarded.

"Captain Felix and Lieutenant Volker," Fox gave a quick salute to two guards stationed outside of Dr. Klein's room. "We are here to question Fritz Klein."

"Can I see your papers?" the guard requested and Hanns noticed that both were armed with semi-automatic rifles and seemed a little on edge.

Without a word, Fox handed the documents to the guards who checked them over quickly.

"Make it brief," the guard unlocked the door for them.

Why brief? Hanns wondered as he followed Fox inside to find that the room was brightly lit. There was a tranquility that made Hanns cringe with resentment. The doctor was being well taken care of with this private room and he was receiving better treatment than anyone that he had presided over.

Hanns and Fox took a seat near the bed of Fritz Klein and Hanns noted that the Nazi doctor was skinny with yellowing skin. It was then that Hanns recognized him as the very doctor that the Allies had forced to watch the mass graves at Belsen. They had nearly worked him to death by forcing him to help bury the bodies.

"How are you feeling?" Hanns asked the doctor, but more for the state of his mental capacity, rather than concern for the doctor's health.

"Exhausted," the doctor replied, understanding the intent of the question.

"How did you come to work at Auschwitz?"

"I'm from Romania," Fitz replied, pointing in the direction of his home country. "I joined the SS and was sent to Yugoslavia to recruit doctors. Afterwards, I was sent to Auschwitz to assist with the selections."

"You knew of the gas chambers at Auschwitz?"

"Yes," the doctor nodded somberly.

"Who was sent to the gas chambers?"

"Those who were unfit for work were selected by the doctors."

"Doctors such as yourself?"

"Yes," the doctor closed his eyes as he seemed full of regret, but Hanns felt that he was being disingenuous in his remorse.

"You selected the prisoners knowing full well that you were sending them to their deaths at the gas chambers?"

"Yes," Fritz replied while his eyes remained closed.

"Was this on your authority?"

"No," Fritz shook his head quickly. "Of course not! I only acted upon the orders I received. I took no pleasure in the job assigned me."

"Then who?"

"My orders came from Dr. Mengele, but where he got his orders from, I don't know. Nothing was ever written down. All orders came verbally."

"Did anyone else partake in the selections?"

"No!" Fritz held up his finger and then pointed it repeatedly at his chest. "It was me and the other doctors, not those good boys who were only there on orders."

"I think you and I have different definitions of good," Hanns clenched his jaw.

"Why did you not try to stop the selections?" Captain Fox interjected.

"What could I do?" Fritz frowned. "I'm just a doctor, and in the army. It's not right to protest when orders are given."

"Do you believe these orders came from authorities higher up within the Nazi party?"

"It's undoubtable," Fritz spoke quietly as if the room was bugged. "Himmler himself was at the camp."

Sensing that there was more to the story, Fox and Hanns kept quiet.

"But I don't think the gas was Himmler's idea."

"What do you mean?" Hanns leaned in.

"Himmler gave the orders for the extermination, but I don't believe he cared how it was completed. Commandant Hoess, Rudolph Hoess that is, invented the method of the gassing."

"Are you telling me that Rudolph Hoess is responsible for the gassing?" Hanns couldn't believe what he was hearing.

"Shooting the elderly and children are taxing on the soldier," Fritz spoke with calculation. "Rudolph developed a method which removed that burden."

"Let me through!" a shout erupted from outside the room and Hanns turned to see the guards holding a man away from the door. His face was red with rage and he was glaring at the doctor with all the hatred he could muster.

"Let me through!" the man continued to scream as the guards struggled to contain him.

"That man is a demon! He's straight from hell!" the man screamed.

"We can't allow you to enter," the guard replied.

"Do you want to know what he did?!" the man panted. "He injected my wife with petrol. He put gasoline into her veins to watch her die slowly and gruesomely. By God, let me kill him with my own hands."

"Sir," the guard pushed him back, "I'm on orders to only allow entry to those with the proper authority."

"I'll kill him myself!" the man pressed. "How can you permit him another breath?!"

"Go get backup," the guard requested his fellow guard while he contained the man.

"Is this true?" Hanns turned towards the doctor to find that he was sitting upright and concerned about the man at the door.

The doctor didn't reply but, again, looked down as though he were remorseful.

"How does this not contravene the Hippocratic oath?" Hanns spoke softly, though he was full of rage.

"If a patient arrives with a gangrenous appendix, I must harm them to cut it out," the doctor looked at Hanns as his remorse began to dissipate and his true, malicious self emerged. "The Jews are the gangrenous appendix of mankind. That is why I cut them out."

"Just give me a minute with him!" the man outside shouted again which frightened Fritz and he tried to stand up.

"You son of a bitch!" Hanns grabbed the doctor by the collar and threw him back onto the bed as he shouted in agony.

"Lieutenant!" Fox pulled Hanns away.

"I should let that man in here," Hanns pointed to the door as he sat back down. "It's what you deserve."

"Mercy, please!" Fritz begged, his voice full of panic. "What is going to happen to me?"

"There will be a trial, by summer's end," Hanns panted as he put his hands onto his hips. "Hopefully they will hang you and bury you in an unmarked grave. As for what will happen to your soul, you need to have been born with one in the first place."

Chapter Ten:
Revelation

In the end, we will remember not the words of our enemies, but the silence of our friends.

Martin Luther King Jr.

Eleonore rubbed her eyes as she sat on the edge of her bed. The sun was painting the sky a beautiful array of oranges and pinks and, if not for her exhaustion, Eleonore would've appreciated the spectacle. She glanced at her clock as it ticked away in its ignorance at the torture it was causing her. She would have to endure the day without sleep as she had done so many times back in Auschwitz.

I don't believe one ever gets used to this tiredness, Eleonore shook her head as she prepared herself for the day. *Mrs. Meyers will be awake in ten minutes and I must not reveal how weary I am. Still, I can't help but wonder why Jung was here? Or did I imagine it? No, Mr. Mattaliano mentioned that he saw the man as well. I wish I was certain either way if it actually was Jung.*

With a deep breath, Eleonore stood before her door, preparing to take the plunge. Opening the door, Eleonore was surprised to see Eva standing in the doorway.

"Eva?" Eleonore looked at her with wide eyes.

"Sorry," Eva held her hand to her chest. "I assumed that you had a rough night and thought that it might be kind of me to wake you."

"That is kind," Eleonore nodded, unable to afford further affection.

"Would you like company on your walk?" Eva's face lit up with excitement.

"It's a pretty short walk," Eleonore grew annoyed. Not that she minded company, but she was too tired to entertain.

"I understand," Eva waved, but Eleonore caught the disappointment in her eyes.

"I didn't say no," Eleonore corrected, though still sounding a little short.

"Oh!" Eva tried to contain her happiness but failed.

Eleonore waited for Eva to move but she remained standing in the doorway with what Eleonore could only describe as a 'stupid grin'. Lowering her head and raising her eyebrows, Eleonore waited for Eva to register the hint, but it soon became evident that this was beyond her grasp.

"Shall we?" Eleonore held out her arm for Eva who immediately wrapped her own arm around Eleonore's with a slight giggle.

"You're not a morning person, are you?" Eva squeezed Eleonore's arm as they headed to the stairs.

"I usually am," Eleonore huffed, "but I do much better when I sleep first."

"I hope that wasn't on account of me?" Eva turned to Eleonore with distraught. "I would feel dreadful if it was."

"No, of course not," Eleonore frowned.

"Then what was it?" Eva looked intensely at Eleonore.

"It's a long story," Eleonore dismissed the subject as she rubbed her sore eyes with her free hand.

"You don't trust me?" Eva stopped when they had come to the top of the winding staircase and threw her fists onto her hips as she looked angrily at Eleonore.

"After last night?" Eleonore looked Eva up and down in disbelief. "After you tried to gain information from me on behalf of Mr. Mattaliano?"

Unable to decipher Eleonore's hinting, Eva awaited her direct answer with eager expectation.

"No!" Eleonore shook her head with incredulity at this girl's lack of perception.

"I told you that he put me up to it," Eva crossed her arms as she scowled.

"After I procured the truth," Eleonore mirrored Eva by crossing her own arms. "Anyways, this will have to wait until later. Mrs. Meyers is expecting me."

"No, she's not," Eva shook her head.

"What do you mean?" Eleonore frowned in her confusion.

"She went out for the morning."

In a panic, Eleonore felt her pocket for the key, which she was relieved to find was still there, and then glanced curiously at Eva who gave a brief, yet scoffing smile.

"You weren't acting on Mr. Mattaliano's request," Eleonore sighed. "You were after the key. Was that why you visited me last night? So that you could get me drunk?"

Eleonore watched in horror as her suspicions were confirmed. Eva's innocence slowly morphed into a scornful, contemptuous loathing.

"Not at first," Eva clicked her tongue. "I was, honestly, just trying to be friendly. But then I saw your reaction when I mentioned Mr. Mattaliano."

"And?" Eleonore shook her head.

"You like him," Eva pinched her lips and examined Eleonore with jealousy.

"I most certainly do not!" Eleonore couldn't believe what she was hearing. "Why does everyone assume they know my most intimate affections?"

"I also saw you two talking last night out front," Eva spoke with seething resentment. "He's mine."

"That's not a problem," Eleonore frowned, wondering where Eva was deriving her fabrications. "You can have him."

"Don't pretend," Eva swayed her shoulders slightly, readying herself for a fight.

"I see," Eleonore stared at her feet as she thought for a moment. "You think that if you find Mrs. Meyers' will, then you will be able to win his affection? Or at least his attention?"

"Give me the key," Eva spoke with a deep, rumbling voice.

"No," Eleonore placed her hand into her pocket as she began to walk backwards.

"Eleonore," Eva gritted her teeth, "this doesn't have to turn ugly."

"It's plenty ugly now."

"Miss Hodys!" Mr. Mattaliano shouted from the bottom of the winding staircase. "It's Mrs. Meyers! Come! Quickly!"

"This isn't over," Eva glared as she watched Eleonore descend the winding staircase.

Eleonore sped down the stairs as she marveled at the turn of events and desperate to find if Mrs. Meyers was alright. *What could possibly be wrong?* Eleonore wondered as she followed behind a panic-stricken Mr. Mattaliano out of the west wing, to the foyer, and then up the stairs to the second floor. Out of breath by time she reached the top, Eleonore panted as she half-ran to Mrs. Meyers' room.

"What's the matter?" Eleonore asked as she tried to catch her breath.

"Listen?" Mr. Mattaliano pointed at the door.

Holding her breath, Eleonore turned her ear towards the door but all she could hear was the thumping of her heartbeat.

"I don't hear anything," Eleonore shrugged.

"Exactly," Mr. Mattaliano looked at Eleonore anxiously.

"I'm not sure that you've explained yourself as well as you believe you have," Eleonore pinched her fingers together as she grew impatient.

"She's usually grumbling and muttering away to herself," Mr. Mattaliano elaborated, "but this morning, there's nothing. I can't even tell if she is moving around in there."

"I think you would be delighted to discover that she is in a better mood today," Eleonore eyed him curiously.

"Just open the door," the butler waved his hand for her to hurry.

"You must stand back," Eleonore grabbed the key, but waited for him to move.

"I know, I know," he raised his hands as he took a few angry steps away.

"You'll be the first to be informed if there is any concern," Eleonore nodded.

Mr. Mattaliano didn't reply but paced anxiously with his gaze locked on his feet.

Unlocking the door, Eleonore entered to a pitch-black room. The curtains had been drawn, blocking out the light from the awakening sun. Closing the door behind her, Eleonore set herself in the darkness and listened intently for any sound. Nothing. She strained to hear if Mrs. Meyers was breathing, but she could only hear the rustling of the wind from the open window. Eleonore began to wonder if Mrs. Meyers was even in the room.

Starting to believe that something sinister had occurred in the night, Eleonore's imagination wandered, and she began to accuse Jung of various misdemeanors and treacheries. Walking slowly towards the bed, or at least where she remembered the bed to be, the floor creaked underneath her.

"Henry?" Mrs. Meyers called out for her husband. "What are you doing up so early?"

"It's me, ma'am," Eleonore called softly.

"Who?" Mrs. Meyers could be heard shuffling around in the bed.

"Eleonore. The woman you hired yesterday."

"Oh, right, Miss Hodys," Mrs. Meyers spoke groggily.

"That's correct, ma'am," Eleonore stopped when she felt the edge of the bed against her thigh.

"That *is* correct, not that's correct," Mrs. Meyers scolded. "I warned you once. I do not make a habit of repeating myself."

"Understood," Eleonore replied politely but rolled her eyes under the cover of darkness.

"You are dismissed," Mrs. Meyers slumped back down under the sheets.

"Dismissed? Ma'am?" Eleonore wondered if she had heard her correctly.

"I shall remain in bed for the day," Mrs. Meyers stated while absent of emotion. Eleonore, however, understood that her grief was the driving force behind such a decision.

"I can't…cannot allow that to happen," Eleonore cleared her throat.

"I beg your pardon?!" Mrs. Meyers grew indignant.

"You hired me to help you, and help you I shall," Eleonore felt her heart pounding in her chest, suspecting that she was making a fatal error.

"I hired you to help me with daily duties, not forbid my wishes," Mrs. Meyers sat up.

"There are no daily duties if you remain confined to your room," Eleonore argued, though she fought against the urge to agree with Mrs. Meyers and simply take the day to rest.

"This is outrageous!" Mrs. Meyers nearly spit as the words shot like arrows at Eleonore.

Still, Eleonore persisted and, taking the liberty upon herself, walked towards the windows.

"What are you doing?!" Mrs. Meyers called after Eleonore, who didn't respond.

"Is everything alright in there?" Mr. Mattaliano rattled his knuckles against the door.

"Quite fine, thank you!" Eleonore shouted back.

"Don't come in!" Mrs. Meyers shouted.

"Ah, here they are," Eleonore took hold of the drapes and threw them open as the orange and pinks filled the room while Mrs. Meyers shielded her eyes like a creature scorning the light.

"Get out!" Mrs. Meyers demanded as she pointed towards the door. "You are fired! And you can expect no reference from me!"

"Mrs. Meyers," Eleonore walked briskly towards her mistress and sat at the edge of the bed and looked at her with compassion, "why did you hire me?"

"Does it matter? Get out!"

"Everyone else in this house will obey your every command, even if it means letting your grief swallow you whole. But I'm here to help you, that is what you hired me for, even if that means going against your wishes."

Mrs. Meyers began to shake with rage as her eyes bulged with fury, "How could you be so insolent as to speak of my grief? What do you understand of sorrow? I hired you because you are stupid."

The words cut into Eleonore and she nearly jumped backwards at the rising hatred.

"I hired you because I thought you were not clever enough to realize what was happening at this house, and even now I believe that you are unaware."

"Mr. Mattaliano is expecting to be named your heir, is he not?" Eleonore spoke quietly as she glanced at the door.

"Well, yes, actually," Mrs. Meyers squinted at Eleonore as she was caught off guard, "but that is not what I was alluding to."

"I believe he is worried about your fortune disappearing," Eleonore chuckled slightly, but Mrs. Meyers remained unmoved.

"And you?" Mrs. Meyers turned her nose upwards and Eleonore watched as her rage began to dissolve. "You are not interested in my fortune?"

"I would be lying if I said that I was immune to such temptations," Eleonore thought for a moment before continuing, "but I had money, at one time, and it did not bring me what I desired."

"And what do you desire now?" Mrs. Meyers remained expressionless.

"Purpose," Eleonore stared intently into Mrs. Meyers' eyes. "I desire purpose."

Still unmoved, Mrs. Meyers turned her attention to the uniform of her husband beside her on the bed.

"I have a task for you," Mrs. Meyers stared at the uniform as she talked to Eleonore, "and once again I must ask for your discretion."

"Of course," Eleonore nodded.

"There is an envelope in the drawer," she pointed to the little table beside the bed. "I need you to pay the gardener."

"Alright," Eleonore frowned at the odd request.

Opening the drawer, Eleonore pulled out the envelope and was surprised by how heavy it was. Curiosity gnawed at her and she began to open the envelope to see how much money was packed inside.

"Not here!" Mrs. Meyers waved her hand frantically. "Do you have any sense of propriety?"

"Apologies," Eleonore clutched the envelope to her chest.

"Give it to the gardener," Mrs. Meyers yawned and crawled back under the bedsheets. "Then return to me and help me prepare for the day."

"As you wish, ma'am," Eleonore gave a quick curtsy as she left Mrs. Meyers and closed the door behind her.

"Well?" Mr. Mattaliano squeezed his hand against the back of his neck, unable to handle the stress as he had been waiting anxiously.

"She's fine," Eleonore held the envelope slightly behind her back.

"What've you got there?" the butler pointed.

"Just an errand," Eleonore tried to appear casual, but feared that she overcompensated.

"But she's alright?" Mr. Mattaliano pointed to the room.

"Yes," Eleonore smiled at his concern.

"Alright, alright," he threw his hands onto his hips as he stared off in thought. Then, muttering to himself, returned to the foyer and disappeared out the front doors.

Chuckling to herself, Eleonore found his concern amusing. *I do not like him!* Eleonore shook her head adamantly as Eva's assumptions reverberated in the back of her mind.

I wonder how much is in here, Eleonore felt the weight of the envelope. *This is all rather odd. Why would she give so much to a gardener? If his wage is that demanding, I'm sure there are plenty who could take his place. Odd that Mrs. Meyers would fire me then simultaneously entrust me with so much. Really doesn't make sense, though I doubt her threat of termination was sincere, but rather, a ploy to make me leave the room.*

Checking that she was alone, Eleonore opened the envelope. With a slight gasp, Eleonore almost dropped the envelope on the floor. There was enough money inside to buy the whole manor twice over.

I could have a fresh start, Eleonore shook her head in wonder. *I could walk out the front door and begin a new life.*

Closing the envelope, Eleonore shut out such thoughts and began her trek towards the garden. Returning to the foyer, Eleonore spotted Mr. Mattaliano outside the main doors arguing with a delivery boy about where to transport his produce for the kitchen. Trying to appear as nonchalant as possible, Eleonore held the envelope just behind her right thigh as she climbed down the stairs. Passing through the kitchen, Eleonore saw Eva wiping down the table and setting the chairs in perfect position, ignorant as to Eleonore's presence. *If only they knew what I was carrying,* Eleonore mused.

With a brief sigh of relief, Eleonore finally left the house and entered the garden. It was then that Eleonore noticed something rather peculiar. From a distance, the garden seemed to be rather kept, but now that she was close enough to examine the detail, Eleonore noticed its blemishes. Weeds had overrun the flower beds, the grass had been poorly cut, and there was a wildness to the vegetation.

Be careful, Eleonore, she spoke to herself. *I don't think this man is a gardener. I should report this to Hanns at once. What if Jung is nearby?* the thought crept into her mind and a terror froze Eleonore in place.

Suddenly, the gate just to the right of the house opened, and Eleonore locked eyes with the gardener who was quick to notice the envelope. Still frozen in terror, Eleonore looked at him with wide, frightful eyes as he approached her slowly. There was a steeliness in his look, an unwavering gaze with bright, blue eyes that reminded Eleonore of the guards at Auschwitz. She knew, beyond a shadow of a doubt, that this man was, in some way, involved with all the cruelty she had known at the camp.

Walking up to Eleonore, the gardener glared at her with an empty stare. Then, holding out his hand, he gestured for Eleonore to give him the money. Slowly, Eleonore complied, and handed him the envelope. She didn't know what the money was for, or why Mrs. Meyers had asked her to give it to this man, but she was certain that it was for an ill purpose.

Opening the envelope briefly, the gardener flipped through the bills, checking to see that everything was accounted for. With the envelope still open, he stared at Eleonore in such a way that she began to feel guilty for a crime that she didn't commit. Then, the gardener walked slowly past Eleonore without so much as a second thought.

What have I done? Eleonore wondered and returned through the house, a little shaken, and again invisible to Eva who was lost to perfecting her duties. Returning to the foyer, Eleonore saw that Mr. Mattaliano was still arguing with the delivery boy, but now the conversation had become heated.

"Sei un idiota!" Mr. Mattaliano shouted.

"Mr. Mattaliano!" Eleonore snapped and opened the door quickly, almost as surprised as the butler was by her outburst.

Both Mr. Mattaliano and the delivery boy, who was not much older than fifteen, stared at Eleonore in shock at her eruption. And Eleonore, for her part, hadn't the slightest idea of what she was going to say next. She merely scolded his anger and was not prepared to address it further.

"Yes?" Mr. Mattaliano threw his hand outwards.

"Be respectful," Eleonore nodded firmly and let the door slowly close behind her.

Her cheeks burned crimson with embarrassment as she continued up the stairs to return to Mrs. Meyers. But despite what she felt, Mr. Mattaliano had ceased his shouting and was addressing the delivery boy with greater civility.

Returning to the room, Eleonore entered to see Mrs. Meyers standing by the window. Even in her nightgown, Eleonore thought Mrs. Meyers to be the most beautiful of women. She appeared to Eleonore as if some goddess of old that had lived for thousands of years and knew the wisdom of the ancients. The light from the window enshrouded Mrs. Meyers, causing her to appear divine.

"Shall we dress for the day?" Eleonore asked softly as she approached Mrs. Meyers, but there was no reply as she remained staring out the window.

"Ma'am?" Eleonore asked again as she stood beside her and, if Eleonore wasn't mistaken, believed that she saw a slight smile.

"My husband loved this house for this very reason," Mrs. Meyers spoke candidly.

"How so?"

"The sunrise," Mrs. Meyers replied sharply, removing any trace of sentiment.

It was at this moment that Eleonore began to understand. Mrs. Meyers lived in this house absent of what made it important to her. Emotions were impossible for Mrs. Meyers to handle. She had to silence them and keep them suppressed. Any emotion could lead to an uncomfortable memory which would then cause Mrs. Meyers to lose control and she was much too proud for such humiliation.

"May I ask," Eleonore cleared her throat, "is that why you cover the windows?"

Turning towards Eleonore, Mrs. Meyers gave a stern yet forgiving look before stating, "I like you, Miss Hodys. You are not as spineless as I initially understood you to be, but do not ask the obvious."

"Understood," Eleonore glanced down at her feet.

"Chin up," Mrs. Meyers clapped as she brushed past Eleonore. "Do not be given over so easily to the moving of the soul."

Says the woman who refused to leave her bed this morning, Eleonore bit her tongue.

"Who was shouting downstairs?" Mrs. Meyers asked as she stood by the bed, waiting to be dressed.

"Pardon?" Eleonore asked as she followed her mistress.

"I could have sworn that I heard shouting downstairs, just before you came up to the room."

"Oh, right," Eleonore shook her head. "That was Mr. Mattaliano. He was calling the delivery boy an idiot in his native tongue."

"You speak Italian?" Mrs. Meyers glanced at Eleonore in surprise.

"A little," Eleonore shrugged timidly. "But even the basic understanding of the language would allow one to translate what he was saying."

"Hmm," Mrs. Meyers became lost in thought as Eleonore dressed her. Then, after a moment, she asked, "What is your opinion of Mr. Mattaliano?"

"My opinion?" Eleonore threw her head back in shock at the question.

"Yes," Mrs. Meyers sighed, already growing impatient.

"I'm not certain that it is my place to have an opinion," Eleonore stood back and looked at Mrs. Meyers apologetically.

Mrs. Meyers offered Eleonore a glare that warned she would not tolerate her evading the question.

"Alright," Eleonore exhaled before continuing, "he's rather rude. He's jealous of my proximity to you and the trust that you've shown me. He's selfish, unkind, and unwelcoming."

"Interesting," Mrs. Meyers narrowed her gaze as she peered into Eleonore who was beginning to feel uncomfortable. "And what about his looks?"

"His looks?!" Eleonore threw her eyes wide open.

Again, Mrs. Meyers glanced at Eleonore with increasing impatience.

"Uh," Eleonore gave a slow shrug, "I suppose he's handsome."

"Good," Mrs. Meyers gave an emphatic nod before moving over to the vanity and sitting in front of the mirror where her jewelry was laid out.

Following her mistress, Eleonore took the black cross necklace and placed it around Mrs. Meyers' neck, who then inspected herself in the mirror.

"He will need a wife when I am gone," Mrs. Meyers glanced quickly at Eleonore who froze at the candid suggestion of such a union. Not only had she just met the man, but she detested him.

"Having the manor all to himself would be rather troublesome I should think. Not to mention lonely," Mrs. Meyers adjusted her necklace so that the cross sat perfectly in the center.

"Eva," Eleonore cleared her throat which had suddenly run dry, "expressed her interest in Mr. Mattaliano."

"Eva is not capable of running a house of this grandeur," Mrs. Meyers shook her head.

"So, you are naming him your heir?" Eleonore watched Mrs. Meyers in awe.

"It is already done," Mrs. Meyers nodded but then pointed her finger in the mirror at Eleonore. "I have not told him yet, and you must not either."

"I promise," Eleonore raised her hand quickly.

"You perceive him as selfish and rude, but these are the byproducts of care. He seems rude because he is passionate about the state of the house. He is a man of honor. He gave up marriage, office, and prestige to serve my family. This house, the family name, are all he will ever have. This is how my husband would have wanted it," Mrs. Meyers nodded firmly as she began to well up.

Then, suddenly, Mrs. Meyers put her head into her hands as she began to weep. "I need to stop doing that," Mrs. Meyers collected herself as she grabbed a handkerchief from her pocket and blew into it.

"I don't think that you do," Eleonore placed her hand slightly on Mrs. Meyers' back who glanced up at Eleonore, annoyed by the familiarity.

"What do you mean?" Mrs. Meyers frowned.

"I may not understand grief on your level, but I'm intimate with trauma."

"How?" Mrs. Meyers scoffed.

"The camps."

"I will not hear another word," Mrs. Meyers warned with a raised finger and a stern gaze.

"You must," Eleonore persisted. "You need to understand what they did to Germany, what their impact still has upon our sacred land. Many mothers are in your position because of the cruelty of the Nazi regime."

"Bah!" Mrs. Meyers grunted and waved her hand. "I am hungry. We can discuss this nonsense at another time."

Chapter Eleven:
The Cello

They sowed the wind, and now they are going to reap the whirlwind.

British Air Marshall 'Bomber' Harris

What I'd do for a hot shower right about now, Hanns rubbed his arms, feeling the chill of the cool morning as they arrived at the Allied camp in Belsen. The drive from the hospital was brief, about thirty minutes, but it felt much longer.

"Help me with these," Captain Fox barked as he grabbed the satchels from the back of the truck.

They had spent the night at the hospital going through the affidavits after their interrogation of Dr. Klein. The lack of sleep, and the content of what they had to read continually, had soured Fox's mood drastically.

"I did offer to drive," Hanns grabbed one of the satchels.

"I know," Captain Fox grumbled.

"You told me that you could handle it," Hanns continued.

"I know!" Captain Fox glared at him as he grabbed two satchels and marched towards the administration offices.

"Well what's the problem then?" Hanns caught up to Fox and stopped him.

"The problem is that you're supposed to fight about such things," Fox continued towards the office.

"I don't understand," Hanns stared at his feet in confusion as they walked.

"You're supposed to insist," Fox pointed at Hanns. "When we both are clearly exhausted, and I say that I can drive even after you've offered, you're supposed to insist."

"That doesn't make any sense," Hanns shook his head. "Why would you say something that you don't mean?"

"I'm English! There's no sense about it!" Captain Fox burst through the main doors and all eyes turned towards them as the two continued their spat past the rooms with their large, open windows.

"I'm not a mind reader," Hanns continued after Fox as he sped along. "I'm not accustomed to every English idiosyncrasy."

"Clearly!" Fox shouted over his shoulder.

"Hey, hey," Hanns grabbed Fox's arm and stopped him again. "How can I make this up to you? I didn't know. Honest."

"I just need some sleep," Fox nodded a slight apology, but then continued bitterly. "Let's deliver these to Genn, then I will find some lukewarm food, a stupidly cold shower, and fight the insomnia for a couple hours until I give up and start the day again," Fox turned and stormed towards Genn's office.

Hanns trailed Fox as he burst into Genn's office to find a startled Lieutenant Colonel looking over correspondence. Apart from a photo of the King hanging on the wall, the office was entirely bare. The desk was kept so tidy that, if Genn suddenly were to disappear, no one would've known that the office had ever been used. A single, dull lamp was the only light in the windowless room which Genn used to read his mail. Yet despite the gloominess of the cramped office, Hanns sensed that Genn didn't mind being isolated. In fact, he seemed to thrive in this solitude.

"Here," Fox dropped the satchels down onto the desk, and Genn gave an annoyed glare for the introduction of chaos into his perfectly ordered office.

"That many?" Genn stood and opened the satchels as he leafed through the papers.

"I will report tomorrow morning," Fox saluted sarcastically and, spinning on his heels, stormed away in protest.

"Forgive him," Hanns watched Fox stomp away.

"What's the matter with him?" Genn asked quietly as he remained studying the documents.

"He's English," Hanns set his satchels down on the desk as well, though with less drama than Fox.

"Usually that wouldn't pardon his misconduct, but I'll release him from judgement because he does good work," Genn huffed as he set the satchels beside the desk in an orderly fashion.

Out of breath, Hanns sat down on a chair just to the left of Genn's desk.

"Yes?" the Lieutenant Colonel looked down his nose at Hanns.

"Pardon?" Hanns frowned.

"What can I do for you?" Genn elaborated, though with great irritation.

"I see," a slight smile formed on the corner of Hanns' mouth, "this is one of those English things where the question is cryptic. You're not actually asking what you can do for me."

"How perceptive," Genn remained unamused.

"I'm wondering what my next assignment is?" Hanns asked.

"These need to be formalized," Genn gave a slight pat against a satchel. "They need to be typed up, properly, and then sent to the prisoners who made the statements and signed in the presence of a witness."

"One of the clerks can do that," Hanns waved his hand. "We need to be hunting down those who are still at large."

"What a peculiar morning," Genn glanced at his watch. "It's not even seven and already I've had an officer insult me with his theatrics, and another lecturing me on strategy."

"I apologize for the liberal behavior," Hanns collected himself. "It's just that this work is mind-numbing. I need to be out there, trying to catch people like Rudolph Hoess. I feel helpless about those who are getting away. I would like to request permission to pursue them. For every guard or doctor that we interrogate, another three or four are implicated, yet we have no one searching for them."

"What are your qualifications?" Genn asked.

"Sir?" Hanns sighed, knowing the direction Genn was taking.

"What police experience do you have? Do you know where Rudolph Hoess is? Do you have any leads? How will you get there? What tactical support do you have?"

"I understand," Hanns nodded.

"But do you?" Genn took a couple steps towards Hanns and stood over him as he crossed his arms. "If these documents are not done properly, then the Belsen trials, which are approaching at an alarming speed, will fail. And if these trials fail, then it won't matter who we catch. If this is successful, we will see more funding, greater manpower, and then us little dogs can start chasing the big ones."

"I'm not doubting the significance of this work," Hanns lowered his gaze. "I just believe that my talents are being wasted here. Have the clerks complete these while I hunt Nazis."

"You are the son of a doctor and you only recently took up the banking trade in England," Genn leaned over. "You have no experience in detective work or police procedures. You have no leads, no clues and, may I remind you, you don't have the authority to arrest anyone. If you do, it's an illegal arrest."

Hanns scratched his head, too exhausted for a sharp reply, though he felt defeated by his inability to argue his case.

"Good," Genn returned to his chair. "You have the day off, anyways. See to it that you get the proper rest so that you can apply your energy to completing these."

"Sir," Hanns stood and saluted before exiting.

"Howard," Genn held up his hand to stop him from leaving, "please understand that my hands are tied here. I'm not saying never. I'm just saying that right now, this is essential."

"Understood," Hanns nodded firmly.

"Dismissed," Genn rolled his finger for Hanns to close the door on his way out.

Fuming inwardly, Hanns marched into the briefing room where the team had first been assembled. Desks were lined up in rows and the other interrogators and typists were hastily typing up the statements that they had taken. The room resounded with the dings and strokes of the typewriters which had been provided, begrudgingly, by some of the nearby towns. Smoke billowed about the room from the cigarettes and the atmosphere was one of organized and frenzied chaos as the teams pressed themselves to have the documents ready in time for the trials.

A board was set at the front of the room and a diagram had been created to help the investigators identify those responsible for the atrocities. A depression set in Hanns' soul as he looked helplessly at the diagram. It remained almost entirely bare. While Hitler sat at the top, and Himmler was directly below him, there were only a few lower level guards pinned against the board. Hitler, unfortunately, had escaped his judgement by taking his own life and Himmler remained at large. The other suspected positions remained disturbingly empty.

Raging as he walked to the front of the office, all eyes turned towards Hanns and a hush fell over the room as they wondered as to his purpose. Taking the photograph of Rudolph out of his pocket, Hanns slammed it against the board and pinned it in place. Then, taking a pen, he wrote underneath the photo, 'Rudolph Hoess, Commandant of Auschwitz,' and stood back as he brooded.

"Is everything alright lieutenant?" Smallwood came to stand beside Hanns, and the room returned to commotion, disregarding the recent drama.

"He's getting away," Hanns shook his head as he looked at Rudolph's photograph.

"I doubt that," Smallwood spoke plainly.

"How do you know?" Hanns turned and looked at Smallwood with slight annoyance.

"These came for you," Smallwood ignored Hanns' question and held out a couple letters in his hand.

"Oh," Hanns sighed when he noticed that they were all from Ann. "You're delivering mail now? Do you have that much free time?"

"Of course not," Smallwood replied bluntly, "but these letters are of international interest."

Hanns frowned at Smallwood as he grew curious.

"She's taken to writing Lieutenant Colonel Genn," Smallwood spoke quietly.

"She's what?!" Hanns' felt a sharp pang in his chest.

"Don't worry," Smallwood gave a slight smile and handed Hanns another letter, "I've responded on your behalf without burdening the Lieutenant Colonel."

"Thank you!" Hanns put his hand on Smallwood's shoulder.

"You should read the letter before thanking me," Smallwood offered a mischievous grin.

In a panic, Hanns read Ann's letter to Genn:

This is not going to be a proper letter but merely a few lines full of complaints which, the writer sincerely hopes, will produce the necessary effect. Lieutenant Volker's writing efforts during the last few weeks, not to mention months, have been absolutely appalling. Please see what you can do to satisfy the writer or else the undersigned will have to take drastic steps.

Yours sincerely,

Ann Graetz

"Well her English has improved," Hanns chuckled nervously as he began to read Smallwood's reply.

Dear Madam:

I must apologize for his behavior. Adding to Lieutenant Volker's long list of admirable qualities is his willingness to undertake any challenge. In fact, at this moment, he is on assignment from my office to investigate a German harem. No doubt this will keep him working at high pressure by day and night, but in spite of working single-handedly, it is anticipated that his enthusiasm and drive for the job should be completed in time for a well earned rest in order that he may replenish the lead in his pencil.

I am, Madam, your obedient servant.

Major Smallwood.

P.S. Actually, Howard has no excuse, so if I were you, I'd make your next letter even stronger.

"You bastard!" Hanns slapped Smallwood's shoulder who by now was laughing heartily.

"You're corrupt," Hanns rubbed his worried head as Smallwood continued to laugh liberally. "I would think that the damage you've done is irreversible. I should write to her as soon as possible."

"Well, maybe wait until after you talk with your brother," Smallwood settled a little.

"What do you mean? How did you know that I have a brother?" Hanns studied Smallwood in awe.

"Paul is coming to Belsen to collect some SS prisoners that were in the hospital here and have made a miraculous recovery," Smallwood mocked.

"Really? Paul is coming here? When?"

"He's on his way."

"How do you know all this?" Hanns examined the little man in front of him.

"Mr. Volker, this is an intelligence agency. It's important that I know a thing or two," Smallwood raised an eyebrow, but then added, "Also, I sent for him."

"You sent for him?" Hanns became perplexed. "Why?"

"For the prisoners, of course," Smallwood shrugged, but then patted Hanns' arm as he walked away. "I also thought you could use some cheer. It is your day off, after all. I'll tell him to find you at the hall this afternoon."

"What an odd little man," Hanns muttered to himself as he watched Smallwood disappear out of the room.

Then, folding up the letters from Ann, Hanns placed them securely in his pocket as he made way for the barracks. The morning sun beat down on him as he left the administration office and walked past the mass graves which stood as permanent reminders as to his purpose. Many mourners still stood outside the unofficial cemetery, handkerchiefs at the ready, as they talked to their loved ones buried underneath. It was a harrowing sight, and Hanns' heart broke for their suffering.

While Belsen looked nothing like the camp it had once been under Nazi control, there was still a sorrow present. Nearly ten thousand former inmates resided at Belsen as they had nowhere to go. The old barracks and buildings had been burnt to the ground and new, improved structures were erected in their place.

The inmates were fed, clothed, and most of their needs were looked after, but still, there was a general feeling of unease as many were anxious to leave. Yet where could they go? Their families had been murdered which left them without anyone to turn to, their homes had been destroyed, and they were penniless. Not to mention, traveling around Europe without the appropriate papers was impossible, making Belsen seem like it would host its dependents forever.

Returning to the barracks, Hanns set himself on his squeaky, uncomfortable cot. Retrieving his stale rations, Hanns ate as he watched the other soldiers laughing and playing games. Some were reading, others were writing letters, and some were sleeping. But Hanns refused to participate in their activities or waste time reading novels. Instead, he studied the extra picture he had of Rudolph Hoess, examined the copies of the affidavits while searching for some clue or lead, and obsessed over maps while trying to guess where these men could be.

I'm so tired, Hanns rubbed his eyes and laid down as he read the affidavits. Sleep began to crawl over him, but Hanns shook himself awake and read, again, the statement from Dr. Klein.

"Hey, Howard," a soldier called out from the group playing dice.

"Ya?" Hanns replied while still studying the statement.

"We need a fifth person," the soldier waved for him to join. "Percy had to leave."

"Did he now?" Hanns replied absentmindedly.

"Are you coming or what?"

"What?" Hanns frowned as he looked at the soldier.

"I said we need a fifth," the soldier became agitated.

"Ask Somerhough," Hanns pointed to a man on a top bunk a few rows down who was smoking and staring at the ceiling. He was the same, round-faced gentlemen that Smallwood had pointed out during the briefing. Anthony Somerhough was a larger man, about the same height as Hanns but nearly twice his weight and not the sort who took pleasure in games.

"Tony cheats," the soldier replied, but watched Anthony cautiously who continued to stare at the ceiling as though he was not the subject of conversation nor was his integrity in question.

"Who says that I don't cheat?" Hanns snickered.

"I would've noticed," the soldier snorted. "I'd think that you'd win more if you were cheating."

"Ha!" Hanns chortled. "You wouldn't notice even if the dice told you themselves. Why do you think that you've never won a single game? They're all cheating you."

At this, the soldier looked at those around him in the group and was shocked to find that Hanns was telling the truth.

"I can't believe you're all in on it!" the soldier stood up and barged out of the barracks which began to grumble and begged him to return. They had lost their avenue to quick and easy money.

Smiling to himself, Hanns returned to reading but felt sleep approaching. This time, however, he was powerless to resist and was pulled into oblivion.

The barrack's door slammed shut and Hanns shot awake. Wondering what time it was, Hanns glanced at his watch to find that it was only 1:00 PM and he had likely not missed Paul. Sitting upright, Hanns felt as though the nap had done nothing for his exhaustion. *A cold shower might wake me up,* Hanns shrugged.

Grabbing his small, sandpaper-like towel and his diminishing bar of soap, Hanns left the barracks. Heading towards the shower, which was a hastily made wooden stall with a curtain across its entrance, Hanns grumbled when he saw a lineup. There were about four men waiting their turn, and Tin Eye Stephens stood at the front with a scowl of disappointment.

"Hurry it up!" Tin Eye shouted at a younger soldier who was assisting the officer while straining with a full bucket of water.

Then, removing his clothes without care that everyone should see his nakedness, but keeping his monocle affixed, Tin Eye entered the 'shower' and pulled the curtain across. Which, Hanns mused, was rather pointless since he had just stripped in full view of everyone.

"Pour the water in!" Tin Eye barked at the soldier who struggled to lift the bucket above his head and the water slushed over the sides.

Finally, the soldier rested the bucket on the corner of the shower and began to pour slowly. But with the weight of the water, and the awkward angle, the poor, young soldier overcompensated, and the bucket fell into the shower and landed squarely on Tin Eyes' foot.

"Jenkins!" Tin Eye stormed out of the shower in full view of the camp and threw his hands onto his hips as he stared down the panic-stricken young man.

The others waiting in line began to snicker at the sight of him, naked and deprived of his 'intimidation'. His rage held little threat with scrawny little legs under a wrinkled, sagging torso.

"Go get some more!" Tin Eye pointed in the direction for the boy to run, and then retreated to the cover of the shower as his audience was now laughing hysterically.

Seizing the opportunity for mischief, Hanns ran and caught up to Jenkins.

"Hey," Hanns stopped the young man. "Give me the bucket."

"What? Why?" the soldier glanced back in terror at the shower.

"Just, trust me," Hanns gestured for him to give the bucket.

"Alright," Jenkins agreed. He was a rather simple creature who appeared to Hanns like an owl with permanent, wide-set eyes.

"Now, do you know where any flour is?" Hanns grinned.

"Yes, but why?" Jenkins frowned.

"No reason," Hanns shook his head and tried to hide his smile. "Can you get it?"

"Now?" the soldier glanced back at the shower.

"Yes," Hanns nodded adamantly.

"Alright," the soldier shrugged and ran off.

We really do need to get some running water, Hanns pumped the lever to fill the bucket. *But this will teach Tin Eye for not getting it himself and ordering about this hapless fellow.*

Finally filling the bucket, Hanns grunted as he lifted it and the thin steel handle cut into his fingers.

"I've got the flour," the soldier panted as he returned holding the bag high.

"Perfect," Hanns groaned under the weight.

"Want me to carry that?" the soldier asked.

"Nope," Hanns shook his head quickly, but strained to talk. "I've got it."

Realizing what Hanns was planning, the other men in line quickly joined in on the fun and helped Hanns heave the bucket of water over the edge of the shower, drenching Tin Eye.

"Jenkins!" Tin Eye shouted as he drew a sharp breath from the cold shock. "Not all at once damn you!"

"Here's some soap," Hanns opened the bag of flour and poured it over top as the dust flew in the air.

"Hey!" Tin Eye screamed.

"Who did that?!" Tin Eye demanded as he burst out of the shower, caked in a sticky paste.

"Run!" Hanns grabbed Jenkins and the group scattered in jovial terror.

"I'm a dead man," Jenkins shook as they ran.

"Nonsense," Hanns chuckled. "Come with me. Let's blow off some steam."

"Where?"

"The dance hall," Hanns pointed in the direction but then slowed his pace when they walked past a group of refugees, remembering to be respectful. But he was happy, at least, to find that he had brought some of them joy as they laughed at Tin Eye's expense as he was now forced to trek through the camp in his state to refill the bucket.

Hanns and Jenkins continued briskly through the camp towards the dance hall and Hanns wondered if his brother was already there. They had been inseparable growing up, and this had been the longest that they had been apart.

As they approached the dance hall, Hanns heard the thumping of bass which carried throughout the camp in joyous triumph. It was a simple, yet powerful statement that even though the Nazis took their lives, their homes, their land, they could not break their spirit.

Entering the dance hall, Hanns saw that it was full of people happily and giddily dancing. Allied officers and soldiers danced with the rescued inmates, silly games were being played by different groups huddled together, and the atmosphere was electric. If anyone had told Hanns that this place had once been a concentration camp, he would've never believed them.

"Go have some fun," Hanns gave Jenkins a slight pat on his backside and sped him along who, again, obeyed mindlessly.

Poor Jenkins, Hanns thought as he stood at the back, smiling as he watched the merriment, inspecting the pretty girls in their new dresses with their hair curled and their bright red lipstick.

But then Hanns saw something that stole his attention. In the corner, sitting by herself, was a young woman who seemed to be taking no pleasure in the liveliness around her. She sat up straight as she clutched a small leather bag on her lap. She was unadorned with makeup, and her dress was a simple, dark blue which contrasted the lively reds and yellows of the other girls.

Slowly, Hanns walked towards her but noticed that she was trying to ignore his approach. He pushed through the crowd and watched as the girl's unease grew with each step he took. She was different than the other girls and he had to talk to her.

"May I sit with you?" Hanns held his hands casually in his pockets as he stood beside her.

"Yep," the girl replied quickly, remaining polite although Hanns assumed that she would prefer him to leave her alone.

"So," Hanns sat on the wooden chair beside her, and inched it closer, "why aren't you dancing?"

"Not my kind of music," the girl stared straight ahead.

"And what would that be?" Hanns shouted over the noise.

"Pardon?" the girl asked, still refusing the courtesy of eye contact.

"What kind of music do you like?" Hanns asked again.

"Classical," the girl replied, hoping that this would be enough to scare Hanns off.

"Oh, me too!" Hanns tapped his chest, and the girl looked at him in surprise.

"Really?" she frowned slightly.

"Honest," Hanns held up his hand in affirmation.

"So, why are you here then?" she asked.

"I could ask you the same thing," Hanns smiled.

"I play after this," she pointed to the stage.

"You sing?"

"Cello," she replied shyly.

"Really?" Hanns was impressed. "One of my favorite instruments."

"Mine too," the girl smiled, but then returned to solemnity. "Kept me alive."

"How so?" Hanns leaned in.

"I played the cello in the orchestra at Auschwitz," she glanced down at her hands as she fidgeted nervously with her fingers. "Otherwise I don't think I would've made it."

"I know that it's difficult to talk about," Hanns waved as he understood. "Would you like to dance?"

"No," she chuckled.

"Why not?" Hanns pressed.

"A guy like you has a girl at home," she shrugged. "I won't be the one who breaks her heart."

"I was just asking to dance is all," Hanns professed his innocence. "Nothing more."

"Dancing is a judgment of mating capabilities," the girl replied frankly. "When men and women dance together, they are assessing whether their partner would make a good mate. Also, it's a way to become comfortable, physically."

"That's ridiculous," Hanns scoffed and turned away as he studied the men and women pairing up and dancing cheerfully together, realizing how correct she was.

"Can I at least have your name?" Hanns continued. "As a friend only."

"Anita," she replied and extended her hand in friendship, which Hanns thought was odd behavior for a girl, but he shook it nonetheless.

"Well, Anita," Hanns took a deep breath, "is it so wrong for them to seek distraction?"

"Distractions only put off the sorrow," Anita shrugged. "You will have to deal with it now or later, but you can never escape."

"So, you'd rather them be gloomy and remember all that they lost?"

"I'd rather they control their natures and understand that this will not help them. Honestly, sir, you'll have a better chance with one of the other girls. You don't need to waste your time on me."

"Nonsense," Hanns shook his head. "I'd much rather visit with a girl like you who reminds me of everything that I want to forget."

Anita chuckled slightly which made Hanns proud. If he was honest, he would love to enjoy a quick romance with one of the other girls. What man wouldn't? But there was something about this Anita that he found incredibly attractive. And while it started as an amorous pursuit, Hanns found himself enjoying her company rather from friendship.

"So," Anita leaned in, "what sorrows does a Nazi hunter need distracting from?"

"How did you know?" Hanns looked at her in surprise.

"Know what?"

"That I'm a Nazi hunter?"

"I've seen you around the camp with other war crimes officers," she explained. "So, how's hunting?"

"Nonexistent," Hanns shook his head in frustration.

"What do you mean?" Anita frowned.

"Politics are getting involved," Hanns gestured, not wanting to elaborate further.

"That's terrible," Anita grew angry. "You mean they're getting away?"

"I have my orders," Hanns shrugged, but the minute the words came out of his mouth he regretted them.

"So did the-"

"I know, I know," Hanns threw up his hands. "But what do you want me to do? I don't have the authority to arrest."

"You're telling me that if you brought in someone like Rudolph Hoess that they'd turn him free because you don't have the authority to arrest him?!"

"Well, I'm sure if-"

"Damn your orders!" Anita clenched her hands into fists and Hanns felt a fear in his soul for the fiery spirit that was arising before him. "I'll hunt him myself if you don't!"

"You?" Hanns chuckled. "And what are you going to do once you find him? Play your cello?"

"That's uncalled for!" Anita raised her finger in warning.

"Alright, alright," Hanns raised his hands to apologize. "Let's think about this. What-"

"What's there to think about?" Anita interrupted. "You need leads, you need something substantial."

"If I go hunting Nazis while shirking my duties, I could be court-martialed. Then what would I do? Besides, my superiors are right, the work that is being done to prepare for the trials is of vital importance."

"Then don't do it during your work hours," Anita slapped Hanns on the arm as if the answer was obvious.

"What do you mean?"

"Do it during your free time. Do it now! Don't distract yourself with this pitiful dance. Get out there!"

Studying her for a moment, Hanns felt his spirit swelling with purpose, but then reality set back in as he remembered Genn's warning.

"I don't have any leads," Hanns sulked.

"Go talk to the towns," Anita threw her hands out in a rage. "Talk to citizens, policemen, anyone! You silly boy! A woman should be doing this work!"

"You know what?" Hanns stood in his excitement. "You're right! I should be getting out there!"

"Of course I am!" Anita stood as well, imitating Hanns' excitement.

"We need to toast this," Hanns looked around and spotted the punch bowl at the far end of the dance hall.

"I've got something we can spike our drinks with," Anita gave a quick wink.

"Good, good," Hanns clapped quickly and then rushed off to the punch table.

Pushing his way through the dance floor, Hanns felt an excitement coursing through his veins. This was it. This was his purpose. He would find those devils and bring them to justice with or without his superior's consent.

"Lieutenant," Smallwood approached Hanns as he poured the punch.

"Sir," Hanns glanced at Smallwood, but continued to pour the drinks.

Smallwood stood beside Hanns, a little too close for comfort, and Hanns gave him a curious look for the intrusion.

"How can I be of service?" Hanns eventually asked.

"You're in two places at once," Smallwood replied.

"Pardon?" Hanns frowned.

"My intelligence failed me in one regard: I didn't know that your brother was also your twin," Smallwood pointed towards the door.

"Paul's here?!" Hanns spun around with excitement, but his joy faded quickly when he noticed that his brother was talking with Anita.

Suddenly, Paul grabbed Anita by the waist and playfully dipped her over and planted the largest kiss on her lips.

"Hey!" Hanns shouted so fiercely that the band stopped playing and the hall became deathly quiet as they watched him intently.

Anita, surprised by Paul's violent passion, turned to see Hanns and a horror fell over her as she looked back to see Paul with an ignorant, yet mischievous smile.

"Oh, you horrible man!" Anita gave Paul a quick slap across his face and stormed back to the corner where she was seated.

"Worth it!" Paul held his sore cheek as he shouted after her and the hall exploded in laughter and returned to their distractions as the band resumed.

"Typical Paul, I do all the heavy lifting and you reap the easy rewards," Hanns looked crossly at his brother, but then, abruptly the two embraced and laughed as the punch Hanns was holding spilled everywhere.

"Do I care to ask what that was about?" Paul asked as the two sat at a table.

"I was chatting her up while I was waiting for you," Hanns shook his head in pretend disapproval.

"Ah!" Paul laughed. "She thought I was you then. No wonder that was so easy."

"I do feel a little bad for her," Hanns confessed as he studied a red-faced Anita with crossed arms and a foul glare.

"No, you don't," Paul shook his head.

"I should though," Hanns laughed.

"Reminds me of when we were younger switching places in school," Paul glanced at Hanns.

"You were such a terrible influence on me that they separated us so that we couldn't be in the same class," Hanns chuckled.

"But then you'd stand in for me in French, and I'd take over for you in Mathematics," Paul laughed. "And they were none the wiser."

"Didn't help our scores much," Hanns laughed.

"You know," Paul began, and by the tone of his voice, Hanns braced for what he knew would come next, "thinking back to our younger years, we had it really good."

"You had it good," Hanns huffed. "You'd trick the nanny into thinking that you were me so she'd feed you twice," Hanns reached over and poked Paul's belly who swatted his hand away.

"I'm trying to be serious," Paul gave an annoyed glance.

"Is that what you're doing?" Hanns smiled, trying to lighten the tension. While he was close with his brother, the two didn't often engage in serious or heavy discussions, and Hanns needed the diversion of his brother's good spirits.

"You can't joke your way out of this one," Paul looked at him sternly, and then continued. "Our Jewishness was never something that I thought of, really. I mean, I understood that we were different, but we only went to the synagogue once a year. Other than that, our lives were identical to everyone else's."

"Identical?" Hanns shot Paul a glance. "Paul, we had to sneak into hockey games."

"Only once the Nazis took over," Paul grew annoyed. "But before then there was little difference."

"Did you come here to argue?!" Hanns leaned back in his chair as he shouted over the noise of the band. "I was hoping to chat with my brother, not talk with our dad."

"Looks like our friend is up," Paul pointed as the band ceased and bowed to a warm round of applause as Anita took the stage.

With a quick, heated glance at the two brothers, Anita tuned her cello and then closed her eyes as she prepared to play. The dance hall became still and Hanns had turned in his chair as they waited anxiously to be charmed by her skills.

With passionate intensity, Anita began playing Edward Elgar's Cello Concerto. A tear fell from Hanns' eye as he listened to the beautiful composition being played so masterfully.

He felt, in that moment, all the sorrow that he had been striving to avoid. The tears streamed down his face unchecked as the strings reached into his heart. Yet this release wasn't bitter or hateful, but rather, a relinquishing of a burden that he couldn't carry any longer. The pranking, the jesting, and his nonchalance were merely distractions for what he could no longer escape. The bittersweet melody permitted a warmth to enter his spirit, calming him with the assurance that he was allowed to experience these emotions. He was allowed to question, and it wasn't wrong to have doubts.

"Boo!" a callous man from the back called. "Play something we can dance to."

Shocked at the interruption, Anita stopped playing. Immediately, Hanns and Paul stormed onto the dance floor with their fists at the ready.

"Who said that?!" Hanns demanded as he scanned the crowd for the culprit.

No one dared to take credit for the blunder, and the hall watched the two brothers with the petrified understanding that they were ready to enact violence.

"Come forward you coward!" Hanns called but was again met with silence. "You have plenty of time to dance, but take the moment," Hanns began as passion swelled in his voice, "a single, precious moment of reflection."

With one last survey of the crowd, Hanns gave a swift, decisive nod and the two returned to their seat. With a smile and a look of thanks from Anita, grateful to have the brothers on her side, she continued in the complexity of the cello concerto.

"So," Hanns cleared his throat as he spoke to Paul, "what have they assigned you to now?"

"I help run the POW camp which, I might add, is filling up quite nicely," Paul raised his punch in the air in salute.

"I think it's time I began hunting, properly that is," Hanns studied the table in front of him as he became reflective.

"Where will you start?" Paul asked.

"You think there are many Nazis here?" Hanns glanced around jokingly. "I'd wager that the inbred disaster who booed Anita might be one."

"No," Paul pounded back his punch and wiped his mouth before continuing, "but I know where some are."

"Really?" Hanns frowned. "Where?"

"Drink up," Paul stood.

Obeying gladly, Hanns finished his drink quickly and followed Paul out of the dance hall. But Hanns looked over his shoulder and began to walk backwards as he watched Anita performing with all the energy she could muster.

"Howard!" a shout arose from near the barracks.

"Who's that?" Paul studied a man trudging his way towards them.

"That's Tin Eye Stephens," Hanns panicked, but with a mischievous grin. "We've got to go. Now!"

"The truck is by the entrance," Paul began to run as Hanns followed closely beside him.

"I don't think he's up for the chase," Hanns glanced behind him to see Tin Eye had given up the pursuit.

"Why's he so angry, anyways?" Paul watched his brother curiously as they climbed into his truck.

"Ah, just a stupid prank," Hanns brushed off the subject. "Smallwood said that he had some prisoners for you to take back?"

"They're in Celle," Paul started the truck and they exited the camp. "They were captured a couple nights ago."

"Anyone of interest?"

"That's your job to find out," Paul glanced at Hanns.

"Have you heard from anyone back home recently?" Hanns shuffled down in his seat as he settled in for the drive.

"Ya, actually," Paul nodded. "Father is doing well. The food is still being rationed, as is the petrol, but he's been renting out flats to build up his practice."

"That man is relentless," Hanns smiled with pride.

"Did you hear about Bella?" Paul asked cautiously.

"I did," Hanns frowned. "Our poor sister. She's going to have her hands full raising those two little boys on her own."

"Agreed," Paul shook his head. "Just a tragedy the way it happened. A week after VE Day, when we should all be celebrating that we survived this mess, her husband is killed by a plane that overshot the runway."

"At least mother is around to help," Hanns stared out the window as he felt for his sister.

"Anyone else you're concerned with?" Paul nudged Hanns.

"What do you mean?" Hanns glanced at his brother.

"Oh, come on!" Paul laughed. "What about Ann?"

"What about her?" Hanns frowned.

"She's been writing to me, begging to hear from you," Paul slapped his brother on the chest.

"Ah, ya," Hanns blushed slightly.

"So? Are you going to write to her or what?"

"I'll write," Hanns nodded. "Tonight, I promise."

"Good," Paul nodded and stared out the window in thought. "She's keeping busy, you know."

"Oh I know," Hanns sighed. "She's a proud member of the League of Jewish Women."

"They're a ferocious bunch," Paul shuddered. "Should've sent them to fight the Nazis. No mercy in them, let me tell ya."

"Don't they just deliver food and visit the elderly?" Hanns frowned.

"Yes," Paul nodded, "but don't repeat my mistake of discrediting their services as non-vital. They do not take kindly to being patronized."

The two returned to silence as they drove, but Hanns took notice that Paul was smirking.

"What?" Hanns squinted, knowing that his brother had left something unsaid.

"What?" Paul glanced at Hanns and played dumb.

"There's something on your mind," Hanns continued to squint.

"Are you going to marry her?" Paul snickered.

"I don't know," Hanns shook his head.

"Why not?!" Paul shrugged.

"It's complicated!" Hanns threw his hand into the air.

"I won't bother you about it," Paul chuckled.

"Good," Hanns rested his chin on his fist as he stared out the window. "I'm the older brother, anyways. I deserve respect."

"By fifteen minutes!" Paul shouted.

"Still older," Hanns muttered.

"And what has that fifteen extra minutes of life experience taught you?" Paul grunted before adding, "This is a tiresome argument."

"What about Aunt Bing?" Hanns turned to Paul. "Did you find out anything in Frankfurt?"

"I was hoping that you weren't going to ask," Paul looked at Hanns with concern.

"Why? What happened?" Hanns sat up straight. "That stubborn woman should've come with us when we asked her to."

"You know her," Paul glanced at Hanns, "resolute to the end."

"So, what happened?"

Paul took a deep breath before continuing, "Well, I went to her hotel in Frankfurt but there was no record of her departure and the police were clueless. The Red Cross, at least, provided me with some useful information."

"And? Out with it!"

"She was taken to Theresienstadt," Paul gave a quick glance at Hanns who slouched back into his seat.

"From what I've heard," Paul continued, "Theresienstadt was not as terrible as the other camps. It's where the Nazis got most of their propaganda from. They even called it a 'spa town' where elderly Jews could go to retire as part of their 'resettlement project'."

"We both know that's a lie," Hanns looked intensely at his brother. "The Nazis would take a few photos of some smiling Jews, then ship them off to Auschwitz to be gassed."

"Whatever the case," Paul spoke softly. "I don't think that she suffered for long."

"There's not much hope then," Hanns sighed. "Have you told anyone else?"

"I'm not sure how to tell our parents," Paul cleared his throat. "I don't think mother would handle the news well and I'd rather not upset her."

"Do you think things would've been different if the German population knew what was really happening at the camps?" Hanns rubbed his chin.

"Honestly," Paul glanced at this brother, "I don't know. I mean, when they were told it was a resettlement project, and millions of people were displaced from their homes, they didn't protest. I can't imagine they would've protested either way."

"You're probably right," Hanns grew solemn.

"We're coming up on the prison," Paul pointed out the window.

They arrived at the back of the prison and Paul handed the guards some documents to state their purpose. Waved through, Hanns noticed a barbed-wire pen in the courtyard of the prison. Inside the pen were about fifty prisoners of war. There were no toilets, nowhere to clean oneself, they were exposed to the elements, and there was nothing but the concrete to sleep on.

"That does the heart some good," Hanns sat up straight as he inspected the POWs, "to see these SS scum herded like animals."

Exiting the vehicle, the two approached the barbed wire pen as the SS guards, soldiers, and officers watched them warily. Many were dirty with their hands caked in dried mud, some were wounded with bandages around their injuries, others were sitting and staring vacantly into the concrete at their feet.

"You," Hanns pointed to a soldier.

Standing slowly, the soldier stood and grudgingly walked over to the fence. He looked back at Hanns with tired, red eyes but seemed to be not entirely certain of where he was or why.

"Roll up your sleeve," Hanns demanded as he lit his Dunhill pipe.

Obeying, the soldier revealed the SS tattoo on his arm.

"Sit back down," Hanns waved. "You," he pointed to another. "Come here."

Again, another soldier obeyed, showed Hanns his tattoo, and was dismissed. Again, Hanns did this to another soldier, and another, and another.

"What are you looking for?" Paul whispered to Hanns.

"Someone without the tattoo," Hanns whispered back. "And someone who doesn't stand up so slowly."

"Why would that matter?" Paul grew curious.

"The men I'm after wouldn't have been on drugs," Hanns puffed his pipe. "They're all going through withdrawal."

"Drugs?"

"Pervitin," Hanns explained. "Lowers their empathy and makes them almost immune to exhaustion. That's how they marched for three days straight into France."

"I remember that," Paul replied slowly as he looked at each of the prisoners in a new light.

"I'm after those who didn't take the drug, yet still lack empathy," Hanns scanned over the group of soldiers. "These are small catch. I'm after the bigger names. You can keep these."

"Your generosity knows no bounds," Paul smirked.

Chapter Twelve:
Cucina

I have nothing to offer but blood, toil, tears, and sweat.

Winston Churchill

What a day, Eleonore thought as she returned to her room later that evening. After Mrs. Meyers' emotional display in the morning, the mistress of the manor had resumed her propriety and remained as withdrawn as ever.

Turning on the little lamp between her bed and the window, Eleonore paused when the light came on, remembering the events of last night. Quickly, she shut the light off again and, carefully, used her finger to make the slightest opening in the curtains. Certain that she had not been spotted, Eleonore made a larger opening and pressed her face against the glass as she looked to the left and to the right and sighed her relief when she saw no one.

I'm starving, Eleonore held her stomach as it growled, but then felt conflicted for such a selfish thought. *I'd probably be livid if I heard anyone else exaggerating about their hunger,* Eleonore mused, recalling her time in the standing cell. *I can eat in the morning,* Eleonore thought as she looked longingly at the bed. *I haven't slept since I arrived here. At this point, I don't even care all that much if Jung is, in fact, out there. I just need to rest.*

Grumbling as she struggled to undress and put on her nightgown, Eleonore felt the aches and pangs of hunger. Not even a week had passed since she had left the camps, but a part of her wanted to remember what it truly was to be hungry. She didn't want to forget the fear, the anxiety, the starvation, and, yes, even the death. These would serve as testaments and permanent reminders to refine her character. Financial stress seemed so trivial and the pressures of society appeared so flimsy in comparison to the suffering at Auschwitz. Economic status counted for nothing and, with material possessions stripped, all that mattered was character, ingenuity, and chance. She would honor those who had been murdered by living as selflessly as she was able.

She found it odd thinking about her old life and how concerned she was with the frivolous. How inconsequential it now appeared when she recalled being frustrated at a poor design for a dress, or that she didn't have her brand of tea, or that she worried at all about money. Her horrific experience at Auschwitz had, at least, shown her what was important in life and nothing mattered more than the relationships she had with others.

Also, Eleonore was a living declaration to the atrocities. She was the warning of the evil that had swelled in the heart of her beloved country and could rise again if people weren't careful. She hated how difficult it was for her to talk openly about the camps. While she had no difficulty attesting to the fact that they did exist, explaining the details of the hospital, or how the Hoess family lived in such luxury, or the conditions at the barracks, or the extended time she spent in the isolated cell caused her the greatest anxiety.

Lying in bed, Eleonore placed her hands over her stomach as she breathed in and out, feeling the rise and fall of her belly. It was impossible for her to keep a smile away as she wiggled her weary toes under the sheets.

Suddenly, a light flickered at the edge of her bed. Frightened, Eleonore sat up and tucked her feet to her chest. She could feel someone's presence in the room, but they were shrouded in the darkness.

"Who's there?" she whispered harshly.

Silence.

Eleonore held her breath as she listened intently, but the only sound was her heart pounding in her chest.

Then, the light flickered again, and Eleonore saw the shadow of a man holding a lighter. Raising the lighter to his face, the man revealed his identity. Behind a cruel, sinister smile, was Rudolph Hoess returning for another nocturnal visit.

Eleonore tried to scream but her jaw was frozen shut. She was petrified by fear and unable to move. Then, Eleonore realized that Rudolph was naked, but his body was famished and mere skin and bones like a prisoner from Auschwitz. Slowly, Rudolph's countenance changed to sorrow, and his body contorted as he slouched over and stood like a withered tree.

Dropping the lighter onto the floor, Rudolph began to laugh as the room was engulfed in flames. The cries of thousands rose with the blaze and Eleonore could hear the screams of Alex and Ruth and the pleas for mercy from Em. Rudolph glared at her with a heartless, empty stare.

A dark, burnt hand reached out of the fire, crawling its way to Eleonore who was powerless to scream or even move. Then the hand reached up from the side of her bed and grabbed Eleonore. The host of the hand screamed as she crawled out from under the bed. It was Ella, and her face was severely burnt.

Eleonore jerked awake.

Throwing off the covers, Eleonore reached over to the lamp and turned it on as she inspected the room for Rudolph. Satisfied that she was alone, Eleonore put her fingers to her neck as she felt her pulse raging. Then, suddenly, Eleonore grew irate and slammed her fist repeatedly against the bed. This was her one chance for sleep and, grabbing the pillow, she screamed into it with all her might.

I could really use a cigarette, Eleonore thought to herself after she had calmed a little. *Even now, Rudolph won't leave me alone,* Eleonore stood and dressed herself in a rush, desperate to escape. *The one chance I get to sleep, peacefully, and he interrupts it. And Ella,* Eleonore paused as the tears welled, *I'm sorry I couldn't save you. I'm sorry I couldn't keep you from the grave.*

Leaving her room, Eleonore walked briskly back to the foyer hoping to find Mr. Mattaliano smoking outside. But to Eleonore's disappointment, Mr. Mattaliano was nowhere to be seen. Aimlessly, Eleonore stood in the foyer and rubbed her tired eyes.

Then, Eleonore noticed a light on in the kitchen. *I do need to eat,* she shrugged, *that might help me rest a little.* But as she headed towards the kitchen, Eleonore caught a shadow moving from inside. *Oh good,* Eleonore smiled, *Mr. Mattaliano is awake. I can eat and borrow a smoke from him as well.* With a slight bounce in her step, Eleonore sped onward with purpose.

But when Eleonore entered the kitchen there was no one. It was vacant. She felt her heart rate rising, terrified that someone was hiding, or worse: she had gone mad. She glanced at the door leading to the garden and noticed that it was locked. The entrance to the dining room and the garden were the only two ways in which someone could enter the kitchen, yet she was alone.

"I know what I saw," Eleonore whispered to herself.

"You're just hungry," Ella's voice spoke to Eleonore.

"I do need to eat," Eleonore shrugged.

Passing by the large stove and the island in the center with all the pots and pans, Eleonore wasn't sure exactly what she was after but knew that there had to be something of substance.

Ah! Bread! Eleonore smiled when she saw a roll of French bread, the same loaf that had been delivered that morning by the boy who Mr. Mattaliano was shouting at.

"Now I just need a knife to cut it with," Eleonore rubbed her hands together excitedly as she surveyed.

"Aha!" Eleonore rushed over to the knife block on an otherwise empty table beside the walk-in cold storage. The table was still stained red from what Eleonore assumed were the remnants of Mrs. Meyers' supper.

This would go perfect with just a touch of butter, Eleonore began to salivate. *I suppose it's in the cold storage.*

Grabbing the door handle, Eleonore froze when she heard movement from inside. Again, her heart pounded in her chest as she wondered as to the correct course of action. Holding the knife in her free hand, Eleonore committed and threw the door open.

"Hey! Hey!" Mr. Mattaliano jumped up from where he was sitting on a wooden crate.

"What are you doing in here?!" Eleonore half-shouted, annoyed and relieved at the same time.

"Having an uninterrupted smoke," the butler spoke through gritted teeth before stomping out the cigarette.

"Were you hiding from me?" Eleonore threw her hands onto her hips.

"No, no, don't flatter yourself," Mr. Mattaliano waved his hand. "It's too windy tonight. I sometimes smoke in here as well."

"Well you scared me to death!" Eleonore ran her hand over her tired eyes, feeling the discomforts of her insomnia.

"I scared you?!" Mr. Mattaliano looked at her with incredulity.

"I heard movement inside. I thought maybe you were an animal…or someone else."

"What are you doing here anyways?" Mr. Mattaliano studied her curiously.

"I'm hungry," Eleonore glanced back at the bread which was begging to be sliced and slathered in butter.

"You could just eat with us servants," Mr. Mattaliano glanced at his pocket watch. "Instead of at this ungodly hour."

"I haven't slept in a few days," Eleonore sighed. "I thought it would be wise to get some rest first, but that didn't work so well."

Watching Eleonore for a moment, Mr. Mattaliano looked at her with understanding, "Nightmares?"

"Ya," Eleonore frowned. "How did you know?"

"Just a guess," he gave her a quick, sympathetic smile. "Well, let's get you something decent to eat, then."

"What do you mean?" Eleonore asked as he exited the cold storage room and went over to the sink where he began washing his hands.

"I'll make you something," he spoke plainly.

"You're going to cook...for me?" Eleonore wondered if the nightmare was still ongoing.

"I'm Italian," he smirked and glanced at her. "Cooking is as part of my nature, just as poor humor is to you Germans."

"Austrian, actually," Eleonore smiled as she set the knife back into the block and leaned against the table as she watched the butler with amusement. She wondered how a man could be so rude and yet so kind.

"What are you making?" she asked as he put a frying pan on the stove.

"Something to accompany your bread," he pointed to the loaf behind her and then called out as he returned to the cold storage room. "Cut yourself two slices."

"Alright," Eleonore raised an eyebrow as she couldn't resist a little smirk. She found it exciting, to an extent, to have someone cook something secretive for her. *As long as he doesn't use onions,* she prayed. It was the one and only ingredient that she detested.

"Here we are," he returned from the cold storage with some sliced prosciutto, two eggs, and a block of Parmesan cheese.

"Nothing too fancy I hope," Eleonore looked at his supplies in surprise. She wasn't about to refuse his cooking, but she didn't want him to go to great lengths on her behalf.

"It's not a fuss," he shook his head and Eleonore was certain she saw him smile.

With a long match, Mr. Mattaliano lit an element and began cooking the eggs. The smell and sizzle warmed Eleonore's heart as she stood, silently, watching the butter melt on the pan. It was an odd thing, she thought, to be so comfortable with him. She didn't know Mr. Mattaliano well enough to carry a decent conversation, yet his character had a calming influence, at certain times that is.

"You're familiar with prosciutto?" Mr. Mattaliano broke the silence as he began removing a few slices from its paper wrapping.

"My father used to cook with it," Eleonore nodded.

"Is that right?" the butler smiled at her warmly. "Mine too."

"When did you leave Italy?" Eleonore tilted her head.

"Pardon?" the butler glanced up at her quickly and then back at the food. He seemed to be rather unnerved by the question and pretended that he didn't hear her properly so that he could play for time in crafting a fabrication.

"I asked when you left Italy."

"Long time, long time," he waved, and Eleonore noticed he became immensely uncomfortable.

"Do you know the story of prosciutto?" he cleared his throat as he changed the subject.

"I never knew it had a history," Eleonore chuckled. "At least not one worthy of mention."

"Oh yes," Mr. Mattaliano nodded adamantly. "I…I come from Parma, you see, and-"

"That's in Northern Italy?" Eleonore squinted.

"Correct!" Mr. Mattaliano tilted his head in pleasant surprise. "Anyways, my father used to tell me how prosciutto was created many centuries ago. It's an art form in Parma. Basically, the delicacy is made by curing the meat and removing the moisture. Sometimes the legs hang for months and even years. And I have it on good authority that the meat you are about to enjoy is a year and a half old."

"Really?!" Eleonore grew excited.

"Si, si!" he nodded eagerly. "Come, come," he waved to her and grabbed a small slice of the meat.

"Here," he handed the prosciutto to her as if it was a fragile jewel. "Eat!"

Taking the prosciutto, Eleonore raised it to her mouth as Mr. Mattaliano watched impatiently and even opened his mouth in imitation.

"Oh, that is wonderful!" Eleonore's eyes flew wide as she savored the meat. "I've had prosciutto before, but never one so rich!"

"È perfetto, si?" Mr. Mattaliano returned to cooking.

"It really is," Eleonore closed her eyes as she relished the taste.

"One of the many benefits of working here. Bring the bread," Mr. Mattaliano snapped his fingers.

"Right!" Eleonore rushed back to the table and grabbed her two slices.

"Here," he took a spatula and grabbed the fried eggs as he placed them carefully onto the bread. Then, grabbing the prosciutto he placed two slices on each egg. Finally, he grabbed the block of Parmesan and a small cheese grater and crowned each slice with a thin layer of the white cheese.

"Grazie!" Eleonore grabbed one and began to eat it immediately as Mr. Mattaliano watched her expectantly.

"And?" he grew impatient.

"Why are you a butler?" Eleonore gave him a limp slap on his arm. "You should be a professional cook."

At this, his smile evaporated, and Eleonore gathered that, in some unknowing way, she had overstepped and caused unintentional offence.

"I should retire for the evening," Mr. Mattaliano wiped his hands on the towel beside the stove.

"I'm sorry," Eleonore grabbed him by the arm to stop him.

"Nothing to apologize for," he shook his head as he prepared to leave.

"Please!" Eleonore spoke sharply, and Mr. Mattaliano's eyes flew wide with astonishment that such a little woman could produce such a commanding voice.

"Just stay with me while I eat," she pleaded.

Shaking his head slightly, the butler rubbed his eyes in exhaustion.

"We don't have to talk," Eleonore persisted. "I just can't be alone right now."

Watching her for a moment and, remembering why she had come down in the first place, Mr. Mattaliano nodded and then pointed to two chairs by a small table in front of the window where the single orchid sat.

"Thank you," Eleonore sighed her relief and grabbed the other sandwich.

"You said no talking," Mr. Mattaliano spoke sternly, and Eleonore glanced up at him to see a cheeky smile emerging.

Sitting at the table, the two remained silent as Mr. Mattaliano rested his head against the glass while Eleonore ate in happy silence. The moonlight streamed into the kitchen which reminded Eleonore of the night in Berlin when she was arrested. It seemed to her that every pleasant experience was marred with a sour memory.

"If only I had used my senses," Eleonore muttered.

"Pardon?" Mr. Mattaliano looked at her.

"Oh," Eleonore chuckled awkwardly, "nothing. Just talking to myself."

The two returned to silence as Eleonore finished her sandwiches with the greatest pleasure. She delighted her taste buds and filled her belly with some much-craved nourishment.

"You ready?" Mr. Mattaliano sighed.

"Almost," Eleonore bit her cheek.

"What now?" he frowned.

"I could, um, I could use a smoke."

"I think I could as well," he stood as he dug into his pocket for his pack of cigarettes.

"The wind has died down a little," Eleonore glanced outside. "Should we stand out front?"

"Lead the way," he held his hand out for Eleonore to go before him.

Returning to the front of the house, the two stood outside under the dim light of the porch lamp as they smoked.

"Do...do you ever wonder why?" Eleonore glanced nervously at Mr. Mattaliano, feeling a bond growing between them that she would've never believed could've formed.

"Why what?" Mr. Mattaliano shook his head.

"Why you, why me?"

"I believe there is some context that you're not including here," the butler took a puff of his cigarette.

"Sorry," Eleonore chuckled. "I'm a little nervous. I mean, do you ever wonder why you survived while others didn't? I never had much of a chance to think about it until now."

"Survival of the fittest," he shrugged.

"Look at me," Eleonore raised her eyebrows. "I'm not the fittest. And there were plenty of the fittest that saw their end at Auschwitz."

"Auschwitz?"

"The camp where I was held prisoner.

"The camps," Mr. Mattaliano scoffed. "Don't mention those to Mrs. Meyers."

"I know, I've tried. Why is she so against hearing the truth?"

"Well, her brother was taken to Buchenwald and she hasn't heard from him since."

"Her brother?!" Eleonore shot Mr. Mattaliano a surprised look. "I don't understand."

"There were rumors that he, well, enjoyed the company of men," Mr. Mattaliano cleared his throat.

"Really?!" Eleonore frowned in disbelief.

"Yes, and that particular camp was alleged to have experimented on men of his disposition to try and cure them."

"That's terrible," Eleonore sighed and stared at her feet. She thought that Mrs. Meyers maybe held Nazi sympathies, but now realized that there was more to the mistress than she assumed.

"That it is," Mr. Mattaliano puffed.

"Can I ask," Eleonore glanced at the butler, "why are there no photos?"

"No photos?" the butler glanced back her curiously.

"There's none in the foyer, the dining room, the dressing room, the master bedroom, or in any of the wings. Why would Mrs. Meyers take them down?"

"She took down the photos the minute they left for the war," Mr. Mattaliano began.

"Why would she do that?"

"She was against the war. She opposed Hitler and everything that he stood for. Except for the smoking," Mr. Mattaliano looked at his cigarette with peculiarity. "That, for some reason, she agreed with him on."

"I still don't understand why she would take the photos down?"

"I can't say that I understand, either," Mr. Mattaliano shrugged, "but she was upset that the Nazis had stolen her boys, even before they died. Maybe it's too painful for her to look at their photos?"

"But she still sets the table for all six of them?" Eleonore shook her head in confusion.

"Grief is complex," Mr. Mattaliano looked at her sympathetically.

"And what about the youngest, Paul, what happened to him?"

"Ah, yes," Mr. Mattaliano sighed. "He wanted to be a pilot, ever since he first saw a plane. He was assigned to the Luftwaffe, but his plane was faulty and he crash-landed during training. First time he sat in that cockpit, and he wasn't even in the air for five minutes before the engine cut and he plummeted to the earth."

"That's awful," Eleonore looked back at the manor as she began to feel a new sense of understanding.

"You know, I believe that I may have misjudged you, Miss Hodys," Mr. Mattaliano spoke softly and flicked his cigarette onto the ground.

"And I you," Eleonore took a puff from her smoke as she avoided eye contact. "To be fair. I perceived you as a selfish, rude man, but Mrs. Meyers set the record straight for me."

"She defended me?" Mr. Mattaliano threw his lips upside down in surprise.

"Rather adamantly," Eleonore chuckled remembering the conversation.

"This family has always been kind to me," Mr. Mattaliano looked up at the house with fondness.

"Why is that?" Eleonore studied him. "And how does an Italian come to work at a manor in Northern Germany?"

"There were some problems in Parma," he began and looked out at the stars as he remembered home. "I had to flee. I had no money, nowhere to stay, so I lied on my application and joined the German army during the great war, or first world war as they're calling it now."

"And no one noticed that you were an Italian?" Eleonore looked at him in disbelief.

"I can hide it rather well," Mr. Mattaliano spoke with a perfect German accent and Eleonore was shocked at the precision. "And the army wasn't about to turn away volunteers."

"So, when did you stop pretending?"

"I served under Mr. Meyers in the first war. That's where I met him actually," Mr. Mattaliano smiled as he reminisced. "I mispronounced his name and gave myself away."

"And he didn't report you?"

"I was a good soldier," Mr. Mattaliano boasted. "Otherwise things may have been different. He kept my secret, and after the war he hired me on as his butler."

"That was kind," Eleonore studied Mr. Mattaliano, wondering what secrets he had left unsaid.

"I miss those days," Mr. Mattaliano mused.

"You miss the war?" Eleonore shot him a surprised glance.

"No, of course not," Mr. Mattaliano returned a stern glare. "I haven't slept a full night since," he grew solemn.

"Then what do you mean?" Eleonore persisted.

"I…" Mr. Mattaliano took a deep breath in. "I miss purpose. I miss knowing exactly what I needed to do. Somehow, when I was so close to death, I felt quite the opposite. It was hard, and still is really, to go on with life as though nothing had happened. As though your friends simply vanished."

"Now imagine how those in the camp felt," Eleonore began passionately, "being ripped from their homes and facing death every day. Imagine what would happen if someone came along and told you that your very nature, not your character, was enough to stuff you into stock cars brimming with people, strip you naked, shave off all your hair, force you into rickety old barracks without any heat, kill you off at random, and then cover it up as propaganda."

"You've made me think, Miss Hodys," Mr. Mattaliano looked at Eleonore with growing interest as he retrieved another cigarette. "I don't like to speculate. I'm a practical man. I just keep my head down and do my work."

"You know," Eleonore paused, "I feel a little embarrassed to ask again, but I would like to know your first name."

The butler chewed his lip pensively as he studied Eleonore intensely.

Then, taking a quick breath, "You can't make fun of it."

"I would never!" Eleonore professed, offended that he would even assume that she would be so childish.

"It's…it's Benito."

"Benito?" Eleonore tried to hide her smile, but the butler caught it creeping on her face.

"Don't!" he warned.

"Like Benito Mussolini?" Eleonore chuckled.

"You promised!" Benito grew embarrassed.

"I'm sorry," Eleonore calmed herself a little. "Well what's your middle name? Could I call you that instead?"

"I don't have a middle name," Benito glanced at her.

"What? Really?!" Eleonore frowned. "An Italian without a middle name?!"

"What's yours?" Benito shifted the focus to Eleonore, growing tired of being the spectacle.

"Nora," Eleonore replied proudly.

"That's beautiful," Benito grinned slightly. "What does it mean?"

"What does it mean?" Eleonore smiled brightly.

"Ya," Benito cleared his throat.

"It means light. It's short for the Greek Eleanora. What about yours?"

"Benito comes from Benedictus, meaning blessed. I think the meaning behind a name gives it weight," Benito nodded firmly.

"Agreed! So, if I can't call you by your first name, what can I call you?"

Staring into the earth in thought, Benito grinned slightly, "Ben will do."

"Well, Ben, why did you and I survive?" Eleonore pressed. "There has to be something more to it then survival of the fittest or pure chance. There has to be."

"Who says?" Ben narrowed his gaze.

"Everything inside me," Eleonore's voice swelled with passion. "Besides, it's better to live as though there was purpose than to abandon it altogether."

"You mentioned someone named Ella," Ben puffed his cigarette, "who was she?"

"The greatest woman I had ever met," Eleonore smiled as she remembered her friend.

The two talked late into the night as Eleonore described, in length, her trials and misfortunes. She bragged of the heroism of Ella and Roza, shuddered as she recalled the barbarity of the camp, and surprised Ben with the inequality of the Villa. Yet Eleonore didn't trust Ben with the details of Rudolph. She knew that no one could know. She told Hanns as she knew it would be beneficial for the trial, but no one else would understand.

Ben would assume just as Hanns had: that she had been a willing mistress to the Commandant of Auschwitz. He'd react like Hanns as well: how could she be involved with him? He'd assume that if he was in her position that he'd be strong, he'd refuse Rudolph even at the cost of torture or death. But, like Eleonore, if he were in that situation, she knew that he'd be like her, or worse. Only a few were as strong as Ella. Even fewer were as brave.

Chapter Thirteen:
On Morality

We do not merely destroy our enemies; we change them.

George Orwell – 1984

My dear Poppet,

This letter is long overdue, but I trust that you'll understand. In fact, the very paper with which I'm writing this letter to you is a token of proof for how occupied I've been. This stationery was stolen from an SS official. The man himself is of little consequence, but it gives me joy that a Jew who hunted him down is now using his notepaper to write to his love who also happens to be Jewish.

My greatest pleasure, besides thinking of your sweetness, is chasing these SS about. I unfortunately haven't been able to catch anyone of interest, but I'm not entirely convinced that this is my fault. Officially, I'm not permitted to hunt down these villains. During my free time, however, I have been making short forays into the countryside.

These past few weeks have shown me a Germany that is still very much under Hitler's shadow. The police are too scared to discuss any information, most civilians won't even look at me while I wear the British uniform, and the ones who are eager to converse with me have little in the way of useful information. Still, I'm determined to continue.

My father wrote to advise that his practice now boasts 1800 patients! Jolly good show, as the English would say. I only hope that I can make 1800 SS swing, but with the way things are progressing here that may never happen.

I should, I suppose, address your main concern with regards to our relationship. While I remain committed to you in every way, I don't have an answer on your pressing question of marriage. If I should take leave, then I should only be permitted ten days. To leave the continent, get married, honeymoon, and then return within ten days would not be an enjoyable start to our union. If things should begin to settle down here at Belsen, then I'd be more than happy to consider an extended leave.

All my love,

Hanns

Sitting on the edge of the desk in the administration office, Hanns rubbed his chin as he studied the diagram of the suspects on the board. With a cigarette in hand, Hanns took advantage of the isolation provided by the early morning. A single lamp was lit by the corner of the diagram and papers lay scattered across the desks and floor.

The administration office had been turned into a sort of mock police station. The diagram was becoming complete with photographs of the suspects and had been arranged in the hierarchy that they assumed existed from the guard's statements.

A righteous fury rose in Hanns as he studied the photograph of Rudolph smiling, holding a cigar in one hand, and appearing as if he had no care in the world. *How can he be so removed?* Hanns wondered, but knew that he was not a man, but rather, a beast without a soul. There was no conviction in him. Rudolph had justified his position, as many others had as well, but only to shift the blame.

Beside the diagram was a map of Germany and the surrounding areas, ready to be filled in with the speculated locations of these criminals. But not a single pin had been placed on the map. Both Himmler and Rudolph were still at large, Hitler had killed himself, and none of the major characters behind the genocide were captured or on trial. Even most of the doctors had gone missing. There were no clues, no leads. Nothing.

"I don't think you'll find them staring at their pictures," Smallwood handed Hanns a cup of coffee.

"No," Hanns took a careful sip, "I fear not."

Joining Hanns, Smallwood sat on the edge of the table beside him. The two sipped on their coffees and smoked their cigarettes in the dim light, devising ambitious plans to hunt down the men pictured before them.

Hanns, for all his cunning, felt at a complete loss. Yet, there was something else at work within Hanns. Something he didn't quite understand. It felt to him as though some breakthrough idea, or lead, was just a thought away. It felt tangible, like a dark cloud hovering over his head that he could poke with a knife and release the rain. He didn't know how, or when, but he knew that it would be him who found these men. It had to be him.

"It's hard for me to understand why we aren't going after them," Hanns broke the silence. "I mean, I understand what we're doing is important, but if men like Himmler and Rudolph escape, then I'll regret it for the rest of my life."

"Himmler didn't escape," Smallwood glanced at Hanns.

"What do you mean?" Hanns turned towards Smallwood.

"It was in the paper this morning," Smallwood adjusted his glasses.

"Nobody informed me! What happened? Is he in custody?"

"They caught him at a checkpoint trying to escape Germany," Smallwood took a sip of his coffee.

"And?!"

"When he admitted who he was, he was taken for medical examination but then bit into a cyanide pill and killed himself," Smallwood took another sip.

"That bastard," Hanns slunk down.

"He took the easy way out," Smallwood spoke without much emotion.

"Damn him!" Hanns picked up a chair and threw it against the wall with a loud crash. "If I had been out there, then I could've caught him! I could've brought him to justice!"

"He would've used the pill either way," Smallwood remained unmoved. He had grown well accustomed to Hanns' outbursts.

"I can't stay here," Hanns shook his head in despair.

"Then get out there."

"I have been," Hanns leaned over and put his hands on the desk, "but it seems that everyone I speak with doesn't want anything to do with me. They either ignore me altogether, don't trust me, or refuse to have any dealings with Jews."

"Maybe you need to make some arrests," Smallwood shrugged.

"I don't have that authority," Hanns scoffed.

"They don't know that," Smallwood leaned in.

"I wish," Hanns sighed. "I need to be out there. I can't be here much longer."

"You know what I find the most difficult to believe?" Smallwood shook his head.

"What's that?"

"How they didn't know."

"Who?" Hanns shot a glance at Smallwood.

"The towns near these camps," Smallwood glanced at his feet and Hanns, for the first time, thought that he saw some emotion from his calculated comrade.

"You think they were aware?" Hanns sat beside his friend.

"How could they not be?" Smallwood scoffed. "The ash from human remains was falling all over their town. Auschwitz and Buchenwald both knew."

"Howard!" Genn burst into the room and rushed over to Hanns.

"Whatever is the matter?" Hanns stood in a panic.

"Josef Kramer," Genn tried to catch his breath, "he would like to make a statement."

"We already have one," Hanns looked at him curiously. "He testified that he didn't know anything."

"Yes," Genn stood up straight, "but he would like to amend his original report."

"Really?"

"I told you the work that you were doing was important," Genn smiled his relief and his victory. "With the rising tide of testimonies and witnesses that you have collected, Josef can't deny any longer that he knew exactly what was happening at Auschwitz. I'm putting my best men on this. You and Captain Fox must travel to Celle at once. Josef Kramer is instrumental."

"I'll leave immediately," Hanns grabbed his satchel by the end of the table.

"Howard," Genn called after him.

"Yes?" Hanns stopped.

"If this is what I think it is, then you'll be out in the field shortly."

Full of vigor, Hanns gave an energetic salute. That was all the motivation he needed. To know that Himmler had taken his own life enraged Hanns to no end. He wouldn't permit another one of the devils the convenience of a cowardly death.

Lighting his Dunhill pipe, Hanns let the smoke swell in the small cell. It was the same room that they had interviewed Irma Grese and some of the other prisoners. Yet, this time Hanns was even more nervous than before. This statement would have to be perfect.

"Look at this," Fox whispered as he leafed through Josef's file.

"What's that?" Hanns asked.

"It says here that Josef was known as 'The Beast of Belsen.'"

"Let me see that," Hanns grabbed the folder from Fox.

"Doesn't say why," Fox muttered. "I can't imagine I want to know either."

"Regardless," Hanns drew a deep breath, "Kramer needs to provide an account which identifies that he was, and is, sufficiently morally aware."

"Agreed," Fox put the folder back on the table. "We have enough of the details, now we need to examine his conscience, or lack thereof."

"I don't know if Josef is doing this from genuine guilt, though," Hanns frowned as he stared at the table pensively.

"How so?"

"Well, with the amount of testimonies coming forth, sooner or later it will be revealed what he did. I think he realized that it would look better if he confessed now instead of his involvement being discovered later. Either way," Hanns took another puff of his pipe, "he won't be saved from the gallows."

The door to the cell swung open, startling Hanns.

Ushered into the cell was a large man with a thick jaw and an ugly scar on his left cheek. There was a coldness to his glare, even when seemingly repentant, and it was evident to Hanns that Josef was after nothing else but self-preservation. *I can use that against him,* Hanns thought. *Remember, don't react to what he says, even if it's intolerable. Just take down the information so that the prosecution can do their job properly.*

"I'm Lieutenant Volker," Hanns began as he puffed his pipe after Josef had been seated, "and this is my associate, Captain Felix."

Josef nodded his acknowledgement as he sat up straight, though Hanns thought he detected the slightest trembling.

"You may begin," Fox signaled to Josef.

"I want to revise my testimony," Josef rubbed his hand across his face.

"Understood. We have prepared some questions as well which we would like to add to your amendment. Please state your full name," Fox asked as he stared at his page.

"Josef Kramer."

"Date of birth?"

"November 10, 1906."

"Why did you join the SS and what kind of work did you do?" Hanns asked.

"I was unemployed," Josef shifted in his chair slightly, "and the SS were hiring. I attended parades and did some clerical work, but that was the extent of it, initially."

"When did you begin working at the concentration camps?"

"Fall of 1934," Josef glanced at the ceiling as he searched his memory. "I worked at Natzweiler before being transferred to Auschwitz, which I was not keen on."

"Why?" Hanns frowned curiously.

"Auschwitz was in poor order and not tidy and there was the Polish element as well," Josef replied and Hanns noted that he held no reservation for his disgusting bias.

"When you arrived at Auschwitz, who was the Commandant?" Hanns asked.

"Rudolph Hoess," Josef nodded.

"What was your position at the camp?"

"I was the Commandant of Camp No. 2, also called Birkenau."

"I'm going to read you the statement which you originally made," Hanns retrieved the document from Josef's file and cleared his throat before continuing, "'I have heard of the allegations of former prisoners in Auschwitz referring to a gas chamber there, the mass executions and whippings, the cruelty of the guards employed, and that all this took place either in my presence or with my knowledge. All I can say to all this is that it is untrue from beginning to end.'"

"That was my original statement, yes," Kramer swallowed, "but I want to amend that I didn't know anything about the gas chambers. I did, in fact, inspect the crematoriums and I was present when the first victims were selected. To be clear, however, I received written orders from Hoess that, although the crematoriums were in Birkenau, they were in no way under my jurisdiction."

"Why are you amending your statement?" Hanns asked as he set the document back into Kramer's folder.

"Why?" Josef glanced at Hanns and swallowed.

"Why amend your statement now?" Hanns watched Josef patiently and then tapped the folder. "To reverse this sworn affidavit carries serious implications."

Staring at his hands as he rubbed them together nervously, Josef seemed to be debating whether he should tell the truth. Hanns assumed that Josef was pinned into a corner and, while there was no way to free himself, he hoped to lessen his sentence.

"Can I have a cigarette?" Josef cleared his throat and Hanns noticed that his breathing was beginning to labor and his forehead was perspiring.

Glancing at Fox, who gave a nod of approval, Hanns agreed to provide the prisoner with his wish. Slowly, Hanns stood and retrieved a smoke and a match for Josef. Trembling, Josef lit his cigarette and inhaled deeply as his leg bounced anxiously.

"So," Hanns sighed and gestured for Josef to continue.

"There are two reasons for the discrepancy," Josef took a deep breath. "One is that the prisoners advised that these gas chambers were under my command which is false. Secondly, and more importantly," Josef shifted again in his chair. "I swore on my honor that I would not speak of the gas chambers."

"And now, four months later, you don't feel bound to this word of honor any longer?" Hanns shook his head as he frowned.

"My first statement was taken when the results of the war were unknown. Now that those who I've sworn to, Hitler and Himmler, are dead, I'm no longer bound by my word of honor," Josef explained, though Hanns still didn't detect any true signs of remorse.

"I was under the impression that there were no written orders in relation to the gas chambers," Hanns squinted. "Why would Rudolph then write to you to advise that they aren't under your jurisdiction?"

"I believe he understood my conscience was conflicted," Josef replied and Hanns could see his pulse raging in his neck.

"Josef," Hanns spoke softly, "this is a sworn statement. Do you understand the implication of being dishonest? Why would Rudolph disobey orders by writing to you just to ease your conscience? Are you not simply shifting the blame?"

"It is as I said it was," Josef nodded firmly, and both Hanns and Fox glanced at each other with the understanding that the man before them was blatantly lying.

"Were you aware of the selections?" Fox asked.

"Yes, most of the transports arrived near Birkenau and, if I was on inspection, I would see the transports arrive and the selections being made."

"You've been accused of selecting prisoners yourself," Hanns leaned in. "Is that true?"

"No," Josef shook his head quickly. "Only the doctors made the selections. Usually it was Dr. Mengele."

"We have witnesses who have sworn that you were selecting prisoners to be sent to the gas chambers," Hanns pressed.

"Not possible," Josef shook his head. "As I stated, the crematoriums were not under my jurisdiction so neither I, nor my staff, took any part in the selections."

"Why didn't Hoess stop the killings?" Hanns asked.

"He's the one who gave the orders," Josef shrugged while avoiding eye contact. "But I'm convinced that the orders came from Berlin."

"How so?"

"I know Hoess quite well," Josef cleared his throat. "He wouldn't have thought of such things on his own."

"What do you mean?" Fox glared at Josef.

"He was just following orders," Josef spoke quietly but shifted in his seat as he grew uncomfortable.

"As you were just following orders?" Hanns pressed. "If you were in his position, what would you have done?"

"I believe I would've acted as Rudolph had. If Rudolph protested, or if I protested, then we would just be taken prisoner ourselves."

"Josef Kramer," Hanns folded his hands and stared intently at the prisoner as he was becoming impatient with the measured replies, "I firmly believe that you are amending this statement for a reason entirely outside of honor. I'm not sure if you intend to be honest with the hopes that your sentencing may be reduced or if you're afraid that soon your involvement will be found out. Either way, you will be judged on your personal oversight as a Commandant and I require you to answer as such. Now, can you advise us as to your personal feelings on the gas chambers?"

Hanns and Fox remained silent as Josef closed his eyes while he tried to gather his thoughts.

"I was surprised when I received the orders to kill those who were unfit," Josef paused.

"Go on," Hanns said softly. He wanted to appear friendly to this demon to try and elicit his trust so that he would reveal the damning details.

"I asked myself if it was right that this was happening and how those who signed the orders to kill that many people would be able to answer for it," Josef continued as he clenched his jaw, not relishing the implication of guilt.

"Did anyone else feel this way? Did they tell you such?"

"They didn't have to," Josef scoffed. "Many of my men killed themselves or drank until they were in a continuous stupor."

"I heard that there were some revolts. Were you Commandant during this time?" Hanns asked as he began to shake with rage.

"There were a few, yes," Josef nodded. "There was a woman once. A ballerina, I think, who knew what the gas chambers were. She took a gun from one of Rudolph's officers, shot the officer and a few others before she was locked inside the chambers. There was also a revolt that killed a good number of SS guards and destroyed a few of the crematorium. Others didn't fight at all."

"At Natzweiler," Fox removed a document from the folder, "there was a gas chamber, correct?"

"Yes."

"And at Natzweiler was this gas chamber under your jurisdiction?"

"Yes, I constructed the gas chamber and received a written order for a special transport of about eighty women that I was to kill at this gas chamber," Kramer spoke plainly which infuriated Hanns.

"Who did the order come from?" Fox asked, and Hanns noticed that he, too, was struggling to remain calm.

"Himmler," Kramer replied dryly.

"And this was a legal practice?" Hanns asked but had to stare at the page in front of him to hide his emotions. Still, after all this time of hearing the insurmountable death and atrocities, he found it nearly impossible to contain his reactions. But Hanns knew that Josef Kramer's statement could not, in any way, be impeded.

"Legal? That I'm not certain of," Josef shook his head.

"You don't know if this order was legal, yet you carried it out?" Hanns frowned.

"The order came from the highest military authority," Josef shrugged.

"But you must've understood that this was a crime?" Hanns pressed. "You must've understood that to kill eighty women by gassing could not fall under any law?"

"I followed orders," Josef swallowed. "Though if it was right, I don't know. All I know is that I had to follow orders."

"You didn't ask your superiors?" Fox asked with a hint of incredulity.

"We never spoke of such things," Josef shook his head. "We spoke of orders, nothing else."

"Was it because you understood that this was an outrage against decency?" Hanns narrowed his gaze.

"No," Josef stared at his feet.

"What was the purpose of the gas chambers?" Hanns asked as he watched for Josef's reaction.

"That was never explained to me," Josef remained staring at his feet.

"Was it not the doctrine of the Nazi party to exterminate all Jews?"

"As I said," Josef cleared his throat, "we didn't talk about such things."

"But a central doctrine of the Nazi party, the party to which you have sworn allegiance, is the extermination of the Jewish race. Is it not?"

Josef remained silent for a moment as he stared at Hanns before reluctantly replying, "Yes."

"Why, at Belsen, was nothing done to provide the inmates with food or water?" Hanns folded his hands as he leaned forward.

"I only had a limited supply of food," Josef replied quickly. "I could not feed so many with so little."

"What about the water?" Hanns squinted. "There is a river only about four hundred meters from the camp. Why was this water not provided to the inmates?"

"I had no means to bring the water into the camp."

"Could you not have let the prisoners go to the river instead?"

"I was advised that the water was not safe for drinking."

"Really?" Hanns scoffed and glanced at Fox. "Because this is the same water that we are using for the camp now."

Josef remained silent.

"Josef," Hanns cleared his throat, "your wife provided a brief statement."

"My wife?" Josef grew nervous.

"Rosina Kramer is your wife, correct?"

"Yes."

"She was asked if you ever talked to her of what happened in the camp, and, according to her, you mentioned that those responsible for all these deaths likely did not sleep lightly. Is that true?"

"I believe I mentioned that, yes," Josef nodded.

"We believe that the person responsible," Hanns paused, "is you."

Josef remained quiet as his breathing returned to laboring. Hanns knew that he had cornered Josef, and now he only needed this ex-Commandant to admit to his guilt.

"You knew that this was wrong, correct?"

"It was my order," Josef swallowed.

"But, naturally, you knew that it was wrong. Your conscience must've weighed heavily."

"Yes."

"Lastly, Josef," Hanns cleared his throat, "why were you sent as the Commandant of Birkenau?"

"I don't know," Josef shook his head. "I received the orders and complied."

"I have a theory," Hanns glared at Josef. "I believe that when you were at Natzweiler you entered into a sort of apprenticeship in the craft of mass murdering innocent people. You constructed the gas chamber yourself, where you then gassed the innocents by your own hands. Your superiors recognized your skills and selected you as the Commandant of the largest death camp in Birkenau. It strains credulity when you advise that you do not know why you were chosen for the position of Commandant. They knew that, in you, they had a Commandant who they could rely on to carry out the dirty work with the utmost secrecy."

Josef remained silent as he sweat profusely and returned Hanns' glare.

"In you, Josef, I believe the Nazi party found a man willing to carry out orders and to carry them out explicitly. Is that true?"

"What was I supposed to do?" Josef fumbled with his hands.

"You are a man with free will," Fox replied. "I understand it may have been difficult to resist your orders, but when this evil was proposed, you had two options: oppose and face the consequences, or blindly follow orders. We ask you, again, do you believe that what you did was wrong?"

Josef remained silent as he stared at both Hanns and Fox. Then, slowly, he nodded his head.

"We require an answer," Hanns pressed.

"As I stated," Josef cleared his throat, "I don't know if it was right or not."

"That's all," Fox nodded and signaled to the guards to take Josef away.

Hanns and Fox sat quietly as Josef was ushered out of the cell. The door closed slowly behind Josef and the two interrogators were left in the room by themselves to absorb the information. Neither Hanns nor Fox dared to move as they sat quietly, listening to the hum of the pale orange light above them.

"Howard," Fox spoke softly, almost as a whisper.

"Ya?" Hanns glanced at Fox with tears in his eyes.

"We got it!" Captain Fox stood in a rush and embraced Hanns as the two wept.

"This is the final nail in the coffin," Hanns felt a lump in his throat. "This is a moral statement. This proves that they knew what they were doing was wrong."

"We should provide this to Genn at once!" Fox rubbed his hands together with excitement.

Chapter Fourteen:
The Belsen Trials

If everyone is thinking alike, someone isn't thinking.

General George Patton

Hanns walked with Fox as they approached the gymnasium-turned-courtroom. Lüneburg had been gracious enough to host the trials in their town, but knew that the courtroom would not be substantial enough to hold the sheer volume of defendants, judges, lawyers, and spectators. While the alternative was unconventional, the space provided by this irregular venue was necessary to serve the purposes of the trial.

Arriving at the gymnasium, Hanns spotted a large group of press with their cameras and notepads, government officials smoking liberally, and high-ranking military staff standing outside and chatting excitedly. The world had come to Lüneburg, and an excitement grew within Hanns that he was awarded the opportunity to be at the center of it all.

"Do you suppose this is the place?" Hanns tapped Fox and pointed at a large sign hung outside the gymnasium with big, bold letters which read 'COURTROOM'.

Fox chuckled nervously, and Hanns knew that he shouldn't be making jest in such circumstances, but he was glad, at least, to see that he wasn't alone. The crowd of military personnel and press that had gathered were laughing and talking loudly as if they were waiting to watch a sporting event and not about to witness a gruesome trial.

But then Hanns noticed another group that had gathered outside as well, and they weren't too fond of the British presence. This other crowd consisted mostly of women, accompanied by a few elderly gentlemen, whom Hanns detected still held strong Nazi sympathies. The women clung tightly to their daughters, not letting anyone out of their sight while the men gripped their canes as their knuckles turned white from outrage.

Pressing their way through the crowd, Hanns and Fox came to the entrance where they were stopped by some guards who signaled for them to spread their arms while they patted them down. The women, Hanns noticed, were also being checked by some female guards who were making thorough inspections.

"I think we're in the wrong line," Hanns nodded and Fox looked over his shoulder to see one of the female guards patting down the female officials and citizens.

Shaking his head, Fox couldn't help a smile and, after being cleared, the two were about to enter when a shout arose from down the street. Curious, Hanns watched as some others began to shout as well and he left to investigate. By now, everyone in the crowd had migrated over to the disturbance and Hanns watched as two trucks drove towards the back of the courtroom which were being chased by the press with their cameras rolling. It was, without question, unanimously understood that these vehicles were transporting the accused.

"Howard!" Fox shouted and Hanns turned to see that Fox remained by the doors.

"I want to see them!" Hanns shouted back.

"You'll get a better view in here!" Fox waved.

Agreeing, Hanns joined Fox as they entered the makeshift courtroom and found a spot near the front. It was a peculiar set-up and Hanns now understood why a traditional courtroom, where only one person is on trial, would not suffice. Booths that were three rows deep were set up facing each other at the far end of the gymnasium to accommodate the number of defendants. Lamps and headphones were affixed to each seat which were to be used for translation as the trials would take place in English. Facing the judge's booth, in the center of the courtroom, was a podium which Hanns assumed was where the prosecution and witnesses would appear.

Apart from Fox and Hanns, the courtroom was almost empty as everyone was distracted by the excitement outside. The two sat silently as they stared at the booths and an unease set in Hanns' spirit as he imagined how the proceedings would take place.

"Told you," Fox pointed to the back of the room where the prisoners were ushered into their booths. The press were following closely behind and showing no concern for personal space as their cameras were capturing every blemish.

First into the room was Josef Kramer who looked stern yet concerned as he was taken to his seat. The number 1 was hung around his chest, signifying his trial number. Glancing over, Josef made quick eye contact with Hanns, but then looked away and stared straight ahead. Next to him was Dr. Klein, wearing the number 2 and appearing feeble, but Hanns assumed that he was performing a little in order to elicit some sympathy. Down the line from them was Irma Grese, wearing the number 9 and sitting with her arms crossed and her jaw jutting out. Still, with all her authority stripped, she acted as if the room belonged to her.

Then, bursting into the courtroom were those who had chased the truck down the street and were now anxious to get a decent view. Hanns nodded his thankfulness to Fox for getting them prime seating.

The unease in the room was one that Hanns had never experienced before and one that he would be happy to forget.

Many about the room stared at the defendants with a permanent scowl, ready and willing to enact justice themselves. The defendants were tense, knowing that they likely had little to no chance of escaping their fate. A fate which depended largely on the statements Hanns and Fox and other members of 1WCIT had collected.

"Do you think they're adequate?" Fox asked solemnly.

"What are?" Hanns replied, though he was rather distracted.

"The statements we took."

"Of course they are," Hanns drew his attention to Fox.

"You're right," Fox took a deep breath. "Just feels intimidating to have the whole world watching, hanging upon our diligence."

"They won't escape justice," Hanns gave a knowing look at Fox. "Our work is adequate. What we need to rely on now is the efficiency and effectiveness of the prosecution."

"To order," came the call and everyone was seated shortly as the military judges, five in all, took their place at the head of the booths.

Whatever excitement Hanns was feeling about the trials was soon quashed by the extended formalities. He felt himself slipping into an inescapable boredom as the order convening the court was read, the names of the defendants were announced while they acknowledged their presence, the president and members of the court were duly sworn, the shorthand writers were duly sworn, the interpreters were duly sworn, the prosecutors and defence lawyers were announced, and applications were submitted to have certain defendants put on trial separately which were subsequently dismissed.

Finally, the initial proceedings had ended and Hanns felt the exhilaration swelling within him again as they were about to commence with the trial. This was the culmination of months of his work and the thankless underpaid and undervalued servitude from thousands who sought justice.

"The charges are as follows," the Judge Advocate began as he looked over his glasses and Hanns thought that he seemed rather ceremonial and impartial; not the merciless and vindictive man that he was hoping to find. "Count One. At Bergen-Belsen, Germany, between the 1st of October, 1942, and the 30th of April, 1945, when members of the staff of Bergen-Belsen Concentration Camp responsible for the well-being of the persons interned there, in violation of the law and usages of war, were together concerned as parties to the ill-treatment and deaths of Allied Nationals."

A stillness settled on the courtroom as the Judge Advocate let the charge resonate, and to give time for the charges to be interpreted properly to the defendants.

"The second count," the Judge Advocated continued. "At Auschwitz, Poland, between the 1st of October, 1942, and the 30th of April, 1945, when members of the staff of Auschwitz Concentration Camp responsible for the well-being of the persons interned there, in violation of the law and usages of war, were together concerned as parties to the ill-treatment and deaths of Allied Nationals."

Again, the Judge Advocate allowed for a brief moment for the defendants to understand the charges properly.

"How do the accused plea?" the Judge Advocate asked.

The defence lawyer, who Hanns thought was a weaselly-looking creature, took the stand and the room became deathly silent as they awaited the pleas. He appeared to be gathering his thoughts, leaving the world in suspense. He looked towards one of the defendants, then to the judges, and then he turned and looked at the cameras behind him. There was a defiance in his gaze, and a pit grew in Hanns' stomach as he guessed what was to follow.

"That's Major Cranfield," Fox whispered, "one of the British lawyers provided to the defendants. Rather intelligent man. The prosecution will have their work cut out for them."

"May it please the Court," Cranfield returned to looking at the judges, "For Joseph Kramer…not guilty."

A murmur rushed around the room as no one could believe what they had heard. Hanns clenched his jaw and squeezed his hand into a fist at the arrogance of such a plea.

"Order!" the Judge Advocate demanded, and his face grew red with wrath.

"Continue," he spoke to the lawyer once the room had quieted.

"For Dr. Klein," Major Cranfield paused, bracing for the response from the crowd, "not guilty."

The murmur grew louder and Hanns felt his heart pounding within his chest. He had been to the camps and seen what had happened. He had helped bury, in mass graves, his own people. How could these degenerates dare say that they were not guilty for such crimes?

But Major Cranfield continued to shock the courtroom, and the world, as he read out forty-five 'not guilty' pleas.

"It's just a tactic," Fox leaned over. "Don't worry, they're not getting away with anything."

"The Prosecution may make its opening statements," the Judge Advocate gestured and then folded his hands as he leaned over in reserved anticipation.

Everyone in the court sat up as straight as possible to get a glimpse of their 'champion' as he approached. With relief, Hanns watched as a large man with big, burly hands and a thick mustache took the stand. There was a ferocity in this man's stride and Hanns was glad, at least, that he was on their side.

"That's Colonel Thomas Backhouse," Fox whispered. "This should be good."

Mimicking the defence lawyer, Colonel Thomas Backhouse stood silently as he studied the defendants. Hanns thought that he could see the defence lawyer squirming in his seat and smiled at the thought of justice arriving swiftly. Then, Backhouse retrieved a written statement from his clipboard, and placed it squarely on the podium. For a quick moment, Hanns thought that he caught a hint of nervousness in Backhouse, but it was buried under a resounding conviction to speak the truth.

"May it please the Court," Backhouse read with a loud, booming voice. "The prosecution is stating that there was a deliberate, cold-blooded extermination of millions. These forty-five before us are accused in the first place of committing individual murders and mistreatments, and in the second place of having knowingly participated in a common plan to operate a system of ill-treatment and murder. Every member bore a share in the treatment they knew would cause death and physical suffering.

"We will produce an overwhelming amount of evidence that they committed deliberate acts of cruelty and willful murder. Those who were responsible for the well-being of the prisoners interned, in violation of the law and usages of war, were together concerned, as parties, to the ill-treatment of those under their care. I ask that the Court view the evidence as a whole and that each defendant must not only bear the responsibility for his own actions, but also for those of his criminal gang. The causes of death were mainly starvation, thirst and ill-treatment, beating to death and shooting, but starvation was undoubtedly killing every person in that camp. If a man did not die directly of starvation, he was so weakened that he had no resistance whatsoever to disease. If he did not die of either, he died of overwork or of the beatings that he received.

"You will hear, for example, that in Block 13 the average life of a man there was twelve days from arrival. The food situation was such that the ordinary rations in a concentration camp, quite apart from any peculiarities which may arise, was a cup of weak ersatz coffee for breakfast, some turnip soup with sometimes a little bread for midday meal, and nothing for the evening meal. The English witness, which I will bring forward, will tell you that the sum total of the food he received during the first four days, for the whole of four days, amounted to less than half a litre of soup, and no bread, and half a mugful of water. During the last five days before the liberation, he received neither food nor water, and he was required, with the other prisoners in the camp, to work twelve hours a day dragging corpses. Although they did not have the strength to carry them, they had to move fast because the moment they faltered, they were beaten or shot."

Hanns felt his shoulders tightening and he wondered how he would manage to endure the days that this trial would extend, let alone the next hour hearing, again, the barbarities that happened to his people.

"I would like to address an individual story," Backhouse rested his hands on the stand as he leaned over and read. "Mr. Le Druillenec was arrested in Jersey one day before D-day because his sister had helped a Russian officer to escape. He was put into various prisons and concentration camps and finally came here to Lüneburg by train. From Lüneburg he was taken by truck and arrived at Belsen about half-past ten at night on the 5th of April, 1945.

"In a concentration camp, you are not very sure of either date or time because you have no belongings of your own. Everything you try to keep, even your pocket handkerchiefs, are taken away from you and you are beaten for having them. You have no name, but instead, you have a number tattooed on your arm and you are known by that number. When Mr. Le Druillenec arrived at the camp, he was offered some soup in exchange for any cigarettes or bread he had brought, and since he could not produce such articles, he received no soup. He was locked in his block with six hundred other prisoners. The floor was wet and indescribably foul, having been used as a latrine by people who were too weak to move.

"They were so overcrowded that he had to sleep sitting up because he could not lie down. They were kept locked in there during the night. Eight or nine of them died every night that he was there. The corpses, of course, were not taken out and stayed there with the living. At 3:30 in the morning he was called out of his block, being assisted by the usual beating. He was then forced, with the other prisoners, on to their miserable selections without anything to eat. They were then kept standing at attention till eight o'clock. Anybody who moved was beaten. Some fell, and then they were kicked and beaten on the ground.

"The first day they did little. The next day they were dragged out again at an early hour and divided into fours. They then set off in groups of four and had to drag the corpses and put them in the large burial pits. Eventually they piled the corpses up because there was nowhere to bury them.

"Every guard carried a stick or a piece of wood and the orderlies, whom I term prefects, lined the road and beat anybody who faltered. For twelve solid hours that miserable procession dragged on. They passed one of the water reservoirs each time they went round, and you can imagine the dust as they dragged these corpses. They were not allowed to stop, and they were not allowed to have a drink at all throughout the day.

"If they faltered a yard or so behind the man in front, they were beaten till they got up. That is how he spent the first four days, and that is all that he had to eat during these four days. The last five days he had neither food nor water. The one and only thing that kept him alive was the fact that he could hear the Allied guns, and he felt that if he could keep alive for one more day, then possibly someone would come to their aid. All day you would hear shots going off about the camp and you would see the guards amusing themselves by shooting the internees for no apparent reason at all.

"You have got to try and imagine the type of men that were prepared for this mass murder of every person unfit to serve the Reich. There were occasions when selections, as they were called, were made on arrival. The transports arrived and before people were posted to their blocks, selections were made and the old, children, pregnant women, weak or sick, or those showing signs of unfitness, never went into the camp at all. Instead, they were loaded on lorries and taken straight to the gas chambers where they were murdered on an industrial scale.

"Everyone in the camp knew about it, every one of the accused who was at Auschwitz knew about it, and you will hear that the majority of them took an active part in the selection of victims for the gas chamber. In November of 1944, in one transport of fourteen hundred people only one hundred were accepted as fit and the remainder were taken and gassed straight away. In another transport of five thousand persons, forty-five hundred were gassed. Forty-Five thousand Greek Jews were taken to that camp, and when they were evacuating the prison, only sixty were left out of that number.

"You have precisely the same position at Belsen. You have not the gas chambers, but you have conditions created there which may well have been worse than any gas chamber. You have people dying in very drawn out agony, which was not thought of in Auschwitz. It is immaterial, in my submission, whether that was deliberate, because these people were no longer fit to work for the Reich and therefore they were left to starve, or whether it was the result of gross neglect of the persons who were placed in their charge. Again, I suggest that if a person took part in such an enterprise, if they were the Commandant, such as Kramer was, or if they were lower level guards, as were some of these Kapos who joined it possibly to save their skins, they cannot avoid their responsibility. I say if you are satisfied that they did take part in it, however small, then they are guilty of the charge.

"This Court is doing justice. If you have any reasonable doubt in the case of any of the accused quite rightly, you will acquit them, providing of course that doubt is in fact a reasonable doubt. If, on the other hand, you are satisfied in respect of all or any of these persons that they knew what was happening, that they realized that these people were dying of neglect, and they took part in it then, in my submission, there can be only one other verdict on whichever charge it may be, and that is that they are guilty.

"If you are satisfied on the evidence that these conditions did exist in Belsen and in Auschwitz, then the Prosecution have amply made out a case against each one of those prisoners who took an active part at either of those camps, however small it may be. It is the duty of the Prosecution to prove the guilt of the accused beyond any reasonable doubt, and unless the Prosecution have fulfilled that burden of proof then it will be your duty to acquit any one of these persons you may be in doubt about. If you are satisfied that they in fact acquiesced to and took part in the atrocities of which you will be told, that they created conditions which you will see in so far as they can be seen on a film, that they were responsible for the mass murders both at Belsen and at Auschwitz, then the Prosecution say that they have made out their case, and that the charges which have been put before you have been fully proved. I conclude with the unimaginable assertion that a conservative total of at least one million had been killed by gassing or starvation or disease or murder at these two camps."

A tear fell from Hanns' eye. He knew that the death toll was high, but he refused to allow himself to ponder the number. It would be too much for him to bear. Yet, now, he was forced to face the certainty and his heart became a raging sea of sorrow and anger.

"That number can't be right," someone whispered in front of Hanns.

"They must be exaggerating," another bickered.

"No," another chimed in, "I don't think the number is high enough."

"The defence," the Judge Advocate pointed to the stand.

"May it please the Court," Major Cranfield began, and Hanns wondered what kind of man would have the stomach to defend such evil people, "I would argue against the Prosecution's charges that these men and women before you share in the blame. I have read the witness statements and affidavits collected by the War Crimes Investigation Team, and I'm shocked to find that none of the SS guards who fled Auschwitz are here before us, and, to my knowledge, no one is pursuing them. The incompetence of the Prosecution is so detrimental that, in fact, one of the defendants, Oskar Schmitz," the lawyer motioned to a rather panic-stricken man in the defendant's bench, "was an inmate of the camp and not a guard or responsible by any means. Yet the poor organization of the Prosecution has placed him under these strenuous circumstances instead of returning him to his family. Such an erroneous misjudgment of this defendant will display the level of mismanagement and should bring the entire operation into question. Not only so, but the arrest of these individuals is illegal as it has contravened the promise of withdrawal in the ceasefire agreement.

"Perspective, I believe, will allow us to understand the condition in which these men and women have been placed. In the defence of Dr. Klein, the order which he was given and which he carried out, was in itself lawful under Nazi law. Namely, to divide prisoners into those fit for work and those unfit for work. If he had refused to make the selections himself then other doctors would have done so in his stead. By contrast, a British soldier could refuse to obey an order and he would face a Court Martial when he had an opportunity of contesting the lawfulness or unlawfulness of the order which he had been given. Dr. Klein had no such protection.

"For Josef Kramer, the evidence of Irma Grese will show that beating was done without his authority and without his knowledge. Counsel invited the Court to consider the many difficulties that arose in the course of roll-calls and the people who had to cope with them, and to accept Kramer's word against the uncorroborated allegations contained in some of the affidavits. As to Kramer's responsibility for conditions at Belsen, Counsel maintained that the Court had placed before it sufficient evidence to have a picture of Belsen during the period of December of 1944, until the liberation, when the order which Kramer established changed into disorder, and when disorder changed into chaos.

"Belsen, in itself, was an example of what was happening to Germany as a whole country. More and more people were sent to the camp and Kramer was inadequately provided with medical facilities. Even when he closed the camp in order to avoid further sick people from contracting typhus, he was ordered to keep it open. On the 1st of March, he realized that nothing was going to be done, and so he wrote a dispatch to his superior officer, Glücks, telling him what the present situation was at that date and prophesying a catastrophe.

"Counsel submitted that if blame could be attached to anybody in these chaotic months before V.E. day, it should be laid at the feet of the men who left Kramer in the lurch.

"If the evidence regarding food shortage was analyzed, it would be clear that the evidence relates to the period from about the last week in March to the date of the liberation. At the beginning of April, food was scarce in Germany as a whole. The numbers entering Belsen were meanwhile ever increasing.

"When Kramer came to Belsen, the roll-calls began. Roll-calls were a part of concentration camp life and it was the only way of being able to make out a strength return for rations, especially when transports were coming in at an alarming rate. Counsel will point out the evidence of Grese which showed that roll-calls were not unreasonably frequent or oppressively administered.

"Regarding beatings, Counsel claimed that certain force was necessary to restrain the internees, particularly when there was a shortage of food. It is suggested that the story, by two witnesses, of the kicking of the four Russians and the possible death of one, was a pure invention for the sole purpose of exercising revenge on Kramer. It was also for this reason that these two witnesses accused him of taking an active part in the selections at Auschwitz.

"Dr. Klein was a locum at Belsen for ten days in January and when he returned he was under Dr. Horstmann's orders and was not the senior doctor. Dr. Klein has stated that Dr. Horstmann specifically allocated to him the task of looking after the SS troops and SS personnel. It was only three days before the British came that Dr. Klein became the chief medical officer and, I might add, the only medical officer at Belsen concentration camp.

"I would place before the Court that the evidence will show that the real war criminals are not in this courtroom and are still at large. These accused are being made to serve as examples when the British Administration should be pursuing those responsible for the atrocities of Auschwitz and Belsen."

"That's the only point I agree with him on," Hanns whispered to Fox.

"That's one more point than me," Fox replied.

"The Prosecution," the judge called dispassionately. Hanns knew that he was required to be impartial, but it drove him mad.

"May it please the Court," Backhouse stood and waved to a couple men to shut off the lights, "the Prosecution would like to present video evidence from Belsen. This film was taken when the British authorities went into the camp, and it will give you some idea of the conditions and the degradation to which humanity can descend. You will see the thousands of corpses lying about and the condition of those bodies. You will also see the well-fed condition of the SS who were stationed there. You will see people fishing for water with tins in a small tank. What you will not see is that the water was foul and that there were bodies in it. That was all the water that was available to drink. You will see the dead, you will see the living, and you will actually see the dying. What the film cannot provide is the abominable smell and the filth and squalor of the whole place. If there is any one of the accused who suggests that he did not know what the conditions were, if you will merely draw the only possible inference when you have seen the film, the Prosecution will ask you to say that it is a hopeless lie for anyone to suggest that he did not know what was happening in that camp."

The film began to roll as the courtroom, with the exception of a stifled gasp, became deathly silent. The world watched the images of bodies piled upon bodies, Dr. Klein standing before the mass graves, and the survivors who were mere skin and bones. The skeptical Germans who were watching in the courtroom now had to face the cold facts that were displayed before them. The firm belief that these camps had been nothing more than propaganda was stripped away by the rising tide of evidence. In contrast, the survivors and relatives watched with tears streaming down their faces. Some, unable to stomach another image, excused themselves and left the courtroom. Regardless of background, demographic, nationality, or sex, everyone who was watching the film experienced something that would never leave them.

The film stopped, the lights were turned back on, and Backhouse returned to his seat as he adjusted his uniform.

"The defence," the judge called.

Hanns watched with delight as Major Cranfield shook his head slightly.

"There's no way he can defend that!" Hanns leaned over to Fox.

"Of course not," Fox replied. "Cranfield isn't defending the concentration camps as a whole. He's defending the specific charges brought against the individuals accused."

"Hmm," Hanns frowned.

"May it please the Court," Backhouse stood, "the Prosecution would like to call the first witness to the stand."

Hanns strained his neck as he watched a petite woman approach while clutching her purse tightly. A man also approached with her and stood just to her right, but far enough away that Hanns understood their relationship to be purely professional.

"Please state your name," Backhouse began as he stood near the witness with his hands in his pockets. He seemed much too casual for Hanns' liking.

At this, the man standing beside her spoke to her and Hanns understood that he was her interpreter.

"Ilona Stein," the woman replied timidly and Hanns noticed that she had a strong Hungarian accent.

"Where are you from?" Backhouse asked. "And please state your age."

"Gyongyos, Hungary. Twenty-one," she replied in English, though she spoke slowly.

"And you were taken to the camps?"

"Yes."

"Why?"

"I am a Jewess," Ilona cleared her throat. "I was taken to Auschwitz, and then sent to Belsen. I worked in the kitchen at Auschwitz."

"And what was your assignment in Belsen?"

"I was part of smaller working groups."

"Did you ever see the selections for the gas chambers?"

"Yes," Ilona began to tremble, "but the selections happened so often that I'm afraid I'm unable to give an accurate accounting."

"Your affidavit testifies to ill-treatment such as beatings and starvation. Can you identify those responsible for the camp and for the trials you and many others endured?"

While quivering, Ilona pointed at Irma and then at Josef, "No. 1 is Josef Kramer, and No. 9 is Irma Grese."

"Thank you, Miss Stein," Backhouse strolled slowly over to the defendant's bench. "How do you know them?"

"Everyone at the camp knew them."

"You saw this woman," Backhouse pointed at Irma, "beating other prisoners?"

"That's correct. She beat prisoners regularly at Auschwitz, though not as much in Belsen."

"Did she ever beat you?"

"On one occasion, yes," Ilona nodded.

"Can you describe the circumstance?"

"She saw me talking with a friend through the barbed-wire fence and she immediately started beating me."

"What did she beat you with?"

"Her belt."

"Your statement also mentions another tragedy where your friend was murdered. Can you explain?"

"My friend was shot by No. 16, Francioh," she pointed at the defendant, "while we were near the kitchen."

"And why were you near the kitchen, Miss Stein?"

"It was the only way to get some extra food," Ilona shrugged. "We were starving."

"Yet you've heard the defence state that they did not have adequate food to feed everyone. Can you attest to this?"

"I worked in the kitchen at Auschwitz," Ilona swallowed, and Hanns could see, even from a distance, that her heart was racing as she recalled her horrible experiences. "I saw the food that Kramer and Irma ate, and the food that was given to us prisoners. The inequality was startling. None of the SS went malnourished."

"The defence may cross-examine her now," Backhouse nodded his thanks to Ilona.

"Miss Stein," Major Cranfield stood and walked over to her as he stared at his feet thoughtfully, "you described in your testament, which I have read over carefully, that you witnessed defendant No. 16, Francioh, shooting prisoners."

Ilona glanced at the interpreter for some assistance. While she could speak English, Hanns noticed that her level of comprehension was moderate at best. Especially under these circumstances with all attention being concentrated on her.

"That's correct," Ilona nodded after conferring.

"Was she Hungarian?"

"Yes."

"Where was the shooting?"

"Outside the kitchen."

"Why were you outside the kitchen?" Cranfield asked quickly which upset Hanns. The defence lawyer was taking advantage of her competency with a foreign language to confound the accuracy of her answers.

"The best work is in the kitchen. It's where one can get an extra drop of soup," Ilona replied just as quickly and Hanns was pleased that she handled herself well under pressure.

"But, from what you stated, you weren't allowed near the kitchen."

"No one was," Ilona's voice trembled. "If one dared get too close it would elicit a beating."

"So why were you near the kitchen if you knew that the result would be a beating?"

"Again, it was the only chance to get some more soup. We were starving."

"And it was during one of these 'gatherings' near the kitchen that you stated that Francioh began shooting."

"That's correct."

"And you stated that he shot your friend."

"That he did," Ilona glared at Francioh who glared back with no emotion.

"What happened when he started shooting?"

"I turned and ran away."

"Did your friend run?"

"I was concerned about getting away as soon as possible. I didn't see if she ran away or not."

"So you didn't see with your own eyes what happened to your friend?"

"I didn't, but a few minutes later they were taking away my friend's body. It's quite clear to me who killed her."

"Was the body taken away by stretcher?"

"When someone died at the camp, which happened quite often, their body was placed into a blanket and dragged away."

"And you're sure it was this man who killed her," Cranfield pointed at Francioh.

"Of course."

"But there were many SS cooks in the kitchen, how can you be sure it was he?"

"There was only one man in charge of the kitchen, and that was Francioh. He started shooting."

"But you didn't see your friend die?"

"No."

"Yet you swore, in your statement," Cranfield lifted the affidavit, "that you saw your friend be shot by this man."

"She came towards the kitchen with an empty container and that man drew his pistol and began shooting. Then she was dead."

"As I have demonstrated in my opening remarks, there was a food shortage and Kramer was given the unimaginable task of feeding many with little. Didn't you understand that the food rations needed to be guarded severely?"

Ilona didn't answer.

"Irma Grese," Cranfield changed direction, "you stated that you saw her beating prisoners with her belt."

"That's correct," Ilona nodded.

"I have here a belt worn by Irma," Cranfield waved to one of his attendants who ran up to him with a thin, black belt.

"Now, you can see how flimsy this belt is," Cranfield folded it and swung it around in the air before striking it hard against his own arm. It landed lightly against his flesh despite the strength he put into the swing. "This was the standard belt issued to all guards. As I have demonstrated, this belt would cause no harm whatsoever."

"This may have been an issue with translation. I was referring to the custom-made whip that she would beat prisoners with," Ilona replied. "There was no reason for the beatings. None of us had stolen anything. We were simply standing about, hoping for some extra food."

"You reported that Irma would force the prisoners to stand for hours on end when even one of the prisoners was missing from roll call."

"That's correct."

"You also stated that she would force sick prisoners to attend roll call, even if they had fevers."

"Yes."

"How did you know that they had fevers? Did you take their temperatures? Do you have any medical experience?"

"I can only speak to my own experience," she cleared her throat. "A girl in my block was feverish. I took her pulse and felt her forehead and knew that she must've been close to forty degrees. She fainted during the roll call, but Irma threw freezing cold water on her to bring her back to consciousness and forced her to stand."

"You told the court that you were upset that she would report prisoners as sick to the hospital instead of forcing them to work?"

"The hospital was a temporary holding cell for the people they would send to the gas chambers."

"So, you would rather that Irma forced the prisoners to work. What would you have done in her place?"

"I would've reported the sick people as having certain duties. I would've found a way to keep as many alive as possible. At Birkenau, I have seen Grese making selections with Dr. Mengele of people to be sent to the gas chamber. In one selection, there were between two to three thousand who were selected. At this selection, Grese and Mengele were responsible for selecting those for the gas chamber. People chosen would sometimes sneak away from the roll call and hide themselves under their beds. Grese would go and find them, beat them until they collapsed and then drag them back into line again. I have seen everything I describe. It was general knowledge in this camp that persons selected in this way went to the gas chamber."

"Thank you," Cranfield gave a slight nod. "The defence would like to call Irma Grese to the stand."

"I don't hear her singing today," Fox whispered to Hanns as he mocked her.

"Still, she looks as defiant as ever," Hanns replied as he watched Irma walk towards the stand, guided by the guards.

"Irma Grese," Cranfield began with his hands behind his back. "How many prisoners were in your care at Auschwitz in camp 'C'?"

"About thirty thousand."

"And how many huts were there?"

"There were about twenty-eight living huts."

"And how many could a single hut accommodate?"

"Anywhere from one hundred to a maximum of three hundred."

"Yet you had thirty thousand people that you were required to house? That means that each hut housed around one thousand prisoners?"

"Correct. In the beginning, when there were smaller numbers and sufficient rations, the prisoners behaved civilly. Later, when the population grew to about thirty thousand, they behaved like animals. When the food became scarce, they waited, in groups of twenty to thirty people, to pounce on the kitchen workers and take their food away. In regards to sanitation, in the beginning the camp was well kept. Later, when the population increased, the prisoners seemed to find it acceptable to use anywhere for a latrine. The proper latrines were ruined when they threw junk inside and they ceased to function."

"How could anyone possibly believe her?" Hanns shook his head.

"Just wait until Backhouse gets to her," Fox leaned over with a smile of anticipation.

"You received orders for what has been called 'selection parades'," Cranfield continued. "Did you know what this was for?"

"No," Irma replied curtly as if the very question was offensive.

"What were the prisoners supposed to do when the whistle went?"

"Fall in fives, and it was my duty to see that they did so. Dr. Mengele then came and made the selection. As I was responsible for the camp my duties were to know how many people were leaving and I had to count them, and I kept the figures in a strength book. After the selection took place they were sent into "B" Camp, and I was told that they had gone to another camp in Germany for working purposes or for special treatment, which I thought was the gas chamber. I then put in my strength book either so many for transfer to another camp, or so many for the gas chamber."

"Were you told anything about the gas chamber by your senior officers?"

"No, I found out from the prisoners."

"But you were accused of choosing prisoners to be sent to the gas chambers."

"That's a lie."

"When these prisoners were paraded, they were often naked and inspected like cattle. Is that true?"

"Not like cattle," Irma replied with just enough sarcasm that Hanns was required to strain his violent wishes towards her.

"You were there keeping order, were you not, and if one ran away you brought her back and gave her a beating?"

"Yes."

"Did you beat them with a specially made whip?"

"Yes, one made of cellophane. It was a light whip, but still effective. Kramer forbid the use of the whips, but we continued regardless."

"Will you explain to the Court on what occasions you struck prisoners, and the reason why you did it?"

"In the beginning I did not use anything at all, but when the crowds became larger, a great deal was stolen and prisoners did not obey my orders. Even when they were simple orders, I was forced to take action. Every day I received complaints of things stolen in the kitchen. On those occasions, I used my whip."

"Have you ever taken an individual prisoner and beaten her until she was bleeding or fell senseless to the ground, or have you ever kicked a prisoner whom you have struck to the ground?"

"At Auschwitz, never. But at Belsen, the condition of the prisoners was so bad that one had almost a horror of them. One had to be ruthless to keep order."

"At Auschwitz did you ever have a dog?"

"No. There were trained dogs, but I had nothing to do with them."

"Ilona Stein, in her affidavit, alleged that there was an incident when a mother was talking to her daughter over the wire between two compounds, and that you beat the mother so severely until she fell to the ground where you began kicking her?"

"I do not deny that I beat her, but I did not beat her until she fell to the ground, and I did not kick her either."

"Miss Stein, also in her affidavit, accused you of setting your dog on to her. Is this true?"

"I never had a dog."

Growing frustrated, Hanns leaned over to Fox, "Why didn't he bring this up with Stein while she was at the stand?"

"Probably because he knows that this is true, and he doesn't want to give Stein the opportunity to give credibility," Fox shrugged. "That's what I would've done if I were in his position."

"Will you tell the Court," Cranfield began pacing, "what the conditions at Belsen were like when you arrived there at the beginning of March this year, and what they were between then and the arrival of the British?"

"Transports arrived almost daily, and the camps became overcrowded. I was horrified because the prisoners were so dirty and sick. I had to attend the roll call twice a week, and every time I came back from the camp I felt horrified."

"At Auschwitz, did you ever consult or plan with Kramer or Dr. Klein as to who was to go to the gas chamber?"

"We never talked about these things. Kramer and Dr. Klein were my superior officers, and if Kramer came into the camp I had to make out my report as was my duty, and nothing else."

"Have you ever planned with Kramer or any other person to put to death in any way or to ill-treat deliberately any person at Auschwitz?"

"No. I am not capable of making plans and I never made a plan to kill prisoners."

"Have you ever planned with them the death or deliberate ill-treatment of a prisoner at Belsen?"

"Never."

"The defence has finished with their cross-examination," Cranfield nodded to the Judge Advocate and sat back down.

"Watch this," Fox almost sounded giddy as he whispered to Hanns. "Backhouse will call her out on her lies."

"Miss Grese," Backhouse studied her with an unrelenting indignation and Hanns smiled with eagerness, "were you not in charge of a group working at a sand-pit?"

"As I explained in my affidavit to Major Cranfield, I was in charge for two days of a work group that brought in stones from outside the camp."

"I'm aware of what you said," Backhouse narrowed his gaze as he raised his voice slightly, "but I'm suggesting that you did not speak the truth. There was also a great deal of sand brought into the camp for the road, was there not?"

"I don't know," Irma looked at Backhouse and Hanns thought that she might be shaking with rage.

"But you were with the group building the roads?"

"I don't know."

"Don't you know what your prisoners were doing while you were in charge?"

"They were putting stones in the ground and hammering them for the purpose of road-making."

"So you never saw the sand-pit?"

"That's correct."

"I would suggest that while you were at the sand-pit, you knew of the wire placed around the perimeter which, if a prisoner crossed over, they would be shot by a guard. I would also suggest that you used to amuse yourself by sending women outside the wire so that they would be shot. Is that true?"

"You can think what you like, but that is a lie," Irma clenched her jaw.

"She doesn't like him much does she?" Fox whispered to Hanns who smiled back at him.

"Did you not have a dog to guard these working parties?" Backhouse continued.

"No."

"But they were trained to watch the Kommandos going out of the camp. Why weren't you allowed to have one?"

"I didn't want one."

"But you did, in fact, have a dog and you used this animal to round up stragglers," Backhouse's voice swelled with conviction.

"I should know better whether or not I had a dog," Irma began to shift in the stand as she glared at Backhouse, and Hanns wondered if she wished that she still had her dog now.

"I have here the affidavit of the witness Rozenwayg," Backhouse held the file high in the air, "who stated that you set your dog on her and it bit her on the shoulder."

"She might have been bitten by a dog, and it may have bitten her on the shoulder," Irma matched Backhouse's fervor, "but since I never had a dog I couldn't have set it upon anybody."

"I suggest that when you went out on these working parties, you made a habit of beating and kicking women and you enjoyed it?"

"And I would suggest that you have been woefully misinformed."

"Gertrud Diament," Backhouse held up another file, "in her disposition said that your favorite habit was to beat women until they fell to the ground where you would then kick them as hard as you could with your heavy boots."

"Perhaps it is Gertrud's habit to lie," Irma clenched her jaw.

"The whip that you made out of cellophane, did others have these whips made too?"

"No."

"So it was just your bright idea then?" Backhouse glared at her.

"Yes," Irma replied dryly.

"Was it not a practice, at Auschwitz, to have the officers to be of different nationalities than those assigned to them so that they could confuse the prisoners?"

"That's not the case at all. When the Hungarians arrived, they came at one thousand per block. I used the experienced officers from previous transports so that proper order would be kept."

"But even experienced officers would be inadequate to organize a block of one thousand people meant to fit only one to three hundred," Backhouse shook his head.

"That was only at the beginning, for about two weeks."

"Why, were they killed off quickly?"

"They were strong people," Irma glared at Backhouse. "They went out on working parties."

"Lebowitz in her affidavit says she often saw you with Dr. Mengele selecting people for the gas chamber and for forced work in Germany, and that if you saw relations trying to get together in selections for forced work you beat them until they were unconscious and left them lying on the ground. Is that true?"

"It is true that when they ran away I brought them back and I might have beaten them," Irma swallowed nervously, "but it is imagination to say I have beaten them till they lay on the ground or until they were bleeding or perhaps until they were dead."

"The witness Ilona Stein said that prisoners that tried to escape were shot if they got far, or were brought back and were terribly beaten, and were put back in their lines again. Is that true?"

"Why should one shoot people inside the camp?" Irma shook her head as she spoke defiantly. "There is barbed wire around the camp so they cannot escape."

"When people were sent to the gas chamber, you entered that in your logbooks as 'special treatment'. Were you forbidden to speak outside the camp about the mass killings?"

"I do not know whether it was allowed, but it was already kept secret through the fact that you were never allowed to leave the camp because it was closed on account of typhus."

"Did you often keep prisoners as long as three and four hours on roll-call?"

"As an exception, but it was usually one to two hours."

"And you made people stand still then, did you not?"

"Of course."

"If they moved they were beaten, were they not?"

"That is nonsense," Irma scoffed. "I did not say that they were not allowed to move."

"If people did not behave as you wanted them to, did you sometimes make them kneel?"

"Yes."

"On other occasions did you not make some people hold stones above their heads?"

"No, that is a fabrication."

"I suggest that if any of these internees did not stand still on the roll-call you either made them kneel or hold stones above their heads for a long time, and if they faltered you beat them?"

"No."

"Several witnesses in their depositions say that you were the worst SS woman in the camp."

"They are all lying. These people exaggerated and made an elephant out of a small fly."

"Do you or do you not remember the incident when a mother was trying to talk to her daughter across the wire and you beat her until she fell to the ground?"

"No."

"Have you beaten so many women that you cannot remember whether it happened or not?"

"I do not remember this incident, and I did not beat so many women that I would not be able to remember."

"The witness Ilona Stein speaks of an incident when you kicked her too. I suggest to you that you regularly kicked people and it was all part and parcel of this business of swaggering around in top-boots?"

"I would like to know who has seen me swaggering in the camp. I have never kicked anyone."

"Did you not regularly beat people at that gate?"

"I would like to ask you to leave out this word 'regularly'."

"Did you regularly," Backhouse paid special attention to the word, "carry your whip at Belsen?"

"No."

"Did you realize that people were dying all around you at Belsen?"

"Of course I realized it."

"Did you realize the amount of food that these prisoners were getting, and did you think that that was a proper way to treat them?"

"No."

"I suggest to you that you gloried in your jackboots and your pistol and your whip?"

"Gloried? I wouldn't say so."

"And that you beat and ill-treated prisoners to such an extent that even you were told to stop carrying a whip, and that you continued to do it?"

"I have beaten prisoners, but I have not ill-treated them, and it was not prohibited for me personally to carry a whip. It was a general order emanating from Kramer that whips were not to be carried anymore."

"You are aware that your sister, Helene Grese, provided a testimony?"

"Of course."

"In her testimony," Backhouse paused as he rubbed his chin and Hanns could sense that he was building up to a grand conclusion, "your sister stated that you and your father quarreled. Why?"

"I was part of the SS and he didn't approve," Irma replied, and Hanns detected that she wasn't appreciative of such a personal question.

"And you were about fourteen years of age when you left home, correct?"

"Yes."

"Your mother committed suicide, correct?"

"I don't understand how this is relevant," Irma spoke softly.

"Please answer the question," Backhouse pressed.

"Yes."

"Your father was having an affair and your mother discovered this which drove her to end her life, correct?"

Irma nodded.

"I require an answer, Miss Grese," Backhouse persisted unapologetically.

"Yes," Irma gritted her teeth.

"Let me put this finally to you," Backhouse paused again. "According to your sister, you were a frightened, cowardly young girl. You are exactly the sort that the SS recruits. Because, with the SS, you found yourself for the first time in a position where you could strike others and they were unable to strike you back."

"I might have been, as my sister said, cowardly as a child, but I grew up in the meantime," Irma's knuckles flushed white as she gripped the bars on the stand.

"In conclusion," Backhouse cleared his throat, "with the insurmountable evidence and testimonies exposing your brutality, I put it to you that you have lied. You did work at the sand pits where you entertained yourself by killing women through tricking them to cross the barbed wire, you did have a dog that you used to terrorize those under your care, and you did regularly beat and mistreat women so badly that they were unable to stand. Is this not true?!" Backhouse slammed his hand on the stand in front of Irma.

"No," Irma replied bitterly.

"I have no further questions," Backhouse returned to his seat.

"The Court shall take a brief recess," the Judge Advocate waved as Irma left the stand and returned to her booth. "Then we shall hear from other witnesses who will take the stand."

At once, the court burst into heated chatter as everyone had waited patiently to share their opinions. The exits became clogged as the spectators clamored to get outside. A shout or two erupted from the crowded hallways as disagreements broke out between the German spectators and the 'occupiers'.

"I think I've seen enough for one day," Hanns spoke to Fox as he wrapped his jacket over his arm.

"Take the truck," Fox nodded. "I'll catch a ride back."

"You sure?"

"Ya I'd like to stay for the closing statements," Fox gave a slight pat on Hanns' arm who looked at his Captain curiously for the gesture.

"You alright?" Hanns pressed.

"Of course," Fox replied quickly.

"Is this one of those English things where you're being modest?" Hanns leaned in.

"No," Fox laughed nervously. "It's just...I...I'm fine."

"You sure?"

"Ya, you head on out," Fox gave another pat on Hanns' shoulder.

"Howard?" a familiar voice called from the crowd and Hanns turned to see Genn pushing his way through the aisle towards him.

"Lieutenant Colonel," Hanns gave a quick salute when Genn had arrived.

"Glad you made it," Genn smiled briefly, but looked around the courtroom and seemed to be tense.

"Is there something that I can help you with?" Hanns asked.

"Why don't we have a chat outside," Genn pointed over his shoulder.

"Sure," Hanns shrugged. "Everything alright?"

"Yep," Genn replied quickly as he headed for the door.

Curious at what this fuss was about, Hanns followed silently behind Genn as they slowly moved their way through the crowd and exited the 'courtroom'.

"There looks decent," Genn pointed to a bench under some trees about a hundred yards away.

"After you," Hanns replied, still intrigued by the irregular behavior displayed by both Fox and Genn. He felt rather like he had as a schoolboy being sent to the principal's office for some misdemeanor and assumed he was about to be scolded.

Sitting on the bench, Genn retrieved a cigarette and began smoking as Hanns sat beside him. Glancing at Genn, Hanns noticed that he was avoiding eye contact and fidgeting with his hands.

"Sir?" Hanns leaned in.

"Yes?" Genn glanced at him quickly.

"The suspense is killing me here," Hanns pressed.

"Just wanted to chat is all," Genn gave a light backhanded slap on Hanns' leg. "You know, they're about to read the statement you took from Josef Kramer."

"How can they defend those men?" Hanns rubbed his eyes.

"It's important that they do," Genn looked at Hanns earnestly. "As hard as that is to understand."

"What do you mean?" Hanns frowned.

"When Hitler took power, he abolished Habeas Corpus. It's imperative that it is returned to Germany."

"But not for degenerates like them," Hanns glanced back at the 'courtroom'.

"Yes, but the danger arrives from those who decide what constitutes a 'degenerate' person," Genn raised an eyebrow. "To you and me, those in there are, yes, degenerate and not deserving of a fair trial. If I had my way, I'd shoot each and every one of them myself. But when the wrong people take power, as we've seen, and decent people are labeled as 'degenerate' because of the coincidence of their birth, then the world quickly goes to hell. It's vital that they get a fair trial, and not for their sakes, but for the benefit of those who deserve one. Even when the guilt is obvious, it needs to be recorded, proven, and given proper jurisprudence. The German people need to have their transgressions made bare and the world to be their jury. The Nazis fed this country with so many lies, and twisted the truth to such a degree, that the population is confused. They must see the truth through just and fair means."

Hanns pondered quietly as he watched Genn and was thankful beyond words for his friendship. His commanding officer could be stern and unyielding, but when it mattered the most, Genn was a dear friend.

"Though, I think I share some of the defence lawyer's concerns."

"Like what?" Hanns frowned and turned towards Genn sharply.

"The organization for the prosecution was sloppy, for which I take the blame."

"Sloppy?!" Hanns chuckled ironically. "Lieutenant Colonel, only two on our team had any police experience. The rest, including the two of us, are laymen with no understanding of the complexities of the legal system. The British government is to blame, not you."

"Speaking of which," Genn looked at Hanns with a promising grin, "I have excellent news for you."

"Really?" Hanns looked at him in surprise.

"I didn't really bring you out here just to chat," Genn beamed. "The British government has been chastised in front of the whole world for its lack of resources towards hunting down Nazis."

"Are you telling me what I think you're telling me?" Hanns sat up straight as his excitement grew.

"That's right," Genn smiled playfully. "You now have authority to go wherever you want to hunt and arrest any SS or Nazi criminals you find."

"That's such great news!" Hanns stood and began to pace as his mind ran wild.

"That it is," Genn laughed heartily.

"Where shall I start?"

"Do you remember Miss Hodys?" Genn tried to return to solemnity, but his happiness was impossible to contain.

"Who could forget her?" Hanns huffed as he continued to pace, not entirely paying attention as his mind was filling with ambition.

"Remember that town where we bought her that dress?"

"I do," Hanns nodded, still not paying much attention.

"Gustav Simon," Genn looked off into the distance. "He is your first assignment."

"The Gauleiter of Luxembourg?" Hanns couldn't believe what he was hearing. "Are you certain?"

"Entirely," Genn nodded.

"This is huge," Hanns shook his head in bewilderment. "Gustav Simon is one of the most hated men in all the Third Reich. Any leads on his whereabouts?"

"None whatsoever," Genn looked at him with a slight smile, "but thanks to Eleonore Hodys, we have a clue to where his son might be. We know that the Gauleiter's son is in hiding and that he visited that town. If we can capture the son, I have faith that we can squeeze out the father."

"What about Hoess?"

"Do you have any information on him? Because if you do, we should start there," Genn scoffed. "Gustav Simon is your target. Show them that we are capable, then hopefully they will give us resources or intelligence that will lead to Rudolph. Also, you've been promoted to Captain," Genn stood and extended his hand towards Hanns who shook it vibrantly.

"When can I get started?" Hanns asked eagerly.

"Start now," Genn shrugged. "At the office are travel permits, handcuffs, a pistol, and a list of wanted criminals. They are for you."

"You knew about my assignment already, didn't you?" Hanns squinted.

"I was going to keep it to myself until the end of today," Genn chuckled, "but I suppose it's best that someone of your mischievous nature remains occupied. Besides, I'm as anxious as you to begin the hunt."

"I'm sure you've thought of a clever name for this operation?" Hanns crossed his arms as he grinned.

"Operation Haystack," Genn nodded. "You, Hanns Volker, are to find the needle. You are the first Nazi hunter in history. By the way, do you know what day it is today?"

"Yom Kippur," Hanns smiled cheekily.

"The Jewish day of atonement," Genn smiled back. "Quite fitting, I believe."

Chapter Fifteen: Memories

Tis better to have loved and lost than to never have loved at all.

Alfred Lord Tennyson

Eleonore awoke to the blissful chirping of birds outside her window. With a stretch and a yawn, she looked at the clock to see that it was still 4:30AM. With a smile, she snuggled into her pillow to enjoy a few more heavenly minutes of sleep. Months had passed by as she served Mrs. Meyers in her tightly regulated schedule. With the arrival of fall - Eleonore's favorite season – there was a tranquility in the manor which hadn't been felt since she had arrived.

Eleonore had found a new home and maybe, just maybe, she was starting to develop affection for Ben. Her nights were still filled with nightmarish manifestations of Rudolph and Ella, but Eleonore would wake up and head to the kitchen or the front of the manor where she would smoke and talk with the butler who was tormented by his own dreams. She had pressed to discover the reason for his insomnia, but he refused to divulge any secrets of his past to her. Still, he was a comfort to Eleonore and she looked forward to their nightly chats. She supposed it appeared rather scandalous, but the truth was, unfortunately, rather boring. They would visit, smoke, eat, and then withdraw without any hint of affection.

Maybe that's why I'm drawn to him, she pondered. *He doesn't feign affection for carnal purposes. He simply enjoys my company as I have come to welcome his.*

Mr. Mattaliano wasn't the sort of man that she would typically have seen herself 'falling for', but still, she found herself thinking about him while he wasn't around. He would look at her with a smile that was kind, not like the smile she had witnessed from Rudolph or even Jung at times. He would cook an Italian dish for her most nights, and Eleonore would take a turn here and there cooking for him. Eventually, his insistence on cooking led Eleonore to believe that the culinary arts were not her calling and his polite way of letting her down easy.

Jung, or whoever the man was that night, had not reappeared since Eleonore first saw him. She would've believed that she had fabricated him altogether had Ben not said anything. Still, her pact with the butler held true and he protected her as she held onto the knowledge of his future with the manor. But as time passed, Ben seemed less and less concerned with his material prospects and Eleonore hoped that she held some influence in this regard.

A knock came to the door, stirring Eleonore from her pleasant rest.

"Eleonore?" Eva called and sounded rather flustered.

"Yes?" Eleonore sat up quickly, worried that something terrible had happened to Ben. She found it odd that her thoughts leapt to some tragedy, but in the back of her mind she was cautiously optimistic about the future, knowing how it felt to have all joy stripped away from her.

"It's Mrs. Meyers," Eva replied, her voice still wavering.

"What about her?" Eleonore threw her robe over her shoulders as she opened the door.

"She's in a terrible state," Eva looked at Eleonore with the deepest concern.

"How so?" Eleonore gave a suspicious glance out into the hallway.

"She's demanding to speak with you at once."

"Where is she?" Eleonore frowned.

"She's downstairs, in the foyer."

"The foyer?!" Eleonore turned her head slightly, holding her conclusion in reserve.

"I know that I haven't given you reason to trust me," Eva looked remorseful, "but I'm telling you the truth."

"Miss Hodys!" Ben called from the bottom of the winding stairs.

"Coming!" Eleonore shouted as she waved for Eva to make way.

Locking the door behind her, Eleonore burst towards the stairs and quickly descended, covered in only her nightgown and robe. Only when she saw Ben beside Mrs. Meyers in the foyer did she become painfully aware of her disheveled hair and the lines on her face from the pillow.

But Eleonore's concerns were diverted to Mrs. Meyers who was standing before the doors, already dressed for the day and holding an umbrella at her side. Eleonore approached the mistress carefully as one approaches a wounded animal.

"Mrs. Meyers?" Eleonore asked cautiously.

"I want to go for a walk," Mrs. Meyers raised her umbrella and tapped the glass of the door with the metal end.

"Really?!" Eleonore threw her head back in shock but then gave a smile to Ben who returned the excitement.

"I do not repeat myself," Mrs. Meyers gave a steel glance at Eleonore who, at the time, though maybe inappropriate, thought it was rather ironic that she had heard that phrase more than a handful of times.

"I'll get dressed immediately," Eleonore bounded up the stairs, followed by an eager Eva.

"What are you doing?" Eleonore asked Eva.

"I'm helping you," Eva nodded and seemed to be genuinely excited.

"I can manage on my own," Eleonore growled, and a disappointed Eva stopped in her tracks and returned to the foyer.

I've put on a few pounds, Eleonore grumbled as she returned to the room and struggled with her dress which was tighter than usual. *Though I suppose, given the circumstances, that this a good sign that I'm returning to my previous weight.*

After dressing quickly, Eleonore rushed back downstairs and was at once by Mrs. Meyers' side. Still, Mrs. Meyers remained idle, staring nervously out the front doors. Ben and Eva stood at a distance, watching with eager anticipation. Even the cook had heard about the peculiarity and withdrew from his greasy sanctuary to witness the spectacle.

"Mrs. Meyers?" Eleonore whispered as she held out her arm.

"What are you doing?" Mrs. Meyers glanced at Eleonore's arm.

"Take it," Eleonore moved it closer to her.

"I can do this on my own," Mrs. Meyers held her chin high.

"I know," Eleonore nodded sympathetically, "but you don't have to."

With a tear in her eye, Mrs. Meyers glanced again at Eleonore and then down at her arm. Slowly, Mrs. Meyers put her arm around Eleonore's and the two took a step towards the door.

Mrs. Meyers paused as she put her hand to the door and a tear rolled down her cheek. Eleonore understood that for Mrs. Meyers to leave the manor, this would be instrumental in her path towards healing. This would be her first step towards letting her husband and sons rest, and Eleonore knew how impossible this task was for her.

"It's just a door," Eleonore whispered.

At this, Mrs. Meyers burst into a short laugh and smiled at Eleonore. Removing her handkerchief, Mrs. Meyers gave a quick blow, took a deep breath, and pushed the door open as she walked briskly outwards. Ben, Eva, and even the cook began clapping as the door closed behind them.

"I wish they would not indulge," Mrs. Meyers grumbled.

"They are proud of you," Eleonore gave a light tap with her free hand on Mrs. Meyers' arm.

"They are patronizing me," Mrs. Meyers began to fume.

"You're being silly," Eleonore discarded her concerns. "They love you and you should appreciate having such people in your life."

"You are welcome to agree with me from time to time," Mrs. Meyers gave a slight smile. "We mustn't always disagree."

"Did you just use a contraction?" Eleonore looked at Mrs. Meyers in awe.

"It seems that you're having a rather poor influence on me," Mrs. Meyers smiled slightly then, suddenly, when they were standing on the stone bridge overlooking the stream, she froze.

"What's wrong?" Eleonore stopped.

"This bridge," Mrs. Meyers spoke quietly. "Recollections I thought long forgotten or buried seem to have found their way to the surface."

"All the walks you took with your husband?"

Mrs. Meyers gave a quick nod as it was all she could offer while barely containing her emotions.

"Take a minute," Eleonore helped Mrs. Meyers over to the stone wall on the bridge where the two of them sat.

Eleonore waited patiently as they listened to the babbling of the stream underneath while Mrs. Meyers' memories floated by.

"I cannot live this way," Mrs. Meyers held her handkerchief by her face as she caught the tears that escaped. "There is so much pressure on my chest. It feels like someone is sitting on me."

Eleonore's heart broke for this woman whose grief had no end. She recalled the loss of her mother and how broken she had been; she couldn't imagine the pain of losing a husband and children. She remembered how surprised she had been that grief was physical more than it was emotional, and she assumed that Mrs. Meyers was still feeling the tangible heartache.

"I don't mean to be dramatic," Mrs. Meyers calmed a little and spoke as she sniffled, "but I don't feel like going on."

Reaching over, Eleonore took her hand in hers and looked earnestly at her mistress. She understood that there was nothing which she could say to lessen the pain and, maybe, the simple act of listening was more beneficial.

"Everything that I took pleasure in has been robbed from me," Mrs. Meyers finally lost control as she wept. "This road is nothing but a painful reminder of what once was. We were happy, you know, we were happier than most families. I was the grumpy one out of the lot," she chuckled slightly through the sobbing. "My sons would know just what to say to correct my scowl. They were such teases, those boys. Even my husband was amused by their tomfoolery."

"And do you think your husband would want you to be sad now?" Eleonore pressed.

"His emotions were rather cryptic," Mrs. Meyers glanced at Eleonore as she calmed a little. "It was hard to decipher what he was thinking. But he was raised with the perception that emotions are weakness."

"I understand that this is difficult, but-"

"Oh what do you know?!" Mrs. Meyers turned to sudden rage.

Eleonore had grown accustomed to her outbursts and wasn't bothered in the slightest. She knew how difficult it was for Mrs. Meyers to have these forthright discussions. Her instinct was to push Eleonore away like someone who was in darkness having to cover their eyes at the sudden break of light.

"I know that you feel lost," Eleonore began. "I know that grief is a journey we take alone. I know that you're tired and desperate for this suffering to end. I can't promise you that this will ever lessen, or that your trials will ease, but I can promise you that I know what is right."

"And what's that?" Mrs. Meyers looked deep into Eleonore's eyes as her lips trembled.

"Getting up," Eleonore's lips trembled as well, "and taking one step after the other, and realizing that you're not alone on this road. You've got a friend to help keep your balance and to catch you if you stumble."

"I can't go on," Mrs. Meyers burst into sobs.

"When I was in the camps," Eleonore began.

"I told you I won't hear a word of it," Mrs. Meyers shook her head vehemently.

"You must," Eleonore spoke as a tear rolled down her cheek. "You must face this."

Shaking, Mrs. Meyers held her head in her hands, abandoning propriety as she wept openly.

"When I was in the camps, there was a Jewish woman who worked in the hospital. She spent her days encouraging those who had lost everything, and everyone, to keep going. I watched her once in awe as she convinced a man to not take his own life. So, I will be that woman to you. Don't focus on the years that lay ahead, or the months, but focus on the next hour. Can you give me an hour to walk this road into town, as impossible as that may seem? Don't think about the return journey, just focus on the way into town."

"That I can do," Mrs. Meyers blew into her handkerchief.

"C'mon," Eleonore stood and held her hand out to Mrs. Meyers.

Taking her hand with an iron grip, Mrs. Meyers stood tall and walked towards town as the tears rolled down her cheeks. Like waves crashing upon the shore, Mrs. Meyers would suddenly burst into emotional fits, but then she would swiftly retreat to a detached state as if all emotion was foreign. Then, again, she would burst into tears. It was heartbreaking to watch, but Eleonore stood by her mistress with patient understanding.

Eventually, Mrs. Meyers seemed to settle and the two of them walked and listened to the surrounding countryside. The crisp fall air was a perfect temperature and Eleonore closed her eyes as she breathed deeply. She recalled the times, as a girl, when her father would make a pile of leaves for her to jump into. The two of them would spend hours running around and playing in nature, and Eleonore wished that she could return to such simplicity.

"My Paul could name each of the creatures you hear," Mrs. Meyers reminisced with a smile as they were serenaded by the critters and frogs from the nearby stream. "He was a clever lad. He could even name the exact genus."

"You two were rather close, weren't you?" Eleonore studied Mrs. Meyers.

"Inseparable," Mrs. Meyers' lips trembled as she paused before continuing. "He was quite unlike his older brothers. Not that I loved them any less, but he was more 'my speed'. Paul was calculated and pensive while his brothers were reactive and more energetic than I could, at most times, manage."

"Sounds like a handful," Eleonore smiled sympathetically.

"They were," Mrs. Meyers looked at her feet as they walked. "But what I would give to catch them being mischievous again. Simply put, they terrorized the manor. They once cut through a painting of my husband's when they were re-enacting the battle scene it depicted. Another time they took his priceless model ships and sent them racing down the stream."

Eleonore smiled as she listened to Mrs. Meyers and wondered if she would've made a good mother to boys of such a wild disposition. From her mistress' description of her sons, Eleonore wished that she could've met them and maybe this, she mused, was indication enough.

"Paul, I believe, was their only voice of reason," Mrs. Meyers began again. "He would try to caution them against their excited plans, but they would never listen. They were much bigger than Paul, being that he was the youngest, and took no pains to hide their bullying. Of course, their sins would find them out and Paul would be punished alongside them as he would be dragged into their excursions."

"I'm sure you could fill a book with their stories," Eleonore grinned.

"A book?" Mrs. Meyers huffed. "I could fill a whole library."

Eleonore laughed.

"I...I think..." Mrs. Meyers paused for a brief moment and Eleonore waited patiently for her to continue, "I think I was so close to Paul because there was something familiar about him."

"How so?" Eleonore frowned.

"Well, he often reminded me of my brother," Mrs. Meyers choked.

"Mr. Mattaliano told me about him," Eleonore spoke softly and gave the slightest squeeze on Mrs. Meyers' hand.

"I am not convinced that Paul was of the same...nature as my brother, but he was of the same character and temperament, if you understand me."

"I believe I do," Eleonore nodded.

"They were both gentle souls," Mrs. Meyers trembled as she spoke, "and I feel a tremendous amount of guilt for not telling my brother that I loved him for who he was. His affiliation was of little consequence to me. Now, you could possibly be convinced that I am lying, being that I am a woman whose primary concern is propriety and my standing in society, but the truth is quite the opposite. I loved him, dearly, and I barely gave his…nature…much consideration. I pretended, Miss Hodys," Mrs. Meyers drew a deep breath, "I pretended that it bothered me when other ladies would whisper their gossip, and I believe that in doing so I wounded him deeply. When the Nazis took him, I realized that I had squandered the opportunity. I wish that I could have held him in my arms and told him that I loved him as he was."

"I'm sure he knows," Eleonore nodded slightly.

"They entrapped him," Mrs. Meyers' countenance devolved into wrath, "the Nazis planted a man to seduce my brother and when he agreed to the compromising proposal, they arrested him. They took my sons. They took my husband. They took everything. And for what?"

"May I ask," Eleonore paused before inquiring, hoping that she wasn't about to cause offence, "why did you take down their photos?"

Glancing at Eleonore, Mrs. Meyers frowned as her breathing labored and Eleonore assumed that she was gathering her thoughts.

"When Paul left to become a pilot," Mrs. Meyers nodded as her eyes welled, "that is when I took them down. I understood that I could do nothing to stop my husband and my other boys from joining; they were preparing for war since they left my womb. But Paul, he was the furthest thing from a soldier. When he was conscripted that was unbearable. I know what war does to a man. The Nazis had killed off my family before they even left to fight."

"You're a strong woman, Mrs. Meyers," Eleonore looked at her in amazement, but Mrs. Meyers huffed.

The two continued down the road and, as they approached the town, Eleonore was nearly startled to death when the horn of a car honked abruptly as it passed by. It had been months since she had heard the ruckus of a motor vehicle and, in that moment, wished that they had never been invented at all. The excellence of nature was drowned out by man's demand for expedience.

Eventually, they arrived at the little town to find scaffolds set against churches and wooden planks resting against houses. Yet, despite the promise of restoration, Eleonore found the town eerily quiet. No one was working and even the shops were closed. Apart from the car which had raced past them, Eleonore would've believed that the town was deserted.

"Do you know what?" Mrs. Meyers stopped in her tracks and closed her eyes as an embarrassed smile crept onto her face.

"What's that?" Eleonore frowned curiously.

"Today is Sunday," Mrs. Meyers opened her eyes and then burst into laughter.

"Oh," Eleonore giggled, "none of the shops are open."

"That was silly," Mrs. Meyers reached out her hand for Eleonore to steady her and the two returned in the direction of the manor.

"Still," Eleonore leaned in, "there is nothing wrong with a good walk, even if the destination was in vain."

"How right you are," Mrs. Meyers smiled. "You know, I believe my husband would have liked you quite a bit."

"That's very kind," Eleonore grinned. "What makes you say that?"

"You have an agreeable temperament, quite unlike myself. I am certain that he would have found you refreshing. Of course, I would have been driven mad with jealousy," Mrs. Meyers looked down her nose in warning at Eleonore for a transgression she could never commit. "I was careful to only have older women as my maids while he was around."

"Well," Eleonore blushed at the compliment, "I'm not exactly youthful."

"Trust me," Mrs. Meyers patted Eleonore's arm, "when you are my age, everyone is youthful."

Eleonore giggled and felt a bond deepening between her and this woman which she had spent nearly every waking minute with over the past few months. Her severity, Eleonore understood, was out of necessity as her love had been spent in its entirety.

As they returned to the manor, Eleonore's heart stopped when she spotted the gardener standing on the front steps, smoking a large cigar. She wondered what Mrs. Meyers' reaction would be, given her disdain for the habit.

"What is it?" Mrs. Meyers noticed Eleonore's concern.

"There's something not right about him," Eleonore nodded towards the gardener.

"Never you mind him," Mrs. Meyers spoke quietly with a concealed indignation.

They turned the corner to cross over the stone bridge, but when the gardener spotted them, he didn't so much as flinch a muscle. He remained standing on the steps as he smoked his cigar without any concern that he had been spotted.

Mrs. Meyers locked eyes with him and the tension was palpable as they approached the front doors as neither Mrs. Meyers, nor the gardener, would let down their guard. With a puff, the gardener enshrouded Mrs. Meyers in a cloud of smoke.

"How dare you!" Eleonore was appalled.

"Miss Hodys!" Mrs. Meyers turned towards her, stopping any further outrage. "Inside at once!"

Fuming, Eleonore glared at the gardener as he gave a cocky smile.

"How could you let him get away with such disrespect?" Eleonore threw her hands onto her hips after the door had closed behind her.

"This is not your concern," Mrs. Meyers brushed her dress off and set her umbrella by the door.

"I wonder where everyone is?" Mrs. Meyers looked around curiously when Mr. Mattaliano was nowhere to be seen.

"They might have taken advantage of your absence," Eleonore shrugged, though she was still outraged by the gardener's behavior and Mrs. Meyers' quick dismissal of his insolence.

"No matter," Mrs. Meyers waved. "Would you grab us a bottle of wine?"

"Really?!" Eleonore's eyes flew wide. A glass of wine would fit the morning perfectly, though she did feel a slight tinge of guilt for indulging so early in the day.

"The cellar," Mrs. Meyers pointed to a door just underneath the stairs.

"I'll be right back," Eleonore walked briskly.

"I will meet you in the dining room," Mrs. Meyers spoke plainly, showing no excitement.

Opening the heavy cellar door, Eleonore was surprised at how smoothly it glided once momentum was in its favor.

The lights are on, Eleonore noticed the peculiarity as she descended the stairs and found that the cellar was not what she expected. It was furnished with shelves upon shelves that were brimming with bottles of wine that sat collecting dust. At the bottom of the stairs were rifles, at least ten altogether, on a rack.

Grabbing one of the rifles, Eleonore inspected its intricacy with great interest. It was an antique from the Napoleonic era, yet it was decorated with golden leaves that ran along the whole length of the barrel. Holding it by her shoulder, Eleonore aimed at one of the bottles of wine and pretended to fire. Setting it back down, she grabbed another rifle, one that was better suited for hunting, and smiled as she felt its weight in her hands. How she missed hunting with her father. It was one of the few things that they had in common. Their natures were kindred, but there few activities that they could share together.

It's loaded, Eleonore frowned. *Why would it be loaded?*

Suddenly, the door to a storage room at the other end of the cellar opened. Eleonore's heart shattered as she watched Eva, holding Ben's hand, giggling as the two walked out. Ben was carrying his vest slung over his arm, Eva's hair was loose by her shoulders, and their faces were flushed crimson.

"Oh my god!" Eva threw her hand over her mouth when she spotted Eleonore.

"Eleonore?!" Ben panicked, frantically searching for a plausible explanation.

"I suppose this is why you were so eager to have us out for the day?" Eleonore fumed as she looked at them while still holding the rifle.

Neither butler nor maidservant knew what to say and they looked at Eleonore with the utmost regret and shame.

"Please don't mention anything to Mrs. Meyers," Ben raised his hand slightly and glanced at the gun she was holding.

"It's loaded," Eleonore hinted at her malicious desire.

"She's bluffing, right?" Eva stood slightly behind Ben.

"They're always loaded," Ben nodded, and Eva shot him a sharp look.

"Why's that?" Eleonore raised the gun slightly as the two jumped back. She would never harm them, but she relished the power that she had over them in this moment.

"Mr. Meyers, uh," Ben swallowed and dabbed the sweat off his forehead, "he thought it prudent to always be ready."

"Interesting," Eleonore set the rifle down again on the rack.

"You won't tell Mrs. Meyers, will you?" Eva began to tear up as she pleaded.

"Save your tears," Eleonore rolled her eyes.

"Oh grazie!" Ben rushed over to Eleonore and grabbed her hand.

"You disgust me," Eleonore withdrew and grabbed a bottle of wine at random before stomping back upstairs.

She knew that, officially, she had no reason to be upset with them as Ben had made no profession of love or affection. He was not committed to Eleonore in any way, nor were they romantically involved. Still, Eleonore took this as a betrayal and the look on Ben's face revealed that he had shamed himself in her eyes.

Chapter Sixteen:
Breadcrumbs

Like so many of our people, we have now had a personal experience of German barbarity which only strengthens the resolution of all of us to fight through to final victory.

King George VI

Arriving at a police station in Koblenz – the town where they had purchased Eleonore's blue dress – Hanns thought it would be best to seek the professional support of the local police force. Maybe they had caught some SS trying to flee and were unsure of how to process them. It would strain credulity to assume that he could be so fortunate, but Hanns was determined to try nonetheless.

A meagre one-story brick building, the police station was rather humble, and fittingly so for the size of the town. Yet, to Hanns, it appeared much like the stations that he had seen in some of the American films. Thick, iron bars were installed in the windows and the exterior was deteriorating from exposure to the elements.

Knocking on the rickety, wooden door, Hanns stood back as he waited. A few anxious seconds passed, but there was no answer. An elderly couple walked sluggishly by as he stood outside. Hanns gave a quick nod and stepped out of their way, but they continued their gradual journey as though he didn't exist. Curious as to why his knock had not received an answer, Hanns glanced into the dusty window, and thought that he saw the silhouette of a man sitting at a desk.

Knocking again, and louder, Hanns waited a few more seconds. Pulling out his notebook, he pretended to be reading through it as he felt the discomfort of being unanswered. Glancing again into the window, Hanns saw that the man hadn't moved.

This is ridiculous, Hanns shook his head in frustration. Trying the door, he noticed that it was unlocked so he opened it and walked inside.

The man behind the desk glanced up from an old, leathery book as he took a cautious sip of hot coffee. Studying Hanns for a moment, who was awaiting a greeting and a damn good explanation, the man set his coffee mug back down and returned to reading.

"I was knocking," Hanns pointed at the door, slightly irritated by the inhospitality.

"It was open," the man replied dryly as he looked down his nose through his glasses as he read.

"I would like to speak with a constable or someone in charge of this station," Hanns cleared his throat.

"He's busy," the man continued in his dry tone.

"When will he be back?" Hanns glimpsed at his watch.

"I didn't say that he was absent," the man set his book down momentarily and gave Hanns an annoyed look.

"I see," Hanns clicked his tongue thoughtfully. Then, grabbing a chair beside the desk, he sat down rather forcefully and glared at the constable who was unconcerned with Hanns' aggression.

To be fair, the man was, as far as Hanns could tell, about the same height as him, but with thick shoulders and beefy hands that were covered in dark hair. The years spent at his desk duties, however, revealed themselves in his swelling belly. Still, he carried the look of one who had devoted their life in the field and, in no way, had his desk duties impeded his physical aptitude, despite his size.

"I have some questions," Hanns began and opened his notebook, pen at the ready.

"That's a British uniform," the man looked him up and down.

"That's correct," Hanns nodded. "The English took me in after my own country threatened to murder me for the coincidence of my birth."

The constable's gaze narrowed at the announcement of his Jewishness, and Hanns sensed the hate boiling within him. Closing his book slowly, the constable set it down to the side and removed his glasses as he folded them with harbored violence.

"I'm looking for a certain young man who, I have on good authority, has been through this area," Hanns continued, unimpeded by this man's prejudice.

Suddenly, the man turned in his chair and bent over to grab something behind the desk. Hanns hovered over his pistol, prepared to draw if necessary. To his relief, yet shock, the man grabbed crutches that were set on the ground and, standing with their assistance, he walked to the side of the desk where Hanns was stunned to see that he only had one leg.

"This is the fruit of the men wearing that uniform," the constable used one of his crutches and pointed it at Hanns' chest. "While you wear those colors, I won't assist you."

Realizing that he wouldn't get anywhere with this constable, Hanns returned his notepad to his breast pocket, stood slowly, and walked towards the door. But as he reached for the handle, something stirred within him. Images of the bodies piled into mass graves flashed before his eyes. He remembered Eleonore, and the thousands of others, in their starved state, and he felt them calling to him, crying out for justice.

"No," Hanns returned and stood across from the constable who was still leaning on his crutches. "You are going to give me the information I seek, and you will comply."

"On whose authority?" the constable scoffed. "This is my jurisdiction."

"On this authority," Hanns retrieved the letter from his jacket which stated he had the power to arrest. "You are impeding my investigation," Hanns continued as the constable read the letter with growing concern.

"You'll have to arrest me," he held his chin high, but shuffled his jaw awkwardly which Hanns understood as nervousness. The battle of wits, he detected, had already been won and all that remained was collecting the spoils.

"You don't want that," Hanns shook his head. "The prisons are run by the same people whom the Nazis ordered to be killed in the millions. The prisons are run by Jews, British, Americans, and all sorts of decent people that your previous leaders would designate as degenerate."

"I understand," the constable's voice trembled ever so slightly as he spoke.

"Oh, I don't think you do," Hanns took a step forward as he delved into his embellishment. "You see, the people running these prisons are a vengeful sort. They don't take kindly to the folks like you who rounded up us Jews like we were animals. I have on good authority that one officer in particular, Tin Eye Stephens they call him, is disobeying the order to withhold force upon those he interrogates and instead is employing it most creatively and liberally."

The constable breathed heavily as he glared at Hanns who wondered what the man would be capable of should he have the full use of his limbs.

"The ones who are responsible for the removal of your leg," Hanns spoke with a bit of compassion, "are not the English, or the Americans, but they are the ones who professed to have saved Germany."

"What information do you need?" the constable finally relented as he swallowed.

"I'm after Gustav Simon," Hanns retrieved the photograph and showed it to the constable who, surprisingly, began to smile after recognizing the man in the picture. "And I believe his son came through here."

"I've heard the name," the constable hobbled back to his chair.

"Has he been through here?" Hanns leaned over the desk.

"No," the constable shook his head, but then he began to chuckle.

"I'm aware that you are in possession of some information that may assist me," Hanns glared at the officer with a veiled threat.

The constable then burst out in a haughty laugh and Hanns began to feel uncomfortable being the brunt of whatever joke this was.

"Gustav has not been through here," the constable calmed a little, "because he killed himself nearly two months ago."

"What?!" Hanns stood back from the desk in shock.

"The Frankfurt paper wrote about it," the constable wiped a tear from his eye.

"How can this be?" Hanns muttered to himself.

Then, again, the constable burst into laughter, "This is the best the British intelligence can offer? Chasing the ghost of a man who died two months ago?"

"I appreciate your service to your country," Hanns spoke sarcastically as he stormed out of the police station.

Fuming as he drove, Hanns delved into an unforgiving pit of rage as he gripped the steering wheel with all his might. He shouldn't have to threaten a police officer to elicit information about Nazis on the run. Hanns was beginning to understand that the process to bring Germany out of Hitler's shadow would be long and painful. In his heart, he knew that there was little left for him in the country of his birth.

Arriving late in the afternoon at the newspaper office in Frankfurt, Hanns wasted little time as he ran inside, not caring that the rain should soak him. Standing in the foyer, Hanns removed his cap and looked around briefly as he noticed the recent repairs to the building. All that remained to complete the restoration was the painting. Otherwise, the contractors had done excellent work to bring the office back to its original splendor.

"How may I help you?" a clerk asked without looking up from his desk. He was a skinny man with a plain, dark gray suit who clearly took pride in his appearance and the perfection of his work.

"I'm looking for an archived edition," Hanns explained as he continued to inspect the renewal of the building.

"As you can see," the clerk responded indifferently, "the office was subject to bombing. It may be difficult to find some papers."

"This one was written about two months ago," Hanns ran his hand through his wet hair.

"Do you know the date?" the clerk asked, still without looking up at Hanns.

"No," Hanns huffed, "but it is regarding the death of Gustav Simon."

At this, the clerk gave a startled look up at Hanns, but his interest morphed into disgust when he noticed that Hanns was soaking wet.

"You're familiar with the name?" Hanns asked as he leaned on the desk.

"I am," the clerk nodded, but gave a foul look for the disregard that his desk was now being saturated by Hanns, "but if Gustav Simon was indeed dead, then I would be the first to know."

"What do you mean?" Hanns studied him.

"I'm one of the Jews that he 'cleansed' from Luxemburg," the clerk grew animated. "He killed someone very important to me."

"So, this office never wrote about his suicide?" Hanns pressed.

"We did not," the clerk shook his head quickly. "But when the day comes, I cannot wait to pen the words."

"I understand," Hanns dropped his shoulders in despair with the confirmation of the constable's deception.

"What is your purpose with him?" the clerk continued.

"Justice," Hanns threw his hands onto his hips as he walked away from the desk and began to pace aimlessly.

"Who told you that he had killed himself?"

"Someone I assumed, incorrectly, to be of a benefit in my pursuit."

"May I offer you some advice?" the clerk removed his glasses and held his hands flat by his sides.

"Of course," Hanns nodded.

"When you're hunting Nazis, don't trust anyone. The Werwolf Resistance is larger than we would like to believe. Even those who aren't part of the movement still may have sympathies to the Nazi party."

"Werwolf Resistance?" Hanns squinted. "Like the creature?"

"Yes, but spelt differently. Here," the clerk rummaged through his desk and retrieved a pamphlet which he handed to Hanns.

"What's this?" Hanns asked as he flipped through the pamphlet.

"Some of their propaganda," the clerk threw his hands behind his back as he watched Hanns. "Operation Werwolf, again not to be confused with the mythological werewolf creature, was started by Himmler when the Allies began gaining ground. It's a guerrilla operation meant to disrupt the Allied efforts and ultimately restore Nazi power."

"Hmm," Hanns closed the pamphlet and slapped it against the palm of his hand as he sighed.

"Where are you off to next?" the clerk asked with increasing interest.

"To arrest the constable who gave me false information," Hanns turned and stormed out of the building.

"Captain!" the clerk ran after Hanns and caught up to him in the rain.

"What?!" Hanns shouted over the downpour.

"Don't go back to the constable," the clerk shook his head.

"Why not?!"

"Don't give Gustav any more time."

"The constable deserves to spend the rest of his days behind bars!" Hanns defended.

"Of course he does! But he's just a distraction. If you process the constable, you're just giving Gustav that much more time to get away."

"Well if you have any leads, I'm happy to hear them," Hanns let his hands fall to his sides in desperation.

"What town was the constable stationed?"

"Koblenz," Hanns pointed in the direction of the town.

"Go talk to the mayor," the clerk nodded. "And in the future, avoid any local police. Most were criminals during the war and I doubt that they've abandoned their previous loyalties."

"Maybe you should be doing my job," Hanns smiled.

"No," the clerk laughed nervously. "I'm afraid that is the extent of my wisdom."

"Well, thank you," Hanns extended his hand and the clerk shook it.

"When you find Gustav," the clerk pulled Hanns towards him, "I want to be the first to know."

"Understood," Hanns nodded and retreated to the shelter of his truck as he watched the clerk race back inside the office.

Speeding towards Koblenz, Hanns was eager to reach the mayor before the day was out and was thankful that he was one of the only vehicles on the road. Even though the war had ended months ago, the impact was still palpable. A few farmers walked by with their horses, a handful of kids could be seen playing on the empty streets, but otherwise the towns were deserted. Hitler had sacrificed everything for his wicked ideology.

Arriving back at Koblenz within the hour, Hanns parked just outside of Jesuit Square which housed a few local municipal buildings and, most importantly, the town hall. Racing through the rain, Hanns found the architecture of the square rather impressive and, if he was afforded the time, would've loved to investigate its rich history.

Entering the town hall, Hanns was met with the familiar scent of aging wood that was so customary with buildings of this era. But Hanns' attention was stolen by the interior decorations which were ill-matched to a town hall of this size. Gold plates hung underneath elaborate paintings which made Hanns suspicious as to how and when the art was collected.

"May I help you?" a receptionist called from behind a curved desk, much too modern in comparison with the rest of the town.

"Yes," Hanns handed his papers to the receptionist. "I'm Captain Volker from the War Crimes Investigation Team. I would like to speak with the mayor."

"Ah, yes. Follow me," the receptionist stood and began to walk towards a hallway. "He's been expecting you."

"He has?" Hanns shot his head back with surprise.

Regardless, Hanns followed the receptionist down a narrow hallway with bright, cedar walls and a thick, gray carpet. Again, this hallway was full of paintings and some even rested on the ground where there was no room to hang them.

Knocking on a large, double door, the receptionist opened them slightly as she leaned in and whispered something inaudible.

"Good, good," a voice boomed from inside, and the receptionist pushed the doors wide open and signaled for Hanns to enter.

Complying, Hanns entered a large office that was richly decorated. Marble busts of Roman Emperors were lined up neatly against in front of large windows, and on the wall behind the mayor was a broad sword that was held in place by an extravagant coat of arms. But what stole Hanns attention was the man behind the spacious desk.

The war, while causing others to be nearly famished, seemed to have not been much of a burden to the mayor. Half a sandwich lay eaten on the desk in front of a man twice the width of Hanns and then some.

"Ah, Captain," the mayor struggled to stand.

"Thank you for meeting with me," Hanns reached forward but the mayor hesitated to shake his hand.

"Beautiful office," Hanns looked around but noticed that the mayor wiped his hand on his pants when he thought the captain wouldn't see.

"Yes," the major chuckled slightly, "I'm very fortunate."

"Can I ask," Hanns moved over to one of the busts, "where did this come from?"

"That?" The mayor replied and rolled his hands in the air as he, unmistakably, tried to elicit some fabrication. "Ah, that was a gift."

"A gift from whom?" Hanns turned his attention to the mayor, sensing his unease.

"Well, that I can't say," the mayor again chuckled as his whole belly heaved.

"How so?"

"Well, it was before my time, you see."

"Ah," Hanns nodded. "Do you mind if I ask you some questions?" Hanns took a seat in the chair in front of the mayor's desk.

"Not at all," the mayor spoke timidly as he slowly sat back down and folded his hands across his belly.

"I'm looking for some fugitives," Hanns passed the list of names across the desk to the mayor. "Most importantly, I'm looking for Gustav Simon."

"I'm sorry," the mayor looked over the list briefly before passing it back to Hanns, "but we haven't had many traveling through here. Especially not any SS or the like."

"Do you know the whereabouts of Gustav Simon?" Hanns pressed.

"No," the mayor spoke quickly.

"What about his son?" Hanns continued.

"You know," the mayor again struggled to stand, "you may have more success with these types of questions down at the police station. I'll have the receptionist phone ahead for you."

"Sir," Hanns raised his voice in warning, "I require your full cooperation."

"Now look here," the mayor rumbled and leaned on his desk with his fists. "We didn't have much dealing with the SS because we didn't have your people amongst us. No Jew has ever lived in Koblenz, so there was no need for such extreme measures."

"Need?!" Hanns scoffed and shook his head. "You know, I spoke with your chief of police who, oddly enough, was about as *indulgent* as you are."

"I beg your pardon?!" the mayor's eyes bulged with indignation.

"I wouldn't make such a rude statement if my suspicions weren't roused," Hanns took out a cigarette and lit it.

"There's no smoking in here," the mayor pounded his fist on the desk.

"Every other person that I've passed by in this town is malnourished, yet you and the chief of police seem to be the only two who have thrived."

"If you have a problem with the chief of police," the mayor leaned over the desk as his cheeks shook from rage, "then I suggest you deal with the district police instead."

"A fine suggestion," Hanns threw his eyebrow up, surprised that hadn't thought of that himself.

"I must ask you to leave," the mayor pointed emphatically at the door.

"Thank you for your time. I'll let you get back to your lunch," Hanns spoke sarcastically as he stood and rushed out of the office and returned to his truck.

Slamming the door, Hanns sat in the truck as he rubbed his eyes from frustration. While the war was over, the impact was long lasting and Hanns knew that he would have to make do with the fact that every town would have pro and anti-Nazi sympathies.

You can't arrest everyone, Hanns shook his head. *Besides, I don't have the authority to arrest citizens. Still, it's obvious where he got those paintings.*

Not allowing himself to waste any more time, Hanns turned on the truck and headed for the district police. Passing through the town, Hanns smiled as some younger boys started to chase the vehicle excitedly. He was a military officer and, quite frankly, they were too young to be concerned with his allegiance. A military man was one that every boy aspired to be, regardless of the colors that they flew.

But, as the boys chased Hanns, he looked in the rear-view mirror to see that one of them had tripped and fallen on the pavement that was slick from the recent rain. Feeling sorry for them, Hanns stopped the truck and ran back to assist.

"Are you alright?" Hanns called and knelt in front of the boy.

"Just a little scratch," the boy tried desperately to remain brave as the blood ran down his leg.

"I've got some bandages in the truck," Hanns stood and was about to run back to the vehicle when his heart dropped.

If the boy had not fallen, Hanns would've never noticed that he was standing outside a Jewish cemetery. *"No Jews have ever lived here,"* Hanns clenched his jaw as he remembered the mayor's statements.

Quickly, Hanns grabbed the first aid kit for the boys and threw the whole pouch at them, insisting that they keep it all. Then, he turned the truck around and raced back through the town until he came to the hall where he drove right on up through the square and made an abrupt stop outside the doors.

Bursting back into the building, Hanns stormed with purpose down the hallway towards the mayor's office.

"He's in a meeting!" the receptionist tried to stop him.

"Mayor!" Hanns opened the door to the office to find him eating the other half of the sandwich.

"I'm sorry," the receptionist panted as she ran in after Hanns. "I tried to stop him."

"What's this then?" the mayor demanded.

"You're under arrest," Hanns took out his handcuffs and walked towards him.

"Whatever for?" the mayor demanded, growing irate.

"For the obstruction of justice."

"What on earth do you mean?" the mayor clung to the pretense of innocence.

"If no Jews lived in your town, then why is there a Jewish cemetery next to the main road?" Hanns questioned.

"You filthy Jew!" the mayor spat at Hanns.

With a swift strike, and a surprised scream from the receptionist, Hanns landed a blow against the mayor's chin who spun and fell face down on his desk. Throwing the mayor's arms behind his back, Hanns quickly handcuffed him.

"Let's go," Hanns pushed the mayor out towards the vehicle.

"Please," the mayor stopped, "use the back entrance."

"The vehicle is out front," Hanns refused and pushed the mayor onward.

Walking towards the truck, Hanns spotted a few watchful eyes out the windows. And, while he couldn't be sure, he was certain that he had seen a smile or two at the sight of the mayor being led away.

"Get up!" Hanns put down the tailgate for the mayor who struggled under his own weight.

"Where are you taking me?" the mayor asked through gritted teeth for the humiliation.

"The district police," Hanns answered as he slammed the gate shut.

Driving as fast as he was able, Hanns paid special attention to any potholes in the road as he made his way to the station, much to the bitter complaint of his prisoner.

"You know," Hanns slowed the vehicle a little as they came to the Jewish cemetery, "I almost drove right by it."

"You won't get away with this," the mayor huffed. "How dare you parade me by their graves as if I'm some common criminal."

"Imprisoning you is not the justice that they deserve," Hanns slowed the vehicle to a near stop as they crawled by the cemetery, "but it's some measure, at the very least."

"This isn't legal," the mayor shook his head. "The ceasefire law forbids you from arresting citizens."

"I know," Hanns spoke casually, "but I don't care. Besides, there's some interpretation to that law. How many Jews lived here?"

"Enough," the mayor spit.

"How many survived?"

"I don't know," the mayor frowned, offended by the very question.

"What happened with their property? Are those paintings or the busts from their houses?"

"What does it matter?" the mayor grunted.

"You're right, you're not some common criminal. You're much worse," Hanns returned to normal speeds as they left the cemetery. "You murdered many and took their possessions."

The mayor didn't reply as he looked crossly out the back of the truck, muttering to himself and cursing Hanns under his breath.

Arriving at the district police station, Hanns pushed the mayor into the building as he grumbled. All eyes turned towards them and the mayor seethed with resentment.

"Can I help you?" a constable eyed him curiously.

"I'm Captain Hanns Volker," he replied proudly. "War Crimes Investigator. I've arrested this detestable man on obstruction of justice."

"It's about time," the constable nodded eagerly to a couple guards who took the mayor into custody.

"This isn't legal!" the mayor shouted as he was led away.

"I was hoping that someone would come," the constable shook Hanns' hand.

"I need information on Gustav Simon or his son," Hanns got straight to the point.

"Sir," the constable chuckled, "we've got a hell of a lot more than information."

Chapter Seventeen:
Intolerance

Who looks outside, dreams; who looks inside, awakes.

Carl Jung

Eleonore stood sheltered on the front porch as it rained. Again, Mrs. Meyers had been a little too liberal with the wine and was now napping to try and recover. Taking advantage of the time afforded her, Eleonore took a moment to catch her breath and reflect on yesterday's events.

How could he? Eleonore fumed. *With someone like Eva? She's only after him because of his possible inheritance. Can't he see that?*

The front door swung open and Eleonore turned to see Ben with a somewhat remorseful countenance. Joining Eleonore, Ben stood at a respectful distance and the two quietly watched the downpour. Eleonore knew that both their thoughts consisted of nothing but each other, yet she refused to acknowledge him.

"It's a bit chilly out here," Ben rubbed his arms as he tried to make some small talk to ease the tension.

"It's cold inside, too, Mr. Mattaliano," Eleonore shot a cutting glare at Ben.

"Listen," the butler began contritely, "about yesterday."

"I don't want to hear it," Eleonore threw her hand up.

"I need to explain," he pressed.

"There's nothing to explain," Eleonore turned towards him.

"I don't understand why this upsets you?" he shook his head in confusion.

"It's...uh..." Eleonore stumbled as she was lost for words. If she confessed her affections for him, it would throw her into possible ridicule. Allowing herself to be vulnerable in this regard was entirely foreign.

"You have feelings for me?" he threw his eyes wide in disbelief, guessing her thoughts.

"Is that so horrible?" Eleonore crossed her arms and returned to staring out into the yard.

"Just...unexpected," Ben studied her in shock.

"Look," Eleonore drew a deep breath, "I've never been in love before-"

"In love?!" Ben withdrew slightly as he began to panic.

"I'm not saying that I'm in love with you," Eleonore held up her finger to correct herself, "but for the first time, truly, I'm developing a genuine affection."

"Miss Hodys," the butler looked at her earnestly, "if I had known…"

"Save it," Eleonore clenched her jaw. "Even if you were aware of my feelings, I would've still found you down in that cellar with Eva. And don't try and deny it," she gave him a fierce scowl.

"No, no, I would've never," Mr. Mattaliano ignored her warning. "Not in my wildest dreams would I have supposed that a woman like you would be interested in me. I believed you to be so far beyond my reach."

Eleonore turned away so as not to give him the satisfaction of seeing her flattered smile. Whether he was being genuine or not, it had been some time since a man had complimented her.

"Continue," she nodded after she had regathered herself.

Studying her for a moment, Ben seemed at a loss for words. Then, looking out at the rain, and acting upon impulse, he left the shelter and stood a few feet out.

"What are you doing?" Eleonore asked dryly, unimpressed by his recklessness.

"I'll stand out in the rain until you forgive me," Ben threw his hands outwards.

"This is ridiculous," Eleonore rolled her eyes.

"Forgive me," Ben begged.

"Or what? Your clothes will get wet?" Eleonore nodded for him to return under the cover. "I think you'll live."

"No," Ben shook his head adamantly, "I won't. I never thought that someone like you could ever have affection for someone like me. I won't leave until you forgive me."

"It's rain," Eleonore shrugged. "You're not exactly making the sacrifice of ages here."

"Then come stand with me," Ben shrugged.

"Absolutely not," Eleonore scoffed and looked away, hoping that no one was witnessing this embarrassing spectacle.

With her gaze diverted, Ben seized the opportunity and, grabbing her hand, pulled her out into the rain.

"Mr. Mattaliano!" Eleonore slapped his chest and he chuckled at her indignation as she was drenched in the downpour.

Yet, for all her rage, something stirred within Eleonore's heart. She was furious with him and disappointed that he wasn't the man of character that she believed him to be. But if he was telling her the truth, and he had been ignorant of her feelings, then maybe she could allow for some clemency. Besides, she was rather withdrawn, and any man would find it difficult to interpret her subtleties.

Lost in the moment, Eleonore forgot her concerns and stared deep into his dark, green eyes and he smiled down at her. Her heart and stomach fluttered as she felt a passion which was unknown to her. She had felt affection before, but this was something she didn't know how to describe.

"Forgive me," Ben spoke quietly as he held her hands gently near his chin.

"What about Eva?" Eleonore asked softly and watched him intensely.

"She's nothing," Ben mimicked throwing away something over his shoulder.

"I'll need time," Eleonore shook her head. She needed to be reasonable, despite the impulsive begging of her heart.

"Take all the time you need," Ben gave a slight bow with his head. Then, turning to face the door, he held out his arm for her and the two returned to the shelter of the porch. Giggling slightly, Eleonore examined the pitiful state that they were in, drenched from head to toe.

"I never knew you had such a silly side," Eleonore grinned but tried to regather her propriety as she stood properly with her hands gently in front of her.

"You're teaching me things about myself I didn't know existed, Miss Hodys," Ben smiled warmly at her.

Eleonore looked away as she smiled bashfully.

"I should change before Mrs. Meyers wakes up," Eleonore chuckled.

But when they walked inside, Eleonore and Ben spotted Eva standing at the top of the stairs. With a scowl, Eva glared down at them and then stomped away in the direction of Mrs. Meyers' room.

"Never mind her," Ben gave a slight pat on her back, and Eleonore felt his touch lingering. "Go dress, I'll meet you later tonight."

But, as Ben began to walk away, Eleonore reached out and grabbed his hand. Surprised, he looked at her in confusion. It was rash, and a little self-serving, but Eleonore was desperate for companionship. She was desperate to be loved, properly, by someone who desired her for who she was.

Leading him by the hand, Eleonore took him back to her wing. Her heart pounded in her chest as the two walked to her room. She knew that it was entirely improper to give herself so soon after she had spotted him with Eva, but reasoning and decency were being silenced by desire.

"Are you sure?" Mr. Mattaliano asked as she unlocked her door.

"No," Eleonore shook her head. "This is probably wrong, but I don't care."

Wrapping his arms around her, Mr. Mattaliano leaned in and began kissing her lips as they backed clumsily into her room. As romantic as this experience was, Eleonore was unimpressed with Ben's technique. He pressed too hard with his chin, his breath smelled of tobacco, and he nearly smothered her as he squeezed tightly. Still, her longing for intimacy muzzled these discrepancies and she returned the passion.

"Help me get this off," Eleonore demanded as she struggled with the wet dress clinging to her skin while balancing her longing to continue kissing.

"Here," Ben grabbed her sleeve and pulled as she leaned away but, as these things often happen in bouts of desire, the dress tore.

"Ben!" Eleonore looked at him in horror.

"What?!" Ben shrugged. "I was trying to help!"

"You tore the dress!" Eleonore looked at him with rage. Suddenly every romantic sentiment had vanished.

"There are plenty of spares. They're in the dresser, bottom drawer," Ben pointed and leaned in for another kiss.

"I know where they are!" Eleonore threw her hands on to her hips. "That's not the point!"

"Do we really want to have this argument?" Ben smiled at her tenderly.

"I suppose not," Eleonore succumbed to his sweet smile and abandoned her dignity as she threw her arms around Ben and kissed him.

Then, suddenly, music began to blare from the gramophone in the dining room. Wagner's *Tristan and Isolde* played over the speaker and, in that instant, Eleonore was back in the Villa at Auschwitz with Rudolph Hoess. It was only for a moment, quicker than she could count, but it was Rudolph standing in front of her in the form of Mr. Mattaliano.

"Stop!" Eleonore put her hand to Ben's chest, believing him to be Rudolph.

"What's wrong?" Ben shook his head, wondering what he had done to offend her.

"Just stop!" Eleonore backed away.

"This was your idea," Ben defended.

"It was a mistake," Eleonore rubbed her eyes. "The music likely woke up Mrs. Meyers. I'll have to get changed immediately. Please leave."

"Of course, but—"

"Leave!" Eleonore pointed to the door as she gathered a fresh dress to change into.

With a slight bow, a confused Mr. Mattaliano closed the door as he left Eleonore alone. She knew that he didn't deserve to be spoken to in that way, and he was likely now baffled by her behavior, but her mind was troubled with the image of Rudolph. She wondered if she could be close to someone again without his face appearing. He plagued her dreams, her thoughts, and now he was interfering with the one thing that she believed would make her whole.

I'd wager that Eva put the gramophone on, Eleonore fumed. *I doubt the cook would be so bold.*

Rushing as she scrambled down the stairs while buttoning up her new dress, Eleonore ran to the gramophone to shut it off. Lifting the needle, Eleonore held her breath as she listened for Mrs. Meyers and hoped that she was not too late to keep her napping.

"Why did you turn it off?" Mrs. Meyers spoke, startling Eleonore who turned to see the madam sitting in the corner of the dining room, veiled in darkness.

"Sorry, I'll turn it back on," Eleonore panicked and was about to set the needle back when, out of the corner of her eye, her attention was stolen by the newspaper beside the gramophone.

The headline read: The Belsen Trials. Rudolph Hoess, The Commandant of Auschwitz, On the Run.

Her heart nearly stopped when she read the title and picked up the paper to inspect it further, believing that he was simply imposing himself on her imagination. But this was no fabrication, and Eleonore shook as she stared at his picture which was plastered across the front page.

They haven't caught him?! Eleonore trembled and her mind started to race with wild possibilities. *What if he's after me? Maybe that was him in the garden and not Jung?!*

"Eleonore!" Mrs. Meyers growled. "Can you not hear me?!"

"Sorry, ma'am," Eleonore shook herself free and looked at Mrs. Meyers with wide, frightful eyes.

"The gramophone," Mrs. Meyers waved.

"Right!" Eleonore spun and put the needle back in place.

Wagner's melody of forbidden love blared, and the world went dark around Eleonore as she felt Rudolph standing behind her. She was paralyzed as a dark fiction played out in her mind, reminding her of the terrible injustice he had done to her.

"Why is your hair so wet?" Rudolph asked as he grabbed her elbow.

Spinning around, Eleonore was relieved to see that it was only Mrs. Meyers.

"Whatever is the matter?" Mrs. Meyers offered a perplexed frown at Eleonore.

"It's nothing," Eleonore gave a limp smile as she shook her head. "I apologize for the distraction. It won't happen again."

"Good," Mrs. Meyers walked past Eleonore, but not before studying her thoroughly. "Bring tea to the drawing room."

"At once," Eleonore ran to the kitchen.

Eleonore wondered what was wrong with her. She knew that it was silly to believe that Rudolph's greatest concern was tracking her down, but still, it wasn't beyond him either. Regardless, she was lost to internal turmoil and stared at her feet as she walked into the kitchen where she nearly plowed into Ben.

"Careful!" Ben put his hands up to stop Eleonore.

"Sorry," Eleonore blushed.

"Don't worry," Ben shook his head, but Eleonore detected that he was a little embittered by their recent 'experience'.

"Listen," Eleonore began. "I would like to explain what happened."

"You don't need to," Ben glanced away, avoiding eye contact.

"No," Eleonore sighed, "no, I think I do. I need someone to talk to and I believe I owe you an explanation. If me and you are going to be involved, then there are some things you should know."

"Alright," Ben nodded, but then left in a manner which made Eleonore believe that he wasn't entirely convinced that a talk would do much good.

Maybe he won't understand, Eleonore shook her head as she put the kettle on. *I could tell him in a way where I don't divulge all the details. He doesn't need to know names. I just need him to recognize that there are other forces at play besides my affections. I'm not some irrational woman who is incapable of knowing what she wants. I need Rudolph to stop interrupting my life,* Eleonore rubbed her eyes, *otherwise I'll be alone forever. Why, in God's name, does he keep appearing? I mean, I know why, but Rudolph is far away, why should I still be so concerned and afraid?*

The kettle screeched and Eleonore grabbed the tea as she headed towards the drawing room. As Eleonore returned to the second floor, she passed by Eva cleaning one of the rooms and continued walking until, grudgingly, her conscience begged her to make things right, if she could. Stopping at the door, Eleonore gave a slight knock against the doorpost.

"What do you want?" Eva asked casually as if she felt no antipathy towards Eleonore.

"I hope that the two of us can come to an agreement," Eleonore spoke tenderly.

"Agreement?" Eva huffed sarcastically and stopped cleaning.

"Yes," Eleonore cleared her throat. "There's no reason that we all can't be civil."

"What does he see in you?" Eva glared at Eleonore with an intense hatred.

"I wonder that myself," Eleonore offered a quick smile to try and dispel the tension, but to no avail.

"This isn't over," Eva spoke bitterly.

"I know why you're doing this," Eleonore persisted.

"You're still as clueless as the day you arrived," Eva shook her head. "You still don't know what the manor is, do you?"

"You believe that Mr. Mattaliano will inherit the property," Eleonore continued, "and you're trying to seduce him to secure a better position."

"And what's wrong with that?" Eva snickered. "Aren't you doing the same thing?"

"Of course not!" Eleonore frowned.

"I think I hit a nerve," Eva flinched her eye. "Why are you attracted to Mr. Mattaliano?"

"I should take Mrs. Meyers her tea before she becomes suspicious," Eleonore spoke with an air of importance for her esteemed duties in contrast with Eva's cleaning.

Yet, as Eleonore continued towards the drawing room, Eva's words rung true. *What does Ben see in me? Eva is young and pretty while I'm old and not as beautiful as I once was.* Still, despite her misgivings, Eleonore felt no real threat from Eva. While from a carnal perspective, Eva had the advantage, Eleonore felt that Mr. Mattaliano was genuinely interested in companionship. In fact, he seemed almost too happy to cut off his involvement with Eva, which was now making Eleonore curious.

But these concerns would have to wait as Eleonore returned to her duties. Entering the drawing room, a smile crept on Eleonore's face when she noticed that some of the curtains had been opened. The fresh, lingering smell of rain filled the room with its wonderful, natural scent.

"Thank you," Mrs. Meyers took the cup from Eleonore who was surprised to hear gratitude from the mistress.

"Will that be all, ma'am?" Eleonore asked as she held her hands gently in front of her.

"I love the rain," Mrs. Meyers sipped her tea. "The smell reminds me of childhood. It was the only time my father would quit working and spend time with us. He would run around and chase us and then sit and read to us by the fireplace. It was never a story that we wanted to hear, but we were just happy to listen to his voice and enjoyed being in his presence. He was a rather silly man, my father, and it was a good thing, too. He had four temperamental girls to keep up with. I should not reminisce," Mrs. Meyers glanced apologetically at Eleonore. "It is impolite to be so dull."

"Not in the slightest. I rather enjoy it," Eleonore smiled. "Reminds me of my own father."

"Though, he could also be quite severe, at times," Mrs. Meyers continued.

"How so?" Eleonore asked as she sat down opposite Mrs. Meyers who looked at her with horror for the impropriety of sitting without asking permission.

"He forbid the staff from having relations," Mrs. Meyers glared at Eleonore.

Speechless, Eleonore felt a lump in her throat as she watched Mrs. Meyers with grave concern.

"He once discovered that the cook and the servant girl were having extramarital relations and he promptly dismissed their services."

"Did Eva tell you?" Eleonore looked out into the hallway with a vengeful glare.

"Eva?" Mrs. Meyers laughed quickly and then raised an eyebrow. "She is the only one getting a proper sleep while you and Mr. Mattaliano are enjoying your nocturnal visits and your filthy smoking."

"How did—"

"My dear," Mrs. Meyers looked down her nose. "There is nothing that happens at the manor of which I am unaware."

Eleonore sat across from Mrs. Meyers feeling rather like a child scolded. She had only just discovered love, or at least the kindling of love, but now she would be forced to defuse it. Though, she didn't believe that she would have the strength to rid herself of such pursuits.

"You may go," Mrs. Meyers spoke with a hint of sympathy as she took another sip of tea.

"May I ask why?" Eleonore cleared her throat.

"You may not!" Mrs. Meyers' eyes bulged with indignation.

"If it's pregnancy you're concerned with, I can promise —"

"Miss Hodys," Mrs. Meyers stood quickly. "You are dismissed for the remainder of the day without remuneration as I consider your future here."

"My future?" Eleonore shook her head in disbelief.

"I will not tolerate insubordination," Mrs. Meyers shook in her rage. "And I cannot fathom how I hired someone with such wanton morals as yourself. To think that you would argue to continue conducting a carnal relationship with another man under my roof is unthinkable. I am running a respectable house. If you want to marry the man, that is another issue altogether."

"Marriage?" Eleonore nearly choked.

"Oh," Mrs. Meyers squinted as her voice grew deep and brooding. "I see how it is. I have had my doubts about Mr. Mattaliano for quite some time, but I remained silent in honor of my husband. Yet now I see that his interests lay elsewhere," she examined Eleonore.

"Ma'am," Eleonore began, but Mrs. Meyers held up her hand to stop her. She wanted to defend Ben, but she understood that any further comment would be detrimental.

"He will not inherit this house," Mrs. Meyers grew cold and returned to staring out the window.

"That's unfair. I —"

"Leave," Mrs. Meyers growled, "before I have you removed entirely from my employment. You have hurt me deeply, Miss Hodys. I shared my most intimate and personal thoughts with someone of your indecency. This cannot be forgiven."

Eleonore nearly ran out of the drawing room as she held back her tears. The injustice was too much for her to bear. Even if she had enjoyed the pleasures of the flesh, this was none of Mrs. Meyers' business.

Eleonore fumed as she stopped briefly in the doorway of the room Eva was cleaning. With her back turned to Eleonore, Eva continued obliviously in her duties. But when Eva spotted Eleonore, and saw the troubled state that she was in, a scornful grin formed. Eleonore knew that Eva was behind everything and she returned a contemptuous glare of her own, promising retaliation. She hadn't survived this long just to be displaced by a licentious and vindictive girl.

Chapter Eighteen:
The Twins of Marburg

Wit is educated insolence.

Aristotle

The next morning, Hanns returned to the district police station to see what information they had for him with regards to Gustav's son. The police were busy processing the mayor's arrest and, having travelled the entire day, Hanns thought it best for him to get some rest first. Though sleep had evaded him as his mind ran rampant with ambition and, he supposed, it would've been better if he had just stayed later last night.

"Constable Becker, at your service," the constable extended his hand in greeting as he led Hanns to the evidence room.

"Nice to meet you," Hanns shook his hand.

"Here we are," the constable unlocked the wired cage which held an abundance of contraband and weapons.

Stepping inside, Hanns shook his head in amazement. SS uniforms, pamphlets, caps, iron crosses, helmets, guns of every variation, and close combat weapons were heaped on the shelves inside a small storage area. Most of the items were dirty and carelessly thrown into piles and it was clear that the district police were clueless as to what needed to be done with them.

"Ah, here it is," the constable retrieved a rucksack from one of the bottom shelves and handed it to Hanns.

"Who does this belong to?" Hanns unbuckled the straps and opened it up.

"See for yourself," Constable Becker grinned.

Excitedly, Hanns pulled out the identity card for none other than Gustav's son, who was also confusingly named Gustav Adolph Simon, a British Ordinance map of Germany, and pamphlets from the Werwolf resistance. This was Hanns' first real and tangible evidence that the son of Gustav had not only traveled through the area, but was actively involved in treason.

"How recently did you obtain this?" Hanns asked as he dug through the rucksack.

"I'd say a few months back," the constable recalled.

"Why have you kept it all this time?" Hanns grew annoyed.

"Between you and me," the constable whispered and looked over his shoulder before continuing, "the men at my station are the only ones I trust."

"I understand," Hanns remembered his recent dealings with the local police. "But you trust me?"

"I don't think the mayor would have been so 'endearing' if he liked you," Becker smirked. "That man was on my list for some time."

Hanns nodded as he rubbed his eyes. While the evidence was vital, it still meant that Gustav and his son had an additional three months to get ahead. If Hanns had come into contact with this conclusive evidence sooner, then he could've already been hunting down these criminals.

"That's not all," Becker waved for Hanns to give him the bag and he dug around the bottom. "There's a train ticket here, with the name Gustav Henning. One-way ticket to Hermeskeil."

"Henning?" Hanns squinted as he looked at the constable.

"That is Gustav's ex-wife's maiden name," Becker bounced his eyes as he followed the trail. "I'm assuming the son took his mother's identity to conceal himself."

"And Hermeskeil?"

"That's where young Gustav's grandparents live. His father and mother divorced some years ago now," Becker nodded and grabbed a small piece of paper and began to write down an address.

"I think you are the single most helpful person that I've met," Hanns stretched out his hand which the constable gladly shook.

"Happy to help," Becker held his hands behind his back as he tried to appear modest but smiled brightly.

"I may have use for your services in the field at a later time," Hanns studied him.

"Nothing would make me happier," Becker chuckled, unable to withhold his gratification.

"We'll talk soon," Hanns gave a quick salute as he left the police station with the rucksack of young Gustav.

This is it, Hanns thought as he started the truck and the adrenaline coursed through his veins. *If I can catch the son, I can lure the father.* He was desperate to prove himself to his superiors and, not to mention, catch these men.

Taking out the piece of paper from his breast pocket as he drove, Hanns read the address again, and then set it on the empty seat beside him. Then, reaching back, Hanns grabbed his lunch kit. Opening it as he tried to keep an eye on the road, Hanns took his breakfast out and bit into a plain, tuna sandwich.

I need some air, Hanns rolled down the window as he drove along and felt the crisp, morning breeze. But, tragically, when the wind rushed through the cabin it grabbed the paper with the address and dragged it out the window.

"No!" Hanns shouted with a mouth full of food as he tried to seize it with his free hand but failed as it swirled past his face and he watched the paper soar into the air.

"Shit!" Hanns slammed his fist against the steering wheel which only increased disaster as the tuna from his sandwich slipped free and landed squarely on his pants.

"Oh, you've got to be kidding me!" Hanns tried to remove the tuna before it stained his clothes.

A horn honked and Hanns looked up to see that he was on the wrong side of the road. Swerving, Hanns just avoided contact with the only other car on the highway. The dirt and gravel swirled about as he slammed on the breaks and came to a stop.

Pay attention, Hanns closed his eyes as he gripped the steering wheel and his heart raced momentarily. Taking a deep breath, Hanns tried to relax himself, but felt his shoulders tightening. *I've been on the road too long,* he shook his head in bewilderment. *I enjoy the driving, I do, but sometimes it can be rather exhausting. One ends up talking to themselves,* Hanns smiled and then began to chuckle at how ridiculous he was being.

Don't worry about anything besides the drive. Just focus on getting to Hermeskeil. Once that is done, I can concentrate on step two, which is finding the Hennings without so much as an address. I really should've memorized it. How will I find them? No! Stop it, you fool! Just drive.

Agreeing with his own logic, Hanns returned to the road as his mind wandered to thoughts of Ann. He recalled the pleasant distractions in England: going to the movies, picnicking in the park, and enjoying each other's company. He wondered if he could return to such a life after everything he had seen. How could he have witnessed the horrors of Belsen and the other camps only to return to England and have a normal life?

I should propose to her, Hanns smiled at the thought. *She has been too patient with me and, really, when will another girl like her be this interested in me? She is quite sweet, my Ann. I should write, at least, to tell her as much. I was just hoping to have a career and a life set up before taking the plunge but, honestly, those things will fall into place.*

Before he knew it, the brief drive to Hermeskeil had transpired and Hanns approached the town as the sun was still rising over the large, rolling hills. It was quite a beautiful town and Hanns was struck by its aesthetics. It seemed to him as though Hermeskeil was kept secret from the world while tucked away in the corner and sheltered.

Descending the hill into town, Hanns was happy, at least, to see plenty of pedestrians about and hoped that he could find an answer from them for the address.

"Excuse me," Hanns rolled down his window and asked a passerby in the street.

"Yes?" the woman looked sheepishly at Hanns, wondering what business an Allied officer had with her.

"This is a bit of a long shot, but do you know where I can find Mr. and Mrs. Henning?"

"Of course!" the woman laughed, which surprised Hanns. "They're the first house on the corner just down that street."

"Thank you," Hanns nodded and began to roll up the window.

"Best of luck," the woman scoffed which Hanns thought was rather curious.

First house on the corner, Hanns recalled as he pulled up to a blue house which was two stories tall yet rather narrow for its height. Squished in with other houses of similar build, the property had a miniature garden and a walkway of about ten feet and was not, in any sense, spacious.

Why did that woman laugh like that? Hanns frowned as he left the vehicle and stretched. Grabbing his satchel, Hanns stood in front of the house as it impressed upon him the significance of his charge. As a reserved person, and being somewhat introverted, Hanns didn't relish the apprehension swirling in his stomach each time he had to knock on someone's door. He wondered if the other investigators felt as he did, or if he was alone in his worries.

I hope that they're willing to talk, Hanns took a deep breath as he opened the little four-foot-tall gate and, in about three steps, was at the door. Knocking loudly, Hanns watched as an elderly man, who was slightly hunched over, waddle towards him.

"Yes?" the man opened the door slightly and looked warily at Hanns.

"Mr. Henning?" Hanns asked.

"That's right," Mr. Henning nodded. "And you are?"

"Who's at the door?!" a woman called from inside.

"I was just about to find out!" the man shouted back.

"If it's that salesman again, just shut the door. Don't be polite," the woman shouted. "Coming around here just before lunch, interrupting our meal, and without a dash of respect for the hard-working people of this town. Does he have no regard for decency? I mean really, a salesman? Just after the war? What kind of profession is that?"

"I'm assuming that's Mrs. Henning?" Hanns whispered to Mr. Henning.

"Well if it's another woman, then I'm a dead man," Mr. Henning threw his eyebrows up and Hanns couldn't help but chuckle.

"I asked you who was at the door!" Mrs. Henning's voice drew closer as she stomped over towards them.

"I just asked him when you started rambling," Mr. Henning defended.

While admirable and brave, Mr. Henning's excuse was foolhardy. Even Hanns, who had known Mrs. Henning for a mere few seconds, knew that Mr. Henning had brought ruin upon himself.

"It's my fault then, is it?" Mrs. Henning's voice grew stern.

"I didn't say anything," Mr. Henning threw his hands up as he retreated.

"Who are y—" Mrs. Henning swung the door open, but was caught off guard by how handsome the gentleman was in front of her and immediately covered up with her housecoat.

"My name is Captain Volker," Hanns began.

"How can I help you, Captain?" Mrs. Henning examined him with lingering eyes.

"I know this is a sensitive topic," Hanns took a deep breath, "but I'm looking for information on your son-in-law."

"Ex-son-in-law," Mrs. Henning's concern for her appearance evaporated as she corrected him firmly.

"That's right," Hanns waved apologetically.

"Well come in, come in," Mrs. Henning gestured but then stopped to scold Mr. Henning. "Quit being so rude to our guest. You should've invited him in ages ago."

Sighing, Mr. Henning ushered Hanns inside and pointed to the living room, which was adjacent to the entryway, indicating that the captain should make himself comfortable.

"Tea?" Mr. Henning asked Hanns but didn't wait for a reply as he headed straight for the kitchen with his head down, carefully placing each foot in front of the other.

"Sit on the chair or the couch. Whatever you find more comfortable," Mrs. Henning shouted as she ran up the stairs. "I'm just going to make myself decent."

Alright, Hanns shook his head at the peculiarity, wishing that his brother Paul was with him to witness this. Sitting on one of the couches, Hanns looked around the little house and noticed that there were many photographs of what he assumed was their daughter and grandchildren, but no photos of Gustav. Given their overwhelming excitement to receive him, Hanns was confident that they would be more than willing to assist his investigation.

The kettle whistled and Mr. Henning half-heartedly returned to the living room with a cup of tea that he handed to Hanns.

"Thank you," Hanns nodded as he set his cup on the coffee table.

With an exaggerated grunt, the kind that grandfathers are chiefly expert at, Mr. Henning sat on the couch opposite Hanns. Less than enthusiastic about starting a conversation, Mr. Henning sat quietly staring into his teacup as he waited for Mrs. Henning. The clock on the wall ticked patiently as the two sat in silence, waiting for what they both knew would be the plummet into a whirlwind of a discussion.

"What's that?" Mr. Henning broke the silence and frowned at Hanns' pants.

"Pardon?" Hanns glanced down and noticed an oily stain. "Oh, right. Some tuna escaped my sandwich."

"Huh," Mr. Henning shrugged and took a sip of tea.

"Coming!" Mrs. Henning shouted as she clumped down the stairs. She was not a large woman in respect to either height or width, but the sound of her heavy tread greatly exaggerated her figure.

"Sorry about that," Mrs. Henning panted as she slumped down on the couch beside Mr. Henning whose eyes flew wide with panic as he kept his tea from spilling.

"As I said at the door," Hanns put his cup down on the table in front of him and held his hands together as he sat on the edge of the couch, "I'm looking for information on Gust-"

"I'd prefer it if you didn't say his name," Mrs. Henning held up her hand, still panting from her excursion.

"Sure," Hanns said slowly. "Do you have anything which could help me?"

"For Gustav?" Mrs. Henning frowned.

"Correct," Hanns nodded, marveling at her ability to break her own rule so quickly.

"Not a thing," Mrs. Henning tilted her head apologetically. "We haven't spoken to him much since the divorce which was, oh, how long ago was that now, dear?"

"Hmm?" Mr. Henning looked up from his tea at Mrs. Henning and it was clear to Hanns that Mr. Henning wasn't involved in much conversation.

"How long ago was the divorce?" Mrs. Henning whispered as if saying the word was forbidden, then gave a slap on his leg. "Pay attention."

"Oh," Mr. Henning threw his lips upside down. "That was maybe —"

"Now I remember," Mrs. Henning interrupted and lifted a finger as she recalled. "That was three or so years ago."

"Hmm," Hanns glanced at Mr. Henning who returned to the tranquil enjoyment of his tea.

"Mr. Henning?" Hanns pressed.

"Yes, Captain?" Mr. Henning glanced at Hanns as if he had awoken him from a trance.

"Do you have anything to add?" Hanns continued.

"I —" Mr. Henning began.

"Oh," Mrs. Henning chuckled, "he's always quiet. Can never get a word in with me around," she laughed.

Mr. Henning shrugged his shoulders as he agreed.

"Believe me," Mrs. Henning put her hand to her chest, "if we had any information, we would gladly give it. That pitiful excuse for a man robbed our daughter of her future. He left her with nothing. Practically kicked her out and abandoned her on the street," Mrs. Henning waved her hands in the air as she became animated.

"Mr. Henning," Hanns ignored Mrs. Henning for a moment. "I've been doing this job for some time now. I can tell when someone is hiding a secret."

"What's he saying?" Mrs. Henning spun on the couch as she looked at Mr. Henning in shock.

"I've been trying to tell you," Mr. Henning began.

"Tell me what?!" Mrs. Henning straightened as she looked at him with wrath.

"The neighbors saw our little Gustav backpacking through the yards with two other girls."

"Our little Gustav? Are you certain?" Mrs. Henning slapped her knee in astonishment and then turned to Hanns, "Little Gustav is our grandson." Then, turning back to her husband, "Why didn't you tell me?"

"I tried. I—"

"Oh," Mrs. Henning leaned back as she put her hand to her head. "This is unbelievable. Our little Gustav. He's gotten himself in quite a bit of trouble."

"Do you know where—" Hanns began.

"He used to be such a good boy," Mrs. Henning interrupted, and the habit was becoming increasingly irritating. Hanns wondered how Mr. Henning had stomached these tendencies for all these years.

"Where can I find him?" Hanns spoke quickly so as not to be interrupted again.

"That I don't know, either," Mrs. Henning shook her head in regret. "I'm afraid we aren't much help."

"But," Mr. Henning spoke, yet seemed surprised when Mrs. Henning remained quiet.

"But what?" Mrs. Henning looked at him crossly.

"We do know where the twins are," he tilted his head.

"Twins? What twins?" Mrs. Henning frowned at Mr. Henning.

"The ones our little Gustav was seen with by the neighbors," Mr. Henning pointed in the direction.

"You didn't say he was with the twins," Mrs. Henning shook her head in frustration.

"Yes, I did," Mr. Henning defended, bravely.

"You said," Mrs. Henning pointed her finger at her husband, "our little Gustav was spotted with two other girls."

"Yes," Mr. Henning pressed, "the twins!"

"Where?" Hanns half shouted and both looked at him in surprise for the raised voice.

"Where can I find these twins?" Hanns cleared his throat.

"They're in Marburg," Mr. Henning replied.

"Where in Marburg?" Hanns set his pen to his notepad.

"Oh," Mr. Henning looked up as he searched his memory, "that I can't help you with."

"Of course," Hanns muttered.

"They're conniving things, these twins," Mrs. Henning shuddered. "They turned our sweet little Gustav rotten like his father. I warned our daughter, didn't I?" she slapped Mr. Henning's knee.

"Warned her of what?" Mr. Henning looked at her with confusion.

"To not marry that wretched man," Mrs. Henning grew cross. "I could sense it," she shook her head. "From the very first time I met him I could sense the evil in him."

"You and Gustav got on rather well at the start," Mr. Henning frowned and was swiftly met by another swat on his knee and a warning glare from his wife.

"Anyways," Mrs. Henning returned to smiling at Hanns, "they will likely try and trick you as they tricked us."

"How so?" Hanns asked.

"Well they told us that our little Gustav was in Dassel. Didn't they?" Mrs. Henning looked at Mr. Henning who confirmed with a nod.

"We sent him a whole care package," Mrs. Henning shook her head. "We received the package back in the mail with a note that he hadn't lived there in nearly five months. Rather cruel thing to tell some worried grandparents. Then we find out that he's part of the resistance."

"You won't hurt him, will you?" Mr. Henning looked at Hanns with concern.

"Of course not," Hanns reassured them. "He's not my target, but I think your grandson may have information on his father."

"Such shame he brought on us," Mrs. Henning grew solemn and stared into the carpet. "My daughter did the right thing in removing herself from his care. She was lucky to have us around, otherwise I don't think she would've gotten far. She lives in near poverty now, but her conscience is clear. Debt is a lighter burden than a doomed soul."

"I'd agree with that," Hanns nodded, but then added. "I should get going. Thank you for the tea and your assistance."

"If there's anything else we can do, don't hesitate to stop by," Mrs. Henning chuckled as she ushered Hanns to the door.

"That's very kind of you."

"Oh, Captain," Mrs. Henning called as Hanns walked towards the truck.

"Yes?" Hanns turned and stopped in the walkway.

"If you do find our little Gustav, can you tell him that his grandparents send their love?"

"That I can do," Hanns smiled.

Thank God those two weren't Nazis, Hanns chuckled as he started the truck. *The interrogations would be awful. I'll have to write Paul about this. Though, I suppose the circumstances call for someone to be present in order to understand the humor of the situation.*

<u>Marburg, seventy miles north of Frankfurt.</u>

Nostalgia washed over Hanns as he pulled up to the town of Marburg. He remembered, as a child, his parents taking him and Paul on an adventure through the town. Of course, as young twins, they didn't care much for the ancient university or the grand architecture of the old churches. But what had caught their attention was the pathway devoted to the Brothers Grimm who had attended the university. The quaint, half-timbered houses accompanied by the enchanting forest and streams nearby were the inspiration for many of the Grimm fairy tales. The city gave off the impression that it had been untouched since knights strolled the cobblestone streets with their valiant steeds. The thick forest hinted that it was alive and hiding witches' huts and goblin holes.

I should get something to eat first, Hanns thought as he walked through the cobblestone market. He was happy to see that it was brimming with life, just as he had remembered it as a child. Vendors shouted for passersby to inspect their produce, and prospective customers passively acknowledged their pleas as they strolled slowly through the market.

Yet now many of the buildings had been damaged during the bombings. Construction was well underway to restore the town to its original glory, and many of the residents went about their days as if this was all normal. Though, Hanns supposed, after living through a war for so many years, one can adapt rather quickly.

Passing through the crowded street market in the square, Hanns kept his eye open for something to eat. He didn't need much, just something to tide him over. Then, after a quick, sentimental viewing of the town, he planned to head to the police station for information on the twins.

"How much?" Hanns asked one of the vendors after he had spotted an apple.

But the vendor didn't reply. The man simply glared at Hanns. He was a large man with a robust beard who looked like he had recently lost a substantial amount of weight. There was a bitterness in his gaze, and Hanns felt confident that he understood the reason.

"Is it the uniform or the fact that I'm Jewish?" Hanns spoke boldly.

Still, the vendor didn't reply; but pointed to a sign beside his stand which stated the price of the fruit.

"That's steep!" Hanns threw his eyebrows up. "I can't afford that for an apple!"

"Then you shouldn't have bombed our warehouses and crashed the economy," the vendor spoke with such venom that Hanns felt as if he was speaking with a demon.

Shaken a little by the encounter, Hanns left the vendor and decided to head back to the truck. But, as he walked, a sharp and unapologetic elbow found its way into Hanns' shoulder.

"Hey!" Hanns turned to see who had hit him, but they had already disappeared into the crowd.

Rubbing his shoulder, Hanns looked around the market and became increasingly aware of the unwelcoming glares. Vendors clenched their jaws and leaned over their stands as they watched him carefully. A familiar fear grew within Hanns: the same terror which caused his family to flee Germany. Because of the coincidence of his birth, the Germans in this market hated him. They didn't know his character, nor did they care. He was a Jew in a British uniform and to them he was responsible for the death of their loved ones, the destruction of their sacred Germany; he was the enemy above all enemies.

Hanns left the market as he nearly ran back to the truck and, once securely inside, he leaned over the steering wheel as he shook slightly. A sorrow grew within Hanns at the realization that, once his task of catching these Nazis was complete, Germany had no place for him. In his heart, he knew that he would likely never return. He had seen hostile crowds before and realized the stupidity of going around a pro-Nazi town by himself. Though, he supposed, it was difficult to tell which town had such sympathies until he arrived.

You'll just have to be more careful, Hanns warned himself and sped off to the police station. Hanns' route took him parallel with the Lahn River that cut the town of Marburg in half. Still, for all its beauty, there was a callousness about the town with its open hostility. Whatever sentiment Hanns had felt for the sweet childhood memories was lost to their hatred, and he couldn't wait to leave for good.

Arriving at the police station, Hanns cautioned himself for the eventuality that he might be met with the same aggression. Taking a deep breath before he exited, Hanns reminded himself of his purpose.

"How can I help you?" the clerk at the desk asked dryly as she completed her paperwork.

"I'm Captain Volker," Hanns began. "From the War Crimes Investigation Team."

"Oh," the clerk looked up quickly and immediately put her pencil down. "Yes, yes. Come with me. The constable received your message."

Following behind the clerk, Hanns walked past a narrow stone corridor. While some of the prison had been updated, it remained medieval in its appearance which Hanns thought could be quite beneficial should the use of intimidation be necessary.

"Constable Hevel?" the clerk opened the door to a small office.

"Yes?" came a quick reply.

"Captain Volker is here."

"Oh, good!" Constable Hevel could be heard shuffling things around on his desk. "How do I look?" he asked the clerk.

"I'll let the Captain decide," she ushered Hanns into the room as Hevel grew embarrassed that his vanity had been overheard.

Sitting beside the desk was a girl, who Hanns assumed was about ten or eleven, and she was happily kicking her legs and brushing the hair of her doll.

"Constable," Hanns extended his hand as he glanced at the peculiarity of the girl in the office.

"Captain," the constable shook his hand and pointed to the chair in front of his desk for him to sit.

"This is my daughter, Gisela," the constable took notice of Hanns' curiosity.

Hanns nodded at Gisela, but she ignored him. He wasn't great with kids, especially not at the age of this girl. He enjoyed younger children, ones that you could wrestle with and tease, but once they began to take life a little more seriously, Hanns was at a loss.

"What can I assist you with?" the constable asked and tried to position himself to look important but failed in this regard and appeared more awkward than anything.

"Is Gisela going to stay with us?" Hanns glanced again at the girl who continued to play with her doll.

"Right," Constable Hevel became flustered as he tapped his daughter on the shoulder. "Gisela, dear, would you mind seeing if Miss Ruth can watch you for a minute?"

Without so much as a word, Gisela jumped out of her seat and walked out of the office.

"Rather quiet," Hanns smiled at Hevel.

"She hasn't spoken since," Hevel cleared his throat, "well, since, her mother passed in a bombing raid."

"I'm sorry," Hanns became uncomfortable for the blunder. "I shouldn't have mentioned anything."

"No, no," Hevel waved him off. "You didn't know. Anyways, to the business at hand. Your message mentioned that you were looking for our assistance?"

"Yes," Hanns cleared his throat, "I'm looking for two girls, twins actually, who may have some information for me."

"What are their names?" Constable Hevel frowned as he tried to appear serious and retrieved a pen and notepad.

"All I know is their last name, unfortunately."

"Which is?" the constable asked.

"Henning," Hanns replied.

"Ah," the constable sat upright without writing anything. "I was afraid of that."

"Oh?" Hanns frowned.

"Anna and Frau Henning," the constable leaned back in his chair and folded his hands. "Those two have been on our radar for some time."

"They've been trouble for you, then?"

"No," the constable glanced at Hanns, "which is why they are so peculiar. We have it on good authority that they are involved with the Werwolf resistance, but they haven't done anything whatsoever to confirm these suspicions."

"Do you think maybe your information is incorrect?"

"No, no," the constable laughed. "They are cunning, very cunning girls. Twins, you see, have this telepathic ability."

"Do they now?" Hanns smiled, *I wonder when I can tell Paul the good news. Or maybe he already knows.*

"Oh yes," the constable continued. "It's been proven, scientifically speaking."

"Do you know where they are now?" Hanns asked.

"As of yesterday," the constable turned in his chair and opened a drawer from his desk where he pulled out a logbook, "they were at home."

"What's the address?" Hanns asked. "I'll go talk to them."

"With all due respect, Captain, you don't know these girls."

"So, what do you suggest?"

"I'll send my men to bring them in and you can question them here."

Hanns thought for a moment as he looked at the wall, "Won't that contravene the law with respect to action towards civilians?"

"I'm not arresting them," the constable smirked. "They're just coming for a tour of the police station and we can ask them a couple questions while they're here."

"Alright," Hanns nodded. "If you think that will work."

"I'll send my best men to collect them," the constable stood excitedly. "Have you eaten?"

"I have not, but food sounds wonderful about now," Hanns grinned.

Hanns sat in the interview room, preparing his questions as he had done dozens of times with the SS guards. Yet, for some reason, Hanns was still tense. And he had good reason, too. This interview was, by nature, illegal. He had no authority to arrest citizens, and it contravened the law. Still, Hanns knew that the girls had information on Gustav's son. He was willing to sacrifice a little of his conscience for the greater good.

Eventually, the door to the interview room opened and two beautiful young ladies in their early twenties were ushered in by Constable Hevel. Both wore matching light blue dresses with matching blue hats and bright, white gloves which were impeccably tidy. One of the twins wore their hat leaning slightly to the left while the other had hers leaning to the right.

Both moved in a synchronized flow and, sitting in front of Hanns, one crossed her legs to the right while the other crossed her legs to the left. Then, both lightly set their hands on their laps in a distinguished manner and gave Hanns a slightly seductive smile. The twins were alluring with stunning, bright blue eyes and they used this to their full advantage.

Clearing his throat, Hanns looked down at his papers as the man within him retreated and a sweaty-palmed adolescent emerged. While he tried his best to hide his boyish discomfort, Hanns delved into a graceless fumbling of his documents with his suddenly fat fingers. The harder he tried to correct his blunder, the further he tunneled into the embarrassing pit of regret.

"You can't arrest us," one of the twins confronted and her rich, northern accent made Hanns weak in the knees.

"We've done nothing wrong," the other chimed in.

"This isn't an arrest," Hanns cleared his throat and folded his hands to try and contain his nervous twitching. "I just want to chat."

"We don't know anything," the first twin groaned.

"First off," Hanns clicked his pen as he prepared to write, "what are your names?"

"I'm Frau Henning," the sister to his left, spoke.

"And I'm Anna Henning," the second replied.

"Frau and Anna," Hanns muttered as he wrote their names down. "Alright, Frau," he turned towards the first twin on his left.

"I'm Anna," she scowled.

"You told me that you were Frau," Hanns squinted.

"No," the second twin defended, "I'm Frau."

Glancing between the two of them, Hanns guessed the game that they were playing and, for the first time, understood the utter frustration that he and his twin brother Paul had caused their teachers. But, thankfully, this little ploy of theirs gave Hanns the sense that he had the upper hand and along with it came the confidence that he so desperately needed.

Leaning in, Hanns glared at Frau on his left, and then turned his attention to Anna on his right. Neither seemed to budge in their stubborn defiance, but both gave off the sense that they had been cornered.

"I'm a twin myself," Hanns whispered, and Constable Hevel's arms fell to his side in shock. "I'm aware of these little tricks. Hell, my brother and I invented most of them."

Realizing that they had been ousted, the twins crossed their arms. Again, they moved in a synchronized manner as if the two had practiced for this very occasion.

"I think it's best if I talk to each of you separately," Hanns signaled for the constable to remove Anna.

"I'm not leaving my sister!" Anna refused to move.

"That's enough!" Hanns pounded his fist on the table and stood as his face grew red with rage. "You are impeding my investigation and I can, and will, arrest you for obstruction of justice."

The twins stared at Hanns wide-eyed. Then, glancing at each other, they burst into laughter and began mocking Hanns with a silly voice, "Impeding my investigation."

"Remove her," Hanns ordered.

"See what I mean," Constable Hevel mumbled to Hanns as he grabbed Anna's arm.

"I'm not leaving her!" Anna shouted as the constable forced her out of the room.

"Now we can continue," Hanns sat back down and calmed a little, though he was quite disappointed that he had failed to intimidate them. Captain Fox's talents for coercion through the threat of violence had not transferred automatically to Hanns.

"I'm not saying a word until my sister is back in the room," Frau stared defiantly at Hanns.

"I have it on good authority that you are part of the Werwolf resistance," Hanns scowled back at her.

Frau remained silent.

"I can't arrest you for treason as I work with the British government, but I'm happy to inform those in your government of your seditious behavior. I am, however, willing to turn a blind eye if you simply provide me with some information."

"What information?" Frau squinted at Hanns.

"Where is Gustav Adolph Simon? Or better yet, where is his father?"

"That's it?" Frau threw her eyebrows up, unimpressed.

"What do you mean 'that's it'?" Hanns frowned back at her.

"I know exactly where he is," Frau shrugged.

"Really?"

"Ya, that idiot took our money and fled. I'll give you his exact address."

"And?" Hanns put his pen to paper, ready to write.

"He's in Dassel."

Sighing, Hanns put his pen down. He recalled the warning from Mr. and Mrs. Henning that they had been incorrectly advised that their grandson was in Dassel.

"Constable Hevel," Hanns shouted as he glared at Frau. "Bring Miss Anna in and remove Miss Frau."

The constable complied and a heated exchange took place as the twins were again separated from each other.

"Frau told me the location of my suspect," Hanns smiled as he studied Anna after she had been seated.

Anna huffed, "I don't believe you."

"You can ask her yourself when we're done."

"Why would she tell you?"

"Because I'm after Gustav Adolph Simon."

"Oh," Anna chuckled, "ya I can see why she told you."

"Well," Hanns shrugged, "where is he?"

"I thought she told you?"

"I just need to confirm that the information is accurate."

"He's in Dassel," Anna nodded.

"Dassel?! That's not what Frau said," Hanns lied.

Anna frowned sharply and her eyes flinched ever so slightly, just enough for Hanns to recognize that the lie had been exposed.

Hanns grew a slight, victorious grin, proving to Anna that he understood the twins' game. But Anna, for all her cunning, refused to allow this momentary slip to defeat her so easily. Crossing her arms, she jutted out her chin and refused to offer another word.

Leaning forward, Hanns glared at her as he grew hateful. He was furious that they thought that they could deceive him. That they would, for all the wrong reasons, aid young Gustav by not telling Hanns the suspect's location. These two beautiful girls, who had privileges many could only dream of, were throwing it away for some insufferable and dying ideology.

"Constable Hevel," Hanns called, realizing that it was useless to question Anna any longer.

"Yes, Captain?" Hevel poked his head into the room.

"Do you have two cells available?"

"Oh yes," the constable nodded eagerly.

"And are they beside each other?"

"They're on opposite sides of the cell block."

"Perfect," Hanns rubbed his hands together. "Take Frau to one and then return for Anna."

"You can't do this!" Anna grew enraged as her eyes bulged with fear.

"Actually, we can," Hanns sat on the desk in front of her. "You see, you're obstructing justice, which is illegal.

We have cause for your arrest. You can tell me the truth now if you'd like?"

"I told you the truth!" Anna clutched her purse tight to her chest.

"Alright then," Hanns grabbed her roughly by the arm and stood her to her feet.

"You're hurting me!" Anna tried to wrench herself free.

"Do you think that your Nazis cared when they killed millions of my people?" Hanns released his grip as he spoke to her softly. "How do you think the resistance will react knowing that you spent the night in jail? They'd assume that you broke and told us something.

"You idiot," Anna slapped him.

"Where is he?" Hanns remained calm, despite the stinging of his flesh. He needed her to believe that the strike caused him no harm.

"I told you," Anna pursed her lips as she grew enraged. "Dassel!"

"You're lying," Hanns leaned in and flinched his eye. "He hasn't been to Dassel in five months."

"I…" Anna was lost for words.

"Constable, if you would be so kind," Hanns gestured for him to take her away.

"Plettenberg. He's in Plettenberg," Anna wept. "Please, I can't spend the night here. If the resistance found out, we'd be killed."

"Where in Plettenberg?" Hanns rushed over to his notepad.

"I don't know!" Anna cried.

"Where?!" Hanns looked at her sternly.

"He's at 38 Dingeringhauser Weg," Anna sobbed.

"The Fuhrer would be most displeased with you," Hanns smiled as he ran out of the cell, followed by an ecstatic Constable Hevel.

"Is there anything I can help with?" Hevel asked.

"I need you and your best men with me," Hanns grabbed him by the shoulder. "We leave in ten minutes."

Chapter Nineteen:
Revelation

We are told that the American soldier does not know what he is fighting for. Now, at least, he will know what he is fighting against.

General Dwight D. Eisenhower (after visiting a Nazi extermination camp)

Eleonore sat on the edge of her bed as the sun began to rise. Sleep had evaded her, again, as she pondered the likelihood of her employment being terminated. Life at the manor, which she had come to love, seemed to be over just as it began. The first man that she had felt any real affection for would lose out on his future because of the kindling of their relationship.

Eleonore grew bitter towards life as she contemplated her trials. She had followed her conscience which led her to being detained at Auschwitz. She experienced horrors no one should ever endure, and still her tribulations were nothing in comparison to what others had suffered.

Now she had followed her heart which was about to lead towards her termination of employment. Because of the moving of her soul, she would become both unemployed and homeless. Existence was unjust, unfair, and she hated that she was being so selfish when many others would beg to be in her position.

With a deep breath, Eleonore made the plunge into the unknown and headed towards Mrs. Meyers' room. Walking down the winding stairs, Eleonore glided her hand on the smooth railing, locking the feeling into memory. Leaving the wing, Eleonore entered the foyer and smiled at the sound of Ben shouting at another delivery boy. Yet, when Ben spotted Eleonore, he grew a little shameful and his demeanor changed as he began to speak with a touch more patience.

Pausing in the foyer, Eleonore inspected the manor as she took in the view for what she assumed would be the last time.

She grinned as she looked at the little, round table where she had eaten and talked with Ben on many sleepless nights. She wished that she could've indulged with a book or two in that spot, but she was never afforded the luxury of time. Besides, any moment that was available to her she found herself with Ben. She glanced at the front porch where she had borrowed more than her share of cigarettes from the butler and he had not so much as complained once.

But then Eleonore spotted Eva in the dining room, setting up the chairs and cleaning the table. The manor, Eleonore understood, brought her warm memories because of Ben, and Eva, in her jealousy, was about to embitter her potential happiness. Eleonore knew that it would be unproductive to confront her, but impulse was guiding her now and she felt that she had little to lose.

Entering the dining room, Eleonore crossed her arms and stood at a distance behind Eva as she watched her with scathing resentment. Eventually, Eva noticed her and, slowly, ceased cleaning as she studied Eleonore warily.

"What do you want?" Eva glared.

"To be honest," Eleonore frowned as she looked at her feet, "I don't know."

"Then why are you here?" Eva shook her head.

"I think," Eleonore cleared her throat, "I think I want you to know that I'll win."

"Pardon?"

"I want you to know that no matter what happens today, whether Mrs. Meyers terminates my employment or keeps me on, that I'll be alright. I won't let you win. I won't let your pettiness have victory over me."

"We'll see about that," Eva gave a cocky smile. "Mr. Mattaliano doesn't know that you were sent to spy on Mrs. Meyers, does he?"

"I'm not here to spy on her," Eleonore scoffed. "Whatever gave you that idea?"

"So, you're not here to investigate why she's giving money to the Werwolf resistance?" Eva raised her eyebrow.

"She's what?!" Eleonore's heart sank.

"Who do you think the gardener is?" Eva snickered. "Who do you think I am?"

"I don't believe you," Eleonore shook her head, but felt her heart pounding and her throat closing.

"You don't have to believe me," Eva grinned. "Though, I am curious what will happen when the war crimes team reads the letter that I sent them explaining that you were complicit in Mrs. Meyers' support of the Werwolf resistance."

"What?!" Eleonore's eyes flew wide. "You're bluffing!"

"Didn't you hand an envelope with money to the gardener?" Eva tilted her head.

"Well...I..."

"That money went to the resistance," Eva shot her eyebrow up.

"You're lying," Eleonore clenched her jaw.

"You can try to deny it," Eva grinned, "but you know, in your heart, that I'm telling the truth."

"That night, when you came to my room," Eleonore trembled slightly as her eyes welled, "why were you really there?"

"To see how much you knew," Eva spoke plainly.

"And that's why you wouldn't tell me anything about your past or how you came to work at the manor," Eleonore closed her eyes as the reality sank in.

"People often hesitate to ask further questions if they believe that the topic is sensitive," Eva grinned. "You're too polite."

"I understand," Eleonore gave a quick nod before leaving Eva. She wasn't as clever as her, but she supposed that was because Eva was sinister while Eleonore would rather believe that people were honest. Still, the world had changed, and Eleonore understood that if she was to survive then she would have to adapt.

Returning to the foyer, Eleonore found that the delivery boy had left, and Ben was standing lazily in front of a few boxes of produce. Sighing, he rubbed the back of his neck as he stared at his chore, not wanting to complete his task.

Yet Eleonore burned with rage as she looked at him in a new light. If he had known what was happening at the manor but hid it from her, then he had wounded her beyond repair.

"Miss Hodys," Ben spoke to her casually as she walked by him, ignorant of her daggering eyes.

But, when Eleonore had climbed a few stairs, the burden of not knowing weighed too heavily on her and, turning, she asked, "Did you know?"

"Know what?" he replied briskly as he remained staring at his duties.

"Look at me," Eleonore asked quietly, but Ben paid her little attention as he was lost to his mental organization.

"Look at me!" Eleonore demanded, and the butler turned to her in surprise.

"What's wrong?" he frowned and moved to the bottom of the stairs as he looked up at her with concern.

"Did you know?" Eleonore tilted her head as she looked eagerly into his eyes, praying that he wouldn't give the answer that she dreaded.

"Know what?" he shrugged and looked back into the dining area, seemingly confused.

"Ben," Eleonore closed her eyes and took measured breaths to calm herself.

"I can explain," Ben spoke tenderly, and Eleonore opened her eyes and watched, in horror, as Ben's expression confirmed her fears.

"How could you?" Eleonore shook her head.

"I haven't done anything," the butler raised his hand in defence.

"You knew that she was funding the resistance, yet you said nothing to me."

"I think we both have some things which need discussing," Ben reached for her hand, but she pulled away.

"I don't think there is anything that could excuse this," Eleonore glared at him.

"Eleonore," Ben reached again for her hand, but she withdrew.

"I'm going to give Mrs. Meyers my resignation," Eleonore turned and climbed the stairs as tears streamed down her face.

"Eleonore!" Ben called, but she ignored him.

Stopping in the hallway, Eleonore paused to collect herself. She felt as though she was the very definition of ignorance for being the only one who didn't realize what was happening. But, in the back of her mind, she supposed that she knew all along. She had suppressed her suspicions with the hope that life here could be what she needed: normal. She knew that the gardener was not who he claimed to be, and it was ridiculous to believe otherwise.

Is Ben part of the resistance? Eleonore's mind began to wander as she questioned her reality. *No, he can't be,* Eleonore shook her head. *It's not possible.*

With a deep breath, Eleonore unlocked Mrs. Meyers' door and entered to find the room was pitch black. The curtains had been drawn, but with the little light that came from the door, Eleonore spotted Mrs. Meyers sitting expectantly on the bed.

"Light a candle," Mrs. Meyers spoke coldly.

"There is something we need to discuss," Eleonore spoke softly after she had lit the candle and then closed the door.

"I have considered your employment," Mrs. Meyers ignored Eleonore.

"About that," Eleonore began as she stood before her mistress as the dim glow of the flame flickered between them.

"You know what you are?" Mrs. Meyers glared at Eleonore.

"Pardon?" Eleonore frowned.

"You are a distraction. Nothing more."

"I don't understand," Eleonore put a hand to her chest.

"Who is the gramophone playing for?" Mrs. Meyers stood and began to walk towards Eleonore who backed away. "Who was that trek into town for? These distractions are nothing but a temporary relief. I know that you tried to heal me, to repair my soul, but there is no fix to this, Miss Hodys. Now there are no more distractions to fill the void, and I am forced to face these ghosts," she pointed towards the urns.

In shock, Eleonore watched Mrs. Meyers at a loss for what to say.

"I have a task for you," Mrs. Meyers calmed a little and opened the drawer beside her bed, "and after it is done, your services are dismissed."

"Mrs. Meyers, I—"

"I am undone," Mrs. Meyers gritted her teeth as she handed a heavy envelope to Eleonore.

"Ma'am," Eleonore spoke softly, "I can't give this to the gardener. I can't ignore the facts any longer."

"I know," Mrs. Meyers sat on the edge of the bed as she remained reserved.

Slowly, and cautiously, Eleonore sat beside Mrs. Meyers and reached out and held her hand. While Mrs. Meyers appeared withdrawn, she didn't protest to Eleonore's familiarity, which led her to believe that she was merely witnessing the collateral damage from an unseen battle.

"I think, on some level," Eleonore began, "you wanted me to find out. I think that you wanted me to turn you in, but I don't understand why?"

"You really are a stupid woman," Mrs. Meyers scoffed, and Eleonore felt her sympathy towards her evaporating.

But it was in this moment that Eleonore withheld what she wished to say and quieted her wrath for the aim of a higher purpose. Mrs. Meyers was grieving and, while all grief is an unshakable burden, hers was complex. Mrs. Meyers was like a wounded creature, snapping their jowls at anyone who got too close.

"It is my fault that they are dead," Mrs. Meyers began, coldly.

"How can you believe that?" Eleonore looked at Mrs. Meyers with incredulity.

"They were infected by Nazi idealism," Mrs. Meyers took a deep breath to try and steady her nerves before continuing quietly. "I warned them that it would lead to the disaster of the country and this house, but they could not see reason. Maybe if I had supported them, then they would be filling these halls and not sitting in jars at the foot of my bed."

"You know that is an irrational thought," Eleonore studied Mrs. Meyers with the greatest sympathy.

"Irrational is all that I am left with," Mrs. Meyers smirked quickly at Eleonore. "Saying it out loud does sound a little ridiculous, I admit, but I will not refuse to honor them in death when I failed to do so in life."

"Funding a resistance which desires to resurrect a wicked regime is not the way," Eleonore pressed. "And I believe you know that, and your conscience is conflicted."

"My conscience was clear until you arrived," Mrs. Meyers pursed her lips. "You had to fill my head with curiosity. I started researching, you know. You made me look at the horror of what they might have been involved with."

"Mrs. Meyers, I—"

"They cannot have died for nothing!" Mrs. Meyers screamed and wept as she slammed her fist into the bed. "I will not have it! It cannot be! It is a mother's job to protect her children and I have failed them in that regard! It is my fault that they are dead and I will pay the punishment for my sins."

Tears streamed from Eleonore's eyes as she watched a woman that she had come to love and adore be given over to this absurdity.

"So, you'll continue to fund the resistance then?" Eleonore closed her eyes, bracing herself for the answer.

"You don't understand," Mrs. Meyers looked away and returned to an expressionless, stern demeanor.

"I cannot give the gardener this money," Eleonore set the envelope on the bed. "I cannot participate in aiding that evil regime."

"I know," Mrs. Meyers bit her cheek. "You'll turn me in, then?"

"No," Eleonore sighed. "You're not doing this out of retribution, but I have to report the gardener. I'm certain that they have been searching for him. May I have his real name?"

Mrs. Meyers studied Eleonore for a moment as her expression was one of regret mixed with relief.

"Gustav Simon," Mrs. Meyers replied.

A chill ran down Eleonore's spine. She had heard that name before. She had read in the papers how Gustav Simon had bragged about 'cleansing' Luxemburg of all Jews. She remembered how, when Hanns and Genn bought her the dress, his son had been through that town.

"Why would someone like you, who, privately, denounced the Nazi party, help a man as wicked as Gustav?" Eleonore shook her head.

"I was unaware of his true identity," Mrs. Meyers cleared her throat. "When Mr. Mattaliano uncovered

Gustav's past, he begged me to banish him at once, but it was too late."

"Why didn't you say anything?" Eleonore squinted.

"I tried," Mrs. Meyers looked back at Eleonore. "I sent a cryptic message to the Allies that former SS guards were in the area. I had to be careful with what I said in case Gustav intercepted the letters. I also sent a request for a lady's maid and they sent you."

"But once I arrived, why didn't you tell me?" Eleonore pressed.

"I did," Mrs. Meyers spoke with little emotion. "I asked you to give an extraordinary sum of money to a man who was clearly not a gardener."

"I was under strict instructions not to contact the office unless I had specifics," Eleonore sighed. "You should've told me, plainly, who Gustav was."

"And if I did," Mrs. Meyers paused as she looked at Eleonore softly, "then you would have left me."

Eleonore watched in astonishment as Mrs. Meyers reached over and grabbed her hand and squeezed tightly. Eleonore believed that she had been of little impact to this woman, but now she understood that Mrs. Meyers cherished her.

"I was under the impression that you thought little of me," Eleonore watched Mrs. Meyers warily.

"On the contrary," Mrs. Meyers took a deep breath before continuing and Eleonore understood that she was uncomfortable with such open discussions, "I am an old woman sitting in darkness, and you are the light which burns my eyes. You are everything I shall never be. You have a strength which I could only dream of."

A chill rippled through her body. She remembered how often she had spoken such similar words when she thought of Ella. Now, someone was admiring her in much the same way.

"I realize that you have to report what is happening at the manor," Mrs. Meyers released her grip.

"I do," Eleonore spoke solemnly.

"They can't have died for nothing," Mrs. Meyers whispered and shook her head in despair. "Please understand that."

"I don't think I could ever understand what you are feeling," Eleonore nodded, "but I will try."

"This is the last of my money," Mrs. Meyers patted the envelope. "And inside is the deed to the manor, to be delivered to Gustav."

"You were never going to give Mr. Mattaliano his inheritance, were you?"

Mrs. Meyers shook her head as she stared at her feet in shame. Eleonore watched and grieved for her. Mrs. Meyers was hurting, deeply. Eleonore understood that all Mrs. Meyers had of her children and her husband was memory. If that memory was tainted, then she would have nothing left and her long-suffering years would count for nothing.

With a sigh, Eleonore took her leave and returned to her room. Searching through her belongings, as limited as they were, Eleonore grabbed the piece of paper that Hanns had given her with the number to the office and mailing address.

Eleonore sat on the edge of her bed as she held the paper in her hands. She knew that she had to make the call, it was the right thing to do, but she also understood that it meant the end of her time as a lady's maid to Mrs. Meyers. Still, she couldn't allow the wicked regime any momentum to rear its ugly head.

Just make the call, Eleonore took a deep breath. *Then, it's out of your hands. Better a light conscience and no job than a heavy one working here. Besides, maybe I can get a position with Hanns' outfit.*

Summoning her courage, Eleonore returned to the dining room. Walking over to the phone by the window, Eleonore looked out into the backyard, checking to see if the gardener, or Gustav Simon, as she now knew him, was around. With the rising sun casting the sky in an array of bright oranges and pinks, it was difficult to see much of anything, but Eleonore was confident that he was not in sight.

"How may I connect you?" the operator answered.

"War Crimes Office, please," Eleonore cleared her throat.

"Which office ma'am?"

"The War Crimes Office," Eleonore repeated and glanced at the card to make sure that she had the name right.

"Yes, ma'am, I meant which War Crimes Office?"

"Ah, I see, uh, Belsen," Eleonore fiddled with the paper awkwardly, feeling rather foolish. "No. 1 War Crimes Investigation Team."

"One moment while I connect you," the operator replied as the line went silent.

Sighing, Eleonore held her hand under her arm as she waited patiently on the phone. The silence on the other end was deafening, and Eleonore wondered if the operator had accidentally disconnected the line.

Glancing again out the window, Eleonore's heart stopped. The outline of two men were approaching in her direction, walking casually with their hands in their pockets and had not noticed Eleonore in the window. One she recognized as the gardener, and the other she knew instinctively, undeniably, was Jung.

What do I do? Eleonore began to panic and turned her back to the men. *Hurry up, hurry up,* Eleonore begged for the phone lines to be connected.

"Belsen, No. 1 War Crime Investigation Team," a woman spoke in English.

"Uh, uh," Eleonore tried to remember her limited English, but panic was setting in and she couldn't think properly.

"Hanns Volker?" Eleonore spit out the name.

"Pardon?" the voice replied calmly, ignorant to the danger that Eleonore was in.

What name did he go by? Eleonore tapped her fingers against her forehead and glanced again out the window as the men drew closer, still unaware of her presence.

"Howard Volker!" Eleonore blurted when she remembered.

"He's..." the operator explained but Eleonore couldn't translate quickly enough.

"Sorry," Eleonore spoke in broken English. "Slower?"

"What?" the receptionist grew annoyed.

"Say slower," Eleonore felt her heart pounding in her chest as the back door to the kitchen opened.

"Howard is currently away."

"Message," Eleonore spoke quietly as she turned her back to the kitchen, hoping beyond hope that Jung had not recognized her. "Message to Howard."

"Ma'am," the receptionist groaned, "you're going to have to speak louder."

"Message to Howard," Eleonore spoke louder and began to shake.

The two men spoke in a hushed tone, and Eleonore could hear footsteps approaching slowly behind her, but she didn't dare turn around. The two men continued to whisper about ten yards behind Eleonore who, at the very least, could tell that the conversation had nothing to do with her.

"What's the message?" the receptionist asked.

"Help," Eleonore shook.

"Is everything alright ma'am? Should you be calling the police?"

Eleonore remained silent, not daring to say another word with the two men behind her.

"Ma'am?"

Suddenly, the conversation behind her stopped, and Eleonore could feel the heat of their gaze.

"Who's calling?" the receptionist asked as she grew concerned.

Eleonore set the phone down slowly, knowing that if she said another word that she would doom herself.

"Who are you speaking to?" Gustav demanded in a cold, heartless voice.

"Just an errand for the mistress," Eleonore remained with her back to him, praying that Jung hadn't recognized her or her voice.

"Eleonore?" Jung spoke, and his words cut into her soul.

Slowly, Eleonore turned and locked eyes with the ex-lieutenant. He was skinny and famished with dark circles under his eyes and an unkempt beard. He looked exactly how Eleonore thought of him: an animal on the run.

"Yes?" Eleonore kept her eyes locked on him as a prey watches their hunter.

"I...I'm not sure what to say. How are you?" Jung studied her with pleasant surprise, but then grew disappointed that her reaction did not match his.

"Who were you talking to on the phone?" Gustav walked closer to her.

Eleonore didn't answer, but simply stood there, shaking before them. She wished that she could hide her emotions and offer some clever fabrication, but seeing Jung again transported Eleonore back to the camps. She remembered witnessing him beat Ella within an inch of her life, how he tried to take advantage of her at the hospital, and discovering that he invented the cruel game to play on the inmates.

"Eleonore," Jung took a step towards her and she immediately stepped back.

"We don't mean you any harm," Jung raised his hands slightly as he looked at her earnestly.

"Speak for yourself," Gustav smiled after a lustful examination of Eleonore, who felt her skin crawling with disgust.

"The mistress needs me," Eleonore tried to brush past them, but Gustav put his arm out to stop her.

"Hold on now," Gustav pushed her back with little effort.

"Let me go," Eleonore looked sternly at Gustav, "or my lady will hear of this."

"I'm not concerned with her opinion," Gustav moved closer to Eleonore.

"Leave her alone," Jung pushed Gustav aside who looked at him in surprise.

"What is she to you?" Gustav frowned.

"Who were you talking to on the phone?" Jung looked at Eleonore as he ignored Gustav.

"As I said, it was an errand for my lady," Eleonore tried to remain calm as she spoke.

"Which was?" Jung squinted.

"That's my lady's business," Eleonore swallowed. "If you'd like to discuss her dealings, you will have to speak with her directly."

"Eleonore, the truth if you will," Jung grew solemn, and Eleonore detected that whatever previous affection he held for her was quickly dissolving.

"What's going on here?" Ben asked as he came through the dining room and saw Eleonore surrounded by the two men.

"Keep on your way, butler," Gustav turned and waved for Ben to disregard them.

"You disgraceful worm," Ben grew indignant and approached Gustav with large, fast strides, ready to deploy his fists.

Spying an opening while Gustav's attention was on Ben, Eleonore slipped by.

"Wait," Jung reached out and grabbed Eleonore's hand, but she wrenched herself free.

"Eleonore!" Jung called after her as she walked away briskly while Ben and Gustav entered a heated discussion.

Glancing over her shoulder, Eleonore noticed that Jung was following her, and he had the look of malice. Opening the door to the cellar, Eleonore ran down the steps, feeling the thumping of Jung hot on her heels. Running to the gun rack, Eleonore picked up the hunting rifle and pointed it at Jung as she backed away further into the cellar.

Her palms sweat as she held the heavy weapon, and she shook as she aimed at Jung. But her father had trained her well, and despite her trepidations, she held the rifle steady and true. She was prepared to give Jung over to death should he give her the slightest reason.

"Listen," Jung held up his hands and spoke slowly. "I just want to talk. Remember that it was me who kept you alive in Auschwitz."

"I'm not that woman anymore," Eleonore breathed heavily. "I'm not the helpless creature that you knew. I don't need to be afraid. Not of him, and not of you."

"Him?" Jung frowned, but then understood. "Oh, Rudolph."

Eleonore didn't reply as she tried to steady her breathing to exact her aim.

"Please," Jung raised his hands higher, "let's talk."

"There's nothing you can say!" Eleonore vibrated as she shouted.

"I didn't even know you were here," Jung took a deep breath and put his hands by his side, signaling for Eleonore to mirror him.

Slowly, Eleonore lowered her rifle, but kept her stance should he try anything rash.

"Listen," Jung took a step forward.

Immediately, Eleonore raised the rifle and aimed.

"Alright, alright," Jung backed away.

"Take another step closer and I will not hesitate," Eleonore threatened.

"Understood," Jung took another step back. "What do you propose we do?"

"I don't know," Eleonore shook her head as she lowered the rifle slightly. "But now that you've seen me, you can't let me live."

"I'm not going to hurt you," Jung tilted his head. "If I wanted to harm you, I could've done so a thousand times at Auschwitz. I brought you food, remember? I saved you from going to the gas chambers. If it wasn't for me, you'd be dead a long time ago."

"I'm grateful," Eleonore trembled as she recalled the standing cell, "but that doesn't absolve you of your other crimes."

"No," Jung relaxed his shoulders, "you're right. I know that I've sinned. But you and I, we are even."

"Even?" Eleonore laughed at the absurdity. "You worked at a death camp. I was locked in a standing cell for longer than I can remember."

"What was I supposed to do?" Jung threw his hands into the air. "I kept you alive. If I had tried anything else, then I would've been shot, or worse."

"Then why are you continuing down this path?" Eleonore pressed.

"Would you prefer that I run?" Jung looked at Eleonore in desperation. "They'll hunt me down and hang me. If I turn myself in, I might be spared the noose, but I'd likely spend the rest of my days in prison. The luxury of choice was never given to me, and now is no different. My only option is with the resistance."

"There's always a choice," Eleonore spoke calmly.

"I know," Jung smiled, remembering their conversation in Auschwitz. "I would've died a long time ago if I had chosen your path."

"You don't know that," Eleonore shook her head.

"But I do," Jung scoffed. "I know better than anyone what happened to the men and women who chose with their conscience."

"I'm not sure what to do next," Eleonore relaxed a little as she saw that Jung meant her no harm. "I have to report you to the British."

"Come with me," Jung smiled slightly and timidly.

"Come with you?" Eleonore couldn't believe what she was hearing.

"I know that you don't love me, and that you never will," Jung took a small step towards her, "but I'll take care of you and I won't ask for your affection in return."

"That's out of the question," Eleonore frowned. "You're a criminal."

"I never thought that I should see you again," Jung took another step forward. "You're just as I remembered you."

"I can't let you go," Eleonore ignored his romanticizing and raised the rifle slowly again.

"I won't say a word," Jung raised his right hand. "I swear it."

"I'm the only one who can identify you," Eleonore stepped forward and cocked the gun. Once the prey, she was now the hunter.

"I will leave this place," Jung sighed. "I will never come back. I will forget you. You will forget me."

"I could never forget you," Eleonore wiped away a tear with her shoulder. "I've tried. I'm still haunted by you. I awake in the middle of the night believing that I'm back in the standing cell."

"Who did you call?" Jung grew tense, realizing his persuasion was failing.

"The men who will take you away to swing from the gallows."

"I can't let them do that," Jung gave a threatening look at Eleonore. "Why would you turn me in after I saved you?"

"You saved me because when you looked at me you saw yourself; you saw the German people. But when you looked at the Jews, you had no compassion. You saved me because I was the last fragments of your conscience. I once thought I could rescue you from that pit and that you would do the right thing, but now that I see you again, I know that you are nothing more than an animal and you deserve worse than the hell you gave Ella, and Em, and Ruth, and Alex."

Footsteps could be heard coming down the cellar stairs and Eleonore pointed the rifle at Jung as she glanced between him and whoever was descending. Eventually, Ben came into view with his hands in the air as Gustav held his pistol firmly against Ben's back.

"Did you find out who she called?" Gustav asked Jung.

"Not yet," Jung lied as he stared longingly at Eleonore.

"You just need to be more persuasive," Gustav cocked his pistol.

"Let Mr. Mattaliano go," Eleonore turned the rifle onto Gustav.

"If I do, you'll either shoot me or turn me in," Gustav replied slowly.

"The first option is the most appealing," Eleonore flinched her eye.

"Lower your rifle and we'll talk," Gustav pushed the end of his pistol into Ben's back who winced with discomfort.

"Let him go!" Eleonore prepared to squeeze the trigger.

"If you dare shoot, you can be sure that my bullet will lodge right in his spine," Gustav gripped Ben's shoulder with his free hand.

"Eleonore," Ben looked at her with a controlled dread, "do as he says."

"If I obey, then he'll just shoot us both," Eleonore replied without wavering from her aim.

Then, taking a slow step forward, Jung stood between Eleonore and Gustav with raised hands.

"What are you doing?!" Eleonore pivoted to keep Gustav in her sights, but Jung moved with her, keeping himself between the two.

"I won't let this end in bloodshed," Jung shook his head.

"That's not your call to make," Eleonore nodded towards Gustav.

"On the count of three," Jung turned so that he could look at both Eleonore and Gustav, "both parties will recoil. Understood?"

Neither Eleonore nor Gustav replied as they kept their eyes locked firmly onto each other.

"Agreed?" Jung asked.

"He won't honor his word," Eleonore shook her head. "As soon as he sees fit, he'll shoot us."

"Eleonore," Ben spoke softly, "please."

Glancing at Ben, Eleonore returned her gaze to Gustav as she judged the correct course of action. Then, Eleonore caught the look of disappointment in Jung's eyes. He recognized the affection between her and Ben. While he had been holding onto the fragment of hope that Eleonore could have feelings towards him, he now knew that hope was lost forever.

Softening her stance a little, Eleonore looked apologetically at Jung. She knew that he still had feelings for her, and that she could never love him in return.

"Alright," Eleonore, slowly, lifted her hand off the trigger and held it up, open palmed.

Then, slowly, Gustav lowered his pistol.

The tension in the room began to give way as Ben heaved a sigh of relief as he walked over to Eleonore and Jung returned to standing near Gustav.

"Now what?" Eleonore asked as the two parties stood in opposition.

"Well," Gustav shifted his jaw as he thought, "since you won't tell us who you called, I believe that means it's not in our best interest."

Eleonore didn't reply.

"So, here's what's going to happen," Gustav pointed his finger at Eleonore. "We are going to take the last of Mrs. Meyers' money and leave."

"I can't let you do that," Eleonore spoke firmly.

"You don't have a choice," Gustav gripped his pistol.

"There's always a choice," Eleonore glanced at Jung knowingly.

"We're leaving," Gustav raised his pistol slightly. "We'll spare your lives and, in return, you won't say a word about us. Sound fair?"

"No," Eleonore shook her head as she also, raised her rifle slightly.

"What are you doing?" Ben whispered harshly at Eleonore.

"We can identify both of them," Eleonore replied as her eyes remained fixed on Gustav. "We're too much of a liability to be left alive. He'll wait until we're most vulnerable and then he'll strike."

"Very perceptive," Gustav narrowed his gaze as he became tense, ready to make his move.

Then, quickly, Gustav raised his pistol much faster than Eleonore could respond. But before he could fire, fate decided to play a hand in her favor. Jung, for all intents and purposes, had no reason to assist Eleonore in any regard. Still, it was this ex-lieutenant who was once again saving her life by grabbing Gustav's arm and throwing him off balance.

Gustav pulled Jung to the ground in retaliation and they wrestled for control of the pistol. Seizing the opportunity, Ben also tried to remove the weapon and gave a swift kick to Gustav's back who screamed in pain. The three soon became involved in a heated, vicious struggle, but Gustav was swifter and more cunning than his opponents and was able to slip away.

Standing as he panted from exhaustion, he aimed the pistol at Jung who was still on the ground.

"Gustav! Stop!" Jung held up his hand to shield himself.

But Eleonore, waiting patiently for the opportune moment, made her aim true and steady. She squeezed the trigger.

Chapter Twenty:
Son of the Werwolf

Courage is knowing what not to fear

Plato

"This is it," Hanns looked out the window as he read the address when they arrived at a distance from a small, detached house on a side street.

"I hope the twins didn't lie," Constable Hevel spoke warily as he stopped the truck.

"They didn't lie," Hanns shook his head and double-checked that his pistol was loaded.

"You're not going to use that, are you?" the constable frowned. "He's only a boy."

"He might not be alone," Hanns cautioned.

"At least we've got the advantage," the constable looked up at the night sky.

"That we do," Hanns exited the vehicle as the other policemen, five in all, climbed out the back of the truck.

"What's the plan," Hevel whispered as the group huddled together.

"I need one man to stay down here in case he makes a run for it," Hanns leaned in, "and another watching the back of the house. Constable Hevel and I, with the rest of you, will storm his room."

"And if he has company?" Hevel asked.

"Don't fire until fired upon," Hanns looked at the policemen and noticed their concern.

Apart from Constable Hevel, they were younger men and most looked shell-shocked as their rifles rattled while they trembled.

"I'll have your back," Hanns looked reassuringly at the men. "The most important thing is that the boy is kept alive. He is the key to his father's location."

Still, the officers seemed unconvinced that they would be free from any danger, and Hanns knew that he couldn't enter the room with them in such a frightened state.

"Gentlemen," Hanns knelt, "today we are making history. If we find out where Gustav is hiding, then one of the most hated men in all the Third Reich will be brought to justice. The world will never know our names, nor will they care, but we can help bring justice to the multitudes affected by this Nazi plague."

"We're with you," one of the officers nodded while still shaking.

"Good," Hanns replied, not entirely convinced.

"Let's move," Constable Hevel ordered.

A rush of adrenaline coursed through Hanns' veins as they ran towards the house. This was a moment, he felt, that he would remember forever. His senses were sharp, and he was acutely aware of his surroundings as he listened to their quick steps against the pavement, noticed their shadows projecting against the brick walls from the dim streetlights above, and felt his heart beating in his ears.

But, oddly enough, there was a calmness in his spirit. He wasn't afraid despite not knowing who or what they would find. He clung to the conviction of the righteousness of his cause, and he could sense that his thankless labor would soon bear fruit. He would finally have the son who would lead him to the father. If he could capture Gustav, alive, then he could bring a measure of justice to thousands of his people.

On Hanns' signal, the men lined up against the fence in front of the house. Gesturing, Hanns sent one man to the back of the house and another to stay put. Then, Hanns crouched as he was followed the steps up to the front door. Trying the door, Hanns noticed that it was unlocked and opened it slowly as it creaked. There was no movement from inside, so Hanns entered as the men, quietly and quickly, followed him with their weapons at the ready.

Apart from the pale light of the moon, the house was pitch black. Still, Hanns could perceive a staircase to his left and a small entryway to his right. A grandfather clock ticked patiently from the living room which was just down a hallway, otherwise the house was completely silent.

"What's the plan now?" Hevel whispered.

"I'll go upsta—"

A woman screamed, startling Hanns and the men with him who all raised their guns in her direction.

"Who are you?!" the woman cried and Hanns made out the silhouette of an elderly lady standing in the hallway with a teapot. "What are you doing?!"

"Lower your weapons!" Hanns whispered harshly and the men obeyed.

"There's nothing to steal!" The woman shouted but remained where she was, petrified.

"We're not here to hurt you," Hanns raised his finger to his lips to quiet her as he holstered his pistol.

"What do you want?!" She began to panic.

"May I turn the light on?" Hanns asked, but proceeded to turn the lamp on without waiting for her permission.

"What do you want?!" the woman asked again and squinted from the brightness while frantically studying the group of men in her house.

"I'm searching for Gustav Adolf Simon," Hanns walked slowly over to her as the police officers held their guns low but remained skittish. "He might be going by the name Gustav Henning."

"Who's asking?" the woman remained wary.

"I'm Captain Volker," Hanns explained quickly, trying not to waste any more time than necessary. "We're with the War Crimes Investigation Team."

"War Crimes?" she frowned. "Are you sure you have the right man?"

"Is he here?" Hanns pressed.

The woman watched Hanns cautiously, and then glanced at the nervous policemen with him.

"Do you swear no harm will come to him?" she asked.

"Promise," Hanns raised his right hand. "We just need to talk."

"He's upstairs," she pointed.

"Which room?" Hanns asked.

"I'll show you," the woman moved as quickly as she was able to a desk near the entrance where she retrieved a key. "I'm the landlady here."

"Odd place to keep a key," Hanns muttered to Constable Hevel who smiled nervously.

"We don't get many break-ins," the landlady glared at Hanns, overhearing his comment. "I'll take you to his room."

Quietly, the men followed behind her as they walked up the creaking stairs. *If her shouting didn't disturb him, then these stairs will,* Hanns thought.

Arriving at the second floor, Hanns noticed a light coming from underneath the door at the end of the hallway. If their target was in that room, and awake, then it was undoubtable that he had heard them downstairs.

Shuffling quietly, the landlady led them to his room and was about to put the key to the door when Hanns stopped her.

"Is there anyone else with him?" he whispered to her, and she shook her head.

Unlocking the door, the landlady opened it quickly and pointed to a boy reading intently on the bed. Seeing the men in the doorway, the boy threw away the book and scrambled to grab something underneath the bed, but Hanns and the men with him seized him immediately and pinned him down.

"Calm yourself!" Hanns ordered and, surprisingly, the boy relaxed and opened his hands to show that he didn't intend to resist.

Seeing that he was no threat, Hanns and the men backed off and the boy sat upright as he looked frightfully at the men pouring into his room. The tension was thick as the policemen kept a shaky hand on their guns and the boy seemed as though he may bolt for the door if the opportunity arose.

"I'm Captain Volker. I'm a British war crimes investigator," Hanns began. "What is your name?"

"I'm…" the boy looked about the room warily. "I'm Gustav Adolf Simon."

Surprised that he had answered honestly, Hanns found young Gustav to be refreshingly unexpected. He was a thin, awkward looking kid in tattered traveling clothes. He had innocent eyes and soft features which made Hanns doubt the information about his target.

"Do you have any identification?" Hanns asked.

"I lost it," the boy replied sheepishly.

"Search the room," Hanns ordered the men who showed no concern or respect for Gustav's belongings as they began to rifle through drawers and turn over the table, chairs, and searched under the bed.

"Just a map," Constable Hevel handed the document to Hanns.

"Looks like another British Ordinance map," Hanns replied.

"What do you want with me?" the boy shook as he sat on the edge of the bed.

"Why do you have this map?" Hanns knelt beside Gustav.

"It was in the room when I got here," Gustav replied, but Hanns caught the slightest flinch from his left eye which indicated, to him, that the boy was lying.

"What have you been busy with since the end of the war?" Hanns continued.

"Working," Gustav shrugged. "Wherever I can."

"And what about your involvement with the resistance?"

"I have nothing to do with politics," the boy scratched the back of his head.

"Where did you lose your identification?" Hanns squinted as he tested the boy's honesty.

"Well if I knew that, it wouldn't be lost," Gustav replied.

"Would you like it back?" Hanns watched young Gustav's every reaction, down to the minuscule, involuntary ones. A flinch of the eye, a flaring of the nostrils, or a widening of the pupils would betray his innermost thoughts.

"What do you mean?" young Gustav swallowed.

Walking over to one of the policemen, Hanns quietly asked them to hand him the bag that he had taken from Constable Becker.

"We found this rucksack with your identification and literature from the Werwolf resistance," Hanns handed the bag to the boy and watched in wonder as his expression morphed from innocence into defiance. Young Gustav had been caught in the lie, and now, as a cornered beast, he was showing his fangs. He had no more use for deception.

"I'm not after you," Hanns sat beside him on the bed. "I'm after your father."

"I haven't seen him in months," the boy replied, almost instinctively.

"I can have you arrested for this," Hanns tapped the map against the boy's leg.

Again, the boy remained silent as an insolent grin grew on his face. He glared at Hanns with a menace that he, as Jew, was all too familiar with from these Nazi scum.

"Listen," Hanns began again, ignoring the threat, "it's admirable that you want to protect your father, but if I catch him without your help, you will be arrested and tried for obstruction of justice."

"What justice?!" the boy scoffed. "You're hunting down these men on baseless accusations. My father is a good man."

"He is responsible for the deaths of thousands of people," Hanns shook his head as he remained calm.

"Degenerates," the boy spit, "not people."

For some odd reason, the boy's wanton denouncement didn't invoke the rage that Hanns usually felt in such circumstances. Instead, he looked at the boy with pity. He had been indoctrinated with the horrible ideology that some people were less than human and, therefore, worthy of death. Yet, in the same breath, Hanns also recalled his conversation with Eleonore and how she instructed him on understanding the villain in order to gain their trust and procure the information. What impacted one person had little effect on another. Hanns grinned as he understood that the boy before him was a frightened, sniveling little rat that would scatter away at even the hint of force.

Grabbing young Gustav by the back of the head, Hanns raised his fist, ready to strike him, but Constable Hevel was at once at action and restrained Hanns.

"Captain!" Hevel struggled as he held Hanns back. "What are you doing?! We need him to talk!"

"He deserves to rot for what he said!" Hanns threw Hevel off of him, and it took the combined strength of the remaining policemen to keep him from harming the boy who had scampered to the other side of his bed. It was all a ruse, of course, but neither young Gustav nor Constable Hevel were aware.

"He's working as a gardener," the boy confessed as Hanns' rage had loosened his tongue.

"Where?!" Hanns shouted as the men continued to restrain him, though with less zeal as he calmed.

"At the manor of Mrs. Meyers."

"Where?!" Hanns' heart stopped.

"The manor belonging to Mrs. Meyers."

"We have to go!" Hanns panicked.

"What if he's lying?" Hevel held up his hand to stop Hanns from leaving.

"We'll leave a man here," Hanns nodded and pointed at an officer at random. "But we have to go! Now!"

Bounding down the stairs, Hanns was trailed by a thoroughly perplexed Constable Hevel.

"Captain!" Hevel shouted after Hanns who was now at a full sprint.

"What the hell is going on?!" Hevel panted as he and the other officers arrived at the truck.

"Give me the keys!" Hanns barked at Hevel who tossed them to him.

"I know someone who works at the manor, and they are likely in grave danger," Hanns eventually explained as he started the truck.

"Really? Who?" Hevel glanced at Hanns as he climbed into the passenger seat.

"Someone important," Hanns glanced back at Hevel as they began to drive. "She provided a statement of Rudolph Hoess' illegal and sexual misconducts. If I can get her to take the stand – when I catch him – it will be a damning piece of evidence."

"And Gustav is also at this manor?" Hevel eyed Hanns curiously.

"Right under my nose," Hanns slapped the wheel in frustration. "We had suspicions that some SS had fled to the area and we hoped that Eleonore would be able to identify them. But now I see that we've put her in an unfortunately precarious position."

"Captain," Hevel spoke solemnly to Hanns, "I think it's time that I ask you a question."

"Yes?" Hanns watched him cautiously.

"What's your intention with Gustav?"

"What do you mean?" Hanns frowned.

"When you find Gustav, what will become of him?"

"We'll arrest him and see that he faces trial," Hanns examined Hevel, wondering as to his intentions.

"That…that can't happen," Hevel scratched his forehead nervously.

"How so?" Hanns grew concerned.

"The men with us," Hevel turned and looked into the back of the truck and Hanns glanced into the rearview mirror, "these are men who once lived in Luxemburg."

"I see," Hanns studied the men in a new light and understood that they weren't nervous from inexperience or shell shock; they were bloodthirsty for revenge.

"I ask again," Hevel cleared his throat. "What is to become of Gustav?"

"My orders are to bring him in alive," Hanns looked apologetically at Hevel.

"I understand," Hevel nodded, but Hanns was unconvinced.

"Do you?" Hanns studied Hevel.

"He deserves to pay for what he did," Hevel spoke bitterly.

"And Gustav will pay," Hanns nodded reassuringly. "Severely."

"You mean pay like they did in the Belsen trials?" Hevel mocked.

"The trials are still ongoing," Hanns shrugged. "I'm confident in the justice system."

"So was I. So were they," Hevel gestured to the men, "but we saw what a 'legal' system did to our people and to our homeland. We don't intend to let Gustav leave the manor alive."

"You're putting me in a rather difficult spot here," Hanns gripped the steering wheel tightly.

"Not at all," Hevel slouched slightly in his seat as he stared out the window. "It's quite simple actually."

"How do you figure?" Hanns asked, hoping that the constable could provide him with a reasonable argument.

"You're just the driver. Whatever happens after we arrive at this manor is beyond your control," Hevel spoke casually.

"That's a slippery slope," Hanns huffed. "How does that make us any different than the Nazis or Gustav?"

"On a few levels," Hevel cleared his throat. "In terms of lawfulness, what we intend is illegal, while Gustav's actions were legal. Legality does not equate to morality."

"But he deserves a state execution, after he has been put on trial for the whole world to see his shame."

"Every minute that man breathes is a minute he doesn't deserve," Hevel glanced at Hanns.

"I can't go against my conscience," Hanns shook his head. "I've done a lot within the 'gray areas' of the law, but killing a man without trial, that I can't allow."

Hevel watched Hanns for a moment then, turning in his seat, he looked into the back of the truck.

"Ludwig," Hevel called and a young, skinny man leaned forward, "tell the Captain where we found you."

"In a floorboard," Ludwig replied with a little embarrassment.

"He fled Luxemburg with his brother," Hevel spoke to Hanns. "His parents were unable to leave, but they sent him and his brother away. The family that took him in, secured him under their floorboard, but then the family was killed and he was locked underneath. When we found him, by chance, he was nearly dead."

"I don't need a lecture of why the Nazis were evil or what they deserve," Hanns defended as he spoke quietly to Hevel.

"What happened to your brother, Ludwig?" Hevel continued.

"They killed him," Ludwig replied quickly.

"How did they kill him?" Hevel pressed.

"They shot him while he was trying to find us some food," Ludwig cleared his throat.

"And you want to save this man?" Hevel squinted at Hanns.

"No," Hanns shook his head adamantly, "I want this man to serve as an example. I want him to pay the ultimate price, but after he's stood in front of the whole world and had his sins broadcasted."

"This is a matter between Jews and Nazis, not the world," Hevel persisted. "Justice for his crimes belongs to us, and us alone."

"Again, if we go through with this, then how are we any different?" Hanns argued. "Believe me, no one would derive greater pleasure than I from putting a bullet in his head, but we have to show the world that we are better than them. We need to have laws that protect us, all of us. We need to have justice, proper justice."

"Like killing him," Hevel nodded.

"We both understand that he deserves this," Hanns became animated, "but if a group of men can collectively decide to take the law into their own hands and kill a man, how does that restore any lawfulness to the world or to Germany?"

"Take the night to think," Hevel shrugged. "It will take some time to drive anyways. This is happening and nothing you can say will change that. It's time you come to peace with that or we will have an issue."

With that, Hevel slouched down and threw his hat over his eyes as he yawned. Soon, he was asleep, leaving Hanns to contemplate the correct course of action. He wondered if he should stop the vehicle, or take a deliberate wrong turn. *Why am I even considering saving a Nazi? I know it's wrong to kill the man in cold blood, but still, he's a terrible, wicked man who deserves it. Paul would know what to do at a time like this.*

Chapter Twenty-One:
Huntress

Peace is only an armistice in an endless war.

Thucydides

The bullet lodged into Gustav's neck, smearing his blood across the brick wall as he fell backwards and slid down. He choked and writhed on the floor, his eyes wide with panic and desperate for survival. Reaching for the bottom step, he pulled himself slowly upwards as he held his neck with his free hand. But his blood gushed all over the stairs, making it too slippery for him to climb, and he slid back down. Eventually, Gustav realized that his death would not wait, and he slumped onto his back as he glared at Eleonore with an intense, unyielding hatred mixed with wide-eyed terror. Slowly, Gustav's arms fell limp to his side as he ceased twitching and he stared past Eleonore into oblivion.

"You saved me?" Jung studied Eleonore with incredulity while he remained petrified on the ground.

"What have I done?" Eleonore looked at the rifle in her hands and felt sick to her stomach.

"You did what was necessary," Ben came to her side after stepping carefully around the blood. "Though, I suppose you could've waited until after the gardener had shot him," he nodded at Jung.

"Jung saved my life at Auschwitz," Eleonore nodded her gratitude. "Now the debt is repaid."

Walking over to Gustav, Eleonore stared into his eyes. An awful, disgusting, rotting pit grew in her stomach, but still, Eleonore couldn't look away. She felt as though a piece of her soul had been chained, and she knew that she would carry this curse for the rest of her life.

She wondered how someone like Gustav could murder thousands and how cold-hearted and wicked one would have to be to endure this experience, unless it was of the utmost necessity. And even then, Eleonore hated the sensation. It was unlike anything that she had felt before and couldn't put into words the decay she was sensing in her spirit.

While killing Gustav to save another was the right thing to do, Eleonore understood that she had also killed a part of herself. She had taken on a permanent and unbending burden.

"What are we going to do?" Ben became frantic.

"We?" Eleonore frowned. "You've got nothing to do with this. I'm going to run. I'll be wanted for manslaughter."

"And leave me as a suspect?" Ben glared at her.

"Tell them the truth," Eleonore set the gun back on the rack as she stepped over Gustav as though he were a piece of furniture in the way.

"Who would believe me?" Ben huffed. "They'll think I killed you too."

"He will corroborate your story," Eleonore glanced at Jung.

"I can't stay here," Jung stood and brushed himself off. "I'm wanted as it is."

"Then I suppose you'll have to come with me," Eleonore smiled slightly at Ben, but felt at any moment that she would vomit.

"I can't leave the manor," Ben became flustered. "I can't abandon Mrs. Meyers."

"She abandoned you," Eleonore looked tenderly at Ben.

"What do you mean?" Ben shook his head.

"There is no inheritance for you," Eleonore spoke slowly and softly.

"I don't understand," Ben frowned. "Who did she give the manor to? Please don't say Eva."

"All her money went to Gustav," Eleonore glanced again at the body.

Ben turned pale as he slouched, "And the house?"

"The deed has been signed over to one of Gustav's fake names. The house is to be used as a base for the resistance."

"It's true," Jung confirmed.

"She might as well have burned it to the ground," Ben slunk to his knees in despair as he studied Gustav's body with a newfound abhorrence.

"She had her reasons," Eleonore knelt beside Ben.

"Like what?!" Ben grew irate. "I told her to be rid of him, but she wouldn't listen."

"I know," Eleonore nodded and touched his shoulder lightly. "We'll talk later. We should pack and leave as soon as possible."

"What about him?" Ben looked at Jung, who studied the two of them warily.

"The right thing to do would be to turn you in," Eleonore rubbed her hands together as she tried to control her shaking, "but that would include turning myself in as well. So, for the sake of my self-preservation, Jung's fate is in his own hands."

"Agreed," Jung spoke quickly. "We should be going."

While still in shock, Eleonore followed the men up the stairs. But when Eleonore reached the top, she turned to look one last time upon her kill to see Gustav's vacant, wide eyes staring back at her. For a moment, she felt pity and guilt rising within her. But then she looked at his crimson-stained hands and wondered how many lives they had destroyed. Gustav's blood was on his own hands, and her conscience was quieted. Closing the cellar door, Eleonore locked it and placed the key back into her pocket.

"I'll go to the kitchen and grab as many supplies as I can," Ben rubbed his arms nervously.

"We need money, too," Eleonore threw her hands onto her hips.

"How are you calmer than I am about all this?" Ben studied her.

Glancing at Ben, Eleonore nodded as if to confirm the peculiarity and she, herself, was puzzled by her demeanor. Gustav's death, although just, was not delivered justly. Still, Eleonore felt at peace for sending him into death's hands as though thousands were crying out from the grave and offering her their thanks.

"I have some money," Ben continued, "but not much."

"I know where we can find some more," Eleonore remembered the envelope that Mrs. Meyers had wanted her to give to Gustav.

"Before you go," Jung asked Eleonore nervously, "can we talk…privately?"

"Alright," Eleonore nodded, "but make it quick."

"I'm not leaving you alone with him," Ben glared at Jung.

"I'll be alright," Eleonore spoke reassuringly.

"There's no way-" Ben began but was interrupted by the slamming of a car door outside the manor.

Eleonore turned to see a military truck had pulled up to the front of the house. While she couldn't determine who they were, the vehicle undoubtedly belonged to the Allies and a handful of men jumped out in a rush.

Eleonore had a mere few seconds to determine her next course of action. She could remain and explain the situation to these men and hope that they would understand. They would arrest her, or so she assumed, and she would likely face execution or spend decades in prison for manslaughter. Even if the killing could be determined as just, she wasn't willing to risk any more time in detainment.

A loud knock came to the door, and Eleonore looked at Ben for direction.

"Go!" Jung pushed Eleonore towards the back, kitchen entrance.

"I can't let you do this!" Eleonore shook her head.

"You're not," Jung pointed wildly at the exit. "This doesn't make amends for my sins, but it's a start."

"Follow me," Ben grabbed her hand and they bolted out the back as the Allies began pounding against the front door.

"How did they know?" Eleonore whispered as they rushed through the garden.

"How did they know what?" Ben replied, only half paying attention to her.

"I called the War Crimes office earlier," Eleonore explained, "but they arrived much too quickly. I didn't give them my name or address. How did they know to come here?"

"I'm not sure," Ben grabbed her hand as he led her through a small opening in the hedges at the far end of the garden.

But, before Eleonore passed through, she heard some shouting coming from inside the manor. Turning, she spotted Allied officers through the kitchen window with their weapons trained on Jung. It was too dark for her to recognize who they were, but Eleonore squinted in the hopes that Hanns was amongst them. Then, maybe, she would be persuaded to stay and explain herself.

"C'mon," Ben waved, "we have to go."

Relenting when she couldn't see Hanns, Eleonore pushed through the hedge and followed behind Ben as they ran over a hill which overlooked the manor. The scenery was breathtaking, and Eleonore took a moment to watch as the sunrise painted the manor's walls in a warm orange. It was the last time she would look upon the manor, but this didn't fill Eleonore with the sorrow that she supposed it would. Ben, she understood, was what made the manor feel like home.

"Eleonore!" Ben called to her when he realized that she had stopped.

"Coming!" Eleonore hiked up her dress as she continued after him. "Where are we going?"

"To my lodgings," Ben pointed to a small, rickety cottage barely hidden by a handful of thick, oak trees at the far end of a field.

"You have a cottage?" Eleonore shook her head in surprise. "Why didn't I know that?"

"I'll explain later," Ben opened the door as he panted from exhaustion.

Entering behind Ben, Eleonore looked around his humble cottage in amazement. She wasn't sure what she had expected to find, seeing as she had just discovered its existence, but she was surprisingly pleased. A meager, one-room dwelling, the cottage carried all the amenities that a bachelor would require, yet it was almost too tidy.

There was a bed, a bath, a desk, and a dresser for his clothes which, Eleonore incorrectly assumed, would be scattered across the floor. But Ben had taken his profession for cleanliness and respectability and applied it to every aspect of his life.

Walking over to the desk while Ben gathered his belongings, Eleonore noticed a pile of unopened letters. The letters on the bottom were worn and tethered while the ones on top appeared to be rather recent. Frayed, brown strings were tied around them, but some had been broken as if the reader had intended to open the letter, but never proceeded past that point.

I should probably be keeping watch, Eleonore thought and peeked her head out the door, but was happy to see that no one had followed them.

"Ready," Ben huffed as he closed his suitcase.

"Ben, wait," Eleonore put her hand up. "I should go back and confess to those men. You shouldn't have to suffer on my account, and Jung shouldn't either. Not that he deserves to escape captivity, but it feels wrong that he should do so on account of my actions."

Taking a deep breath, Ben studied her for a moment, "Mrs. Meyers gave away everything I've worked towards for nearly two decades. There's nothing here for either of us."

"But they'll catch us at the border. I don't have travel papers," Eleonore shrugged, feeling hopeless.

"I do," Ben reached into his pocket and pulled them out as he waved them.

"And how does that help me?" Eleonore rolled her eyes.

"Well, my dear," Ben cleared his throat and looked at her nervously, "that's why we're getting married."

"Married?!" Eleonore shot her head back in surprise.

"This way we can legally change your name and get you the proper papers so that we can leave," Ben shrugged.

"How romantic," Eleonore grew unimpressed.

"Eleonore," Ben paused to restrain himself, "you just killed a Nazi. I doubt this is the appropriate time for romance. I believe we should be considering how to get as far away from here as possible."

"You're right," Eleonore nodded.

"Look," Ben moved over to her and grabbed her hand gently, "we can have a new life, together. We can forget the manor, forget this wretched war, and begin fresh. Doesn't that sound wonderful?"

Eleonore pondered for a moment. The manor had been to her, in a way, a reflection of her own personal tribulations, but also, an echo of what the country had endured as a whole. She had been told by Eva, Ben, and Mrs. Meyers that the camps were mere propaganda. They were in denial that they could be linked to something so sinister. Mrs. Meyers had grieved the loss of those whom she loved dearer than life and was forced to face the uncomfortable truth that their deaths were not for some noble cause, but because of the lies of a regime she had given everything to.

Eleonore understood that it was time to move on. It was time to hope. She needed to heal, and to focus on her own troubles. Mrs. Meyers had been a wonderful crutch in the sense that Eleonore was able to focus on her employer's sorrows rather than focusing on her own. But Eleonore comprehended that it would only be a matter of time and her own grief would soon catch up to her.

"Where will we go?" Eleonore asked.

"Parma," Ben replied apprehensively.

"I thought you had some unpleasant history there?" Eleonore frowned. "Why go back?"

"For one," Ben took a deep breath, "it's where I know that I can start a new life…or restart my old one."

"And?" Eleonore pressed, knowing that he wanted to say more.

"And it's time to face my past," he cleared his throat. "I've run from it for too long."

"I don't know if now is the right time for me to be adding my complexities to someone else's complex life," Eleonore shook her head.

"Let's just focus on getting out of here, together," Ben waved, "then we can discuss the next steps."

Suddenly, some shouting could be heard in the distance and Eleonore glanced back at the door, wondering if it was too late for them to run.

"They're looking for us!" Ben grabbed Eleonore's arm. "So, what do you say? Will you marry me?"

TO BE CONTINUED
IN THE THIRD AND FINAL
INSTALLMENT:

PARADISO

www.ingramcontent.com/pod-product-compliance
Lightning Source LLC
LaVergne TN
LVHW022203190225
804146LV00009B/185